the legends:
Beginnings

BY

ROBERT E. CONNOLLY

ORIGINAL WRITING

978-1-906018-92-4

A CIP catalogue for this book is available from the National
Library.

Published by Original Writing Ltd., Dublin, 2009.

Printed by Cahills, Dublin.

*Dedicated
to the
Teachers and Staff
of
Collinstown Park Community College
and to
Teachers everywhere:
They are true legends.*

Introduction

Ireland is an ancient land with a distant and remote past shrouded in mystery. Brú Na Bóinne or Newgrange as it is commonly known is a Neolithic monument that predates the pyramids of Egypt by 400 years and Stonehenge in England by 1000 years. Each year at the winter solstice the interior chamber of this passage tomb is illuminated by a ray of sun light passing through perfectly aligned openings in the rock structure. The mysteries that surround the construction of Newgrange and the carvings on the tomb's walls and adjacent rocks are the sources of ongoing discussion and debate. It is highly unlikely that there will ever be a definitive solution to these mysteries.

Perhaps that is appropriate because unsolved mysteries reflect the realities of Irish history, an ancient and civilized culture that is verifiably thousands of years old. Whenever such ancient mysteries abound so also do myths and legends. Long before the emergence of the written word, generations of Irish bards and shanachies repeated the stories of their ancient ancestors and, perhaps at some point, reality was blurred in the interest of a good tale. On the other hand, all of these stories were undoubtedly grounded in some element of truth. When and how the truth strayed will never be known because there is no written record.

Partholonians, Fomorians, Nemedians, Fir Bolg, Tuatha de Danann, Milesians and Celts are some of the peoples who, according to legends, conquered and occupied Ireland over the millennia. There are certainly scholars who challenge the truth of the conquest stories, and even the existence of many or, indeed, all of these peoples. Recent studies have questioned the influence of the Celts who have long been considered the bedrock of Irish descent. While some of these investigations appear to be quite scientific and scholarly what is truth and what is legend will never be irrefutably known. Just as it is not possible to fully comprehend Brú Na Bóinne, it is not possible to discover where truth ends and myth begins.

The Legends does not presume to define the line between truth and myth. Rather it applies traditional Irish myths and legends and arrives at a logical if remarkable premise. The son of Cúchulainn, one of the greatest Irish "mythical" heroes, is discovered lying on a hillside in the late twentieth century near Brú Na Bóinne, where his father once roamed. I invite the reader to embark on this flight of possible fantasy, and follow the life and development of this special child.

BOOK ONE

The Age
of
Celtic Heroes

Chapter One

CÚCHULAINN WAS DEAD. Cúchulainn, the greatest champion of Ireland's Heroic Age, the most famous of the legendary Red Branch Knights was dead, poisoned by the black magic of a scorned and defeated enemy.

"A mere scratch," the great champion thought as the lance creased his side, but soon the poison, which tipped the spear made its way toward his heart. Shortly after, Cúchulainn felt a weakness he had never before experienced and he knew that the end was near. With the last ounces of his once magnificent strength he dragged himself toward a small lake where he bent down and took a sup of the clear cold water. As the water cooled his fevered head, he saw on the edge of the lake a pillar marking the grave of some long fallen hero. The grave marker was chiselled from grey granite, about five feet in height, well worn by the wind and the rain. Cúchulainn dragged himself to the stone pillar and pulled his dying body erect for the last time. He then passed the leather strap from the empty quiver across his back around the pillar where it caught in a crack near the top.

As his body slumped, the leather caught and he defied death one last time. Cúchulainn raised his sword to the heavens. With his last ounce of energy he lifted his head and loudly proclaimed to the cowards that lurked nearby, "You may claim my body but never my spirit. I am Cúchulainn and I will live forever."

And then, Cúchulainn was dead. His lifeless body stood tied to the pillar while his precious lifeblood flowed into the shallows of the lake. Even his golden red hair hung limp and lifeless while a crow perched on his shoulder waited to pluck his eyes. A safe distance away his murderers stood watch, still fearful that the famous hero might somehow be rescued by his mythical ancestors and wrack terrible vengeance for their cowardly act in poisoning a man they could not defeat. Fortunately for them, vengeance would wait.

Cúchulainn's last conscious act was to tie himself to that gravestone so that he would die as he had lived, with courage and honour, sword in hand, facing his enemy. Even in death he had one last surprise for the cowardly villains who gloated over their dastardly deed. When Lugaid, one of the murderers, finally moved forward to take the great hero's head, Cúchulainn's sword dropped from his hand and cut off Lugaid's sword welding hand.

Apart from Lugaid's screams, an unnatural quiet fell over the countryside. The breeze stopped singing through the trees, the birds fell silent and even the insects made no sound. It was as if all of nature was shocked into silence by what just occurred, a silence, which would only be broken by a country's mourning the loss of its greatest hero.

In truth, while the word of his death spread quickly, few could actually believe that Cúchulainn's spirit had departed from the world. Cúchulainn was, after all, born to greatness and although his deeds were legendary, he was still a young man. Surely the bards and poets had only just begun to record his noble exploits.

There were even those who said that Cúchulainn was not completely human. The records might show that the mighty hero, who was originally called Setanta, was the son of Sualtim and his wife Dechtire, but those who spoke with whispers and nods told a different story. It seemed that on her wedding night, Dechtire was spirited away by the god Lugh Lámhfáda - Lugh of the Long Hand - to his fairy fortress near Brú Na Boinne. When Dechtire was returned to her husband, she was already with child, and no mere mortal child was he.

While half of his lineage might have been supernatural, the other half was unquestionably regal. The boy's mother, Dechtire, was the sister of Conchubar, the King of Ulster and daughter of Cathbad, the greatest druid of the times. Through Dechtire's veins also flowed the blood of the legendary Tuatha De Danann, a noble race who had in a previous century departed the land and created a powerful kingdom under the ground where they became immortal. Despite their departure, the Tuatha De Danann occasionally intervened in human matters so that all connections with those in the mortal world were not lost and also to ensure the survival of the human race. And so it was that another god, Dagda, was Dechtire's great grandfather, and as a result deified blood flowed through Cúchulainn's veins from both of his parents.

From his early days, Sualtim and Dechtire reared Setanta but the custom among the Celts was that children were fostered to other families. As a result a child would not only have his own family, but also foster parents, brothers and sisters creating a strong bond between families. As was customary, Morann, the chief judge and poet of Ulster decreed that when Setanta reached a sensible age, King Conchubar himself would foster the boy because, after all, royal blood flowed through Setanta's veins. From his earliest days, Setanta had been regaled with tales of the heroism of the king's champions, the Red Branch Knights. Setanta knew that all of these great heroes began their training in the court of the king and because of this no greater honour could be bestowed on a young boy. And so, Setanta dreamed of the day when he too would commence his training and, perhaps one day, join the noble band of champions, the Knights of the Red Branch.

Setanta was only seven when he decided he was old enough to get on with his training and, taking his bronze camán and silver sliotar with him, he set off for his uncle's court at Emain Macha near the present day city of Armagh. To pass the time, young Setanta drove the sliotar as far as it would travel and then he ran under it to catch the ball before it dropped. During the entire journey the sliotar never once touched the ground.

When Setanta arrived at Conchubar's hill fort at Emain Macha, he stopped when he saw a large group of older boys in the midst of a hurling match on a field below the fort. He watched for a moment until he could judge the skill demonstrated by the participants. A short time later, Setanta walked among them and when the sliotar fell to his feet, he expertly flipped the ball onto the end of his hurley and began a long solo run. Despite the slashes and tackles of both teams, he weaved his way down the field until he smashed the sliotar into the back of the net. The older boys were not amused and began to attack the little fellow with their camáns, but Setanta fended them off with his own hurley. Eventually Fergus, one of the king's champions and a famous Red Branch Knight, rescued the boy and brought him before Conchubar. Setanta was properly introduced to his uncle the king and when Fergus told the story of the solo run and the boy's courage against the older boys, Conchubar agreed that the time was right for Setanta's training to begin.

Only a short time later King Conchubar was invited to a feast at Slieve Gallion, the home of Culann, a famous blacksmith well known for making the finest weapons in all of Ulster. As a nephew of the king, Setanta was also invited but he was in the middle of a hurling match and received permission to arrive after the match finished. Conchubar arrived at Culann's house and when the host asked whether the entire party had arrived, Conchubar forgot all about Setanta, and told Culann that they had. Culann closed the gates and set his great hound loose to protect his guests from anyone who might attack while the party was going strong.

Now the hound of Culann, the fiercest beast in Ireland, was known to have the strength of one hundred men and no one was likely to challenge his fierce jaws. With such protection, Culann's guests could freely drink the mead he offered, knowing that they would not be called on to defend themselves while they were impaired by alcohol.

Eventually, Setanta arrived at Culann's house, armed only with his camán and sliotar. Just after he passed through the gate, and turned to make sure it was secure, Setanta heard a low growl. Slowly turning around, the young boy was confronted with the most fearsome set of teeth he had ever seen.

Thinking quickly, Setanta spoke quietly to the animal, "There's a fine dog, taking such good care of the house aren't you.... good dog, there's a good dog."

The beast was momentarily confused at the boy's apparent lack of fear and for a time the teeth were no longer visible and the growling stopped. The great hound tilted his head to the right and left, inspecting the small intruder who seemed to have no fear. Hoping for the best, Setanta began to slowly make his way around the hound, but the movement snapped the dog out of his confusion and reminded him of his duty. Soon the growls turned into frenzied barking. The guests heard the hound's barking and assuming an attack ran out to discover what was happening.

When the door was thrown open, Culann and his guests saw the young boy standing immobile while the mighty hound began his attack. Since the gate was some distance from the door there was little they could do except watch in horror, knowing that the small boy would certainly be torn to pieces. The confrontation ended in a matter of seconds and yet to the witnesses, it seemed like time slowed and every movement was seared on their minds and memories.

The great hound took three quick steps and launched himself into air, intent on clamping his mighty jaws around the boy's throat. Setanta courageously stood his ground and then, at the last instant, took one step back, flipped his sliotar into air and took a mighty puck at the ball. The shot was meant to hit the beast in the head, knocking him unconscious but at the last instant the dog opened his mouth and the ball passed through the gaping jaws, flew down the throat of the beast and into his heart, killing the mighty hound. The dog that very nearly killed the young boy was dead before he hit the ground but Setanta was horrified at what he had done. He immediately ran to the animal, and began rubbing his head in a vain attempt to bring life to his adversary but, of course, no amount of care would bring the dog back.

Meanwhile, the entire party stood in shocked silence, amazed at the strength and courage of the little boy. While everyone was relieved that the boy lived, Culann, who had lost his prize guard-dog, was angry that he would have no dog to guard his house. Even though he would surely have been killed had he not defended himself, Setanta took full responsibility for the dog's death and he volunteered to train another dog from the same line as the slain beast. While the dog was being trained, Setanta announced that he himself would guard Culann's home. When everyone agreed that this was a fair outcome, Cathbad the Druid declared that from that day on, Setanta would be called Cúchulainn, which means "Hound of Culann."

After fulfilling his promise to Culann, Cúchulainn trained diligently under Fergus and the rest of Conchubar's champions and in only a few years, he decided that he was ready to take up arms. This opinion was undoubtedly not shared by either his teachers or the older boys who were much closer to completing their training. One day, Cúchulainn overheard Cathbad the Druid tell the senior students that if any of the young men took up arms for the first time that day, his name would be greater than any other name in Ireland, but his life-span would be short. Now that suited Cúchulainn who was not the slightest bit worried about a short life span but knew he was destined to be a great hero. Cúchulainn approached Conchubar the king and told him that he was taking up arms that very day. Conchubar smiled at the little fellow and said, "Whoever put that idea into your head?"

When Cúchulainn replied that it was Cathbad the Druid, Conchubar responded, "Well, if Cathbad thinks the time is right, I have no reason to think otherwise."

With that, Conchubar ordered that Cúchulainn be given a sword, spears and a shield. Cúchulainn tested several weapons but found that they were weak and they broke in his hands. Finally Conchubar presented Cúchulainn with his own weapons and the young boy agreed that they were strong and true. When Cathbad the Druid saw Cúchulainn with his arms he commented to Conchubar that it seemed the boy was a little too young to take up arms.

Conchubar replied, "Sure wasn't it you who told him to take up arms?"

"You must be jesting," Cathbad responded, "why he's only a little boy."

Cúchulainn was immediately called before the king and the chief druid and he was severely chastised for not telling the truth. Cúchulainn however, was not intimidated and he stood his ground. "With due respect Great Cathbad, I did hear you say that whoever took up arms for the first time that day would have a name greater than any name in Ireland, and that is exactly what I did. So I did not lie to Conchubar, when he asked me who put the idea into my head. In truth you, Cathbad, did put the idea into my head."

Neither Conchubar nor Cathbad could find fault in what Cúchulainn had said and done so the young boy became the youngest person ever to take up arms and shortly after, he began his career as a great champion. Cúchulainn soon reddened his sword against all measure of brigands and thieves who threatened the safety and security of his beloved Ulster. He was still a young man when he became one of the twelve great heroes of Conchubar's Red Branch. So great was his skill that he thought nothing about attacking as many as a hundred enemies at one time. The reason he was able to do this was that he had inherited certain gifts, perhaps from his birth father, the immortal, Lugh of the Long Hand.

Among them was the salmon leap, which enabled Cúchulainn to spring a great distance, perhaps over a river or over a wall, to attack an enemy. The other gift was a fury, which came over him in times of struggle. When the fury, or red mist as it became known, came over Cúchulainn, he entered another dimension and his mortal body seemed to disappear to be replaced by a blinding light. At such times he moved with incredible speed and the only thing an opponent would see was the flash of sword or spear that would end the enemy's life. These were mighty gifts that Cúchulainn would seldom employ in single combat but reserved for those moments when his enemy attacked in mass or without honour or when his life was in mortal peril.

Perhaps the campaign that made the name Cúchulainn famous as the greatest champion in the history of Ireland occurred during the war for the Brown Bull of Cuailgne. While this battle was his greatest triumph, it also created for Cúchulainn a mortal enemy who would eventually cause his death. What happened was that Ailell and Meadhbh, the King and Queen of Connaught, were having an argument over who brought the most wealth to that province. When everything was totted up, Meadhbh discovered that Ailell owned one fine bull that she could not match in her list of possessions. So determine was she that she would win the argument with her husband that Meadhbh sent her messengers throughout the country to locate the finest bull anywhere. As it happened, a great brown bull was discovered in Cuailgne, near the present town of Carlingford so Meadhbh attempted to acquire the bull. When the owner told her he wouldn't sell his prize animal, Meadhbh decided to invade Ulster and take the bull by force.

Meadhbh knew that the army of Ulster would be unable to stop her because Conchubar and his entire court were under a spell that took all their energy leaving them asleep most of the time. The spell was punishment for mistreating a woman who was about to have a baby and so, in truth, it was justified. Of all the knights only Cúchulainn was spared because he had settled in Dundealgan with his wife Emer and not been in the king's court at the time of the incident.

As a result, when Queen Meadhbh attacked, only Cúchulainn stood between the coveted brown bull and the entire army of Connaught. Almost immediately armies from the provinces of Munster and Leinster, which pledged their support to Connaught, joined Meadhbh in the attack.

At first, Cúchulainn waged a guerrilla type war, disposing of the various scouts Meadhbh sent out. Soon she sent champions out to finish the job, but these men met with a similar fate. Still, however, Meadhbh's army moved forward into Ulster toward Cuailgne, the home of the great brown bull. Because she was losing so many men and champions to Cúchulainn, she decided to negotiate with the young champion. First, Meadhbh tried to bribe Cúchulainn to change his allegiance but this offer offended Cúchulainn's sense of honour and so he refused. She then struck a bargain, which she hoped would save her army.

Cúchulainn agreed to fight one champion each day and while the fight was on, Meadhbh's army would be allowed to proceed without delay. If Cúchulainn was successful in defeating the champion, Meadhbh's army would be required to halt their march until the next day and the next champion. After all, Meadhbh concluded, it is better to lose one man each day than to lose one hundred every night, especially as her army could move while the battle progressed. Certainly, she assumed, even if Cúchulainn was successful it would take at least several hours for him to defeat her champions. In that case the bull might well be hers before she even needed to dispose of Cúchulainn.

In the days and weeks that followed champion after champion fell to Cúchulainn's sword and spear. So quickly did he dispose of Meadhbh's soldiers that her army barely broke camp when they were forced to stop for the day. Eventually Meadhbh became impatient and broke her word and began to send two and three men against Cúchulainn, but he destroyed them all. Of course all this fighting began to take its toll on the great champion who had been wounded many times and lost a great deal of blood.

Just as it appeared that he could fight no more, Cúchulainn's birth father, Lugh Lámhfáda, appeared from his fairy fort in the nether world and stood guard to protect his son while Cúchulainn recovered. While Lugh was reluctant to intervene in human affairs, even on behalf of his son, he was angry that Meadhbh had broken her word and he was not about to let his son die a slow and painful death as a result of this treachery. While Lugh stood guard, he also brought women especially trained in the healing arts who treated Cúchulainn's wounds with special herbs so the when the young warrior awoke three days later he was refreshed and cured.

In his absence, however, the boy troop of Ulster, made up of the sons of Ulster champions, stood in Cúchulainn's place and fought against Meadhbh's army. These boys had not participated in dishonouring the pregnant woman so no spell was cast over them. Although they were able to fight, they were mere children fighting against seasoned champions. Unfortunately, although they fought gallantly and killed many of the enemy, the entire boy's army was destroyed by the strength and experience of Meadhbh's champions. Their supreme sacrifice purchased Ulster the time Cúchulainn needed to recover and as a result Meadhbh's army had not moved forward.

When he heard of the death of these boys, many of whom were his friends, the fury - the red mist - came over Cúchulainn and he rode around Meadhbh's army killing hundreds of the enemy in revenge. After that, not one of Meadhbh's champions was interested in fighting Cúchulainn. She began to bribe her champions sending out great numbers against Cúchulainn but he slew them all. Eventually she blackmailed Cúchulainn's old friend and great champion Ferdia by threatening that her bards and poets would spread stories and songs questioning his honour and courage. Because he was Meadhbh's champion long before she began to covet the brown bull and he had pledged himself to her cause, Ferdia believed he had little choice but to fight Cúchulainn.

The two great champions met at the river where Cúchulainn reminded Ferdia of their long friendship, which began when they were young boys training in the court of Conchubar. He also reminded Ferdia of the pledge of eternal friendship they made to each other. Cúchulainn attempted to convince Ferdia that he should not fight because Meadhbh's dishonourable deeds released him from any bond he may have made with the queen of Connaught. In the end he was unable to convince his friend that there was no dishonour is refusing to fight for Meadhbh. The contest that followed was the greatest man to man fight in the history of Ireland and, perhaps, in the history of the world. Day after day the two great champions, and friends, met at the water's edge and fought with swords, spears, slings and rocks. At times they fought with their fists striking each other with fearful blows that would have felled nearly anyone else. Each evening they fell asleep totally exhausted but when the dawn broke, they rose to fight again.

The days of fighting had taken their toll and neither warrior had any strength left when the end finally came. Sensing he own life was about to end, the fury came over Cúchulainn, the hero light shown and before Ferdia could react, Cúchulainn's great spear, Gae Bulg, passed over Ferdia's shield and through his armour. Although he won the battle, and was proclaimed as Ireland's greatest hero Cúchulainn could not enjoy this honour because it came at the death of his closest friend.

The battle with Ferdia effectively ended the siege by the army of Meadhbh and Ailell because soon after the men of Ulster recovered from the spell that had been cast. Faced with a battle against a fresh and superior force, the depleted army of Connaught returned home. Meadhbh, however, never forgot the disgrace brought on her by young Cúchulainn and she vowed that she would have her revenge. In the years that followed Cúchulainn fought many great battles and killed many enemies of Ulster. In time, he became a living legend among the men and women of Ireland even though he was still a very young man who had not yet even grown a proper beard.

The difficulty with being so great a champion is that the families of those who have been defeated will often seek revenge for the death of their loved ones. In one case the sons of Curoi - who Cúchulainn killed in battle - sought revenge for their father's death. First, however, they went to Meadhbh who saw an opportunity to even her own score with Cúchulainn. Meadhbh trained the boys for seven years and then she cast a spell on the young men to give them false courage.

Finally, she sent the sons of Curoi out with poisoned spears to seek revenge. Without the spell, the young men would have been no challenge for the great Cúchulainn because they would have run before they had even thrown the first spear. And, there was no question but that a mere spear thrust would have little effect on the great champion even if it happened to crease his flesh. This time, however, any advantage Cúchulainn might have enjoyed was offset by Meadhbh's deceit and trickery.

The first poisoned spear thrown by a son of Curoi killed Laeg, Cúchulainn's chariot driver and the second killed Macha, Cúchulainn's great war horse. Having lost his loyal friends, perhaps he was a little slow in reacting to the third spear, which brushed against his side and, when the poison told hold, cost Cúchulainn his life.

When the news of Cúchulainn's death spread, all of Ireland mourned the passing of their greatest hero. No one was more distraught than Emer who lost her beloved husband. She could not imagine spending the rest of her days without him and no one could console her on her loss. When Cúchulainn was laid in his grave Emer followed him in and, putting her arms around Cúchulainn for one last time, she died of a broken heart. When the leaders and druids saw what happened, they buried Emer with her husband and champion.

The day the two great lovers were buried was dark and overcast, a perfect reflection of the feeling of the hundreds of people who came to mourn their deaths. Many people stood to present testimonials to the fallen hero and his wife. Conall another great hero announced that the cycle of Cúchulainn's life on earth was complete because he had avenged the death. Conall opened a bloody bag disclosing the heads of not only Lugaid, son of Curoi who had thrown the fatal spear, but several others who participated in the planning and execution of the plot. Those killed in revenge included a son of Meadhbh herself whose hatred of Cúchulainn resulted in the young man's death. Cnall announced that the heads of these fallen enemies were to be lined up near the grave creating an honour guard that would escort the great hero into the next world.

And thus the life of Ireland's greatest hero ended. Cathbad, the greatest of all druids and Cúchulainn's grandfather presided at the burial on that cold, wet and miserable day. The couple's bodies were laid to rest and the bards and poets created their songs and stories, which would be passed on to the generations to come. When Cúchulainn had first taken up arms as a young boy in the court of Conchubar, he had known that although he would be a legendary champion, his life would be short and he had accepted the one with the other. Now, there would be no more legendary feats. Cúchulainn was dead, but the stories of his deeds would be passed from one generation to the next for as long as Irish people respected honour and valour. Just as Cúchulainn had announced when he took his last breath, the great champion's body was dead but his spirit would live forever.

Seemingly lost amidst the grief and mourning accompanying the death of ones so young and so famous, the cycle of life, and indeed Cúchulainn's legacy, continued in a far less abstract manner. Unknown to many, shortly before her own death, Emer had given birth to identical twin boys, Cúchulainn's sons. One of the great disappointments of Cúchulainn's life had always been that his great love for Emer had not produced a child but now, at the end of their lives, two miracle children had been born to the couple.

The babies were called Ferdia, after the great champion and Cúchulainn's best friend who had been killed during the war with Meadhbh, and Fergus, after the great champion who had first trained Cúchulainn. The twins were barely a week old when Cúchulainn was slain and they were already orphans. In the flurry of activity surrounding the death of their parents, the infants were placed in the caring hands of an old woman called Mairéad and wet-nurses were appointed to feed the babies. The children were then largely ignored until the death rituals had been completed.

And so, the cycle of life continued and the great Cúchulainn's blood flowed through the bodies of two new lives. Like their father before them, Fergus and Ferdia boasted an extraordinary lineage. They were, after all the sons of Cúchulainn and Grandsons of the deity Lugh of the Long Hand. On their grandmother's side, they were also descendents of the great god Dagda and the great-grandsons of Cathbad the greatest of all druids.

Chapter Two

THERE WAS A TIME many years earlier when Meadhbh, Queen of Connaught was quite beautiful. She had been tall and slender with long blonde hair, dark almond shaped eyes, and a face, not unlike Helen of Troy's, which could probably have launched a thousand ships. Unlike some beautiful women, Meadhbh was neither shy nor self-conscious about her appearance rather she was vain and conceited. Meadhbh knew that she was beautiful and since she had also been born into great wealth she was quite particular about selecting the man who would be lucky enough to become her husband. Meadhbh craved wealth and power and with her looks she knew that few men would refuse her.

Meadhbh first choice was Conchubar; without question the wealthiest and most powerful man in Ireland. It came as no surprise that she was successful in landing Ulster's great king. Keeping him, however, was another matter entirely. Shortly after their wedding, Conchubar decided that despite her great beauty, he could not tolerate Meadhbh's disagreeable personality and so the marriage ended badly. To add insult to injury, Conchubar then married Meadhbh's sister Ethne who was nearly as beautiful but significantly easier to live with. He later married a second sister called Clothra while a third was, from time to time, his mistress. As a result of the divorce and his subsequent relationships with her sisters, Meadhbh not only acquired an ex-husband but also declared that he was her mortal enemy. Conchubar was amused but not particularly concerned.

Meadhbh's next choice for a partner was Ailell the King of Connaught who, along with Conchubar, was also among the most powerful men in Ireland. Ailell also represented the right combination of wealth and prestige. Meadhbh quickly claimed her second husband.

Unlike Conchubar, Ailell was totally infatuated with his bride and would do anything to please her, even tolerate her nasty disposition. Since she was running out of wealthy and powerful kings, Meadhbh was far more calculating with her second husband and treated him with a bit more respect. She was still quite prepared, however, to take full advantage of Ailell's devotion. The marriage of the two consolidated the great families of Connaught and they ruled jointly, as king and queen of that powerful province. Their stronghold was located at Cruachan near the present day village of Tulsk in County Roscommon.

It did not take long, however, for Meadhbh to assume effective control of the province. While Ailell was content to administer and consolidate his power, Maeve was greedy and she thirsted for even more power and more wealth. To that end, she established an army of great champions equipped with the best chariots and equipment as she looked for her opportunity to bring all of Ireland under her control. Recognizing her superior strength, Munster and Leinster entered alliances with Maeve rather than risk destruction. Soon Ulster, the ultimate jewel in her greedy eyes, stood alone against her. Since the province was ruled by Conchubar, her despised former husband, victory would be particularly sweet. Meadhbh's undoing however, was not a result of a calculated battle against her adversary to the north; rather it started with a silly domestic discussion.

In a bit of friendly banter over breakfast, Ailell suggested to his wife that he brought more wealth to Connaught than she. In her greed and vanity Meadhbh could not accept that her husband was correct, even by the slightest of margins – one great bull. To correct the imbalance, she initiated a cattle raid that turned into a war with Ulster and made Cúchulainn a legend.

And so it was that Meadhbh's once beautiful face became twisted with rage and hatred each time she recalled that her plan of conquest was foiled by a mere child. Her once melodious voice was replaced by a snarl as she had sent champion after champion against Cúchulainn only to hear that they had been defeated. She even saw three of her own sons, including Orlám, die at his hand and her hatred, now clearly etched in her face, knew no bounds.

In the end, she captured the great bull, which coincidentally was immediately killed by another bull, so she crawled back to

Cruachan with any chance of taking Ulster, a distant dream. Her once beautiful face reflected the years of anger, greed and despair. It seemed, to be twisted into a permanent snarl and few people, not even her husband the king, dared look her in the eye. She vowed, however, that no matter how long it took, or by whatever means foul or fair, she would kill Cúchulainn.

One might have thought that her snarl would turn a smile of triumph when she finally succeeded in causing the death of her arch nemesis. Although it had taken several years, she had trained the sons of a man called Curoi – who Cúchulainn also killed. Since she knew that training was not enough, she ordered that a spell be cast that protected them from the fear that would cause them to run when they confronted the great champion. She also ordered that their weapons be tipped with poison so that the slightest scratch on the great champion would be fatal. Meadhbh then sent them out to complete their foul mission and they had been successful, Cúchulainn was dead.

But any show of triumph at the news of the great champion's death was to be short-lived. No sooner had the messenger arrived with that news than a second messenger rode into Cruachan and knelt before her on trembling knees.

Meadhbh pointed a long and bony finger at the unfortunate man and demanded, "What news have you to bring your queen?"

The messenger, having ridden for many miles in the pouring rain croaked in a voice wracked with fever and fear, "Maine Mathremail .... your son.... killed."

Meadhbh's face turned red with rage as spittle leaked from the sides of her mouth. Maine was her favourite son and the apple of her eye. He had been tall, blonde and very attractive, like she had once been, and well known for his skill in training horses. "How?" she growled.

The messenger, whose face was nearly to the ground replied in a voice that could hardly be heard, "Conall.... Revenge... Cúchulainn."

One might have expected a mother to mourn her son's death, but mourning was a weakness that Meadhbh had long since abandoned as a waste of her time and energy. In response to the news her distorted features reflected only fury as she ordered that the messenger be killed for daring to bring her such tidings.

While the messenger was being taken away, Meadhbh called a meeting of her chief druid and nobles. Since they knew well that when such a meeting was called, their lives depended on their immediate presence, it was only a matter of minutes before her advisors were gathered.

"I must avenge my son," Meadhbh announced, each word venomously spat out.

"But Cúchulainn has no sons or daughters," one of the nobles pointed out.

"So at least kill his wife," Meadhbh scowled.

The suggestion may well have brought a look of horror to the faces of advisors in another court but those gathered at Cruachan knew better than to express dissent. They said nothing, and lowered their heads as the queen looked around for a response.

In the back of the room an armed soldier whispered something to one of the nobles and the exchange caught Meadhbh's attention. "Well..." she roared.

The noble cleared his throat before speaking up, "I am informed by this young man that our recently departed messenger, before he was put to the sword, reported that Cúchulainn's wife died when informed of her husband's death."

Meadhbh became more furious, if that was possible, and screamed, "But I must have revenge."

Raising a finger in the air, the noble continued with a wry smile, "...and, it seems that Cúchulainn left a couple of whelps after all. Twins it would appear called Ferdia after your late great champion who you will recall Cúchulainn also killed and Fergus after Conchubar's old champion."

The news obviously pleased Meadhbh and what could arguably be called a smile crossed her twisted face. "Perfect," she said. "And where are these children?"

The noble answered, "The messenger came from Dundealgan, where Cúchulainn lived, and the children were in the care of nurses when he rode out."

"I see," Meadhbh said as she considered the situation. "Organise twenty of our best champions and tell them to ride immediately for Dundealgan. When they find the children, kill them. That shouldn't be any problem. Dundealgan is hardly fortified and even my miserable champions should have no problem with a bunch of wet-nurses.

"They may be moved," one of the advisors suggested. "There can be little doubt that Conchubar would expect you to avenge the death of your son."

Knowing Conchubar as she did, Meadhbh had to agree, "Yes, Yes, of course. Make sure several messengers join the champions and if the brats have been moved, send a messenger back and I will give further orders."

Noting that Meadhbh agreed with something offered by a councillor, an increasingly rare event, another noble rose and said, "With total respect to your royal wishes, isn't Conchubar likely to become rather upset if we kill the infant sons of his greatest champion?"

The queen's immediate reaction was to roar at the noble, "You think I care about Conchubar's feelings? He is a useless old man and will be joining his champion very soon now." But then it dawned on her that the advisor was not talking about feelings at all. If Conchubar decided to fight her army was ill equipped to defend against any sustained attack. Turning her head to one side, Meadhbh stared blankly as she considered the situation.

After a few minutes of silent thought she announced, "Yes. I think that I would prefer that the children be brought to me, rather than killed. Conchubar won't attack while the whelps are held hostage because he knows that I wouldn't hesitate to put them out of their misery. And then they are Cúchulainn's sons, so someday they are bound to be worthy champions. I think it would suit me quite well if I reared them as my own sons, almost as replacements for Maine, and then I will turn them against Ulster. Now that would be sweet revenge indeed."

The advisors said nothing. This was just the sort of thing they might have expected from their queen. If it were Ailell who sought their counsel, they might have suggested that Connaught was still weak from its defeat by Cúchulainn and the Ulster champions. As a result, perhaps it might not be such a good idea to incur the wrath of Conchubar, hostage or no hostage. But Meadhbh was giving the orders. She didn't really want or seek their advice, rather she would listen to any information that might have and expect them to agree with everything she said. In the end it was better for their personal health to potentially incur that wrath of Conchubar rather than subjecting themselves to the certain anger of Meadhbh.

Meanwhile Meadhbh looked around at the silent gathering. "Well" she eventually shouted, "is there something you don't understand? What are you doing sitting there like a flock of sheep? If Conchubar is moving the brats, there is no time to lose. I want our little expedition moving before the sun sets."

There could be no doubt that Meadhbh's wish was her court's command and before the sun set twenty champions in full battle regalia were lined up in their war chariots accompanied by their drivers and grooms. Wagons loaded with supplies stood ready and several mounted messengers were included to keep Meadhbh informed concerning their progress. Although a horseman might complete the journey in less than a day, the entourage would take at least a couple of days as they crossed the midlands through the present day counties of Longford, Cavan and Meath.

The detachment, under the command of a champion called Fineen, departed Cruachan before the sun had set to satisfy the queen. They only travelled a few miles, however, when Fineen ordered the company to halt for the night. The queen and her fury were out of sight and Fineen had no intention of actually travelling in the dark. To do so was foolhardy because not only would they risk damage to their chariots along the rocky roads that crossed the country, but night was a time for the spirits they would prefer not to encounter. While Meadhbh could instil fear in her subjects, she did not inspire devotion to duty or a willingness to do anything more than was absolutely necessary.

Chapter Three

THE OLD WOMAN REACHED DOWN and took the infant Ferdia into her arms. Like many of those who lived at or near Dundealgan, Mairéad was a widow whose husband and sons died in the bloody battles that were frequently fought in the age of Celtic heroes. Although death in battle might have been a heroic end for the legendary Celtic warriors, that was of little consolation to the mothers, wives and children who were left behind. They faced the future with one to support them; totally reliant on the charity of their friends and extended family. Mairéad had been alone for decades and, like many others in her situation, she moved to the security of the stronghold of a champion, exchanging her domestic skills and experience for a place to live and a bite to eat. Although her eyesight was no longer clear, and her arthritic hands could no longer knit and sew, Mairéad shared the wisdom of her years and nearly everyone sought her advice.

Of equal importance, the old woman was wonder with infants and small children. At all hours of the day and night, she could be found rocking one of her many adoptive great-grand children in her arms and comforting them when they cried. And then when they were older, swarms of children would gather at her skirts to learn all measure of wondrous things. Since she had nurtured multiple generations of these young people Mairéad was well respected and treasured by the residents of Cúchulainn's fortified crannog.

With all her experience, there was no question but that Mairéad would assume responsibility for the infant sons of the great Cúchulainn. From the moment Emer placed the little boys in the old woman's arms, as she departed to mourn her husband, Mairéad never left the children's side. Fergus and Ferdia became her life and she observed their every motion, every smile and every change of expression. Mairéad carefully ensured that the wet-nurses properly fed the children and she even remained, snoring softly in her chair, while they slept. Although Mairéad might have said the same thing about every child she assisted, it soon became clear to the old woman that these infants were special.

Even though Fergus and Ferdia were only several days old when they were orphaned, Mairéad could see that there seemed to be a magical aura surrounding the twins. Unlike some babies whose eyes appeared milky during their first weeks, the boys' big blue eyes seemed unusually clear. They took in the world around them with an apparent understanding, unheard of in an infant child who might ordinarily see just shapes and colours. The infants' heads inclined toward the sound of speaking voices and from their expressions they seemed to know what people were saying. This unusual attention suggested that, in the absence of their own speech, Fergus and Ferdia were intent on absorbing every word that was uttered in their presence. The twins never once cried out or shed a tear if they were hungry, thirsty or in discomfort because they seemed to be able to communicate this to Mairéad in a mysterious way that, for all her experience she could not quite explain.

Although only infants, the twins had apparently inherited remarkable physical strength from their famous father. When visitors put their finger into the little fellows' hands they were amazed at the strength of their grips. And when the children were taken from their crib, their neck muscles stood out, supporting their heads unlike any other newborn baby. Fergus and Ferdia were certainly happy, healthy infants, both displaying a mop of golden hair, just like their father. Although the venerable Mairéad jealously guarded the twins, there was no shortage of people who quickly volunteered to adopt the children and rear them as their own.

After Cúchulainn and Emer were buried, many from the funeral party returned to Dundealgan to mourn the couple's passing and to determine what was to become of the little orphans. The group gathered at Cúchulainn's crannog where a meal was prepared. Just before the food was served, Cathbad the Druid suddenly appeared at the head table, almost, it seemed, materialising out of thin air. He was tall and slender and although the top of his head was bald, a long mane of silver hair began at the sides of his head and flowed down his back. A full silver beard matched the colour, silky texture and length of his hair, reaching well down the druid's chest. Cathbad was dressed in plain brown hooded robe cinched at the middle with a black rope. When those gathered had recovered from the surprise of his appearance, Cathbad called for Fergus and Ferdia to be brought to him. Mairéad presented the twins and Cathbad held his great-grandchildren for the first time.

The old man pondered each child, staring deeply into blue eyes that remained totally focused without so much as a blink. The children seemed to stare as intently into Cathbad's eyes as Cathbad searched the boys'. A strange glow came over the unlikely trio and the room fell silent as all social chatter ceased for many minutes. It was clear that something special was taking place and everyone looked to the elder druid with anticipation.

The silence lasted for several more minutes, although to some it seemed like a much longer time. Finally, a young voice from the rear of the room was heard to ask, "Is it the sight? Have you seen a vision? Have you seen the future?"

The question was met a universal "Hush" from the rest of the gathering who knew that no one could rush the process. Cathbad would make a pronouncement in his own time.

After another, seemingly interminable delay, the druid's voice, cracking with age emotion, was finally heard.

"I have seen something magical in the eyes of these children, but for the first time in my life, I do not fully understand what it means."

This statement was met with a collective groan and those present looked at each other in concern and confusion. Cathbad was widely regarded as one of the greatest druids who had ever lived. For as long as any of them remembered, he had been the great oracle whose wisdom was required when any great decision needed to be made. His pronouncements were always delivered with a confidence that inspired everyone who listened but this was the first time those gathered had ever heard Cathbad speak with anything except absolute certainty.

The old man continued, "Perhaps, I am nearing the end of my days on earth and perhaps my powers have begun to desert me."

"No" several people replied, "This cannot be."

One woman spoke, "Noble father, you are the greatest druid who has ever walked the earth. Surely your powers would not desert you when we need your wisdom."

Cathbad continued to consider the young children before holding them both high above his head. After a time he lowered the children and gazed at the group that surrounded him. "I will tell you what I see, and perhaps in time I will understand what it means. It may be that if I seek the wisdom of the trees and the wind, I will understand what I see. If I am not successful in interpreting this vision, it will be up to someone else to stand in my place and this will be the last time I will ever exercise my powers of vision and foresight."

The room again fell silent.

Cathbad began, "I see in these boys a remarkable strength. They will be heroic champions, like their father, but in ways their father would never have dreamed. Their destiny however heroic will not be determined on the field of battle, and unlike Cúchulainn, they will not die a hero's death."

The people murmured among themselves. They were obviously well pleased with the prediction that Fergus and Ferdia would be heroic champions, but what was a heroic champion if not in the image of Cúchulainn? And, if the twins were not to die a hero's death, did this mean they would die a coward, or merely old men? Everyone seemed to have his or her opinion and the din rose as discussions continued.

Cathbad raised his hand and silence again descended, "I see a strange world, one I do not recognise from any story or legend I have heard. I see strange people, dark-skinned people, light-skinned people, and people of all shades in between, dressed in strange clothing gathering to honour Ferdia. But I do not recognise these people. Who are they? Where do they come from? Where are they gathered? These are the things I do not know and I do not understand. That is the reason I will have to ponder what I have seen and consider what is to be done."

"But what of Fergus?" a voice cried from the rear of the room.

Cathbad looked for a time at the second child before replying, "I see a similar destiny for Fergus, but it does not appear to be identical. I see the same strange people and strange clothing but the shadows have descended on my vision and I see little else."

The druid handed the children back to Mairéad and he retired from the room disappearing as mysteriously as he had arrived. The discussions among the guests resumed immediately with everyone asking questions and giving opinions. The feast continued well into the night but by the time the group retired to their sleeping mats, the future of Dundealgan and the young orphan sons of Cúchulainn was no clearer than it had been when their parents died.

The next morning dawned bright and sunny as if Mother Nature, having expressed her sorrow and grief at the loss of Cúchulainn and Emer, was announcing that life must continue. Many of those who had travelled to pay their final respects to the great hero and his wife gathered their belongings and prepared to depart. It seemed, however, that no one was actually leaving; rather they milled around outside the main residence within the crannog talking and looking anxiously for some sign of the chief druid. It was apparent that no one wanted to leave before hearing what Cathbad might have to say, particularly as it related to the fostering of young Fergus and Ferdia.

The sun was nearly at its highest point when Cathbad arrived, this time clad in a white robe, trimmed in gold. Calling for the children, he held them close to his heart and made a pronouncement in a loud and clear voice, quite in contrast to his hesitancy of the prior night.

"I will take Fergus and Ferdia with me to Conchubar's court at Emain Macha and there I will discuss the boys' future with the king. I acknowledge that many of you gathered here would rear these children with love and affection preparing them for their destiny, whatever that may be. Conall, I know that in your care, Fergus and Ferdia would become great champions, as you yourself are. You have avenged the death of Cúchulainn and I have no doubt that you would protect his sons. I know that others, related by blood or fosterage, would also do these children great honour as their foster parents."

Cathbad concluded, "The boys are, however, grand nephews of Conchubar and it is only appropriate that any decisions regarding the fostering of the children must originate with the king. Finally, I fear that we have not heard the end of Meadhbh, whose own son was killed in reparation for the death of Cúchulainn. She may yet try to take the lives of Cúchulainn's sons in further revenge. In my opinion Emain Macha is the safest place for children of their vulnerable years."

Everyone present accepted the wisdom of this pronouncement. Conall, who had avenged Cúchulainn, stood, and speaking for the group, said, "Your counsel, great father, is wise. I am prepared to ride with you to protect the children and yourself from any attempts on their lives, or indeed, on your own."

Cathbad replied, "I thank you for your generous offer, however I think it best that I travel in my own way and I can assure you that we will arrive safely at the court of Conchubar. I will report your kindness and support to the king and I am confident that he will call on you should the occasion require it."

Mairéad then stepped forward, "Brother Cathbad," she began, "I am an old woman and my days in this life are numbered in weeks rather than months or years. I also have a destiny and I have seen visions that will bind me to these children for as long as the fates require. While their future destiny may be determined by your sight, I must attend to these children until it is time for one of us to move on."

Cathbad considered the old woman for a moment and then nodded in agreement. "I will take the children to Conchubar and you can be assured of their safety. As soon as you are prepared to travel, old sister, and proper precautions are made for your own safety, you must follow after me. You can then continue your service to Fergus and Ferdia at Emain Macha."

And so it was that the young boys, heirs of the great Cúchulainn, were taken from Dundealgan to the fort of their great-uncle the king, Conchubar. Cathbad took the children and tucked them into special slings across the old man's chest. The druid followed the secret path off the crannog to the stable where he mounted a grey stallion and galloped off. About two hundred yards later, it appeared as if Cathbad and the horse rode through some type of curtain because suddenly they were no longer visible and all that remained was the faint clattering of hoofs.

Chapter Four

THE GREAT HORSE seemed to fly over the ground covering long distances with each stride. It was only about thirty miles from Dundealgan to Emain Macha, the ancient seat of the kings of Ulster, and although the terrain was rough, Cathbad and his precious burdens arrived at Conchubar's court in less than two hours.

Emain Macha was a massive ring fort whose earthen walls, nearly twenty feet high extended over seventy-five metres from the centre point. The walls formed a great earthen circle several metres beyond the base of a perfectly round and gently sloping hill with only a main gate to permit access to the fort. Emain Macha was the fortress of the great king Conchubar whose residence was in the principal building located at the centre of the ring fort on the summit of the hill. Like the fortress, the king's residence was round, following the contours of the hill. The structure itself was nearly one hundred metres in diameter and from a distance it appeared as a giant thatched cone. This roof was supported by a series of poles, located in concentric circles, with the poles closer to the centre increasing the roof's height, both because they were longer and because they were also located higher on the hill. The centre and tallest post was just under thirty-five feet high. The external set of poles supported a wall constructed of interwoven branches finished with stones and dried mud.

Although the residence was technically only one room, various cloth and animal skin drapes provided privacy for the many members of the king's court who resided within the structure. One principal fire in the centre of the building provided heat and kept the residence reasonably dry. The fire was vented through a small grid in the ceiling, but because of drafts from the sides of the structure the smoke did not always make its way out through the grid. The result was that when the weather was cold and damp, the building was filled with a smoky haze.

Smaller buildings, also round in shape with earthen walls, and poles supporting a thatched roof were scattered at the base of the hill. These buildings provided the support services for the great hall as well as lodgings for many of those associated with the court. Included among the support buildings was a granary where corn was ground into flour, a forge where weapons and farming utensils were fashioned and a kitchen where meals were prepared.

As Cathbad approached Emain Macha, he stopped on an adjacent hill and surveyed the king's fortress for the best part of an hour. Then, satisfied that nothing was amiss at his destination, Cathbad showed himself at the main gate and was escorted with much ceremony up the hill and into the great hall.

The residence of the king was dark and the smell of burning wood contrasted starkly with the sweet fresh air that the travellers had enjoyed. Although the sun shone brightly, it was still early spring and there was little warmth on the hills overlooking the Boyne. In contrast, the great hall was warm as the flames from the great fire in the middle of the room still leaped toward the vent above. Inside the great circular house was a beehive of activity as its residents and staff scurried around attending to their daily chores.

After pausing for a moment just inside the entrance so that he could become accustomed to the dark, Cathbad strode toward the back of the great round house where he knew his son would be seated, tending to his own responsibilities. As Cathbad walked around the great fire, Conchubar Mac Nessa, the high king of Ulster, himself an old man, rose and greeted his father, the great druid.

Conchubar had once been tall and strong as befits one of the greatest kings of Celtic Ireland. He was successful in many battles and had defended the people of Ulster against invasions in time of war and led them to prosperity in times of peace. Conchubar had ruled his kingdom for many, many years but now he was growing old and tired. Age not only shrunk the once great warrior but he was also so badly bent forward that the beard and moustaches flowing from his broad chin, no longer touched his chest. In addition, his body was often wracked with coughing spells and there was no question but that the end of his mortal life was nearly at hand. Despite that, Conchubar maintained a remarkable good humour since, like all Celts, he did not fear death because he knew his soul would live on after his body passed from the earth.

Noting the bundles against the older man's chest Conchubar said with a smile, "Are you putting on a few pounds there, Father?"

"I'm afraid it is you that will be putting on a few pounds," Cathbad replied as he produced young Fergus and Ferdia."

"And who might these little fellows be?" Conchubar inquired pushing the children's gowns down so he could have a better look at their faces.

Cathbad replied, "These are your grandnephews, Fergus and Ferdia, sons of Cúchulainn and Emer and grandsons of your sister Dechtire. It seemed the prudent choice to take them from Dundealgan and deliver them into your protection."

"Indeed," the king replied taking one child and looking down he was captivated for a moment by Ferdia's strangely intense blue eyes. He then looked over at Fergus, offered with extended arms by Cathbad, and stared into an identical pair of eyes. "And I wasn't aware of the existence of any child of my nephew except that young lad Connla who was killed at that unfortunate incident on the seaside."

Cathbad looked at his son with a raised eyebrow. Although he said nothing he thought that "unfortunate" was an interesting choice of words considering it was Conchubar himself who ordered Cúchulainn, despite his champion's objection, to kill the young man. It was only while Connla, the brave young warrior, was in the throes of death that Cúchulainn had discovered his adversary was actually his son by Aoife a princess Cúchulainn dallied with before marrying Emer. Cúchulainn was so completely distraught at the thought that he had killed his only son, that it took Cathbad months to bring him out of his depression.

Rather than reminding the king about the details of that unfortunate incident, Cathbad replied. "It seems that Emer eventually bore Cúchulainn not one but two sons that they always dreamed of but when she died rather than living without her husband, these young lads were left orphans. Since Conall has avenged Cúchulainn by killing Meadhbh's son there is a very real concern that she will want to avenge her son and these little fellows are likely targets. That is the reason I decided to deliver them to your protection."

Conchubar again examined the child. "I see," he replied, "but considering my age and state of health, I'm not sure how long or how well I can protect the children. What happens if I can no longer undertake the children's protection?" As if to emphasize his state of health, the old king was suddenly wracked by a long fit of coughing.

"A fair question," Cathbad responded, "but one for which there is no simple answer. I suggest that we discuss the matter further when I have had an opportunity to rest and reflect on what I have seen. Perhaps then the best interests of these children will become clear."

Conchubar agreed and ordered that the elderly women who lived under the king's protection and were responsible for taking care of infants and small children should be called. After identifying the twins and explaining the importance of their protection, the little fellows were passed into the delighted hands of a group of the women who took turns examining and cuddling the sons of the great Cúchulainn. They were visibly impressed with what they saw and began marvelling at the intelligence of their expressions and their muscular constitution. Amidst the oooing and ahhhing over the babies the two men exchanged mock expressions of exasperation, although they were pleased that the women, who had tended so many infants, were so obviously taken with their most recent charges. And then first Ferdia and then Fergus smiled, winning the hearts of the women as well as their approval. Another chorus of ahhhs rose to the rafters.

Some hours later Cathbad, feeling rested and refreshed, left the fortress and wandered into a sacred oak grove not far from Emain Macha. Such groves were the natural cathedrals in which the great druids communed with nature gaining the strength and insight that would enable them to instruct and guide their people. There, in the quiet and solitude of the forest, Cathbad sat on a large rock, closed his eyes and seemed to enter into a trance. For several hours he sat without moving and if anyone happened across the druid in this state, they might have assumed that his spirit had left his body.

It was nearly dark when Cathbad finally opened his eyes. Slowly he turned his head to the right and left, stretched his arms, and pushed himself to his feet. The combination of the bone-jarring ride and the extended period of motionless meditation left the old man stiff and sore, As he moved awkwardly through the forest he muttered to himself, "I am getting entirely too old for this carryon."

His mind refreshed by his solitude, Cathbad returned to the hill fortress to meet with the king and his advisors. After Cathbad announced his intention, runners were sent out to gather as many nobles as were available on such short notice. When the meeting convened in the great hall a short time later, nearly all of the wise men and women of Conchubar's court, including Sencha, his chief advisor, Amerigan the poet and Morann the chief judge, were present. Also included were several champions, Red Branch Knights, pledged to protect Emain Macha and Ulster, an assortment of druids and druids in training as well as older people who were valued for their wisdom. Many other subjects who had not been invited to the conference gathered outside in the courtyard waiting whatever proclamations might come from the meeting. When everyone had taken their place Cathbad made his appearance to the greetings of all present.

Conchubar opened the proceedings by stating, "I have gathered you here this evening to discuss a matter of grave importance. As you know, our greatest champion, my sister's son Cúchulainn has been treacherously slain and his wife, Emer, has died of a broken heart. While we mourn these tragic losses, the life cycle continues as Emer has given us Cúchulainn's sons, Fergus and Ferdia, who are now orphans."

The king paused, coughed into a cloth that he held in his left hand and took a drink from a goblet at his side. Meanwhile the murmuring among those gathered announced that the presence of an heir to the great Cúchulainn was still very much a surprise to many of the advisors. After a few seconds, Conchubar took a deep breath and continued. "Under normal circumstances there would be no question as to the fosterage of such children. I fostered these boys' father and hundreds of other young men who subsequently served Ulster with courage and dignity, the greatest of who have become Red Branch Knights. I have little doubt that Cúchulainn's children are destined for great things and there is nothing I would rather do than foster these children."

When he had again caught his breath, he spoke in a quiet voice, "Unfortunately, my time on this earth has almost run its course and I sincerely doubt that I will see the children's second year, never mind their twentieth year. For some weeks now, I have heard the voices calling for me and while once they were distant echoes, each day the voices grow stronger and more impatient."

Again he paused and this time shouts were heard from the back of the hall, "No... no... Conchubar will live a thousand years."

The king raised his hand to quiet the group and then he continued, "I have no fear of the next life. I have lived a full life and I am tired. It is nearly time for me to go and none of you should begrudge me the right to die in peace and dignity. However, this conference is not about me or my impending death, rather it is about two lives, new lives, the lives of my grandnephews Fergus and Ferdia. I will not be here to see them become men but a decision must be made by those who might. I have invited all of you to listen to what Cathbad has to say, consider this matter carefully and give whatever counsel and advice you may consider important."

With that, Conchubar slumped into his chair; quite clearly the old and tired man he professed himself to be. Taking yet another drink from the goblet, he turned to his father extending his hand to pass on the proceedings to the chief druid.

Cathbad acknowledged the gesture with a small bow and addressed the gathering. "Well my young son," he began with a smile, "if you think you are old consider that I was old when you were born."

The statement brought an uneasy laugh from the gathering and even Conchubar was forced to smile. "Perhaps," he remarked, "if I spent more time communing with nature and less time trying to avoid having my head lopped off, I would be left to face my later years in a bit healthier state."

This brought a more robust laugh from those gathered who, in better times, had become accustomed to the exchange of witticisms between father and son.

Cathbad, himself leaned his head back and laughed heartily before he continued, "No truer words were ever spoken and I do know that neither of us are what we once were. I would never question that you have heard the voices because that is personal to every one of us. I too, have heard the voices for some years now but so far, they remain distant. I know that while I, and indeed all of us, am eternal in one respect, that eternity will not be experienced forever on the plain that we now share. The day will soon come when my soul will also leave my body and I will not be here to see my daughter's grandsons reach the fullness of age."

Cathbad continued, "My king, however, has spoken the truth when he said that we are not here to consider the end of one, or even two lives on earth. That is a matter for some future gathering. As for Cúchulainn's sons, I have held Fergus and Ferdia in my hands and I have not only looked into their eyes but I have done everything in my power to discover their future destinies so that we might properly determine our present course. I will relate what I have seen and perhaps our combined wisdom will discern what it means."

Cathbad paused for a moment and those present held their breath awaiting the next words.

"I am sorry to say," the druid stated, "that only parts of my vision are clear and even some of those visions defy my attempts at interpretation. I present them at this gathering in the hope that together we can determine the appropriate path."

Those gathered in the room looked at each other in amazement. This was certainly a departure from what they had come to expect from their chief druid. In all the years he had counselled them, his words were spoken with confidence. They had never doubted the wisdom, or indeed truth of his predictions or advice. In fact, much of the younger druids' and druidess' knowledge had been acquired at Cathbad's knee because he was the teacher as well as the practitioner. Now, for the only time in any of their memories, Cathbad was admitting before the entire assembly, that his vision was unclear. Perhaps he was getting old and nearing the end of his life on earth, but in deference to all that he meant to them, those present listened carefully hoping that they would have the right vision that surprisingly, their teacher could not see.

Cathbad understood the confusion his revelation caused but he also knew that to assert a course about which he was not certain, would not be honourable and might even result in the death of Fergus and Ferdia. It was better that the gathering thought him less a druid than he bring dishonour to himself or his profession after so many decades of seeking the truth.

Raising his hand for silence, Cathbad surveyed the gathering for a moment and then began. "First and most importantly, let there be no doubt but that I have seen greatness in the eyes of our youngest champions Fergus and Ferdia sons of Cúchulainn. They will live the lives of champions as befits their blood lineage and in the fullness of time, like their great father before them, Fergus and Ferdia will acquire a status, legendary among men and among all the generations that follow. These things I see as clearly as any vision the gift of sight has ever bestowed upon me."

The gathering responded with an appreciative sigh of relief. Cathbad raised his hand one more time and the room again fell into silence as he continued.

"Perhaps that is enough. Perhaps one should be satisfied in knowing that these young children will be blessed with extraordinary powers, but what of their destinies? It is here that my sight grows confusing. I do not see blue sky and green grass rather I see black skies and a grey firmament. I do not see horses, swords and chariots but strange beasts that whine and rumble. I do not see mountains and fields and forests but peculiar man-made structures of every size and configuration, rising into the sky. I do not recognise this place and I do not recognise anyone who occupies this place where I have no doubt that young Ferdia and, I believe Fergus will be crowned in glory."

The room fell silent as everyone considered what had been said. Finally an elderly druid spoke, "My friend, Cathbad, is there anything in your vision that you do recognise which might help to clarify the vision?"

Cathbad replied, "In truth, I do see a sliotar and camán but I see them in the hands of a young man, perhaps Ferdia or Fergus, so I do not know whether they will become part of one or both of their legends. Perhaps they are mere reminders of the twin's legacy."

The other druid then asked, "You have said that you don't see anyone you recognise. Do you see any other druids with whom we might communicate?"

"No," Cathbad responded, "I see no druids or any other person with whom I might even consider communicating. The people in my vision are strangers with strange dress, strange manners and a strange language. I have never heard or seen the likes of them and as you would well know, I have seen many things in my life."

The room again fell silent as everyone thought about the answer. After a time, a young druidess timidly rose to speak. "I am sorry if what I have to say may seem silly as I have only recently completed my training, however as I have been invited here, perhaps I might say something."

"Of course," Cathbad replied with a smile.

"It seems to me," the young woman said, "that Fergus and Ferdia are to become great champions however perhaps they will achieve their destiny in a land that is far away from Ireland."

"You have spoken wisely," Cathbad responded. "I too have considered the possibility of another land. Perhaps all of the strange things I have seen are not to be taken literally but only represent a culture and society that is totally alien to our own. On the other hand, there are many ways to reflect a foreign land but this vision was so strange and unbelievable that I questioned the possibility that their destinies lay in another land. After all, despite my travels and meetings with people from all over the world, I have never met anyone who has described a land that remotely resembles the land and people of my vision. Despite this, you may well be correct, but that is what is entirely unclear to me."

Prompted by the reception received for the young druidess' suggestion another druid rose to speak. "Father Cathbad, perhaps rather than another land, the twin's destinies are to found in another world. Perhaps there is a world that none of us have ever seen that has been shown to you in your vision."

Cathbad pondered the young man's observation, "Once again, thank you for your comment. I will not say you are wrong, because I do not know. I too have considered the possibility of another world. We know that Cúchulainn was conceived in the land of our ancestors the Tuatha Dé Danann far below the earth. The boys' grandfather is Lugh of the Long Hand, so called because he was a great king whose hand was always extended to help his people. It was Lugh who took his people into a kingdom beneath the earth when the Milesians overcame them many centuries ago. It does follow that the sky beneath the earth is black, the firmament grey and perhaps the Tuatha Dé Danann still enjoy hurling. All of that might suggest that the destiny of this child is to be found in Tuatha Dé Danann or some similar world about which we know nothing."

"However, although none of us have seen this world, legends do not suggest that there is anything strange or peculiar about these people, at least not to the extent of those I have seen in my vision. After all, the people of Dana were once like us and there are those among us, including these children, who are direct descendants of these people. What you say, however, is not without merit and once again, I must admit that I just do not know."

Over the next several hours many of those gathered rose to offer their opinions and suggestions, all of which were respectfully received by Cathbad and the other wise people gathered in the hall. It was nearly dawn when Morann, the chief judge rose from his seat and announced, "We have spent the night discussing Cathbad's vision and we are no nearer to an answer than we were when we began this discussion. Perhaps Cathbad might suggest some course of action to test these theories. It has taken great courage for Cathbad to state that his vision is not clear and each of you has assisted in whatever manner you thought appropriate. Surely neither Cathbad nor any of us can be faulted if, after all of this, the wrong course of action is chosen."

"As befits your station Morann, you have spoken wisely," Cathbad responded. "We should all retire and consider what has been said. I will also retire and in the morning I will once again seek the wisdom of the universe. When we reconvene in the evening, I will announce the course I intend to take and unless all of you believe it to be improper, I will proceed."

The plan met with general agreement and everyone retired for the remainder of the night. There was no sleep for Cathbad, however, and he knew the decision he must make would be the most difficult of his long and distinguished career.

The great druid walked silently into the nursery where Fergus and Ferdia lay together in a double crib and looked in on his great-grandsons. Mairéad, who had apparently not delayed in travelling to Emain Macha and asserting her position as the primary guardian of the children, rose and greeted him.

"Thank you for your diligence, old sister, Cathbad said.

Mairéad bowed her head and replied, "It is not only my destiny but also my privilege. The children are well."

The little fellows were indeed sleeping peacefully and Cathbad uttered a silent prayer that whatever decision he made would be correct. Most of all, however, he prayed that his decision would not harm the only surviving sons of the great Cúchulainn. Just as he was about to leave, Cathbad took one last look at the boys who chose that moment to simultaneously open their big blue eyes. Fergus and Ferdia looked up at the old man and both smiled.

Chapter Five

MEADHBH'S COMPANY OF CHAMPIONS rode steadily to the east for two days arriving in the present day County Louth just as the sun was setting. They knew well that their every move was being tracked by scouts sent out by nobles loyal to King Conchubar. On the other hand, because they were travelling in what was effectively a "no-man's land" near the border between Ulster and Leinster their presence was unlikely to raise any great alarm. Although twenty champions was a significant force, it was hardly an army. As such, it required monitoring but would not be considered a threat, unless it took some aggressive action. Fineen, who led the detachment, realised that questions were being asked about his presence but he knew that if his command moved slowly and purposefully, he would be less likely to be challenged. After all cattle raiders would not bypass prosperous farms in the Boyne Valley, which were much closer to Connaught. Lacking any obviously aggressive purpose, Fineen's force would be seen only as travellers from Connaught to an ally in either Leinster or Munster.

After setting up camp within sight of the Boyne, Fineen sent his own scouts out to talk to the local people and, hopefully discover the whereabouts of his prey. As it happened, he had little difficulty in discovering that Cathbad had taken Cúchulainn's sons to Emain Macha. After all, the events of the last several days were on the lips of the many travellers who were returning from the funeral for the great hero and his wife and they saw little danger in sharing the gossip with anyone else they might encounter.

Fineen considered this intelligence in trying to decide on his next move. While it might have been safe enough for Fineen to travel toward Dundealgan, a turn north in the direction of Emain Macha which arguably could seen as hostile and would create difficulties for his relatively small force. After all, Emain Macha was well fortified and the arrival of Meadhbh's champions would certainly be met with a show of force, particularly in light of Cúchulainn's death at her hand.

Rather than make a wrong move and risking not only the wrath of his queen, but also quite possibly his head, Fineen sent a mounted messenger back to Cruachan to seek specific orders from Queen Meadhbh. The following morning he moved a bit further south and away from Ulster and set up his camp while awaiting her response.

When Meadhbh heard the messenger's report the following day, she was not particularly surprised. The infant sons of any dead hero, and undoubtedly the sons of a famous Red Branch Knight would hardly be left in a residential crannog without a champion to protect it. The most likely destination for such infants would obviously be the stronghold of Ulster's King especially since Cúchulainn was Conchubar's nephew. In sending Fineen and his men out, Meadhbh hoped to move against a soft target like Dundealgan if Conchubar was slow in relocating the children. Even if the twins were no longer there, they might have been able to intercept the children as he travelled to Emain Macha. Since the boys were moved quickly there was little her champions could have done about it and even she could find no fault in their actions.

Resigned as she was to the message she actually received, Meadhbh spared the messenger, even though he bore bad tidings and Meadhbh deplored bad tidings. She had far more important things to consider, the first of which was some other way to kidnap Cúchulainn's whelps. A lesser woman, or one not so driven by revenge, would probably have conceded that the twins were beyond her reach. A lesser woman would have bided her time until an opportunity presented itself to either capture or kill the children. Meadhbh, however, was not such a woman so she considered the various possibilities.

An attack on Emain Macha was totally out of the question. Even if she were to make it through miles of hostile territory to the gate of the fortress, Conchubar's stronghold was heavily fortified. Quite apart from that, her forces were still weakened from their previous battles with Ulster and it was unlikely that her allies in Leinster and Munster would respond favourably to another campaign.

Meadhbh ultimately decided that if she were to succeed in her goal of capturing the infants, it would have to be by trickery or deceit. Now that was certainly not something that was difficult for her to contemplate. Before even planning an operation, Meadhbh knew that she needed better intelligence and so she sent her spies into Conchubar's stronghold at Emain Macha. At the same time, she sent a messenger to Fineen instructing him to remain encamped within striking distance of Emain Macha and await further instructions. Meadhbh reasoned that if she was, somehow, able to spirit the babies out of Conchubar's fortress, perhaps by simply snatching the infants when no one was looking, her force of champions could escort the children to Connaught.

Chapter Six

CATHBAD SPENT THE NIGHT AND MUCH OF THE DAY in the sacred oak grove sleeping, meditating and seeking wisdom from the spirits. Late in the afternoon the great druid slowly rose and raising his eyes toward the tops of the towering trees, he expressed his gratitude for their indulgence. Head down with hands locked behind his back, Cathbad slowly returned to Emain Macha. He knew exactly what he would say and do.

When Cathbad entered the great hall it seemed that nothing had changed from the previous evening. Conchubar's entire court was gathered and everyone returned to nearly the same spot they had occupied twenty four hours earlier. An even greater crowd gathered outside because the word quickly spread that Cathbad was going to announce his decision. Soon after Cathbad took his place near Conchubar's chair, the king arrived, shuffling slowly from his resting place at the back of the great round house.

When everyone had settled, Morann raised his hand for silence. As chief judge he would preside over the meeting and he began by summarising what had occurred. "As our noble king has stated, the time has come to make a decision, whether it be right or wrong. We have discussed the vision revealed to Cathbad and we have agreed that these infants' destiny does not lie in the world, as we know it. I have the greatest faith and confidence in my brother Cathbad. No one has served our people so long and so well, without any thought of personal favour or gain. I think it a measure of Cathbad's greatness that he came before us to seek clarity rather than making a pronouncement about which he was not completely confident. Our extended discussions of Cathbad's vision have not eliminated any possibility so all we now know is that Fergus and Ferdia's destinies, great though they may be, may not unfold before us."

Most of those gathered, nodded their heads agreeing with the summary.

Morann continued, "Cathbad has now consulted with the spirits, meditated on the problem and he has considered an appropriate course of action. I now call upon Cathbad to impart to us his wisdom and counsel."

Rising stiffly from his chair Cathbad looked over the assembly and stroked his beard nodding toward the chief judge before beginning, "Thank you my friend for your kind words. I trust that you will understand not only what I believe to be the appropriate course, but the reason I think it proper."

"First, I believe there are two possible courses of action. The first is to do nothing but allow the children to grow and develop hoping that their destinies will become clearer in time. Unfortunately, since neither Conchubar nor I will be alive to provide guidance we must rely on others to rear the children and, perhaps more importantly, protect them from any revenge Meadhbh might chose to extract. If I were to choose this course, the lives of these infants would be at risk for at least as long as they are unable to protect themselves. Meadhbh will doubtlessly consider that the day will come when Cúchulainn's sons will be a threat to her life. She might well decide to terminate the potential threat before it becomes real. Remember, Meadhbh with her black magic, turned the head of Cúchulainn's best friend, Ferdia, and she was also responsible for the death of Cúchulainn himself. She presents a formidable threat to the young boys' lives, even if they could rely on the protection of Conchubar or me."

Cathbad paused allowing those present to consider what he said and again there were general murmurs of agreement. One young druid rose and timidly asked, "But if the children's destinies are to be great champions, how can it be that they might be killed by Meadhbh, or anyone else for that matter, before they attain that destiny?"

Cathbad was more tolerant in his response than, perhaps, others might have been. "You will learn, my young brother that one's destiny does not develop in isolation but rather is bound up with the lives and actions of others. Because of this there is no guaranty that that each person's destiny will be fulfilled.

Young boys, like Fergus and Ferdia, might be denied their destiny if those who are responsible for their growth and development, make choices that do not foster and protect their destiny and indeed their lives. Their destiny is particularly at risk while they are unable to make decisions for themselves."

"I see," the young druid said as he sheepishly sunk back down into his chair.

"It may well be that ultimately, delay is the only course available and the threats to the twin's lives, are risks that must be taken," Cathbad stated. "However, the course I have chosen allows for the possibility that these children are being called by their grandfather Lugh of the Long Hand, to discover their destiny in the lands of Tuatha Dé Danann. If that is the case, we may never see these boys again. Sad as that may seem, if the world of my vision is the kingdom beneath the earth, that is their destiny and we have no right to deny them what is meant to be."

"My decision," he concluded, "is this. I will first examine the stars to determine a day that is particularly fortunate for these children. On that day, I will take the children to the fairy fort at Brú Na Boinne and call on Lugh Lámhfáda to take the Cúchulainn's sons to the world beneath the earth, if that is what is meant to be. If Lugh does not take the children, I will return with them to Emain Macha. Upon my return we will designate stepparents who will rear and train these boys and chose champions to protect him. If Fergus and Ferdia's destiny is not to be found with the Tuatha Dé Danann, and we will leave that choice the children's grandfather perhaps it will then be revealed in the fullness of time."

Most of those gathered agreed that Cathbad's decision was proper, but Mairéad asserting her role as the boys' protectress, asked in a loud, clear voice, "How do you propose to offer these children to Lugh? If, as you say, Lugh is not interested, I would hope that you will return with a happy and healthy Fergus and Ferdia."

Cathbad smiled, "Ah old sister, do you take me for a barbarian? There will be no bloodletting and no harm will come to the children. The choice will be left to the Tuatha de Danann. We have all heard stories of people who were invited into the fairy forts and no physical harm is involved in the process. So it will be with Fergus and Ferdia. They will be presented at the fairy fort and if an invitation is not forthcoming, they will be returned to Emain Macha in the fullness of their health."

"I knew a fellow," a very old man who was prone to storytelling began – to the groans of many present – "who was invited into a fairy fort. He spent one entire night dancing and singing and drinking the finest mead, and when the morning came he awoke with a ferocious headache, lying in the grass outside the fairy fort."

A number of those gathered had undoubtedly heard the story on any number of occasions, but out of respect for his age, the old fellow was allowed to continue. "Most peculiar thing though, when he went home to his wife he found that she had been dead for nearly fifty years, so she had. And, the wee children he knew before he went into the fairy fort were now old people. So it seemed that one night with the Tuatha Dé Danann was like many, many years on this earth. Sure didn't I meet the man himself some years back? What do you make of that?"

Cathbad responded with a tolerant smile. "Well spoken my friend. I know we are offering Fergus and Ferdia to a world that is so strange we cannot understand even how time passes. But it is also a strange world in which I have seen the boys' future so we must take whatever steps are necessary to allow them to fulfil their destinies, even if it they are be found in so strange a world. And one thing further, if Lugh Lámhfáda offers his hospitality, the children will be beyond the reach of Meadhbh and her revenge."

For several minutes after Cathbad concluded his remarks, those present spoke among themselves. Cathbad stood looking around the gathering waiting to see if anyone had further questions or comments but it appeared that most of the conversations affirmed the wisdom of his decision. After several minutes Cathbad nodded toward Morann. The chief judge leaned over and spoke quietly to Conchubar who inclined his head to more clearly hear what Morann. After some minutes of contemplation, the king rose from his chair and the entire room was immediately silenced.

Conchubar looked around and spoke simply, "So be it." With that, he left the hall.

The word of Cathbad's decision to offer the children to their grandfather, Lugh Lámhfáda, quickly passed from the great hall into the courtyard and it soon became the principal subject of conversation throughout the countryside. When Meadhbh's spies arrived a few days later they had no difficulty discovering what had been decided. They knew that Meadhbh would be delighted to hear that the children would be taken from the security of the stronghold. Unfortunately, they would also have to report that no one, even Cathbad himself, knew when the infants would be moved. That, they knew well, would infuriate their queen. They would also have to report that the chance of snatching the children would be remote at best because of all the attention the infants were attracting as they awaited their journey. After some discussion the two men drew lots to determine who would return to Cruachan with the potentially fatal news while the other waited for further developments. As soon as the sun rose, the unfortunate spy headed west to Connaught.

As the word of the druid's pronouncement spread everyone gathered at Emain Macha accepted the wisdom of Cathbad and the decision of Conchubar. However, the thought of losing the children as they had lost their parents weighed heavily on those who embraced the responsibility for their care. While there were many tears, Mairéad and the infants' other caretakers were determined to make the most of the time they had with the little fellows. When they asked Cathbad whether he could tell them how long the children would remain with them, they were told simply that the day was nearly upon them so the children should be made ready to travel. Knowing this, each day the old women spent with the children became even more precious.

Fergus and Ferdia had been alive for only a couple of weeks and already they had lost their parents. Now they faced a future so uncertain that even the world where they would grow to manhood was entirely unclear. Of course, being infants no one would really expected that the children would appreciate their great loss or the nature of the future they faced.

Surprisingly, however, it appeared that Fergus and Ferdia were aware of far more than might have been expected. The young children, whose bright blue eyes displayed remarkable awareness for ones so small, appeared to absorb everything that was said in their presence. As a result, it seemed that somehow they knew about their impending trip into the underworld.

As their principal caretaker, Mairéad attempted to control the gossip, at least in the children's presence. She tried to explain that Fergus and Ferdia knew what people were saying and they could be causing the twins unnecessary worry. This statement was met with a few raised eyebrows and remarks about the old woman's sanity. However, to keep the peace and in deference to her age and authority, that specific topic of conversation was no longer discussed in the infants' presence.

Despite their concerns for the infants' future, Fergus and Ferdia's attendants showered them with constant love and affection. It was as if these adoptive grandparents meant to ensure that wherever destiny might take the children, their earliest days would be filled with joy and happiness. Perhaps somehow they would remember and be fortified by this love. During every waking minute, Fergus and Ferdia found themselves snuggled in warm embraces of one old woman or another as each would look on the infants with rheumy but unquestionably loving eyes. The women would serenade the children with songs and stories, including the epic adventures of the infants' own father. Other members of the court were also frequently in attendance paying their respects.

Rocmid, the court jester, arrived one day, more out of curiosity than anything else, but when he noticed the Fergus and Ferdia smiled happily at his antics, he made several return visits. If there was one thing Rocmid understood, it was an appreciative audience. Mairéad supervised the attention, understanding that whatever about the close and stagnate atmosphere of the great hall, Fergus and Ferdia would not want for love and affection.

Cathbad the Druid and Conchubar the King also frequently looked in on the infants, holding each child and reminding them of their lineage. For each of the elderly men, this was a new and different experience because normally powerful leaders did not even see infants, much less hold them in their arms and speak quietly to them. They both realised that as the two old men moved toward the end of their earthly existence, they might never have a similar opportunity. Fergus and Ferdia were not babies who cried out or squirmed at a strange touch or voice, rather they seemed to accept that everyone who came in contact with them could provide a new and important experience.

Chapter Seven

IN THE COURT OF QUEEN MEADHBH, her spy returned from Ulster and reported his intelligence. To his relief, the queen took the news with relatively good spirits so for the moment he would live to see another day. Although the children were completely secure in Emain Macha, discovering that they were to be moved was a stroke of good fortune that brought a twisted smile to Meadhbh's face.

Meadhbh called for her chief druid Lugain and explained what her spy reported. "So, my learned friend," she asked, "If you were Cathbad what day might be particularly fortunate for offering Cúchulainn's whelps to Lugh Lámhfáda."

The last thing that Lugain wanted to do was make a pronouncement that would prove to be incorrect so he answered, "It is very difficult to say without knowing everything about the children, including their exact birth date and time."

The queen had grown accustomed to such waffling so she assured her advisor with a sneer, "I am not going to hold you to anything you might suggest so perhaps you could give me some idea, even without all that information you so desperately require."

Although still suspicious and concerned for his own welfare, Lugain responded, "Well I would think that the date would be sooner rather than later. Perhaps someday around the first of May since Beltaine is generally considered a lucky day."

"Now that wasn't too difficult," Meadhbh responded. "Sooner rather than later. And tell me; without further study might you be able to give me some idea as to where Cathbad is likely to offer this sacrifice to the gods."

Lugain's complexion turned dark red with rage at the queen's goading but he knew better than to respond with any comment that might be deemed to be impertinent. He simply said, "I would assume somewhere near Brú na Bóinne but I am aware of at least a dozen possible places stretching for miles along the river. Then again Cathbad might know of some other place entirely so I wouldn't be able to say with any certainty."

Meadhbh closed her eyes and shook her head, "I wish I could figure out why I keep the likes of you around. I can't remember the last time you said anything useful. Please get out of my sight before I become ill."

Turning an even darker shade of red, Lugain said nothing but turned and departed. Did she not know of the mysterious and magical powers possessed by the druids... well most druids? Although Lugain was well trained in the druidic arts he knew that he did not possess the natural instincts that enabled the great druids like Cathbad to exercise amazing power, like controlling the elements. Lugain's training gave him a moderate knowledge and practical skills but he wished he had been blessed with true power. There was nothing he would rather do than laugh in Meadhbh's face and leave her with a curse that would destroy her world. Unfortunately that was only wishful thinking and he was forced to grovel before her to maintain his position in her court.

Assuming that she could rely on the sketchy information Lugain provided, Meadhbh decided that the fates might be arranging themselves to her advantage. As it happened, her champions under Fineen's command were ideally located, encamped not far from the Boyne. Meadhbh doubted that Conchubar would send a large force to support those transporting the children because he had no reason to suspect that she was planning to intercept the twins. As a result, her champions should be able to grab the children after Cathbad's entourage was out of range of Emain Macha's support and before they reached their destination.

Since she didn't want to leave Fineen and his men in the field longer than necessary, "sooner rather than later" was also encouraging. Hopefully Fineen could conclude his mission before his continuing presence so far from Connaught became too suspicious.

Finally, the idea that Lugh of the Long Hand would take Cúchulainn's whelps into the lands of the Tuatha De Danann struck Meadhbh as preposterous. She never heard of such a thing happening before, nor had any of her own druids or advisors. In fact, they laughed at the whole idea. Cathbad might be a powerful magician but she wondered if, perhaps, he was beginning to act the fool in his old age. After all, he was Conchubar's father and Conchubar was ancient. Even if the old druid were able to deliver the children to Brú Na Bóinne before he was intercepted, his plan would certainly fail. Lugh would undoubtedly scoff at the whole idea or ignore him completely and Cathbad would have a long trip back. In that case the druid and his entourage would be an easy target for Fineen and her champions.

Convinced that her goal of capturing Cúchulainn's sons was in sight, Meadhbh sent the spy back to the Ulster stronghold with instructions to notify Fineen as soon as he knew when the children would be moved. Meadhbh also sent a messenger to Fineen informing him of her instructions to the spy and ordering him to move on Cathbad's entourage as soon as it left the protection of Emain Macha.

Chapter Eight

In Conchubar's stronghold, Cathbad had indeed decided that the first of May would be the day that Fergus and Ferdia would be offered to his grandfather. Beltaine was always considered a day of good fortune and people throughout the Celtic world marked the occasion with festivals and celebrations.

Cathbad was shrewd enough to know that the trip to the Boyne was a risk to the children's safety, however remote that risk might seem. Since Beltaine was a holiday nearly everyone would be celebrating with family and friends and, perhaps, be less inclined to threaten the babies. With the excitement and confusion of the festival marking the beginning of summer Cathbad thought it might be easier to slip away and complete his mission. Also, by not announcing the date for his departure to anyone, Cathbad might further reduce the risk because it would be more difficult for an enemy to plan an attack. Cathbad decided that there was no reason to expose the children to any risk, however slight, which could be easily avoided.

In the weeks between Cathbad's pronouncement and the first of May, Fergus and Ferdia grew stronger as those around them grew more despondent at their eventual departure. Mairéad and their other adoptive grandmothers were particularly sad but they never expressed their sorrow in the presence of the children. Knowing the children as they did, Fergus and Ferdia's minders were confident that the boys would be well equipped to face whatever perils lie ahead and that gave the minders a measure of comfort.

Celtic tradition required that all travellers should be welcomed so even before the Beltaine festival began, the butchery, granary and kitchens in Conchubar's stronghold were a beehive of activity. In more normal times the residents of Emain Macha would eat little more than bread, porridge and dairy products but these were not normal times. The influx of travellers meant that the celebration began several days early. Conchubar ordered that food be prepared and drink provided, as it normally would have been only for the great holiday itself.

Great joints of meat were stewed in wood-lined holes which held water heated by hot stones. Game was cooked over open fires; oat and barely loaves were baked while wheaten ale and honey mead were served to visitors and residents alike. Each night the great hall was alive with the sounds of bards and musicians rendering honour to their long serving King as well as to Cúchulainn, their fallen champion. In addition, special songs and poems were written honouring Cúchulainn's orphaned sons and wishing Fergus and Ferdia good fortune in the destinies that awaited them.

Even as the celebrations began, preparations for Fergus and Ferdia's departure were completed. At Cathbad's prompting, Conchubar ordered that a collection of valuable treasures be gathered. Cathbad explained that it would not do for the sons of Ireland's greatest hero to call on their grandfather, the immortal Lugh Lámhfáda, without appropriate gifts. Fergus and Ferdia were, after all, not paupers but wealthy in their own right by virtue of their inheritance from Cúchulainn. Although much of that wealth would, in the children's absence, revert to the king, Fergus and Ferdia would not go into the underworld, hat in hand, rather they went as the sons of a Red Branch Knight.

In addition to the finest robes, several intricately carved gold bracelets and amulets were fashioned at the direction of Cathbad. The pieces were Celtic in design so that, as they grew, the children would be reminded of their origins. Two gold goblets, inset with jewels, were specifically included as a gift for Lugh of the Long Hand. To remind the children of their father, the fallen hero's great sword was also to travel with them to the land of the Tuatha De Danann.

Finally, to protect the children during their journey, two stone cribs were fashioned from slabs of granite. The massive rocks were carefully carved and polished into a large oval shape after which the tops were hollowed to accommodate each child. Even then, it took two strong men to lift each crib. A soft mattress of goose down feathers lined the bottom of the hollow and when Fergus and Ferdia lay deep in their rock chariots, a cloth cover was fitted over the top to protect the children from the elements.

When the preparations were completed all that remained was the trip itself. The festive atmosphere in the fields around Emain Macha grew in intensity as Beltaine approached but within the confines of the great hall, it seemed that the residents knew that the day of Fergus and Ferdia's departure was imminent. At times the hall became unusually quiet and sombre and each day everyone looked to Cathbad in anticipation. Those present, particularly the women who attended the infants, realised that they would probably never see the twins again and they keened for their loss. Fergus and Ferdia, perhaps understanding their sorrow, did not protest as they were passed around and around and smothered with hugs and kisses. Their bright blue eyes moved from one face to another and into each corner of the great room, as they seemed to commit to their memories the sights, sounds and smells of Emain Macha. As dusk settled, they closed their eyes to the quiet weeping of the wonderful family the boys had acquired in only a few short weeks.

Chapter Nine

THE FIRST OF MAY DAWNED, and when Cathbad strode purposefully from his retreat in the forest with a heavy travelling cloak draped over his arm, word quickly spread that the day Fergus and Ferdia would depart finally arrived. The morning was blessed with bright sunshine, much to the relief of many who looked to the skies for some sign that the decision to offer the children to their grandfather was proper.

In Conchubar's stronghold, as Mairéad attended to her morning tasks in caring for the children she noticed that Fergus was abnormally fidgety. On closer examination she felt that his forehead was particularly warm as perhaps he was running a slight fever. Mairéad immediately send word for Cathbad and Áine, a woman trained in the healing arts, to examine the child.

It took Áine only a few minutes to confirm Mairéad's suspicions and she announced that Fergus was not only feverish but appeared to be developing a cold. Cathbad stood aside stroking his long beard considering the impact of the diagnosis. He knew that it was certainly not in the best interests of Fergus to send a sick infant on what could be a long and difficult journey. Alternatively, he was confident that the time for delivering the children to their grandfather had arrived and delay was not appropriate.

Ultimately Cathbad recalled that when he foresaw the strange futures, which awaited the infants, he recognized that their destinies were not identical and so, perhaps, this was the sign that the two children should be separated. As reluctant as he was to separate twins, he also considered that if the children took different paths, the chances that at least one of them would survive would be increased. Summarily, two things were certain; the day had arrived for the children to be presented to their grandfather and he was not prepared to risk the life of Fergus who was obviously ill.

Turning to Mairéad, he announced his decision. "Prepare Ferdia for the journey as planned and instruct Áine to attend to Fergus. He will not be travelling with his brother." Although she was also disheartened at the separation of the twins, Mairéad quietly accepted to wisdom of the decision and she watched as Áine removed Fergus from his crib. The little fellow seemed to look over at his brother, perhaps for the last time, and it seemed that a tear slid down from the corner of his eye. Ferdia watched until his brother, wrapped in Áine's arms, disappeared across the room.

Hiding her own tears, Mairéad fussed over the remaining infant in an attempt to distract him from the fact that for the first time in his life, Fergus was not at his side. Ferdia was taken from his crib, bathed and dressed for the last time, at least among the people of the upper earth. Mairéad then passed the child among all of the women who had been entrusted with his care and for the last time the little fellow was showered with affection while sweet endearments were whispered into his ears. Ferdia apparently knew that something different was about to happen. His eyes seemed to reflect a slightly quizzical expression, particularly at the sight and sound of the women's tears and weeping. In a short time, however, he seemed to accept whatever change was to transpire and the questioning look disappeared. After all present expressed their love and affection, Ferdia was adorned in the gold jewellery that was crafted at Cathbad's direction.

With the preparations completed and farewells whispered, Conchubar himself took the child in his hands and kissed his forehead. "Godspeed my littlest knight," he whispered as the eyes of even the most hardened fighter teared over.

Conchubar then returned the child to Mairéad who tenderly placed Ferdia in his rock crib for the first time. The infant placed his hand on the cold stone looking around with interest at his new surroundings. Satisfied that everything was in proper order, Ferdia closed his eyes and slept. Mairéad adjusted the infant's mattress and tucked a woollen blanket between the mattress and the stone. Satisfied that her charge was comfortable, she pulled the cover over the granite crib.

The heavy crib was the placed on a litter for its journey to the fairy hill located not far from the hill of Knowth at Brú Na Bóinne. The weather remained fine if a bit chilly but as the morning progressed, gathering clouds made it quite clear that although the beginning of the long journey might be pleasant, the end would probably be a different story entirely.

A procession was formed led by Cathbad the Druid adorned in his white robe trimmed in gold. In deference to the chill and coming storm, the robe was covered with an animal skin travelling poncho. Cathbad was followed by seven other druids and druidess of lesser status, similarly clad. Following the druids, seven of Conchubar's handpicked champions led the litter bearing Ferdia as well as second litter carrying the remainder of the treasures that would accompany him to the land of the Tuatha De Danann. Following the litter, providing additional protection, were seven more champions. At the end of the procession were seven men and seven women, representatives of the people, who would witness whatever might transpire.

First among these women was Mairéad. Cathbad gently suggested that perhaps the journey would be too much for the old woman and that, as she had so selflessly and loyally performed her duty, she should remain behind. It was clear in the face of the determined Mairéad, that there was no chance that she would agree. "My destiny," she quietly but firmly insisted, "is with the child."

As the entourage emerged from the gate of Emain Macha, hundreds of well-wishers lined the path leading from the fortress. Meadhbh's spies, stood among the throng and when the last witness passed they slipped away to complete their mission. The first spy was off to Cruachan to report to the queen while the other made his way to Fineen's encampment.

Throughout the morning the procession steadily snaked its way to the south and east toward the sacred site of Brú Na Bóinne. As the day progressed all signs of blue sky disappeared and although the weather warmed slightly, the clouds darkened. By early afternoon the first drops of rain began to fall. The steady progress of the entourage was slowed as many slipped on the wet grass and rocks that marked their path. Remarkably, the one person who seemed totally unaffected by the weather was the ancient Mairéad, who walked straight and strong like a healthy girl sixty or seventy years younger.

It was evening when the hill of Knowth came into view. By that time the weather was perfectly miserable as the darkening sky appeared even blacker because of storm clouds that were not likely to lift in the near future. The rain thickened from a mist to drizzle and finally to a persistent downpour. As a result the procession slowed to a crawl as each participant, soaked to the bone, trod carefully to avoid turning an ankle on the slippery surface. Their progress was further delayed because while most of the journey had been over flat ground, they were now climbing from the Boyne Valley.

Although nearly at their destination, Cathbad had no choice but to order a brief rest so that everyone could catch their breath and prepare for the final climb.

Chapter Ten

FINEEN AND HIS DETACHMENT OF CONNAUGHT CHAMPIONS were also forced to halt their progress after several hours of hard riding in their war chariots. The heavy rains left the ground so sodden that even the relatively light chariots sank nearly to their axels. Fineen cursed his luck, which left him mired in muck rather than celebrating the successful completion of his mission. Of course it had all begun with Meadhbh's insistence that his contingent remain in the field for literally weeks while she awaited word of Cathbad's movements.

Unfortunately, he had his orders from his queen to remain in the field and he knew better than to question, or even worse to disobey those orders. On the other hand, the last thing he wanted was an armed confrontation with a superior force of Ulster Champions and he knew that his lingering did not go unnoticed.

Reasoning that Meadhbh would not know exactly where he had established camp, Fineen decided to move his force south, deeper into Leinster. That province was allied with Connaught so his presence would not be seen as a threat. If anyone asked, he could always say that he was on a training exercise at the queen's command. Although the move would take him some distance from the Boyne, he knew that his chariots could move quickly back when the word came. He reasoned that a short delay was a small price to pay to ensure that his troop was not engaged before he could carry out his mission. Fineen ordered that a couple of trusted men remain in the vicinity of his original camp so that the spy reporting from Emain Macha would find his way to the relocated camp.

Fineen's first stoke of bad luck was that the spy from Emain Macha had difficulty locating the two men he left behind. The spy rode to within view of the earlier camp's location but since he did not see the horses or tents, he assumed that he was mistaken about the location. As a result, he spent the next couple of hours wandering around the general vicinity. Eventually he decided that he was correct the first time and it was only then that he encountered the men who had been left behind, sleeping peacefully in and among the rocks and trees.

When the spy was finally escorted into his camp, Fineen was furious at the delay but delighted to finally be able to begin his mission. Morale in the camp was particularly low because none of the men were happy with living outdoors in the rain and the dampness for weeks on end. As Beltaine approached the queen's champions knew they were missing one of the major celebrations on the Celtic calendar. With the summer coming on, they would far rather be working their fields and living in the comfort of their own homes rather. Instead they were chasing infants on behalf of their noble queen whose sanity was frequently questioned even at the best of times.

Questioning the spy, Fineen was pleased to discover that although fourteen champions were included for defence, the Ulster men would not only be outnumbered but they were also on foot. Certainly they would be no match for his detachment's war chariots. Fineen was quick to give the order to mount up and his champions, relieved to be completing their mission, were quick to obey. In a matter of minutes the forces of Queen Meadhbh were thundering north and east across the Meath and heading for the Boyne.

They travelled only about a mile when the morning sunshine turned into afternoon rain. While chariots moved quickly on dry, hard ground even a light rain caused its share of difficulties. Wet grass or muddy paths did little to slow the horses but chariot wheels had a tendency to slide, especially when it was necessary to make any type of turn. Since the path they were taking followed the terrain, there were plenty of turns and continuing at speed could easily cause a chariot to overturn. Cursing the luck, which found him with chariots instead of riding horses, Fineen had no choice but to order his troops to slow their pace.

As the skies darkened and the rain intensified, the pace of his troop was further slowed by the thickening mud along the pathway to the Boyne. Fineen's men were soaked to the skin cursing loudly at every turn and the horses were breathing heavily at the extra weight they were required to carry. Fineen looked to the west to see if any break in the weather might be on the horizon but was again forced to curse his bad luck.

As any good leader would do, Fineen considered the options that faced him, now that the fates destroyed his original plan. While it didn't look like he would be able to intercept Cathbad before he reached Brú Na Bóinne, he knew that his prey also had to travel in the same conditions. It would therefore do no harm to continue even at a snail's pace. He also remembered what the spy said about Cathbad's mission. Seemingly neither Meadhbh nor her druids actually believed that Lugh of the Long Hand was likely to take the infants into the underworld. Absurd, was the word the spy reported.

Although nearly everyone in Connaught had more faith in Cathbad than they did in any of their own druids, it did seem a bit hard to believe that the child would be in Cathbad's company one minute and gone completely the next, having been spirited away to the land of the Tuatha de Danann. Assuming that Cathbad's disappearing act was not successful, there was apparently no rush because his party would be an easy target as they attempted to return home. As he watched his men slog through the mud, a plan that included waiting for the Ulster men to finish their hopeless task and turn back toward Emain Macha was beginning to sound quite appealing.

Fineen was just about to call for his men to halt and shelter from the storm when one champion pulled up next to him and pointed into the hills above. Shielding his eyes against the rain, Fineen followed the man's finger and saw a large number of people on foot, some distance to the east of his detachment. The group was picking its way up the hills that rose from the river valley. Watching carefully for several minutes, Fineen was confident that his prey was in sight. He was also confident that they had not completed their mission because if they had, the group would be either coming down toward the river or not moving at all. The discovery caused him to reconsider his decision once again and he urged his men forward.

Fineen's detachment continued on the flat path along the river, running parallel with Cathbad's movements well up on the hillside. He had little doubt that Conchubar's champions now knew he was coming but for a time they continued working their way to the east and further up the hill. Turning his attention to his own men it became obvious that the horses pulling the chariots were nearly spent. The path was a spongy mess and if one chariot got stuck the entire troop was impeded. When the chariots were not moving, they slowly sank into the mud. Eventually Fineen recognised that the vehicles were more a hindrance than a help and he ordered his detachment to halt and dismount. If they were to overtake Cathbad, the rest of the journey would have to be on foot.

While the men gathered their weapons for the assault, Fineen again cursed his misfortune. Not only were the chariots useless in any upcoming battle, but his men now faced a long and steep climb after which they would have to fight the Ulster champions who held the higher ground. That alone would eliminate the advantage of his numbers and there was no reason to be confident of a victory.

Once again, the idea of waiting for the results of Cathbad's efforts was beginning to sound like the better course. But then he thought of Meadhbh and her foul temper and he thought of his own wife and children and what might happen to them if he were to be disgraced. Perhaps, with a little luck, which certainly didn't seem to be with him today, someone could grab the children during the battle that would follow. "Right," he thought, "with a little luck." And again he cursed his fate as he urged his men on.

Chapter eleven

As CATHBAD PEERED INTO THE RAIN trying to pick out the landmark that would signal the journey's end, the leader of Conchubar's champions, a man called Lorcan who was guarding the rear of the procession, approached.

"With respect," Lorcan began, "some time ago I noticed a troop of charioteers in the far distance and I have been tracking their progress. They seemed to be following us but it is clear that because they are mounted, they have now closed on us quite quickly. Although the visibility is not great, one of my lads thought he saw the banner of Connaught. It is possible that Meadhbh has sent a troop after the child."

Cathbad was alarmed at the revelation and quickly moved to a vantage point to the rear of the parade so that he could judge the threat. Standing on a rock he peered intently down the hill and raising his arms he closed his eyes as if he could somehow place himself among the trailing force. When he opened his eyes, he calmly announced, "Meadhbh has sent her men to take the child."

The Ulster champion looked down the hill in alarm. "They have abandoned their chariots and are coming up the hill on foot. Do you have any orders?"

Cathbad looked down into the thickening rain and then turned and looked at his goal that he could now see was about fifty yards beyond where his entourage was resting. "Form a battle line here," he ordered. "Keep your men between their forces and that grove of hawthorn bushes at least until I have presented Ferdia to his grandfather. If I am successful and Lugh Lámhfáda takes custody of the child they will have no reason to fight especially since they are far from their home. If I am not successful, you will have to hold them off until we can make our way back to Emain Macha."

Lorcan looked down again at the oncoming troops. "I make it about twenty champions and an equal number of drivers and spear-carriers. Although they outnumber us, we hold the high ground. We will hold," he stated flatly.

Cathbad was pleased with Lorcan's confidence but concerned with the number of enemies who had now closed to within a couple hundred yards. It was decidedly possible that a few of them could slip past Lorcan's battle line and the remainder of his druids and witnesses would be in no position to defend the child. Cathbad then looked to the west and south noting that the clouds were even blacker in that direction. "Perhaps I can buy us a bit more time," he said with a grim smile.

Returning to the rock from which he first viewed Meadhbh's champions, Cathbad removed his heavy cloak revealing the white and gold robe of a great druid and raised his staff to the sky, clutching it with both hands. Turning his head skyward, he began chanting in a language the Lorcan could not understand.

As Fineen and his men struggle up the hill, the Connaught commander looked up and saw Cathbad standing on a rock, his robe and beard bent by the wind and rain, his staff held high, horizontal to the ground. Although he couldn't hear what the druid was saying he knew, as did every man in his detachment, that Cathbad was calling down some misfortune on the men of Connaught.

Just then a distant flash of lightening lit the northern sky providing a backlight for the druid and the Ulster champions who had taking their positions across the hill behind him. Fineen and his men froze in their steps. They knew that Cathbad brought champions to protect the children but in that brief moment of illumination, it was entirely unclear just how many of Ulster's finest stood in their path. Clearly, it was more than a few token warriors and possibly more than the dozen or so they originally estimated. Of greater concern was the old druid standing before them. All of Fineen's men had heard of Cathbad's great power, which dwarfed the skills and abilities of their own druids. Whatever fear they might have felt at the sight of Ulster Champions taking battle positions, was nothing compared with their fear of Cathbad's power.

Just then the rain strengthened and it seemed as if a curtain of water was drawn across the hill above them. All sight of Cathbad and the Ulster men was gone and all they could see was a solid wall of water. The rain now beat down with an intensity none of Meadhbh's men had ever recalled. But it was not just the rain falling from the sky, because streams of water from rain which fell higher on the hill made it seem as if they were wading uphill and against the current in a small stream. Several Connaught champions slipped backwards, scrambling in vain to regain their footing. Others accepted their fate and turning on their backsides to protect themselves, allowed the water to take them down the hill.

Fineen tried to rally those that remained on their feet but he knew there was nothing he could do to contend with the power of Cathbad. His day was cursed by the gods and there was nothing he could do to alter what was fated. All that he could hope for was that Cathbad's power was not strong enough to call on Lugh Lámhfáda to take Cúchulainn's children. Shouting into the wind, he ordered his men to return to the chariots and shelter there until the storm broke.

Because of the intense rain, Lorcan's Ulster champions also lost sight of their adversaries below. Remarkably, although the rain intensified higher up where they had taken their positions, it seemed like a far heavier wall of rain was holding steady some fifty yards down the hill. That wall was the outer limit of their vision. Lorcan ordered his men to hold fast expecting that the Connaught champions would eventually break through the wall and the battle would commence.

Chapter Twelve

SATISFIED THAT HE HAD DONE EVERYTHING POSSIBLE to slow the advance of Meadhbh's warriors, Cathbad hurried back to the remainder of his entourage and urged them to begin the final ascent. Since many of them realised what was transpiring further down the hill, they needed no additional urging and the procession was soon scrambling forward.

A few minutes later, Cathbad led the party toward a grove of hawthorn bushes on a small rise not far from the base of the hill of Knowth. To everyone's relief, Cathbad announced that the journey was at an end. As the party gathered, Cathbad directed them toward a suterrain or passage nearly adjacent to the hawthorn grove. The suterrain appeared to be a small opening amidst the rocks at the base of the hawthorn bushes. This was undoubtedly the portal through which, if invited, Ferdia would pass on the way to his grandfather.

As the people gathered around Cathbad, he instructed the lesser druids to form a semi-circle about ten yards from the suterrain. The remainder of party was told to form behind the druids in the same concentric formation. The litter bearers came forward and carefully placed the heavy granite crib at the mouth of the suterrain.

Cathbad then asked Mairéad and the oldest man from among the witnesses to come forward. While the litter bearers held a cloak over the crib to protect the child from the heavy rain, the two were instructed to make sure Ferdia was comfortable and had not been dislodged during the trip. The cloth cap was drawn back disclosing a smiling infant who apparently wasn't the slightest bit disturbed by a long journey or by the discomfort of a cold and wet day.

Mairéad fussed about the child, readjusting the down mattress, straightening his robe and again tucking the blanket in around the baby. When she was satisfied, she bent down and kissed Ferdia's forehead for the last time and pulled the cover back over the rock crib. Cathbad then instructed that the second set of litter bearers place their burden containing the child's treasures next to the crib. When everything was positioned to his satisfaction in front of the suterrain Cathbad removed his outer garment and handed it to the elderly couple. He instructed the witnesses to spread the cloak over the stone crib and treasures to protect them from the elements.

When this was accomplished, the witnesses and litter bearers returned to their places behind the lesser druids and Cathbad, by now soaked to the skin followed them to a point a few feet in front of the druids and a few feet from the crib.

As soon as everyone had taken their positions, Cathbad raised his arms to the heavens, his stout walking stick clenched tightly in his right fist. The rain continued, soaking his uncovered hair and beard and dripping off his face as he turned it up toward the sky. The storm seemed to intensify once again as the skies opened and the rain bucketed down. In the distance, lightening flashed across the sky. Cathbad held the pose for several moments before he roared:

Lugh Lámhfáda, great god of light hear me.
Great king and your welcoming long hand listen
to me.
Great lord, whose royal blood flows in your
faithful servant heed me.

Cathbad was silent for a moment as his head dropped but his arms remained stiff and strong. He closed his eyes as if expecting a painful blow and then a shudder seemed to pass through his entire body while the wind and the rain beat down even harder. To the witnesses behind him, the great druid appeared as a ghostly shadow, apparent only when lightening illuminated the horizon.

Once again he called out.

Lugh Lámhfáda, do not be angry with your servant
I am merely a messenger seeking your indulgence
Your grandson by the mighty Cúchulainn seeks your protection
Welcome him great god, welcome him.

For several moments the rain and the wind lessened as if the gods were considering Cathbad's plea. For his part, Cathbad remained erect his fists outstretched to the heavens and his face welcoming the cold rain as it poured down from the sky. Most of the witnesses cowered behind the line of druids apparently concerned that they might suffer the anger of the gods against those who dared venture onto sacred ground. Others, particularly the elderly witnesses, with Mairéad at the front, watched fearlessly with solemn interest, fully prepared to accept the will of the gods.

After a few minutes a great sheet of lightening illuminated the northern sky casting strange shadows on the hawthorn grove. The light was followed shortly thereafter by a roar of thunder that shook the earth. Even the bravest of the lesser druids and witnesses cowered at this demonstration of divine power. A second and a third sheet of lighting repeated the process and when the thunder roared once again, Cathbad was thrown face down on the ground, his hands still outstretched as if reaching for the bundle holding the child a few feet beyond his finger tips. Seeing Cathbad so violently flung to the earth, the witnesses also threw themselves on the ground hoping that they might be spared a similar fate. Mairéad alone stood strong, her face raised to the beating rain, a smile on her lips.

For several minutes the rest of the gathering clung to the safety of the earth, hoping perhaps that if they were one with the mud and the dirt, the gods might not notice them and they would be spared. Above them the wind and the rain continued to howl. But then, the storm suddenly broke. In a matter of seconds, the rain stopped falling, the wind stopped blowing and the blanket of heavy cloud disappeared to the east. As the timid witnesses peaked up they were amazed to see a clear night sky full of stars.

The lesser druids, champions and witnesses slowly rose to their feet, brushing off the grass and mud that clung to their cloaks. They quickly noticed that Cathbad remained prone on the ground and it was clear that whether by the hand of the gods or the force of his fall, he had been knocked unconscious. The group gathered around the great druid, concerned for his welfare but at the same time relieved that they emerged un- scathed. Two of the druids moved forward to render assistance their fallen chief.

Just as they reached his side, one druid was distracted by a movement near the suterrain and looking up he exclaimed, "The cloak!"

The attention of the entire group was redirected toward Cath- bad's animal skin outer cloak which once covered the granite crib and chest of treasures. It lay where it had been placed and a gentle breeze moved the corner of the garment. Without question something lay under the cloak as it was not flat on the ground but was draped over two objects. While two dru- ids continued to administer to Cathbad, the remaining druids cautiously approached the garment. The champions and wit- nesses moved forward behind the protection of the druid line each looking over or around those in front so as not to miss whatever lay beneath the cloak.

No one breathed as one of the druids reached down to re- trieve Cathbad's cloak. As he pulled it aside, a collective sigh escaped from many of those gathered behind the druids. The cloak was fully removed disclosing the objects it covered, two great lumps of rock.

The shocked silence of the discovery was soon replaced by the amazed pronouncements and in seconds everyone began speaking at once. The conclusion was universally accepted. Clearly Lugh of the Long Hand had taken custody of his grandson, Ferdia son of Cúchulainn and the treasures of the infant's inheritance.

As the impact of their discovery became clear, a silence again descended on the group and their attention was redirected to the unconscious form of Cathbad the druid. One of the lesser druids propped him up; sitting Cathbad against a stone while another prevented his head from lolling to one side or the other. An older woman, skilled in the healing arts examined his head and determined that he was alive but undoubtedly had been knocked unconscious by a blow to the head. She directed that a wet cloth be applied to his forehead and she began to mix a potion from the bag of herbs tied at her waist.

When she finished preparing the concoction, she mixed it with water and forced some of the mixture into the old druid's mouth. The remainder was held under his nose. Either the vile taste or the vile smell had the desired effect because almost immediately, Cathbad spat out the liquid and moved his head from side to side to escape the odour.

In time, the druid blinked, opened his eyes and slowly regained full consciousness. He looked around at the group and quietly spoke. "I have seen Lugh Lámhfáda. He has taken his grandson and discharged us from our duty to the child. He has promised that the child will be placed in good hands and treated in a manner appropriate to his station. Ferdia will be protected for as long as his safety is threatened by those who would seek to do him harm and for as long as he is unable to protect himself. It is finished."

With great effort, the old druid was assisted to his feet and was draped with the skin that once covered Ferdia and the treasures. The remainder of the group quietly gathered their belongings and prepared to return to Emain Macha. After the initial shock of witnessing such an amazing event, it seemed that each person retreated into the silence of his or her own thoughts. All that remained was the musical night sounds of a peaceful spring evening.

A moment later, however, the stillness of the evening was broken by the grasp of one of the women witnesses. "Mairéad!" she exclaimed.

All eyes turned to the form of the old woman who slowly sat in the wet grass and then fell on her side before finally lying on her back. Cathbad and the woman who treated him, rushed over to her side. As they knelt beside Mairéad, she closed her eyes and a smile lit her face.

"Old Sister," he said clearly distressed. "Can you hear me?"

Mairéad's eyes fluttered and opened slightly. "Yes my brother, I can hear you. You are speaking loud enough to wake the dead."

The remark brought smiles to the faces of the entire group and Cathbad pressed on, "Mairéad, have you hurt yourself? Are you in pain?"

The old woman continued to smile as she replied, "No, I am not in pain. It is just that my light is growing dim and I am being called from this life."

Cathbad put his hand on the old woman's cheek and with tears running down his own face said, "I am sorry I agreed to your joining this journey. Certainly it was too much for you. What have I done?"

"Hush, my friend," Mairéad gasped. "This was my destiny and this is the only way my life on this earth could have ended. I knew when I held that child for the first time that our destinies were bound to each other and so it is proper that we depart this world together. I have no fear of the next world; perhaps I will see Ferdia again. Know this, my brother, I am at peace."

With that Mairéad closed her eyes for the last time.

Chapter Thirteen

IN A BLINK OF YOUNG FERDIA'S EYES, the granite crib and chest of treasures were transported to the land of the Tuatha Dé Danann far beneath the surface of the earth. They settled on a table in the middle of a great field where scores of people gathered. A moment later, the cloth covering the crib was drawn back and child found himself staring into at least six pairs of amazed eyes leaning over his bed. After taking in the scene, Ferdia smiled and let out a gurgle of delight. This broke the silence of the moment and everyone began to smile and laugh.

One pair of eyes remained fixed on the child and a moment later Ferdia found himself being lifted into the air by a tall and powerful man. The stranger had two long blonde moustaches flowing from each side of his upper lip and down over his mouth to where they joined his beard which was groomed well down onto his chest. The man's nose was long and pointed, his eyes, not unlike Ferdia's own, were large and blue and he was dressed in a purple robe trimmed with gold.

"This child my friends," announced a smiling Lugh of the Long Hand, "is my grandson!"

As so it was that Ferdia, Son of Cúchulainn and Grandson of Lugh Lámhfáda came to reside with the Tuatha Dé Danann. These people of the goddess Dana were a cultured and highly civilised race of people. They were extraordinarily skilled in all measure of arts and crafts specifically including magic and the black arts. So great was their power that subsequent races and peoples regarded them as gods and goddesses.

The Tuatha Dé Danann conquered Ireland well over a thousand years before the birth of Christ. Unlike other conquerors, the Tuatha Dé Danann did not sail to the coast of the country, armed and ready for battle. Rather, they arrived in what seemed to be a dark cloud sailing through the air until they landed on a mountain in Connemara. When they blacked out the sun for three days the Firbolgs, who controlled the country at that time had no choice but to fight. A great and famous battle determined the fate of the Firbolgs who fought bravely for four days but in the end, were no match for the magic and skills of the Dé Danann. The Tuatha Dé Danann ruled Ireland for many decades controlling lesser mortals with their amazing power. However, they also shared some of their secret crafts, including the ability to refine metals like bronze and gold, and they introduced science and poetry to the people they ruled.

The Tuatha Dé Danann were regarded as kindly and beneficent rulers and some of the people of Dana even married or had children by lesser mortals. This practice caused a great deal of concern particularly among the elders of the Dé Danann and it ultimately led to the end of their rule in Ireland. These elders were justifiably concerned that if the people intermarried with lesser mortals all of their secrets would be disclosed and they would lose their identity. As a result they would have no power over subsequent invaders.

In time other races, including the Milesians, threatened to conquer Ireland and the Tuatha Dé Danann made a remarkable decision. After a great conference at which everyone had an opportunity to be heard, the majority of the Dé Danann's adult population decided to withdraw from the human race and create their own world deep under the crust of the earth. This move would ensure that the Dé Danann blood would remain pure and that the secrets of their power would not fall into the hands of people who might misuse these gifts.

A large number of the Dé Danann chose not to withdraw from the surface of the earth and so remained behind. Some had established relationships with other peoples and did not want to leave their husbands, wives or children behind. Others with children believed that regardless of their probable status as a conquered people and no longer the ruling class, the best interests of their children lay in the sunshine and fresh air of the Irish countryside. Still others had grown to accept the cycle of life as it unfolded on the earth's surface and were content with birth, life, aging and death.

When the Milesians ultimately invaded Ireland, the Tuatha Dé Danann who remained above on the surface of the earth offered only a token resistance against the invasion and were defeated. In time they mixed their blood with that of the Firbolgs, Milesians and subsequent invaders of Ireland. Thousands of years later, traces of that Dé Danann blood are still reflected in the poetic and artistic nature of the Irish people.

The Milesians, who were the forefathers of the Celtic race, conquered Ireland rather easily because the most of the Dé Danann had retreated into a world where they could perfect and practice their arts and skills in peace and security. That world became the subject of innumerable myths and legends, which became part of the Irish tradition, and they are still discussed three thousand years later. In these Irish legends the world to which the Dé Danann descended became known as the "Land of Youth" or "Tir na nÓg," a peaceful and beautiful place with no sickness or death where the people were always happy and time stands still. In truth, the world created by the Tuatha Dé Danann was not significantly different than the one described in myths and legends.

Quite apart from building an alternative world, perhaps the greatest skill the Tuatha Dé Danann perfected was the ability to slow the passage of time almost to a standstill. A second of human time became many hours beneath the earth and an hour became years and as a result the people of Dana effectively became immortal. The population of this alternative world remained static because although few died, no one was born. The cycle of life was frozen in time and there was no sickness or death.

In the decades that followed their descent, the Dé Danann built their own world increasingly isolating themselves from the human race on the surface of the earth. Occasionally, particularly in the early days after the Milesians took control of Ireland, some of the Dé Danann, still interacted with the surface people.

The reason for this interaction was that the Dé Danann had a great deal of respect and affection for the race they had abandoned. Because of marriages while they were still above ground many of those who lived on the surface of the earth were, in part, people of Dana and so they were related to those who chose Tir na nOg. Cathbad the Druid's remarkable skill, for example, could be traced to his royal blood. The Tuatha Dé Danann also believed that an occasional infusion of their own blood would further ensure the survival of these lesser mortals. Thus, Lugh of the Long Hand sired Cúchulainn. In time, this connection became more and more remote, particularly because generations changed so quickly on the surface of the earth. In time, the Tuatha Dé Danann rarely appeared above ground.

The world into which Ferdia was delivered appeared remarkably similar to the one from which he came. Looking around anyone would have sworn that he or she was out of doors rather than in an incredibly massive cavern. The only apparent difference was that what appeared to be the sky was not blue but, rather, a dark shade of grey, not unlike a wet day above ground. That sky seemed to be a long way off but, of course, that was an optical illusion created by the Dé Danann. Although the roof of the cavern was a great distance from the floor it was patently not as endless as the sky. Like the sky above them, the world the Tuatha Dé Danann created was a remarkable collection of illusion, science, metallurgy, mechanics and magic.

The Tuatha Dé Danann enjoyed daylight during waking hours, just as they had when they were above the ground, thanks to an intricate series of glass and mirrors that stored, reflected and magnified light. This light, and heat, was solar in origin and entered the cavern from any number of minute openings to the world above. Because time passed more slowly under the earth, solar light was stored and then displayed to reflect the passing of days and nights under ground. The same was true with air that entered the underworld. Ireland was, and is, covered with rocks and mounds of rocks many of which protect vents into the land of the Tuatha Dé Danann. Even today, as these rocks are taken away by humans, who are concerned with tillage or developing a nice garden, other rocks are pushed up to take their place.

And, of course, there are hundreds of what are known to surface residents as "Fairy Forts" sprinkled across the Irish Countryside. It is said that to interfere with these fairy forts will bring great misfortune. The reason, quite simply, is that these mounds are not forts at all but are portals or suterrains into the land of the Tuatha Dé Danann and to interfere with these portals would threaten the existence of the people of Dana. To protect themselves the Dé Danann employ their black magic against those who would threaten their existence by tampering with their fairy forts.

With air and light cleverly harvested from above the ground, and water from underground lakes and streams, the Tuatha Dé Danann were able to grow crops and raise livestock necessary to sustain their lives. When not threatened by the intrusions of the race above ground, they live a highly cultured existence in peace and harmony. They work to live but always appreciate the arts, poetry, music and dance. Numerous occasions were marked by grand celebrations of culture or "Feis Ceoils" at which, in addition to music and dance, great quantities of food and drink were consumed because without question the people of Dana had not lost the great art of fermentation.

The sudden presence of Ferdia was hardly an intrusion because he was not a threat to the people. Ferdia had been invited into the underworld by no less than Lugh of the Long Hand. The infant was slowly passed from one person to the next as each marvelled at his perfect form and remarkable good nature. Even by Dé Danann time passage it had been a long time since many of the people had even seen an infant, never mind holding him in their arms. One might have thought that the presence of the infant could cause Dana's people to regret what they had lost when they entered their new world, but that was not the way of the people. Rather, they celebrated what that had and did not regret what was gone. The presence of this child was most certainly a cause for celebration.

Lugh ordered that a Feis Ceoil be organised and immediately scores of people proceeded to their designated tasks. Lugh reclaimed the child and looking into his bright blue eyes said "Now what am I going to do with you?"

An old woman named Muroad stepped forward and gently chastised the great Lugh. "What are you like? Of course you haven't a clue about such a tiny one, even though he is your grandson. I will tend the child and you can preside over the celebrations."

Lugh looked at the woman with a wry smile, "And how long has it been since you held a wee child?"

Muroad reached out and took the child, "Will you go away out of that? Sure didn't I tend you when you were about this size? Some things are just not forgotten."

Lugh put his hand up in mock surrender, "But of course dear Muroad. I wouldn't doubt your skills for even a second."

With that the old woman took the child away to be cleaned and fed and Lugh turned his attention to the Feis. At his direction great quantities of food and drink were laid on, and the musicians were organised to play in shifts so that the music would never stop. A massive marquee was erected, not so much to protect the celebrants from the elements, which were never a problem, but to ensure that the party did not wander from place to place. Long tables were set to hold the feast and other tables were arranged around the perimeter of the great tent for drinking, dining and resting. The marquee was extravagantly decorated with flags, banners and bunting adding an amazing array of colour. Finally the solar light store was opened so that there would be no darkness while the celebration was in full swing.

When all the preparations were finalised and the musicians, instruments tuned, had taken their places, Lugh took his grandson to the head of the marquee and holding Ferdia high, announced in a loud voice. "This is my grandson Ferdia who I have vowed to protect from the forces of evil which occupy the upper world. This child represents the continuation of our race and culture and so we celebrate his birth, his life and his presence among us. I declare that this Feis Ceoil be opened."

With the pronouncement the crowd roared, the music began, the drink began to flow, and the party began. Although time passing was difficult to determine, because there was no darkness to divide days and nights, the Feis unquestionably continued for many Tuatha Dé Danann days. Each person who attended demanded his or her opportunity to present their own tribute to Ferdia, be it in song or story, poem, recital or dance and the sheer number of participants ensured a long and memorable Feis Ceoil. No one needed any urging to take the stage and present their party piece because in a world where life was celebrated frequently, every person's efforts were sincerely appreciated. Between presentations the music and dancing never stopped and the food and refreshments were never allowed to run low. Occasionally someone, particularly an older person, might slip off for a bit of sleep but they soon returned delighted that the Feis was still in full swing.

Ferdia and his grandfather were in constant attendance. The infant was usually found in the arms of Muroad who held him so that he could see the proceedings. She was relieved occasionally by Lugh himself who proudly described the festivities to his grandson and introduced the child to everyone who came forward with a tribute. Although he occasionally napped, particularly after he was fed, Ferdia seemed completely attentive to everything that transpired before him. Just as had been the case when he was in the great hall of Conchubar, the Dé Danann found it amazing that such a small infant would seemingly appreciate and understand the strange world around him.

Eventually, after everyone paid his or her tribute to the guest of honour the Feis began to wind down. When it was all over the entire people agreed that this was a party that would be well remembered, and itself celebrated, among the Tuatha Dé Danann for a long, long time. As the panels of the solar store were closed, the light in the underworld dimmed and the people, exhausted from their extended celebration, slept deep and untroubled for a long time. Ferdia, adapting completely to his new environment, also slept peacefully in the watchful presence of Muroad.

When dawn in the underworld finally broke the people of Dana came to life and returned to their normal daily tasks. The name Ferdia and the magnificent tributes that had been paid to him seemed to be on everyone's lips, and the little fellow was never short of visitors. Apparently, their experiences during the Feis convinced the people that this infant child, remarkably, could understand what they were saying and each of them had some wisdom or advice to offer to Ferdia. The child appeared to listen intently committing the sounds and sights of the underworld to the recesses of his memory.

About three underworld weeks after Ferdia had been delivered to his grandfather, life in the world of the Tuatha Dé Danann returned to normal. Muroad, who assumed the role of nanny for the infant, was his constant companion. She was convinced that the Ferdia was abnormally perceptive for a child of his age, and she never tired of sharing her life, experiences and the history of the people of Dana, with him. Ferdia did appear to take it all in occasionally even nodding his head when asked if he understood. Muroad had never encountered any child quite like Ferdia and she was always ready to describe the infant's special gifts to anyone who would listen.

After a time, however, her audience diminished because having heard what the old woman had to say, further explanations seemed repetitious. This troubled Muroad but for a long time she couldn't quite put her finger on the reason for her concern. She did know that even people who are always happy might tire of an old lady's ramblings but that was not what concerned her. It was something about the child and his life, and she hoped that if she thought about it long enough, the answer would come.

Eventually, after many hours of holding the child, rocking him in her arms, singing him the songs of the people, feeding him and, of course, cleaning up after him, the answer came. Muroad arranged an appointment with Lugh to discuss the problem.

"You know, Lugh, that I love your grandchild as if he were my own flesh and blood and only want what is best for him," Muroad began.

Lugh replied stroking his long facial hair, "I have no doubts whatsoever on that score."

She continued, "I also know that you took him here to protect him from the evil which threatened his life in the world above the ground."

"That I did," Lugh stated.

Muroad paused looking down as she wove the end of her shawl around her hands, "Your motive and actions were, without doubt, both understandable and appropriate."

Lugh looked at the old woman with a quizzical expression, "But?"

Taking a deep breath Muroad looked the king in the eye, and the words poured out of her, "But...what kind of a life will Ferdia have here among the people. Of course he will be safe and well loved, but he will never be more than an infant because his age is virtually frozen here, as is all of ours. He will never develop into a boy and into a man and while he might absorb everything we tell him, he will never be able to pass these things on to his own sons and daughters. Is this what you want for your grandson?"

Lugh sat with one arm across his chest and the other continuing to stroke his luxurious moustaches. He thought about what Muroad said and after some time he responded, "I too have given a great deal of thought to the future of this child and I cannot argue with anything you have said. As much as I value the presence of this child among us, he is only an infant and to keep him here will deprive him of an opportunity to live a full life and experience all the things that we knew during our years above the earth. On the other hand, in accepting this child, I have sworn an oath to protect him from the evils that threatened his life and I must be true to my oath."

Muroad nodded her head in agreement, "It is a difficult matter to balance the two."

"Actually," Lugh continued with a smile, "not so difficult. Let me see whether I can work this out. The evil, which originally threatened Ferdia in the world above, has undoubtedly long since passed. In that world nearly two thousand years have passed since Cathbad presented the child, and Meadhbh, her sons and grandsons, and all the enemies of the child's father have long since died. Unfortunately, although the specific evil that brought Ferdia here is gone, my pledge was to protect the child from evil that threatens him in the world above ground, not just the specific evil that threatened him when he came among us. And so, it seems to me, as long as there is evil in the world above, my pledge must remain intact."

The old woman sighed, "And since there will always be evil in the world above, the child will never be able to leave your protection."

Lugh smiled, "Not necessarily. There are other components to my pledge, the first being that the evil must threaten his life and the second is that the protection was only until he was able to protect himself. Because of that second component we must accept that my pledge anticipated that this child would grow and mature so that one day he could protect himself. That would not be the case if he never left our world. If there were to come a time when society above the earth was relatively safe and Ferdia could grow to manhood with little fear for his own life, he should be returned to the land above the ground."

"So you would allow Ferdia to grow into manhood," Muroad said with a smile.

"Of course I would, and I will." Lugh replied patting the old woman's arm. "I will study the world above and determine the appropriate time and decide what mortals might best foster my grandson. When the circumstances are properly aligned, I will deliver Ferdia to a world where he will grow and mature and fulfil his own destiny."

Muroad hesitated for a moment and then spoke again, "But Lugh, he is your grandson. If he were to leave, you would never see him again. He will be gone and in a short time, as it passes in our world, he will be dead. Will that not bring you great sorrow?"

Lugh smiled at her concern, "It will of course. But Ferdia has his own destiny and as it cannot be fulfilled here, the only other possibility is the world above the earth. I would be less than a proper grandfather if I were to deny him his destiny for my own selfish reasons. Beside, one never knows. Perhaps one day he will return to us."

"Thank you my king," Muroad replied as the tears filled her eyes. "The child will be ready when the time comes."

BOOK TWO

The Age
of
The Celtic Tiger

Chapter Fourteen

THE ELDERLY WIDOW stood on the paving stones outside the farmhouse where she had spent most of her adult life. The June morning was bright and the woman basked in warmth of the early summer sunshine. The paving stones hardly required the brushing they just received but Margaret O'Neill loved the feel of the broom in her hand and the bit of fresh air and exercise was a small pleasure she truly enjoyed.

Her wrinkled eyes smiled as she looked down across the fields toward the River Boyne, twinkling in the sunshine far below. In her mind she remembered standing in this very spot sixty years earlier, a young bride in the arms of her Brendan, tall and strong. She could not have imagine having lived a happier life, but her husband was now passed on these ten long years and her children were off to Australia and the United States pursuing their own happiness.

Margaret loved the peace and quiet of her little cottage particularly on sunny days when the whole valley came to life, but in her own way she looked forward to the day when she would be reunited with Brendan. Of course there were neighbours and friends who frequently called, because that is what people in rural Ireland did in the early 1990s when the Celtic Tiger was only a kitten. Margaret always looked forward to those visits but without her family to mind, something was missing and she believed that she would find it only when she entered into the next life.

Laughing out loud, Margaret scolded herself, "Don't be so morbid...what are you like?" She straightened her back raising her face to the warmth of the sun and looked, once again, down toward the Boyne. "Well old girl," she said continuing her conversation with herself, "at least there's nothing wrong with your eyes - in the distance anyway."

Far below a couple was walking through the fields in the company of a massive dog who romped free, chasing birds, butterflies and whatever took his fancy with little or no chance of ever catching anything. That would be the O'Suileabháins, she thought, out on one of their regular strolls through the Boyne Valley. They were a strangely matched couple, he was tall and lean, a quiet scholarly man, while she was short, broad and full of chat. Cathal and Eibhlín lived about a mile away in an old farm cottage, not unlike her own, and for the most part they were content with each other's company.

The O'Suileabháins clearly took pleasure in their walks and would call on Margaret whenever their path crossed her gate. They were a pleasant couple and Margaret enjoyed their brief visits, particularly because that massive Irish wolfhound called Molly would accompany them. Margaret was well accustomed to dogs but she held a special place in her heart for Molly. As playful as she was in the field, Molly became a perfect lady when she entered on Margaret's property. She would greet her host, her great head nearly chest high on the old woman. Margaret would pat the dog's head and scratch her behind the ears assuring Molly that she was a fine dog. Molly would then follow her host into the kitchen where there would invariably be a bone that Margaret kept stored in the refrigerator for just such an occasion. If the day was fine and the visit took place outside, Molly would sit next to Margaret, otherwise the dog's spot was under the kitchen table. While the human beings visited, Molly enjoyed her treat.

Margaret discovered that Cathal was a professor of Celtic Studies at University College Dublin, while Eibhlín was an artist, designing and manufacturing silver jewellery. On one occasion Eibhlín showed Margaret some of her work and it was easy to see why her neighbour was developing such an excellent reputation. The jewellery was normally silver intricately worked into traditional Celtic designs. As recently as ten years ago some Irish people might have thought her jewellery was old fashioned or better suited for the tourist market. "Naff" was the word, new to her, she had seen somewhere, but it seemed that traditional was now back in style.

Her neighbours explained that their walks, and indeed living as they did in the shadow of Brú Na Bóinne, were important to the couple because few places were so steeped in history as the Boyne Valley. They told her that each walk provided Cathal with another insight into his academic speciality and Eibhlín drew inspiration for her Celtic designs from ancient rock carvings and structures that lay strewn about the valley. Molly, on the other hand, enjoyed the great open spaces and the freedom to run, chasing and exploring whatever required her attention.

Looking down on the trio, Margaret envied them their freedom and health. Unfortunately they had not been blessed with children which, she had been told was not an intentional choice. They were older but, God willing, their day might yet come. In the meanwhile, they strolled through the fields, Cathal slightly stooped with his hands behind his back while Eibhlín, obviously carrying the conversation, speaking as much with her hands as she did with her mouth. "God bless and keep them," Margaret said aloud as she turned to return her broom to its spot behind the door.

In the field below, Eibhlín was indeed advancing a spirited argument for the return of Brehon Laws, which, she insisted, provided far greater equality between men and women. This was not an issue of grave and immediate importance to Cathal and he was attempting to direct the conversation to the beauty of the day.

"All these years," Eibhlín sighed, "and I didn't realise I was married to such a chauvinist."

"Now that's a bit harsh," Cathal replied with an affectionate smile. "I was only enjoying the peace and quiet of a beautiful afternoon in the company of my wonderful, beautiful and, of course, equal partner."

Eibhlín reach over a put her stout arm around her husband's thin waist, "Since you put it that way," she replied, "it is a beautiful day."

The two walked on in companionable silence. Cathal was dressed in the outfit of a country gentleman; brown woollen trousers tucked into his Wellington boots, an argyle sweater waistcoat, tweed jacket with corduroy patches on the sleeves and a flat hat to keep the sun from his eyes. Eibhlín also wore corduroy trousers tucked into her wellies with a grey oversized Aran-knit jumper stretching well down her thighs. Her amazing mop of tightly curled red-blonde hair defied any attempt to contain it in headgear so it danced naturally in the breeze. Eibhlín linked her arm with her husband's and nearly skipped along in stark contrast to his leisurely pace.

The couple continued on, commenting on the beauty of the flora they encountered and laughing at the antics of Molly the wolfhound who, at the time, was being tormented by a magpie. Cathal whistled and Molly obediently deserted the bird and returned to his master's side. "That's a battle you'll not win girl," he told the dog as he rubbed her ear. The magpie flew off and Cathal released to dog who loped off in search of new discoveries.

As Molly neared a copse of hawthorn bushes, she suddenly froze in her tracks, and then glanced back at the O'Suileabháins who were by then at least fifty yards behind and further down the hill. They were accustomed to the dog's habit of keeping an eye on them ensuring, they supposed, that as the couple was in Molly's care she would not want them to wander off. As a result, they paid her little attention and continued on their way. Molly, however, did not move. Rather, she lowered herself onto her forearms and hocks and rested her nose against her find.

It was several minutes before the O'Suileabháins noticed that Molly had disappeared from view. This was of no major concern to the couple because the field was vast and Molly was well trained. She could easily be hidden in a deep dip in the terrain or behind a fence or hedgerow. In fact she was only several yards from them but higher up on the hill and sitting on her haunches in the hawthorn grove. Cathal and Eibhlín slowed their pace and looked around waiting for the dog to reappear but when she failed to emerge, Cathal whistled confident that the dog would take his position at his master's side. Another few moments passed but still the dog did not appear.

Puzzled now, more than concerned, the two slowly retraced their steps trying to determine the last place she had been seen. As they reached the place just below where Molly crouched they heard a strange whine, not a whine of pain or fear but a sound that had never before been part of Molly's communication skills. Turning toward its source, they began their climb up the hill until the dog came into view.

"What is it girl?" Eibhlín asked as Molly inclined his head toward her voice. "What have you found?"

As the couple reached the hawthorn bushes they stopped in shocked silence. There in hollowed out granite stone lined with a small mattress was an infant boy who was certainly not more than several weeks old. The child, who was dressed in a simple gown fashioned from wool, smiled brightly as his right hand touched the big dog's nose. Molly was obviously delighted so she licked his tiny hand.

Eibhlín stood in shock with her hands covering her mouth and repeated over and over again, "Oh my God...Oh my God... how...who could have done this?"

Cathal stood and looked around half expecting to see someone fleeing from the scene. However, just as was the case when he was looking for Molly, not a person or animal was visible for as far as he could see.

Eibhlín soon recovered from her shock and reaching down she picked the child up and cradled him in her arms. He responded with continued smiles and a bit of a gurgle and soon Eibhlín was carrying on a perfectly nonsensical discussion with the infant. Molly meanwhile was justifiably proud of her role in the discovery and insisted that her nose remain in constant range of the infant's hand.

Cathal stood aside stroking his chin, watching his wife's antics. He quickly accepted the fact of the discovery and now he was trying to sort out how it was possible that the child would be left in the middle of a field many hundred yards from any possibility of discovery. Since babies did not just drop out of the sky, someone must have put him in the field. And if someone did leave the baby they must have know that there was only the most remote chance that someone, like the O'Suileabháins, would happen upon the spot. Abandoning an infant in the middle of such a field was tantamount to killing the child. This was undoubtedly a mystery worthy of his favourite author, Arthur Conan Doyle, and Cathal began a clinical evaluation of the matter.

Obviously the child was well fed and clothed and as he was at least a month old, someone must have taken good care of the baby since birth. There was little question but that the child had recently been placed in the bushes because although he wore no nappy, the baby's garment was not soiled. In addition, although it was a bright sunny day, the child's face was pale white with no blush from the warm sunshine. And yet, Cathal and Eibhlín had been leisurely walking these hills, in clear sight of the hawthorn copse, stopping occasionally to examine oddities, for at least an hour and they had seen no one. Cathal looked around for some sign that someone beside his wife and himself had broken the knee-high grasses and weeds leading to the site, but he could see nothing. He could clearly see broken damp grasses showing their own path but it definitely appeared that no one else walked these fields for at least several hours.

And then there was the most peculiar crib in which the child had been found. Cathal reached down to examine the rock and the mattress that lined its indentation. It was quite clear to him that hollowed section was man-made and the rock was hewed out for a specific use, perhaps as a large washbasin. On the other hand, it could just as easily have been fashioned for use as a crib because the mattress, which seemed to be made of rough cloth stuffed with feathers, was obviously custom made for the stone. The child had been secure and comfortable in his bed. Cathal tested the stone's weight and immediately realised that it would take at least two very strong men to even lift the granite stone. To transport it onto the hillside would have required a wheelbarrow or handcart. Whatever about the lack of broken grasses caused by an individual, there was no visible indication that a wheeled vehicle had crossed the field.

While Eibhlín continued to rock the baby and delight in his happy reaction to her attention, Cathal began to search the bushes for anything that may help to identify the baby or his parents. His scientific mind could make no sense of the situation but perhaps someone left something behind, a letter of regrets for example, to explain the child's presence. His preliminary search found nothing but then, he spotted what appeared to be an old woollen blanket on the hill beneath the hawthorn bushes. Cathal missed it at first glance because it was a brownish green that blended with the bushes, but now he climbed up to take a closer look. There were, in fact, two blankets that were bundled around something and tied at the top with rough twine.

Cathal opened the first of the bundles and when the contents spilled out, he stood in shocked amazement. What he saw was to him even more surprising than the sudden discovery of a newborn infant in the middle of a field.

Wrapped in the rough blanket was an assortment of the most amazing Celtic design artefacts that he had ever encountered. The collection included bracelets, broaches, disks, torques, rings and two goblets. They specimens were predominately gold or bronze plated in gold and each was in pristine condition. As a professor of Celtic studies, Cathal had vast experience in studying Celtic treasures that occasionally turned up in Irish bog lands but as incredible as those finds were, they could not hold a candle to what laid in the blanket.

Cathal quickly unwrapped the second bundle disclosing only one additional item, a long sword and leather scabbard, again in pristine condition. From the markings on the handle and scabbard, Cathal knew that the sword was also decorated in a Celtic style and, if authentic, would have dated from a time well before the birth of Christ. Cathal slowly bent and plunked himself on a flat rock, shaking his head in disbelief.

"Darling," he finally said to his wife. "If you have a moment to spare from Molly's baby, perhaps you could have a look at this."

Eibhlín turned a made the short climb to where Cathal sat and stared at the collection laying on the ground.

"Oh my," Eibhlín explained not nearly as taken aback as her husband had been. "What a remarkable collection. There must be a fortune in gold or gold leaf on that blanket. I wonder who crafted them."

Cathal replied, "I thought that maybe you might have some idea. You would know nearly everyone in the country who works with gold."

Eibhlín agreed, picking up an intricately patterned disk about a foot in diameter. "...At least everyone who appears at markets and shows. Although, I have never seen anything like this. The detail and designs are perfect replicas of the authentic article. They couldn't be real, could they?"

"Of course not," Cathal responded. "The leather scabbard could not have survived three thousand years and there is no way the gold would be in such perfect condition. But they are undoubtedly amazing replicas."

As Cathal carefully rewrapped the collection, he looked up at his wife and the baby and said, "Before I saw these bundles I was asking myself how in the world the child arrived here in such clean and perfect condition when we haven't seen a living soul all morning. And now this. There has got to be a connection between the baby and this lot but what could it possibly be?"

Eibhlín shook her head, obviously as baffled as her husband. She looked to the baby and then to the disk and as she did so the baby reached over and wrapped his fingers around the edge of the artefact. "Now then," she said smiling at the baby, "this wouldn't be yours, would it?"

The little fellow's expression was suddenly more serious and he looked straight into Eibhlín's eyes and seemed to nod his head.

"Oh my God," Eibhlín replied, "Oh my God.... Cathal, did you see that?"

"See what?" was the reply.

"I just asked the child if the treasure was his... joking like.... as if he could answer. And he gave me a very serious look and nodded his head."

"Ah, love," her husband replied, "will you go way out of that. Sure the child's only an infant and he doesn't have clue what you are saying, never mind responding."

Eibhlín looked back at the child who rewarded her with a big smile and she in turn kissed his cheek. "I wouldn't be too sure about that," she replied.

Cathal returned to his packing. "Just give me the disk and I'll finished wrapping these up. Then we can get back home and sort the whole thing out. We will have to leave the crib but I don't think it will be going anywhere soon."

Eibhlín attempted to hand the disk to Cathal, but the small matter of the baby's grip interfered. Eibhlín looked at the baby in shock. No month old infant should have been able to grip such a large item so tightly. The baby smiled at Eibhlín, but did not let go.

After an impasse of several seconds, Eibhlín spoke, "Alright, my powerful little fellow, would you please give me your disk so that Cathal can wrap it up and bring it home?"

To Eibhlín's surprise, the baby released his hold and the disk was packed with the other items. To Cathal, she said, "So he doesn't understand a word we say.... right."

Little could the O'Suileabháins have imagined, when they set out on their morning walk only a few hours earlier, that Molly would lead them home with their remarkable bundles. Considering everything that happened, there was little conversation as they retraced their morning route. Cathal was lost in his own thoughts trying to find some logic to the abandonment of the child in the middle of a field and the discovery of the gold. Eibhlín was clearly bonding with the infant she held in her arms and wishing the somehow, someway, the child would be hers. Molly marched proudly ahead, checking back now and then as if to assert her continuing interest in the child.

Chapter Fifteen

Eventually the party reached the O'Suileabháin's home. Not unlike Margaret O'Neill's home, the couple lived in a farm bungalow that was at least one hundred years old. Unlike Margaret's house, the whitewashed structure had been extended on at least a couple of occasions over the years as modern kitchens and plumbing replaced the old ways. The result was a haphazard collection of rooms, added with little apparent consideration for the overall design of the home. Fortunately for the O'Suileabháins the rambling nature of the home suited them perfectly.

The low split front door, painted a bright blue, led into the middle of a large sitting room. In an earlier time the massive fireplace opposite the front door had undoubtedly been used to cook the family meals because the cast-iron potholder was still suspended just below the flue opening. On both sides of the front door were smallish leaded glass windows and under each a table held family photographs and a cut glass vase, which always displayed fresh flowers. Two oversized chairs, each with a hassock, side table and reading lamp, occupied either side of the fireplace. The collection of open books, notepads and sketchbooks in the vicinity of the chairs made it clear that the O'Suileabháins spent many evenings enjoying each other's company in this cosy room. And, of course, the old-fashioned rag rug in front of the fire meant that Molly was never far from her charges.

On the right side of the sitting room was a door that led into a smallish parlour now converted into a study. This room was Cathal's office and although he might have been methodical in his academic pursuits the study looked like it had been hit by a windstorm. Books and papers covered nearly every inch of his desk and worktable as well as a substantial part of the floor. Bookshelves on two walls were stacked in the most haphazard manner with his substantial library while the other walls were adorned with pictures, prints and maps.

Cathal insisted that he knew the location of everything in his office and his strict instructions were that nothing was to be touched for fear something might be misplaced. As a result, the only one who ventured into the office, apart from Cathal himself, was Molly because one corner was equipped with a stuffed mattress so that the great wolfhound could keep him company if she so chose.

On the left side of the sitting room were two further doors that led into the original bedrooms. The O'Suileabháins seldom used these rooms except for storage and on an odd occasion if someone was staying the night. To the left of the fireplace in the corner nearest the bedrooms, a door led into a bathroom and toilet, added when plumbing moved indoors. To the right of the great fireplace another door originally led into the back garden but now provided access to many of the rooms that had been added from time to time.

The first addition was a scullery built behind the sitting room, which had ultimately been expanded into a modern kitchen. The centrepiece of the room was a large Aga built into the wall that backed onto the fireplace keeping the room so warm that in the winter the couple spent as much time in the kitchen as they did in the sitting room. In the middle of kitchen a large light oak table with six chairs provided for their normal dining requirements and opposite the Aga were several old-fashioned cupboards and presses.

Off the kitchen and behind Cathal's study a door opened into the O'Suileabháin's addition to the home, a large master bedroom with en suite toilet and bath. Another doorway at the back left corner of the kitchen now led to a hallway off of which was a new pantry and laundry room. The end of the hallway opened into another large room that Eibhlín claimed as her studio.

Unlike her husband's office, Eibhlín's room was well organised and very tidy. Her design books were neatly lined up on a bookshelf, her tools were in a series of boxes designed for them and her supplies were in clearly marked drawers. While Cathal's office was dark, this room was brightly lit with a pair of velux windows in the ceiling and French doors that led out into a large sun porch at the back of the house. Like Cathal's office, dog mattresses made Molly a welcome companion in each of the rooms.

When the O'Suileabháins returned from their eventful morning stroll they entered the warm sun porch leaving their wellies at the door. "So what do we do now?" Cathal asked as he carefully placed his bundles on a couch.

Eibhlín sat down on a cushioned chair and examined the baby, "Well, first things first," she said. "What do we call the child?"

Cathal looked warily at his wife, "I should think that would be up to the child's parents, who will undoubtedly be located when we hand the child over to the proper authorities."

"Perhaps," Eibhlín said in all innocence, "but we can't just say "hey you" until we do that. I propose that we call him Brian because he is certainly strong. Yes, that's it Brian Boru O'Suileabháin."

"I have no problem with the Brian, even the Brian Boru," Cathal replied shaking his head, "but don't you think that the O'Suileabháin is a bit precipitous."

"Possibly," his wife replied, "but if you think I am going to turn this child over to just anyone, as if he were an animal heading for the shelter, you have another thing coming. All they would do is send him off to a foster home while they search for the parents and we could be as good as any foster home. I am not going to hand him over to anyone until I am certain we are doing the right thing."

"I must insist Dear," Cathal replied. "This is not our child and we cannot pretend that he is. The sooner we get to the bottom of this the less heartache it will cause everyone."

Eibhlín ignored her husband and held the baby close to her chest breathing in that wonderful "baby smell" from the top of his head. Nothing in her life had ever felt quite as perfect as holding Brian in her arms. Deep down she knew that Cathal was probably right but she saw nothing wrong with holding on a little longer. After all, they did not steal the baby from his rightful parents, they found him abandoned in the middle of a field."

"Eibhlín," Cathal repeated, "I must insist."

After another moment, Eibhlín looked up at her husband. "All right, call my brother Paddy. Since he's the Inspector at the Drogheda Garda Station he is without a doubt the proper authorities, as you so callously put it, so we will see what he has to say."

Cathal knew that Paddy would do anything for his little sister but he assumed that his brother-in-law's police training would not allow him to agree to any scheme she might have to hang on to the baby so he agreed to make the call.

It took a couple calls to locate Inspector Paddy Rice who would ordinarily have been home but, as it happened, chose to clean up some paperwork at the station. "Rice," he announced into the telephone.

In response Cathal spoke, "Paddy, Cathal here. We have a bit of a situation over here at the house and we would appreciate it if you would give us a bit of advice."

After listening to the response, Cathal said, "Oh no, nothing at all is wrong, everyone is fine. It's just that... ah... well... I think it would be better if you could come over here and see for yourself. It is a little hard to explain."

"Later this afternoon... Yes that would be perfect."

"Of course I will give your love to Evie. We'll see you this afternoon."

After hanging up the telephone Cathal turned to his wife and said, "Well, there you have it. Paddy will call out later this afternoon, so I guess we wait for him."

"Not exactly" Eibhlín said with a smile. "We are not equipped to entertain a baby regardless of how short or long we may have to keep him. It seems to me that we have a couple of choices. You can go into the city and pick up nappies, formula, a bit of clothing – well you know, all the things a baby needs while I look after our young Brian. Or, you could look after Brian while I head off into Drogheda."

Cathal sighed, "That's quite a choice. I'm not sure that I am able for either job."

"Yes, I suppose that isn't on the curriculum at Trinity or UCD," Eibhlín replied with a mischievous grin. "Well I can hardly do both, particularly since we have nothing to dress him in and no car seat or any way to transport him."

Cathal looked down at the baby who was happily settled in his wife's arms. "I suppose no harm would come of me looking after him, as long as you make the trip quickly. Why don't you just go down to the shops? They should have everything we need for the few hours we will have him."

"Two reasons," Eibhlín responded as she rose from her chair. "The first is how do you propose that I explain my shopping list to Mrs. Nolan down at the shop. You know she will ask and even if she doesn't everyone for miles around will be trying to figure it out within a couple of hours."

"And the second?" he asked.

"There is no guaranty that we will only have him for a couple of hours," she answered evenly, handing her husband the baby and heading for the bedroom to retrieve a pair of shoes, her purse and keys to the car."

Cathal followed her into the bedroom, "And what is that supposed to mean?" he asked.

Eibhlín smiled kissing the baby as she went past her husband, "As I told you, I am not just handing this child over to anyone and we will just have to wait to see what my big brother has to say." With that Eibhlín went out the front door and started the car.

Cathal meanwhile settled into the chair recently vacated by his wife. Molly stretched out beside the chair and dozed in the warm sunshine. Cathal looked at the little child he held in his arms. "You do have the most remarkable blue eyes," he said. "I can see why my wife would become attached to you, but you do understand that there are laws and rules that must be obeyed don't you?"

The baby smiled happily as Cathal shook his head and wondered why he had actually expressed his thoughts out loud to a child who arguably could not understand what he said. As he did so, he suddenly felt unnatural warmth spreading over the left side of his stomach and down his legs. "I suppose you have been holding that for just such an occasion," he said to the baby. The little fellow seemed to giggle as a few bubbles formed on his lips. Cathal closed his eyes, shook his head and laughed.

Cathal looked around helplessly half expecting his wife to appear and relieve him of his wet burden but then he realised that he would have to fend for himself. Removing the child's robe, he took him to the kitchen sink and rinsed the little fellow's lower half with warm water. He then retrieved a bath towel from the linen closet and wrapped the child. Removing his own damp trousers, Cathal donned a dressing robe and returned to his chair to await the return of his wife.

In time Eibhlín returned from her shopping, arriving at the same time as her brother, Paddy. Cathal eyed the two suspiciously as they entered the sun porch wondering if his wife already had a word with the Garda inspector. It wouldn't have been the first time that pair cooked something up without a word to Cathal until the matter was already settled. His concerns were obviously misplaced because Paddy was quite surprised to see the infant in his brother-in-law's arms.

"Good to see you Paddy," Cathal said in greeting, "Pardon me if I don't get up but I have a bit of a bundle."

"So I see," Paddy replied looking curiously at the child.

"What happened to the two of you?" Eibhlín asked as she relieved her husband of the baby.

"A bit of an accident," her husband answered. "After several hours I suppose it was to be expected."

Cuddling the baby, Eibhlín said, "Oh did you piddle all over Daddy, you poor thing you?"

Paddy, looking even more confused than ever, finally had enough, "All right, will one of you please tell me what is going on?"

"Yes, of course," Cathal replied as he directed Paddy to a seat. "The long and the short of it is that we were out walking along a hillside overlooking the Boyne, when we, or should I say Molly, found this baby, obviously abandoned."

Paddy replied, "I see. So you want me to make a report and take the baby to the hospital."

Eibhlín quickly interrupted, "Well it is a little more complicated than that. As you can see for yourself, the baby is as healthy as a horse so there is no need to rush him to a hospital. And then, even though he was apparently abandoned, the place where we found him, the crib that he was left in, and a few things that were left behind are so amazing they... well... they defy belief."

"In what way?" the Inspector asked. "It seems quite straightforward to me."

"Let me start from the beginning," Cathal said, "and see what you think."

With that Cathal described the morning's occurrences from the time the couple left the house until they returned. He also described his observations, from the condition of the child, the size of the crib and the state of the long wet grasses around the site. Cathal then explained that he concluded it was highly unlikely that anyone had been at the site for at least several hours before they arrived and yet, the child was found in bright sunshine without a whisper of sun blush. When he finished, Cathal showed Paddy the gold that had been found in the nearby bushes.

"I see what you mean," the Inspector said, clearly perplexed. "Was the child dowsed in sunblock?"

Eibhlín touched the baby's cheek and forehead and raised him up to her nose. "Not unless they have invented a totally invisible product that cannot be felt or smelled."

"So do you have any ideas as to how the baby arrived at the site?" he asked.

"Believe me," Cathal answered, "I think I have considered every angle but I am at a complete loss. Particularly considering the weight of the crib, the only thing I could think of was that for some reason a helicopter lowered the crib, child and treasures but we were out for a couple hours and we certainly didn't see or hear anything."

Eibhlín added, "You know Paddy, you are a professional and no matter how careful Sherlock Holmes here has considered the matter, maybe it would be better if Cathal took you out there so you could have a look for yourself. The crib is still lying in the field and it isn't that far away. Maybe you will have to cordon off the area for forensic study, or whatever it is they do.

"And what of the baby?" Paddy asked.

"Well, little Brian is certainly safe enough with me, at least until we have sorted this out," Eibhlín replied. "I bought a few things for him and I am sure it is time to give him something to eat."

"Brian, is it?" Paddy said rose from his chair.

"Sure we had to call him something," Cathal replied. "Hold on a minute while I put on a pair of dry pants. And while I'm at it, it might be a good idea to take my camera along."

Chapter Sixteen

Eibhlín O'Suileabháin pushed her pram to Margaret O'Neill's gate. The old woman, forewarned by the happy barks of her good friend Molly the wolfhound, was waiting, a welcoming smile on her wrinkled face.

"Hello Molly," she said scratching the big dog's ears as she had so many times. "Aren't you a grand girl looking after the little fellow so?"

Addressing Eibhlín, she continued the words coming in rapid succession, "You are very welcome... come in, come in – before the heavens open up. The water's on the boil." Reaching into the pram she touched the infant's cheek forgetting for the moment any thought of impending rain. "So this is the little fellow I have heard so much about."

"It is indeed," Eibhlín replied happily, "Brian Boru O'Suileabháin, allow me to introduce you to Mrs. Margaret O'Neill."

"So pleased to meet you, Mr. O'Suileabháin," the old woman replied taking his little hand in her own. "I'm sure we will be great friends."

Molly gave a short bark, reminding Margaret of her tradition of providing him with an appropriate treat, and they all walked through the yard and into the kitchen. The dog was presented with a fine bone and settled under the kitchen table to enjoy her treat, while Margaret prepared the tea.

"Sit down there," she ordered directing Eibhlín to a chair. "You must be exhausted altogether and you up all hours God has given taking care of the little one."

Eibhlín did as she was told, and replied, "In truth, he is no problem at all."

Margaret placed a slice of freshly baked slice of apple tart before her guest and proceeded to pour the tea. "You should know that I am a little cross with you. Here you are with a fine little baby boy and I didn't even know you were expecting. Usually I'm very good at noticing such things," she concluded with a raised eyebrow.

"I am sorry about that," Eibhlín said slightly flustered. "You know I'm a bit large at the best of times so maybe that's it. You also know that I am not as young as I once was – and you never know. Anyway, we didn't tell anyone, even our families, so everyone was surprised, as you can well imagine."

"And a very pleasant surprise it was," Margaret said. "Tell me know, what did your family think?"

"Like you they were very surprised but also very happy for Cathal and me. You know that we have dreamed about this for years but we had long since accepted that we would not be blessed with a child. Believe me when I tell you, Brian came as quite a shock to us as well."

"May I hold him?" Margaret asked.

"But of course," Eibhlín replied as she reached into the pram, removed the baby and passed him to the older woman, "he is amazingly good with strangers."

Margaret accepted the child holding him in the crook of her left arm. Her actions reflected an expertise that was, without question, not lost in the years since she held her own children. She reached out and pulled the shirt, which had ridden up, away from his chin. "Now so then, let us take a good look at you," she said as she looked into his remarkable blue eyes. Margaret was quiet for a several seconds as she studied the baby. Perhaps she intended to make the type of comment that most woman make when presented with a new baby, but instead her words came as a surprise, even to herself. "I know this may sound peculiar, but as I look at this child, I feel that I know him, perhaps I have always known him."

With that, Brian smiled brightly and reached out his hands toward the old lady as if he were asking to give her a hug. Margaret responded to his request and as the child gurgled happily, Eibhlín looked at the pair in amazement.

While the child clung to her neck, Margaret closed her eyes as if she was dreaming and a look of perfect contentment came over her face. Eibhlín had, by then, become accustomed to strange occurrences where the infant was involved, but this had to be the strangest since his discovery. "Perhaps," she said tentatively, "Brian reminds you of Cathal or me, or one of your grandchildren."

"That may be," Margaret replied doubtfully. When the child released his hold on her neck, she returned him to her left arm and thoughtfully traced his face with her hand. After a short time, she looked up at her guest and said. "I hope you will not think me strange or a victim of what do they call it, "senile dementia," but I am going to tell you something that I would not have dreamed I would mention to a living soul."

Eibhlín put her cup down and studied the old woman waiting what Margaret had to say with mounting curiosity. She decided that the last thing in the world she would suspect was that this old woman was senile in any shape or form. To the contrary, Eibhlín wished that she were as sharp as Margaret.

"For the last few weeks," Margaret began, "I have had the strangest dreams. Well let me correct that, dreams while I sleep, yes, but also visions while I am awake, usually while I am out walking these hills. I see myself in those dreams and visions, just as I appear today, an old woman who, perhaps, has outlived her usefulness."

Eibhlín protested, "Now Margaret, please don't say things like that. You are very important to me and any number of people in this community...why just..."

Margaret put her hand up and Eibhlín stopped speaking. "I am not complaining my dear, just stating facts. At any rate, although I am old in my dreams and visions, I do not see myself in today's age but rather in an age that must have been long, long ago. In my dreams there are no houses, as we know them, no cars or even roads, no electricity, no running water, and absolutely none of the conveniences of the modern age. I am dressed in rough clothing as is everyone else, and I am at some kind of feast. I am eating, with my hands, lumps of meat that have been taken from an animal that has been boiled in a pit and I am drinking from a wooden goblet."

She stopped for a moment to wipe a bit of spittle from Brian's chin, then Margaret took a sip of tea and continued, "There are many people present, women with long unkempt hair some holding or nursing infants and men dressed in robes with long moustaches and beards. There are also wealthy kings and nobles with finer robes wearing beautiful golden jewellery. There are also children present, barefoot and dirty, dressed in homespun robes that fall to their knees. I look into each person's face searching for someone I recognise, but no face is familiar to me."

"After a time, a big man with a great long beard, perhaps a king because he is dressed in the finest robes, delivers two infants to me and it is clear that I am, in some way, responsible for these children. I hold each child, speak softly to them, and sing songs in words that I do not recognise and I am at peace. Even though this dream is very strange, I do not find it at all disturbing and, in fact, I find it quite comforting. Although it is completely surreal, I have experienced this dream so many times that it is now familiar to me, almost part of my life. Do you not find this very strange my dear?"

Eibhlín sat, her tea going cold, infatuated by the story. It took her a moment to realise that she had been asked to respond. "Strange, perhaps," she replied, "remarkable, absolutely. Tell me Margaret, do you believe in reincarnation?"

"Reincarnation?" Margaret said. "I don't think so. That would be the kind of thing that would not sit well down at the parish church. Still and all, if there were such a thing, perhaps my dreams show me as I was in some prior life. Do you believe in reincarnation?"

Eibhlín replied, "I don't know whether I do or not. You know my Cathal is a professor of Celtic studies and he greatly respects their way of life. Apparently the early Celts were strong believers in some cycle of life in which a person returns to the earth in another time. And of course I'm sure you have heard many stories about people who have premonitions about being someplace before when they knew that was not the case. I have never had any such experiences but, perhaps, you were an early Celt. Undoubtedly they would have roamed these hills."

"Well I don't know about that," Margaret responded with a smile, "You know that when I was newly married, there was an old man who lived in a house not far from here, which has long since fallen to ruins. We used to visit him and he was full of stories and legends about the people who lived near here. He could tell you about every fairy fort in the country and he had a remarkable collection of tales about encounters with the little people. I often wish we had recorded his stories. I doubt that he read all the legends about Celtic heroes like Fionn MacCumhail, Cúchulainn and the Red Branch Knights but he certainly knew them line and verse and we spent many a long winter's evening listening to his tales. Maybe, after all these years, I am inserting myself into those stories but you would think that I should at least be dreaming that I was a fetching young maiden rather than a great-grandmother. Just my luck,"

Margaret laughed. "It seems strange though, that these dreams should come to me after all these years, and then, only in the last few weeks."

Eibhlín agreed, "It does seem strange. Do you ever remember having such dreams before?"

Margaret thought for a moment and answered, "Definitely not that I can remember. And definitely not with the frequency of these dreams. But the strangest thing of all, my dear - one thing about which I have no doubt in my mind - one of the infant children that I held when I dreamed of myself in that other world, is this child, your son Brian."

Eibhlín sat in silence for a moment considering what Margaret told her. And then, her eyes went wide, she placed her hand over her mouth and her eyes teared over.

Margaret was shocked at the younger woman's reaction and hurriedly apologised. "I am so sorry for causing you pain. And you after just having this baby. I do hope that you will forgive me and not think that I am unstable and not fit to visit with this darling boy. Sure it's only an old woman's ramblings and it means nothing."

This time it was Eibhlín who put her hands up asking Margaret to stop apologising. Eibhlín collected herself and said, "Please Margaret, nothing you have said has made me think any less of you, rather, as amazing as it may seem, you may have confirmed something that is even more difficult to believe than what you have just told me. I am only sorry I was not a bit more forthright, but then maybe you will understand once I explain."

The old woman seemed genuinely relieved but also intrigued. She returned Brian, who was asleep in her arms, to his pram and asked her guest if she would care for a bit more tea.

"I think that might be a good idea," Eibhlín replied. "Or maybe something a bit stronger if you have anything."

"That bad?" Margaret replied, even more intrigued. "I do have a drop of sherry."

"That will do nicely," the younger woman said. "I don't think what I have to say is bad but very difficult to believe."

"As difficult to believe as my reincarnation?" Margaret asked.

"You can be the judge of that," Eibhlín said with a smile.

"In that case, perhaps I will have a small sherry as well."

Margaret poured the two glasses while Eibhlín tucked a blanket around the baby. When the old woman regained her seat she raised her glass to her young visitor and toasted, "To strange stories."

Eibhlín clicked her glass against Margaret's and sat for a moment thinking about what she was going to say. Ultimately, she decided to get the hard bit out of the way quickly. "I guess I have been less than completely honest with you Margaret," she began. "Only three people in the world know about this and you would be the fourth. Well, technically Brian and Molly are also in on the secret but anyway, here goes. While I accept that young Brian is, without question, my child, he was not born to me."

Margaret did not appear particularly shocked by this revelation but she listened quietly as Eibhlín continued.

"In fact," she continued pointing out the kitchen window, "I found him in the middle of that field a couple of weeks ago when Cathal and I were walking along. Well actually Molly found him and Cathal and I accepted responsibility for him. What was completely remarkable was that it appeared that he had been placed in the field minutes before his discovery. He was clean and well fed and despite the heat of the morning sun he did not have even the slightest touch of sunburn. Even stranger, there was no indication that anyone walked through the long grasses for at least several hours before we arrived."

Margaret nodded her head understanding what was said, "I do seem to remember seeing you and himself walking along below with Molly one sunny day a few weeks back, but it must have been before you came upon the child," she stated.

"Well it doesn't exactly end there," Eibhlín continued. "You see, in addition to Brian we discovered a bundle of what appeared at the time to be excellent gold reproductions of Celtic jewellery as well as a replica of a great sword from the same era. We took everything home and, of course, immediately contacted the Garda Síochána."

"Yes, yes – the Gardae," Margaret said obviously agreeing with her decision.

"Well, actually it was my brother Paddy Rice who is an inspector above in Drogheda," Eibhlín admitted sheepishly. "He is the only other person who knows about this. His immediate reaction was to call in the social welfare people but I convinced him that the child was undoubtedly traumatised by his experience so perhaps it was better to let him rest a bit before moving him again. I suppose, being a good big brother Paddy was used to agreeing with my suggestions so he and Cathal and Molly, of course, returned to the hillside to inspect the scene of the crime, as it were."

"So anyway," Eibhlín continued, "I settled the baby and the two of them went off. By that time it was mid-afternoon but since very few people are likely to tramp those hills, neither Paddy nor Cathal thought that the site would have been disturbed. As it turned out they were correct. Oh, yes... I forgot to mention. The one thing that we didn't bring off the hillside was a massive granite rock that had been carved out in the middle. This rock was lined with feathers and cloth, a little mattress almost, and that was where the baby was lying when we found him. Anyway, this crib was too heavy for even two or three people to carry any distance so we left it down there marking the spot."

"Paddy reported that they had no difficulty following our tracks, which were clearly visible in the long grass. Molly seemed to know exactly where they were headed and lead the way directly to the hawthorn bushes where the baby was found. Of course, the granite crib remained just where it had been earlier in the morning. Paddy carefully inspected the area for at least fifty feet in each direction but could detect no trace of anyone. He also asked Cathal to take more pictures confirming his investigation."

"Although he was a bit cynical when we first told him our story, Paddy undoubtedly had a change of heart after examining the place where the child was found. Cathal told me that it was not necessary for him to say anything to my brother because Paddy was even more baffled than we were. He is, after all, a professional dealing with all measure of mysteries and even though Cathal might fancy himself a modern day Sherlock Holmes, he is not a trained police officer."

Margaret sat on the edge of her chair, completely absorbed by the story. "When you told me your story was even stranger than mine," she said, "I had my doubts, but while mine was all in my head, you have a child to show for yours."

"Anyway," Eibhlín continued, "it gets better. Out of pure frustration, Paddy took the little mattress from the crib and called Molly over. Holding her collar, he put the mattress under her nose so that she could fully inhale its scent. Then he let go of the collar and ordered Molly to fetch."

"Now, according to Cathal, Molly, who is a bright dog as you know, looked for a moment at Paddy like he was not the full shilling. But then she apparently began to move, nose down, in concentric circles around the area stopping only where our path to and from the site crossed the circles. Eventually she moved closer to the crib and began to sniff in the immediate vicinity. Apparently she caught a scent right in the thicket of hawthorn bushes and began to growl and push her nose in and among the bushes. They were too thick for her to penetrate so Paddy and Cathal bent down to take a closer look. All they could see was a pile of old rocks around which the bushes had grown so Molly was called off."

Eibhlín concluded, "It was then that Paddy told Cathal, apparently in jest, that the mystery was solved. Clearly the hawthorn bushed guarded the entrance to an old fairy fort. The little people placed the child on the hillside and then returned to their underground world. The two boys had a good laugh over that, but then Paddy agreed, however ridiculous that explanation may sound, he had no other ideas."

Molly, who apparently was listening intently when she heard her name being mentioned, stood up, stretched her long frame and wandered over to accept the accolades of the two women for her role in solving the mystery. When she had been properly thanked, and checked the baby to be sure he was safe, she returned to her spot under the table.

"So what happened then?" Margaret asked eager to hear the rest of the story.

Eibhlín continued, "Well, the boys returned and made their report laughing, of course, at the bit about the leprechauns. They brought the feather mattress along with them but left the granite crib to mark the spot, particularly because it was so heavy. After some discussion Paddy decided, that rather than immediately reporting the incident and turning the child over to the authorities, he would make some discreet inquiries to determine if any children had gone missing. Alternatively, perhaps some young one had a child in the past several weeks... you know how that might go. Paddy said that he could just imagine what the boys down at the station house would say if he tried to explain how we happened upon the abandoned infant."

"Anyway, the long and the short of it was that Paddy found that there were no reports of missing children. He could find no record of any child having been born in the last two months, anywhere in the country or the north for that matter, that was not fully accounted for. Of course, Paddy admitted that it was possible that someone in a rural area, like myself for example, could have a child without notifying the authorities or medical professionals. He told us that although it was not as common as it was twenty or thirty years ago that sort of thing did still happen."

"So at the end of the day, we all decided that Cathal and I would mind the baby unless and until someone came forward with a plausible explanation for the baby's sudden appearance in the middle of a field. Although we all agreed that if, somehow, someone abandoned the infant in such unlikely circumstances, they were hardly likely to admit the crime. If, in fact, no one came forward, we would be the couple who, to anyone who might inquire, delivered a child without notifying the authorities or medical professionals."

"And so that is what has happened," Margaret concluded.

"Yes, you could say that," Eibhlín replied, "although we might have been a little premature in going public. As you would know, Cathal and I don't do a great deal of socialising and as I am not exactly petite so it was easy enough to intimate that I had been pregnant but we were keeping it a secret... except for experts like yourself. Anyway with buying cribs, nappies, formula and clothing no matter what we did, the word was going to get out more quickly than we would have hoped. This community is just too small for no one to take notice."

"What a story!" Margaret marvelled. "If it wasn't the little people, perhaps it was a miracle that the good Lord granted your wish for a child. A little peculiar way of going about it I must say."

Eibhlín smiled, "Well there is one other little bit. You know the gold Celtic jewellery that came with the package?"

"Don't tell me," Margaret said, "it was real."

"I'm afraid so," said. "Cathal took a small ring with a bit of the woollen cloth in which it was wrapped. He had the ring analysed and the woollen cloth carbon dated. He told the staff at the university that he found the ring, wrapped in the bit of wool, on a hillside overlooking the Boyne, which as you know is the complete truth. He just got the report back and it has been authenticated. The most perfect specimen of Celtic or even pre-Celtic jewellery ever discovered – at least three thousand years old. Although metal can't be carbon-dated the bit wool could and it helped to confirm the age of the ring. Of course he turned it over to the national museum and apparently there is going to be some major publicity on the find in the next week or so. I'm afraid the hillside might be overrun with people and their metal detectors although in fairness Cathal didn't say exactly which hillside."

"And what of the other gold and the sword?" Margaret inquired.

"We can only assume that they are also authentic, but we have not told anyone, except Paddy and yourself about it. You see, it may not be ours to give away."

"Of course it is yours. You found it on publicly owned land didn't you?" she asked.

"We did," Eibhlín replied, "but it came with Brian so perhaps it belongs to him. You see Margaret, that is the reason your dreams and visions had such an impact on me. I know that this makes absolutely no sense at least in terms of common sense. Were I to share this story with nearly anyone, I would be the one certified as senile but I, and Cathal and Paddy for that matter, have no other explanation. What you told me is just another thread in the fabric of this story."

"And how is that?" Margaret asked, a puzzled look on her face.

Eibhlín replied slowly, "Suppose, and just suppose that there was an infant in Celtic times who was in some way related to a great king. And suppose, again I know how this sounds, but after all, it is your story as well as mine... suppose you, in a former life were responsible for that child. Now, for background purposes, Cathal can tell you all about the Celtic myths and legends, particularly how it was that many of the Tuatha Dé Danann, when faced with the invasion of the Milesians, abandoned the earth and retreated into a land under the ground where they became immortal."

"Suppose that this infant for some reason, his own protection for example, was spirited into the underworld with these treasures where he became immortal as an infant just as the Tuatha Dé Danann were immortal. But now, three thousand years later, for some reason he is being returned to the mortal world with all the treasures that belong to him."

"What an incredible, amazing story," Margaret exclaimed. "I can certainly see how anyone might say that it is preposterous. Best kept to ourselves, obviously... but then... infants lying in granite cribs don't just appear in perfect health in the middle of a meadow accompanied by perfectly preserved Celtic artefacts that are three thousand years old now do they? Isn't that just as amazing?"

"You understand perfectly, don't you?" Eibhlín asked and Margaret smiled and nodded her head. "I have no way of knowing how any of this is going to turn out, but whatever else, we have this beautiful baby boy who, God willing, we will raise as our son and I hope that you, dear Margaret, will help us take care of the child just as you did three thousand years ago...perhaps."

"You know," Margaret replied, "a few weeks ago I was morbidly considering the end of my life on earth and looking forward to joining my Brendan in the next... not that I would mind that of course... But I must admit that the future of this little fellow, whoever he might be, is far more interesting. Of course I will help to take care of our young Brian."

She looked down at the little fellow who awoke from his slumber and was looking at the older woman. "You would like that, wouldn't you?" she asked.

The little fellow smiled brightly and wiggled his head and shoulders as if nothing could make him happier.

Extract from the Academic Press:

Journal of Natural History: What has been described as among the most significant finds in the twentieth century was publicly displayed for the first time at the National Museum. A perfectly preserved gold ring from the early Celtic era was discovered in the Boyne Valley by Dr. Cathal O'Suileabháin, professor of Celtic Studies at University College Dublin.

Dr. O'Suileabháin explained that he was out walking with his wife in the fields overlooking the Boyne, when he came upon something wrapped in a rough cloth. A closer examination revealed the ring, which O'Suileabháin assumed was a reproduction that someone lost. When he returned home and had an opportunity to examine his find more closely he was so impressed by the detail that he decided to have the ring studied at the university. After a comprehensive examination the experts determined that the ring was around three thousand years old. Remarkably, carbon dating the cloth in which the ring was wrapped confirmed their conclusion.

The find adds another chapter to the mysteries surrounding these discoveries. How, for example, did a piece of cloth survive intact for three thousand years? Dr. O'Suileabháin had no answers but suggested that since the cloth was found among rocks, perhaps it had been embedded for all these years. Wind, rain or a careless step might have ultimately cracked open its resting place.

Dr. O'Suileabháin would not disclose the exact location of the find to the general public so that the integrity of the location might be preserved. Experts from the university will continue to study the area for further clues. Meanwhile the ring is on public display during normal museum hours.

Chapter Seventeen

MARGARET O'NEILL STOOD BY HER SITTING ROOM WINDOW eagerly awaiting the strawberry-blonde head that would soon appear over the hedgerow, bounding toward her door. Brian Boru O'Suileabháin would be followed by that massive dog Molly, who apparently decided that, because she was the one who discovered the boy, she was not about to let him out of her sight. Her one concession was to accompany him to the local national school and then leave Brian to his studies. However she was certainly not going to let him run home alone, particularly when there would probably be a visit to Mrs. O'Neill along the way. Brian's mother explained that Molly knew exactly when classes were over for the day and she would always wait at the school gate to greet her boy.

Few days passed when the Brian did not visit Margaret and the boy also stayed with her on a number of occasions when his parents were attending a conference or having a night out. Margaret cherished each such visit and they were without question the highlight of her day. Even waiting for him to arrive brought a smile to her face.

After that memorable afternoon, my goodness was that five or six years ago, when Eibhlín O'Suileabháin told her the remarkable story of Brian's appearance, the dreams and visions of what she now thought could have been her former life, stopped. Margaret reasoned that these dreams were intended as a message and after she understood what they meant, there was no need for repetition. That did not mean that she didn't think about them because for several months after the Eibhlín's visit Margaret recalled the dreams in vivid detail and committed them to her memory.

Although Margaret still had difficulty believing in reincarnation, the more she thought about it, the more Margaret was convinced that in those ancient times there was a woman whose life had now, somehow, become part of her own. She had even given the ancient woman a name, Mairéad, Irish for Margaret. Even if that woman was not Margaret in a former existence, a possibility that Margaret did not entirely discount, she had undoubtedly established a mystical connection between the two. As a result, Margaret was able to see what the ancient woman saw and feel what she felt.

Margaret strongly believed that this connection was disclosed in those early dreams because her ancient alter ego wanted to tell Margaret about Brian and, more importantly, commit the child to her care. Margaret knew, without question, that this ancient woman loved and cared for the child when he was first born. She was now passing that responsibility on to this twentieth century grandmother. It was a task Margaret accepted with great joy because she knew immediately that she too, loved the little boy.

For Margaret, accepting the role as the child's special guardian meant more than just being a glorified baby-sitter and she gave a great deal of thought to how best she could guide the child. Of course, she would always be there for Brian but Margaret had another idea as well.

To implement her plan she dug into the boxes of books that her family accumulated over the decades. Margaret pulled out every old book she could find that had anything to do with ancient Irish history, the arrival of the Celts in Ireland or Celtic mythology. She also made a point to visit Green's Bookstore whenever she was in Dublin and she always came away with a few more old and worn texts. Margaret even visited an optometrist to acquire a special pair of magnifying glasses to ease the strain on her eyes and then she began to read and study everything she had assembled.

For many months Margaret attacked the task she had appointed for herself with a single-mindedness she would not have thought possible. Even after the initial period of intense study, not a day went by when she didn't spend some time either reading or re-reading some book or article.

Margaret embarked on her studies simply because she wanted to learn everything she could about the times and culture into which Brian was born. This, she reasoned, was an important part of her job as his special guardian. Although the boy may never know that he was the son of a great king or hero, when the time was right she wanted to be able to tell him everything there was to know about these people. Without even realising it, she considered that she might even be telling him about his own parents.

Thinking about the books she read and the library she accumulated, now neatly lined up on a bookshelf Margaret purchased specifically for these special books, gave her a feeling of accomplishment. Laughing to herself she thought that even though she didn't have a fancy degree, there couldn't be too many people who knew more about the subject than she did. She had nearly memorised at least a couple translations of the Tain Bó Cúalnge – the story of the Cattle Raid at Cooley – where only Cúchulainn stood between Ulster and the forces of Queen Meadhbh. In addition she read everything she could find about kings and druids and, of course, the legendary Red Branch Knights.

Reading many of the stories and legends brought back warm memories from her own childhood. She remembered, long before anyone dreamed of a television, gathering at the home of an old storyteller, called a shanachie, who would spin tales and tell stories of those ancient times. Margaret thought, at the time, that the shanachie must have a remarkable imagination to tell such wonderful stories. She now realised that the old man was simply retelling these legends, a tradition that went back hundreds and hundreds of years, long before anything was actually written down. And now, perhaps, she was a bit of a shanachie herself.

Her audience, however, was not a clatter of wide-eyed children but one little boy with sparkling blue eyes who hung on her every word. Although he was entirely too young to understand what Margaret and his mother suspected, she had no difficulty in explaining that Brian, like many modern Celts, was born of an ancient people. His ancestors were a race of great heroes with special gifts who above all did what was honourable and right. As she told those stories, the boy listened in rapt attention and at times she thought she saw a flicker of recognition, a recollection perhaps of something that was buried deep in his forgotten memories. The first time it happened, Margaret decided that she seeing something she expected to see, not something that was actually present. Over the years, however, she thought she saw the same thing many times. Not each time she told him a story, but often enough. Invariably it appeared as a raised eyebrow or a puzzled expression as if he was trying to remember something that was just beyond the edges of his memory.

On most of the little fellow's visits there was no talk of Celtic legends and myths. The events of the day, his adventures at school or on the sporting fields were usually the stories that Brian wanted share over his milk and a sweet and Margaret was an enthusiastic audience, listening carefully and seeking even more detail.

From that first visit when Eibhlín pushed the pram holding its special cargo through her front gate, Margaret thought each visit was special. She remembered the day when Brian and his mother, with Molly of course, walking hand in hand, stopped in after his first day at National School. How cute he looked, with his grey pants and jumper and a bright blue knapsack to hold his books and treasures. When asked whether he enjoyed school he explained, quite seriously, that he thought they spent entirely too much time sitting around but he did enjoy the playtime. Margaret told Brian that she understood perfectly because when she was a little girl she felt the same way. He looked on dubiously as she further explained that if he listened very closely to what the teachers had to say, he would learn all kinds of exciting and magical things.

Later Eibhlín told Margaret that she was afraid Brian would be fidgety for some time to come. He had always been extremely active, always running, always on the move and to ask him to sit quietly would take some getting used to. Early on she consulted with an expert to determine whether he suffered from some attention deficit disorder but she was assured that such hyperactivity was normal in healthy, active little boys. In time, Brian solved the problem in his own way. He explained to Margaret that since most of the other children sat quietly, he decided he could sit just as quietly as they and so in the end, his determination overcame his nature.

About a week after school began, a week arriving at Margaret's gate accompanied by his mother on his way home from school, Brian was confident enough to make his own way, accompanied as usual, by Molly. Eibhlín explained that one afternoon she was in the middle of an intricate silver design when Molly informed her that it was time to retrieve her son. More in jest than anything else, she said, "You go bring him home," and she opened the door for the dog. Molly ran out and down the path before stopping and looking back at Eibhlín who once again told her to go. So, off Molly went. Feeling a bit guilty and concerned, Eibhlín retrieved her cardigan and set off after the dog. By the time she got to Margaret's house, the dog had accomplished his task. Boy and dog were making their way through the gate without a bother.

When Eibhlín joined the party she suddenly felt as if her presence was not really necessary. Perhaps even more than delivering Brian to school for the first time, this experience left her feeling depressed because her son was now asserting his independence for the first time. After that, Eibhlín occasionally joined Molly in collecting Brian, but most of the time it was the boy and the dog that visited their special friend.

Throughout his primary school days, unless Brian had some activity that required his presence elsewhere, Margaret's home was always a stop on the way home. In the course of those visits, the old woman came to understand the difficulties faced by the young boy and she came to admire the way in which dealt with his unique situation. She hoped that, in some small way, she helped Brian work things out.

Extracts from the Local Newspaper:

> **Drogheda News:** The members of the St. Faolán GAA Club are shaking their heads in amazement these days, and all because of a six-year old boy. "I have been involved in hurling since I was in short pants," said octogenarian Tommy Boyle, "and I have never seen the likes of that young fellow." "Puts me in mind of that Tiger Woods fellow when he was on the telly hitting the golf ball two hundred yards at about the same age," added a slightly younger Liam Casey.
>
> The boy, Brian, son of Dr. Cathal and Mrs Eibhlín O'Suileabháin, can only be described as a hurling phenomenon. At a time when most boys his age are barely shuffling the sliotar along the ground, Brian has no difficulty lifting, carrying and accurately striking the ball over the bar from thirty or forty years. He does use a child's size hurley but this makes his ability to strike the ball long distances even more surprising.
>
> When asked about the boy's amazing coordination and talent, Dr. O'Suileabháin could shed little light, "He certainly didn't get it from my side of the family. I enjoy watching the hurling but would have difficulty even hitting a sliotar. Brian's Uncle Paddy Rice gave him a hurley before he could even walk and it seems that it never left his hands."

Unfortunately, there seems to be no place for young Brian on any of the many St. Faolán's team rosters. He is entirely too good to play at his own age level and because he is no bigger than most six year olds, it would be too dangerous for him to play at a level that reflects his skill. Come to think of it, that might be our Inter County Team.

Ger McEvoy, who coordinates the underage teams at the club, told this paper that he hopes young Brian will continue to train at St. Faolán's because the boy has obviously been blessed with remarkable talent. McEvoy said that he was looking forward to the day when Brian is big enough to safely compete in the higher age groups. Meanwhile, Brian Boru O'Suileabháin is a name to remember.

Drogheda News: After several weeks of national, and indeed international, publicity after this newspaper first published the story about Brian O'Suileabháin, the six year old with remarkable hurling talent, Dr. Cathal O'Suileabháin has withdrawn his son from the club at Brian's request. The reason, in the boy's own words, was: "all the other boys and girls love hurling just as much as I do. It isn't fair that everyone thinks I am so good and no one likes them as much."

Dr. O'Suileabháin told this newspaper that he saw no purpose in continuing to subject his son to what amounted to a circus atmosphere, particularly when the boy wasn't having any fun. "I'm not sure how much you can read into Brian's own statement," O'Suileabháin said, "but making friends with children his own age is just as important to him, and to my wife and I, as the game itself but it seems his skill and the attention he is receiving, are making that impossible." When asked whether the boy would be giving up the game entirely, Dr. O'Suileabháin replied, "Not a chance in the world. We will just give him a chance to be a boy and when he gets a bit older, I suspect he will be back."

Chapter eighteen

"THERE IS SOMETHING VERY STRANGE ABOUT THAT CHILD," Millicent Blessington, reported to her husband as she stared out her sitting room window on a sunny Saturday morning.

"And which child might that be?" her husband Nigel queried barely lifting his head from the 'Financial Times'.

"The O'Suileabháin child, of course," she replied. "What other child would I be talking about? This town land isn't exactly crawling with children now is it?"

"Yes, yes," Nigel muttered well accustomed as he was to his wife's habit of keeping an eye on everything around her. "And what is it that makes the child so strange?"

"Well for one thing he spends every waking moment running around like some wild animal with that stick and ball. Isn't that some Irish Sport? Curling or something?"

"Hurling actually," Nigel said under his breath now regretting that this conversation would take him away from his reading.

"And then there is that massive animal," she continued. "I never see him with any other children, only that great beast of a dog. He talks with the dog as if it were human. Come on, come on, and look at him."

Nigel sighed, carefully folded his paper and reluctantly joined his wife at the sitting room window. "I wouldn't be an expert at such things," he commented as he pushed the curtain, "but it seems to me that little boys spend a great deal of time running around, burning off energy or whatever, and boys do love their dogs. I would hardly find that strange."

As he looked down into the field across the laneway at the front of his house, Nigel saw the boy and his dog obviously a massive Irish wolfhound. The boy could not have been more than six or seven but there was no question that he was much quicker and unquestionably more coordinated than any child Nigel had ever seen. He was remarkable actually. He would flick the ball off the end of his stick and then whack it to an incredible height. While the ball was in flight he would dash off to where it would eventually land and jumping high he would pluck the ball out of the air with his free hand. The dog, meanwhile, would run after the boy and compete for the ball. Despite the fact that the dog was taller, the little fellow's jumping ability overcame his height disadvantage and although they crashed into each other on nearly every occasion, it had no effect on the boy's ability to catch the ball. After each catch the boy would laugh and reach around the dog's great neck giving him a big hug as if to encourage the animal to do better the next time. On occasion the boy would drive the ball at the remnants of a stone wall far down the field striking it with amazing consistency and power and the dog would chase the ball down and return it to her master."

Nigel stood mesmerised by the scene before him. "You see what I mean?" Millicent said as if she was daring her husband to disagree.

"I do," Nigel replied, "but the child is not strange, just remarkably talented. Don't you remember the television coverage on him some time back?"

"Vaguely," Millicent replied, her elegant arms crossed over her expensive cardigan.

"He looks like he is having so much fun I think I may join him." Nigel said enthusiastically.

"Humph," his wife replied as she marched off to the kitchen.

Nigel meanwhile reached into the basket behind the door and retrieved a soccer ball that he kept more as a reminder of his past than for any active use. In his younger days, Nigel has been quite a useful soccer player. He had a short run at Liverpool and had played for England's under nineteens before a knee injury sent him back to school and a successful career in banking. Of course he was a keen Liverpool supporter but he enjoyed watching younger players perform and he fancied himself as something of an expert at spotting young talent. He had even arranged for a couple of young men to train with his old club. As he looked across the field at the little boy, he knew he was looking at someone special.

Nigel pulled on his old runners and nudging the soccer ball ahead he wandered out to the brick wall separating his garden from the roadway. When their game brought the boy and his dog to the top of the field, he called out, "Hello there."

The boy stopped and looked over at Nigel, shading his eyes against the bright sunshine, "Hello Mister Blessington," he answered respectfully.

Nigel was slightly taken aback that the boy would know his name but then he supposed that, although he had never met them, the O'Suileabháins would have heard of him just as he knew their name. He smiled pleasantly and replied, "And here you know my name and I don't even know yours."

The boy stood scratching the massive dog's ear for a moment remembering the manners he was taught before responding, "I am Brian Boru O'Suileabháin. I am pleased to meet you."

"And I am certainly pleased to meet you," Nigel responded. "And who is your great friend there?"

"This is Molly," the boy said vigorously rubbing her shoulder. "She is the best dog in the world."

Nigel smiled, "I have no doubt about that. It is a pleasure to meet you as well Molly. You know, Brian, I was watching you play there and I would have to say you are pretty handy with the hurley."

"Thank you Mister," the boy said. "Me Da says it must be in my blood."

"Ah yes, and did he play the game."

A puzzled look crossed the boys face as he responded, "I don't think so. It must be some other blood."

Nigel replied, "Of course. Tell me Brian Boru, have you ever played soccer?"

"No," the boy said seriously, "but me Da and I watch it on the telly. We are Liverpool supporters."

"Are you now?" Nigel said, "And would you believe, so am I. Would you like to have a go?"

The young boy looked dubiously as Nigel expertly flipped the ball into the air, catching it on his chest before allowing it to roll back to his feet. Nigel encouraged the boy opening his front gate, "Come on then."

Brian and Molly walked through the gate into the garden. Brian instructed Molly to sit near the entrance and guard his hurley and ball. Molly seemed to understand perfectly and she lay down with her massive paws draped over the stick. Brian trotted to a spot about ten feet from Nigel who was juggling the ball with his feet.

"Now then," Nigel instructed as he allowed the ball to drop to the ground, "you don't kick the ball with your toes but you use the inside of the foot to pass the ball and the top of the foot to shoot." With that he sent a slow pass in the direction of the small boy and was amazed when it was returned firmly and accurately to his right foot. He noticed that the boy's balance was instinctively perfect, head down, left foot properly planted and leaning over the ball. So much for the first lesson he said to himself.

The two passed the ball back and forth without allowing it to stop and Nigel saw that not only was the child well balanced but his feet also demonstrated a remarkable quickness that allowed him to adjust to any unexpected misdirection or hop of the ball. Nigel directed several passes to the boy's left foot but the result was, once again, a perfect return. It was impossible for the former professional to decide whether the young boy was naturally right footed or left footed. Nigel also tried a few step-over passes and Brian repeated the move without difficulty and heel passes met with a similar response. "Are you sure you haven't played soccer before?" Nigel asked in amazement.

"Yes, Mister," the boy replied seriously, "but sure it's only kicking a wee ball now isn't it."

"Quite right," Nigel said as he caromed a strong shot off the front wall. The ball bounced to the child's chest and he calmly absorbed the shot, just as he had seen on television, allowing it to fall to his feet before delivering a strong left-footed shot against the wall. The ball arrived a bit too quickly at the older man's feet and for the first time the ball strayed from what he had intended.

The two delivered several ricochet shots, all of which were handled expertly by the young boy. After a time, Nigel began to feel the heat of the sun and decided that while the child might be able to do this all day, he could not. When the final shot was delivered, he stopped the ball at his feet, put his hands on his hips and looked down at the boy. "I don't think I have ever played with a young fellow who was quite as talented as you are," he said ... thinking - or an older fellow as well. "I think that you could play for Liverpool when you get older if you wanted to."

The boy beamed, "Thank you mister. Ireland as well?"

Nigel replied messing the young boys already wild head of red-blonde hair, "of course Ireland as well. Thank you for playing with me but I think my misses has some jobs for me to do. Perhaps we could do this again some time."

"That would be nice," Brian replied as he picked up his camán and balancing the sliotar on its boss, ran down the laneway with the great Molly in hot pursuit.

Nigel retreated to the comfort of his house shaking his head and muttering "incredible" as he walked. On entering his home he flipped the soccer ball into its basket and stood with his back to the door thinking about what he had seen. Millicent appeared at the entrance to the kitchen wiping her hands in her apron before crossing her arms. "Well, is he strange or what?"

Nigel looked aside considering the questions, "Strange is not the word. That child, even at his young age, is an incredibly gifted athlete. I have never seen a fifteen or sixteen year old that was as natural with the ball as he is and yet he has never played or practiced. If the truth be known, I am having a great deal of difficulty figuring out how it is possible for a child to be so co-ordinated so, perhaps, it is strange. I must have a word with his father. If you don't mind, I just might wander down there on the off chance he might be around. No time like the present, what?"

With that, Nigel took a jumper off the coat stand near the front door and proceeded toward the front gate. His wife's terse reminder that lunch would be ready in an hour sent him on his way. Nigel strolled down the laneway in the direction of the O'Suileabháins' home hoping that the boy's father would be out tending his garden or performing some similar outdoor chore on such a fine morning. He was rewarded in his effort when he rounded a bend and saw a tall man deadheading roses in front of his whitewashed cottage. As Nigel approached the man removed his hat wiping his balding head with an old rag that had hung from his pocket.

"Grand morning," Nigel said amiably.

The tall man walked toward the stonewall surrounding his front garden and replied, "tis that, thanks be to God," he replied.

"Nigel Blessington," Nigel said offering his hand, which was warmly taken by the tall man. "I apologise for not introducing myself earlier but my wife and I only moved here a few months back and it seemed to me that people here pretty much keep to themselves."

"Cathal O'Suileabháin," the tall man replied. "A pleasure to meet you. I suppose you are right, people don't move to a remote townland if they are looking for constant company. But I think you will find people here to be pleasant enough. And if you don't mind my asking, what brings you to the wilds of County Louth?"

Nigel replied, "I took a position with the Ulster Bank in Drogheda. My wife is a country girl – well big house country - and she got tired of living in big cities. She fell in love with the bungalow up the road so here we are."

"I can understand that," Cathal replied, "my wife and I have been here for a dozen years or so. Fell in love with the peace and quiet, at least until the little fellow came along."

"Ah yes, that would be Brian Boru," Nigel said with a smile. "I met him earlier this morning. Quite a remarkable young man, if you don't mind my saying that."

Cathal stroked his chin and gave his guest a wry smile, "Remarkable yes. The wife and I never thought we would have a child at all. We met late and after a few years of marriage it appeared that it just wasn't in the cards. But then you never know."

Nigel nodded in agreement, "I know what you mean. Millicent and I were the same, but I'm afraid we weren't so fortunate. Still and all we have a pile of nieces and nephews and a good life so there are no complaints. Your son, though, is special. I kicked the soccer ball around with him and I must say he is remarkably gifted athletically. Were you an athlete?"

"Not at all, not at all," the tall man said with a smile. "Neither was Eibhlín for that matter. But then there must have been some athletic blood somewhere back in the distant past because I have no other explanation for him. It is almost embarrassing at times."

"A while back," he continued, "we took him down to the GAA club to play hurling with the toddlers. Well toddlers playing hurling might be a stretch; it is more like a bunch of helmets playing an elementary form of field hockey. Anyway, putting Brian among them was like a county player competing with under eights, except of course that he was the same size as all the other toddlers. He couldn't understand why they wouldn't let him lift and shoot when all the other little ones could barely push the sliotar along the ground. We had to take him off before some child got in the way of his shot. So they moved him up with older children and he completely dominated them as well. The other children became frustrated with his skills, particularly because of his size so he took a few belts."

"I recall the press coverage," Nigel replied.

"Of course, the press," Cathal said. "Then you know we all came to the conclusion that it was in everyone's best interest to let him grow a bit before he wins his first all-Ireland medal."

"Perfectly reasonable," Nigel replied. "After watching him out in the field it doesn't seem to have slowed his training."

Cathal responded, "Well now, the one thing Brian loves is his hurling, and sport in general I would have to say."

Nigel agreed, "Yes, yes. I would know a good bit about soccer and I have never seen anyone, even lads ten years older than the young fellow, who has the balance and agility and natural skill of your Brian. Has he played soccer?"

Cathal replied, "No he hasn't. I'm sure if he did it would be the same thing again. He would be far too good for his own age group and far too small for his skill level. As disappointed as he was over the hurling, I wouldn't want him to have the same experience with soccer, so we will just have to wait on that as well. It is a bit of a shame though because he loves sport so much. He doesn't have many friends because older kids don't want to be around a small boy and younger children can't play at his level. Fortunately, he has his Molly and he is generally a happy boy. Now if he had only inherited a few more academic genes..."

Nigel shook his head, "Amazing in this day and age that a child's natural ability would restrict what he can do."

"Well, I suppose we could look at the half full glass of water," Cathal said. "With no organised sport, we can spend a little more time on his education and when he gets a bit older he can always become more involved in sport, if that is what he wants. Maybe it is just a phase he is going through and when he grows his athletic skills will level off."

"Possibly," Nigel replied, "But in all my years of watching young men grow and develop on the soccer pitch, I have never seen the likes of young Brian. And after watching his training regiment with the hurley and ball, I suspect that he will only improve. Meanwhile, if he ever wants someone to just kick a ball around with, I hope you don't mind him stopping in to see me."

Cathal smiled, extending his hand, "Not at all, not at all. In fact, it is all a bit embarrassing for me. I enjoy the sport on the telly and I have taken him to Lansdowne Road, Croke Park and everywhere in between, but as far as actually kicking, catching or hitting a ball, I am totally hopeless."

"Well, we all have different gifts," Nigel said as he stepped back from the wall. "From my brief time with him, Brian strikes me as a great little fellow, a credit to your wife and yourself, and I am sure everything will work out for the best."

Chapter Nineteen

MARGARET O'NEILL put the large glass of milk and two or three of her special chocolate chip cookies on the plate in front of her young friend. While she scurried to the refrigerator to retrieve a soup bone for Molly, she asked, "And how was school today?"

Brian, who was usually much more animated, said nothing for a moment, concentrating on eating around the chocolate chips so that he could save as many of them as possibly for the last bite.

"That bad?" Margaret asked sitting in her customary seat at the round table, next to him.

From the moment she first held Brian in her arms, Margaret experienced a strange kinship with the boy and she not only knew when he was upset, but usually she knew the reason. Brian's immediate problem, if you wanted to call it that, was sport. One day, while Cathal O'Suileabháin was taking his son to a match, Eibhlín called around to discuss the matter.

"It appears," she began, "that our Brian has inherited a remarkable physical constitution from his ancient parents and grandparents. When we took him to our GP before starting school, the doctor said he had never seen a child with Brian's muscle tone, reflexes, eye sight and a number of other more complicated things that escape me at the moment. I asked if this presented a problem and was told, not at all, in fact he could not imagine a healthier child."

"Well that is undoubtedly good news," Margaret replied.

Eibhlín said, "Yes and no. As you know from all that media coverage a while back, these traits have apparently given him athletic skills and abilities that are far superior to anyone his age, or for that matter, children several years older than he. You remember those legends of Cúchulainn, or Setanta, as a young boy having unbelievable skill with the hurley and sliotar. Well, maybe our Brian is the son of Cúchulainn or one of the

Red Branch Knights because apparently that is the level of his skill, and he is only a small child. I realise he nearly lives with his hurley but the people at St. Faolán GAA say that no amount of practice could produce such natural ability, especially for a child that young. It seems that he can also run faster, jump higher and is remarkably more coordinated than children many years older than he."

At the time Margaret had not quite seen the difficulties this gift could create, "Well that should certainly serve him well in years to come," she offered.

"Perhaps," Eibhlín replied, "but for the present, he is not allowed to compete. His skills are so superior to those of others his age that neither the management at the GAA nor ourselves for that matter had any choice. Our little boy has been sacrificed for the good of the many who apparently would not improve or enjoy the sport if they had to compete with the likes of Brian. And then he is not allowed to play in older divisions because, not only is he even better than they are, but there is a concern he would embarrass older children and possibly be hurt, intentionally or by accident."

"The GAA was most apologetic but their only advice was to bring him back in a few years. So the bottom line is that we have a little boy who is an incredible athlete but has no outlet for his skills and abilities."

Margaret finally appreciated the problem. "So how does he cope?"

"Brian spends a great deal of time off on his own, with Molly of course, playing games he has invented. I suppose you could say he competes against himself."

"My goodness," Margaret replied, "I'm not so sure that is a good thing."

"Well, it's not the end of the world," Eibhlín said sipping her tea, "but it does present other problems. It seems that everyone for miles around has heard the story and that means it is a fertile source of gossip and dinner table conversation. You know how children interpret perfectly innocent remarks, or remarks that are meant to be humorous that they hear from their parents…well you can imagine what the parents are saying about our little boy. Apparently some children look on Brian as some sort of freak so he is shunned."

"As a result Brian won't play in schoolyard games because, he says, it wouldn't be fun for him and it would be unfair to the other children. I believe, however, that he is just not invited. Little boys make friends with other little boys by playing and roughhousing on the playgrounds and he can't do that. To be honest, I am concerned that he will become some type of introvert, not only in the games he plays but in his entire social life."

Margaret thought about what Eibhlín told her. "Surely there are children on the other end of the scale who may be very shy or overweight or handicapped in some way and they get on with other children."

"Yes, of course," the younger woman replied. "It seems that children have a remarkable capacity for accepting those less fortunate. They have difficulty with gifted children, perhaps because either they don't encounter them very often or when they do, they don't realise it… and that is our Brian."

After Eibhlín departed, Margaret spent a great deal of time thinking about what she had been told. Brian had always been a bright and happy little boy and the last thing she wanted was for him to lose interest in school and become withdrawn. She wished there was something constructive that she could do to help him, but nothing came to mind. Well… perhaps one thing. She could talk to him about it. Margaret knew that Brian was a bright little fellow and she believed that, with a little encouragement, he would sort things out in his own mind. She hoped she would say the right thing.

Margaret looked at the boy sitting quietly at her table, his hands on his forehead. Margaret had never known Brian to cry, but she could see that he was as near to tears as the child could be and it almost broke her heart. Almost sensing his despair, Molly abandoned her treat and sat next to the boy with her great head on his lap.

"I don't think I like school anymore," he said quietly.

"Did something happen today that made you sad?" Margaret asked.

Brian thought about that for a while and encouraged by the old woman's kindly smile, he replied. "No, not really. It is just that I would rather be out in the fields. Sometimes I dream I have a brother to play with and pretend that we are playing games together but mostly I play with Molly because she is always around."

Margaret nodded her head, "I can understand that, but sometimes everyone has to do things they don't really want to do. Why would you rather be in the fields when there is so much to learn in school?"

"Because Molly is my friend and I have no friends in the school," he replied without hesitation.

"Oh," Margaret said, "that is sad. I think you are a grand wee boy and I can't imagine why you have no friends. Could you help me to understand?"

"I don't know," was the solemn reply. "In school I try to be like the other boys and girls. I sit and listen carefully and do my work even though I feel like getting up or doing something else. I keep telling myself that as long as they can sit and listen, so can I. But then we go onto the playground and everyone is running around talking and playing games. When I try to play like them or talk to them they turn and walk away. So I stand by myself and think in my mind that I am off in the fields with my brother and Molly."

"Thank you, Brian," Margaret said. "Now I do understand. But, you know, I have an idea. Tomorrow, don't even try to play with the other children, or even talk to them. But don't think about playing with Molly either. What I think you should do is stand at the side of the playground and look around very carefully. And see if you can see anyone else who is standing alone, not playing or talking with anyone. If you see someone like that, you should go over to them and tell them your name and start talking to them. Would you try that for me?"

The little boy looked up at Margaret with what she could only describe as a small expression of optimism and he said, "I think I could try that Mrs. O'Neill."

When he visited her the following day, Brian reverted to his happy form. The story spilled from the young boy who couldn't wait to tell Margaret all about his experience. He found a new friend, a girl called Libby. Brian explained that he had introduced himself, just like Margaret suggested, and she didn't run away so they started to talk. Brian told the old woman that even though it was sometimes hard for him to understand what Libby was saying she was very nice and had a lovely smile. He told Margaret that the two of them stood together and laughed at the silly things some of the other children were doing. Apparently Libby's sister called Katie came over and tried to drag Libby away from Brian but Libby said she wouldn't go because she was having too much fun, so Katie left and Libby and Brian talked away.

Margaret was thrilled with his happiness. "Now you must always remember," she told him, "how sad you were when you had no friends and how Libby became your first friend."

"After Molly, of course," he replied happily as the big dog wagged her tail.

The next day brought more good news. Brian reported that he and Libby were having such a good time that Katie came over and instead of trying to take Libby away, she joined in. Katie was apparently very pretty with long dark hair but she didn't smile nearly as much as Libby. Katie was one of the smartest kids in the class and it turned out that she was very nice as well. After that, it seemed that Brian acquired a few more friends, all girls except for one little fellow in a wheel chair. While he wasn't playing with the other lads, he was having great chats with his new friends.

On one occasion, Margaret asked him whether he felt sad that the boys still ignored him but he was very philosophical about the whole thing. "After talking to Katie and Libby and everyone, playing silly games with the boys didn't look like that much fun anymore. Besides, a couple of the girls know more about sport than I do so we don't just talk about girly things. On girl supports Arsenal and another Leeds and I back Liverpool so we have a great time arguing over which team is better. You know what I think," he concluded, "I think that a friend is a friend and it doesn't make any difference whether it is a boy or girl."

From then on, Margaret looked forward to the news of Brian's new friends. She always asked about Libby and it became clear that among Brian's other endearing qualities, he was loyal to his first friend.

"Oh she's in great form," he said one day. "Libby is always smiling even though she is a bit heavy and can't run around very much and she is not nearly as smart as Katie. Sometimes some of the kids make fun of her like calling her a retard, but when I threaten to sort them out unless they apologise, they usually say they are sorry."

"You wouldn't push or hit another child, would you?" Margaret said with some concern.

"Of course not," Brian replied with a smile. "Sure my Da would kill me. I suppose that is one good thing about being stronger than everyone else. Other boys get in fights now and again but nobody comes near me. Anyway, the only time I ever say anything is if someone is mean to Libby or one of my other friends."

"Very good," Margaret replied. "I'm sure Libby is very happy to have a friend like you as well."

"Oh, I don't do much," Brian said. "Libby's sister Katie is very pretty and very popular and I think that most of the kids would be more worried about her being angry with them than they would be worried about me."

"And what about the school work?" Margaret asked.

"I try my best but sometimes it is a little confusing," Brian confessed. "My ma and da make me work for ages every night and so eventually I work things out, but there is no way I could ever be as smart as Katie."

"You see, Brian," Margaret counselled patting his arm, "you should never compare yourself to Katie or Libby or anyone else.

You just work hard and do the best you can and no one will complain about whether you are smart or not."

Brian looked up at the old woman his bright blue eyes sparkling. As he looked into her aging eyes, Margaret knew that the young boy was completely receptive to everything she said. Somehow she suspected that a bond between the two had been created in a time and place many centuries before. Although he may not have been conscious of their deep connection, he knew that he could trust Margaret and her wisdom without hesitation. Margaret prayed that she would always be worthy of that trust.

Excerpt from the Local Newspaper:

Drogheda News: Regular readers will remember our story a few years back on Brian O'Suileabháin, a young boy with a remarkable hurling talent. The story generated national publicity and the television stations descended on St. Faolán's GAA Club to film the boy in action. The boy's father, Dr. Cathal O'Suileabháin, a professor of Celtic Studies at UCD, subsequently withdrew his son from the club and the "circus atmosphere" the boy's talent created.

Although everyone agreed that the proper decision was taken at the time, there were many at the club who were concerned that they boy's remarkable talent might be wasted if he was not allowed to compete. The people of Louth will be happy to hear that, potentially, their greatest hurler since Cúchulainn himself has, in fact, improved considerably in the four years since his last public appearance with the camán and sliotar. In a session at St. Faolán's GAA pitch last week the nine year old worked out with the club's senior team. Now that bit bigger and stronger, using a full size hurley, Brian O'Suileabháin reportedly dominated every aspect of the game, running through tackles, out jumping players a foot taller than he, making pin point passes and pointing from great distances. Apparently the young man is both faster and quicker than any player on the Louth side. Long time club member Tommy Boyle told this newspaper that it looked to him like young O'Suileabháin could score at will but instead chose to involve other players in the action.

When asked to confirm these reports, St. Faolán's underage manager, Ger McEvoy said, "Well now, you have to take what old Tommy has to say with a grain of salt, but I will say that Brian O'Suileabháin is an incredible talent. There should be no concern that his lack of competition has impeded his development, quite the contrary in fact. Even though he is still very young, he is the finest talent I have ever seen." When asked when this young man would debut for St. Faolán's McEvoy replied that there was no rush and that young Brian would continue to grow and develop at his own pace. So there you have it readers. Can the emergence of Louth as a hurling power to challenge Cork, Kilkenny and Tipperary be far away?

Chapter Twenty

NIGEL BLESSINGTON genuinely looked forward to his sessions with young Brian O'Suileabháin. At least a couple Saturdays a month the two would meet and either train or dissect the game, depending on the weather conditions. Of course the constant presence of a huge Irish Wolfhound named Molly took some getting used to, but she was extraordinarily well behaved, and if Brian told her to sit, she was happy to watch quietly while the two went about their business.

If the weather was fine, the two would head over to the soccer pitches behind one of the local schools for a training session. These sessions became an important part of Nigel's schedule for two reasons. First, apart from an occasional game of golf, he realised that he spent entirely too much time sitting around and despite the fact that he only recently turned forty he was seriously out of shape. Although Nigel could hardly expect to keep up with young Brian O'Suileabháin, there was a certain satisfaction in being completely worn out after each session knowing his muscles would be sore the next morning.

Far more important, was the time he spent with young Brian. Nigel was not going to pretend that the boy was the son he would never have, but he genuinely enjoyed teaching and sharing his experiences with a talented and receptive young man. Nigel had long since decided that when the demands of his employment allowed, he would become active in coaching youth soccer and Brian was without question the impetus for his decision. Nigel recognized that he would never coach a player with the skills and abilities of young O'Suileabháin but the boy rekindled his love of the game and he knew that even after Brian moved on, he would continue to coach.

During the first few field sessions, Nigel concentrated on teaching basic techniques but Brian learned so quickly that he could soon drop the ball on the corner of the box from great distances, bend the ball with either foot and chip with remarkable dexterity. Other skills like heading, trapping and throwing followed and there was no doubt in Nigel's mind that the young man was a natural. Remarkably, for a normal to small sized boy, Brain had an amazing vertical leap as well as the timing to direct the ball wherever he chose. In time, Nigel knew, the boy's neck muscles would strengthen and, as a consequence, so would his power on headers but there was no questioning his technique.

Brian needed little assistance with basic ball handling skills because he had obviously

taken it upon himself to perfect all of the juggling skills he saw on the television as well as inventing others that Nigel might not have thought possible. The first time the boy rolled the ball down his back and kicked it back over his head with his heel, Nigel's jaw literally dropped in surprise. These juggling skills also meant that Brian developed the ability to control the ball at his feet to such an extent that Nigel was seldom, if ever, able to take the ball from him. As time passed Brian also developed all the tricks from crossover dribbles to heel-flips and Nigel could only imagine what would happen were he to appear on a field of his peers.

In short, Brian quickly became as technically proficient as any player with whom the former professional footballer had ever been associated. Nigel realised that he had no way of knowing how the young man might develop and change as he grew and matured, or for that matter, whether he would even continue to be interested in the sport.

Blessington was personally familiar with several players who demonstrated amazing ability at a young age but then were injured, lost interest or simply "burned out" and never approached the potential their early abilities suggested. Perhaps Brian would be like that but Nigel believed that if the game remained for him just that, a game, the young man would never lose his passion for playing. To that end, Nigel did everything he could to make the Saturday sessions great fun. Between the games he invented to challenge his prize pupil and the banter for every success or failure, the two got on famously and the Saturday mornings were full of laughter.

When the Saturday was rainy or miserable, a condition that was not infrequent, the training session remained indoors. Nigel remembered that no matter how much he loved the game, training sessions in the rain and muck were occasionally necessary but never enjoyed so on those days, the two talked soccer. Over the years Blessington acquired a number of match videos and after he began his sessions with Brian, Nigel located instructional videos, which could also explain the game. On those cold wet days, the two sat in the Blessington's sitting room watching the videos and talking about what they saw while drinking Millicent's special hot chocolate. Much to his delight, Nigel's normally reserved wife apparently took a shine to Brian's quiet nature and good manners. What was even more shocking was that Millicent didn't seem to mind the presence of the massive Molly who sat quietly by the fire as the two talked soccer. During these sessions, Nigel kept the remote handy to stop or replay important segments and Brian soon acquired an appreciation for the finer points of the game.

Unfortunately for all the coaching, both on and off the pitch, Nigel knew that until Brian could actually play the game, there were limits to the boy's development. He also knew that there was nothing Brian would rather do than compete. Nigel remembered his discussion with the boy's father and he recognized that if Brian were to play with boys his own age, or even those substantially older, neither Brian nor his team mates would enjoy the experience. Although it was frustrating for the young man, Nigel believed that Brian understood his unique situation just as he realised that his competition on a hurling pitch would also have to wait.

"You see Brian," he explained one wet Saturday, "as you know I have seen and played with many, many soccer players in the years since I was your age so I know about these things. The thing is, just like in hurling, God has given you far more skills in soccer than He has given most boys your age or even much older."

"I guess I knew that Mr. Blessington," Brian said humbly, "but why would He do that?"

"That's a tough one," Nigel responded with a smile. "God works in strange ways that none of us will ever understand. I suppose He gave you these gifts because He knew that you would use them well. I'm sure you know people who were blessed with other gifts, like being very smart for example. Maybe He gave them that gift so they could help other people. Maybe He gave you your gift so that you could be part of a team and you would help your teammates be better players and better people as well. Whatever the reason, you were blessed and it is up to you to use your gifts properly."

"And how will I know I am doing that?" Brian asked.

"Another tough one – you do ask hard questions," Nigel said. "I suppose the biggest thing is to always remember that you are part of a team. Maybe you have the skill to score a goal every time but that may not be the best thing to do."

Brian looked at his mentor with a quizzical expression, "But I thought the idea was for the team to win the match and surely scoring goals would help to win the match and help the team."

Nigel held up his hand, "Ah, but you see winning is nice, but it is not the only thing, not even the most important thing. Playing as a team is far more important than winning or losing. Competing well and playing fairly is also far more important than winning or losing. Draws aside, for every winning team there will also be a losing team and if winning were the only thing, all those other teams would be wasting their time. If you were to score every time you got hold of the ball, your team might win but it wouldn't be much of a team now would it?"

"No, I suppose not," Brian agreed. "But I can't very well not try my best because that wouldn't be fair to the team either."

"Of course not," Nigel said, "you must always try your best. But let's say you had a great opportunity to score but then you saw another teammate was open as well. Even though your teammate is not as skilful as you are and he or she may not score, the thing to do is to make the pass because that is best for the team. When you are on a team, you should use your skills to make sure that everyone is involved because that is what makes a team. They may not do things as well as you but if you give them a chance they will become more confident and they will improve and the team will also get better. Do you understand?"

"I think I do," Brian replied obviously thinking hard about what Nigel said.

"How about this," Nigel said. "Let's say that a big match is coming up but something happens and you are not able to be there. Let's say ah...your Mom's car breaks down. The team had to play on without you and of course you are not there to score those goals that are so easy for you. Your team-mates don't have the confidence to play without you so they don't play well and they get hammered and that is the end of the big match. Now if, when you were playing, you involved them in other games, they may have had the confidence to win. But, even if they lost, at least they could play well, compete and enjoy the game and that's what makes any sport special. That's what makes a team."

Brian nodded his head and Nigel could see that he understood. "All right now," he continued, "who's your favourite player on the Irish team?"

"You know that, Mr. Blessington," Brian said with a smile. "Roy Keane, deffo."

"And does Roy Keane score lots of goals?" Nigel asked.

"No, but he makes great passes and Niall Quinn or someone else scores the goals."

"You see that's the thing about a team." Nigel concluded. "Everyone makes a contribution and no one is more important than anyone else. That is the way a team works. A keeper is not likely to score goals, but where would a team be without one."

Thinking about the conversation later made Nigel appreciate the young man even more. Of course he was talented and perhaps even Brian realised how talented he was. But that did not stop him from listening, understanding and learning. No coach could ask for more in a player than a combination of God-given ability, love of the game and a willingness to learn. The only thing that was missing was competition.

One Saturday afternoon several months after the two began their training sessions, an opportunity arose for at least some level of competition. The regularity of their practice sessions was apparently not lost on several other children who began to hang around the school pitch. While most of the other young people played soccer at some organised level they seemed to be particularly attracted by the fun that Nigel and Brian were having and soon there were several young fellows and a couple of girls as well who joined in the games.

Nigel recognized that his ability to assist in the improvement of Brian's physical skills and techniques was nearly at an end so the interaction with other children gave Nigel an opportunity to see just how much his prize pupil had learned about the game itself. It soon became clear that not only had Brian listened to what Nigel said, but the young man was quite prepared to apply it as well. Nigel could see that Brian was initially frustrated with his new playmates' lack of skills, but he soon adjusted and it was clear to Nigel that Brian genuinely enjoyed playing.

With the arrival of the first few children, Nigel was able to work with multiple passes, including a figure eight with three players. The middle player would make a short pass to one of the wing players and then follow around the back of that player. The receiving player would pass the ball to the remaining player and then follow around the recipient. The process would be repeated as the three moved in tandem down the field. Brian flawlessly took each pass, at least those that were remotely accurate and delivered his own pass perfectly, however the remaining passes were usually an adventure. It was Brian himself who suggested to his partners that they start by going very slowly, barely walking and that worked quite well. Gradually the three moved a little more quickly and soon the figure eight advanced with reasonable speed.

After watching this interaction Nigel knew, without question, that Brian would be more than merely a great player. In making his suggestion the young man did not appear bossy or superior, rather he made the suggestions as if either of the other two might also have come up with the idea. Brian did not make the suggestion out of disdain for his teammates' abilities but because he thought it would make it easier for the three to work together. And, the other youngsters accepted the idea without question and were thrilled with their resulting progress.

As more children joined the group, Nigel organised games of man-in-the-middle. Even though, technically, it could not be said that Brian was responsible for ever losing the ball, he accepted the howls of protest from other children and took his place in the middle with good grace. Although it must have been clear to the other children that Brian was not playing at full tilt, his good humour and the fun that everyone was having kept the group coming back. In time there were enough children for relay races and short field matches with four-a-side, then five, and then six.

Because most of the children had some formal coaching, they were a bit beyond the stage where the entire group chased after the ball, but there did seem to be an occasional relapse. Nigel was delighted to see that, without saying a word, Brian went a long way toward sorting that out. When the ball came to him, he simply held possession until he saw someone who moved into an open position and then he made the appropriate pass. Soon nearly everyone was moving into an open spot knowing that they would get a pass, and it didn't even have to be Brian who had the ball.

Eventually, what began as a man and a boy practicing by themselves became a large group of laughing children training with games and competitions, which concluded with a full scrimmage usually with far more than eleven on a side. Molly, the wolfhound was always present, nearly a mascot to the goings on because all the children got to know her and greet her when they arrived. Somehow Molly seemed to know that the pitch was for the children so she either roamed the sidelines with Nigel barking occasional encouragement, or sitting quietly keeping a close eye on the competition.

In all those games, Nigel never saw his protégé score a goal and yet, established in the middle of the field, he completely controlled the play of his team. Nigel could see that Brian had excellent field vision making good through passes so that his teammates could run onto the ball, although what happened at the end of the pass was always a surprise. Even though he was undoubtedly capable of passing over the heads of the children, most of the games were played on the ground and Brian appeared to be quite the expert at picking out the appropriate passing lanes.

Although the Saturday sessions were not particularly competitive, which might have pushed Brian to perform to his capabilities, for Nigel they were the next best thing. Brian had an opportunity to actually play the game, develop his field vision and interact with other players irrespective of their skill levels. Most of all, Brian seemed to enjoy the experience and he was accepted by the other children even though they all realised that he was a far superior player.

As frequently happens, all good things must come to an end and so it was with the Saturday sessions. The sheer size of the gathering brought other curious onlookers including a few parents who came along to see what their children were so excited about. Nigel spoke with a couple of parents and was gratified to be told that the session was the highlight of the week for several of the children. One father explained that his daughter had been entirely put off soccer because she was not having any fun in the league where she was playing. He was delighted to see how much she enjoyed her playing on Saturday.

Another parent wondered exactly how it all came about, and Nigel explained that he was just working out with a local child, having a bit of fun, and soon the news spread. He insisted that he wasn't doing any coaching at all, only supervising a bit of mayhem. That mother explained that she didn't know that much about the game but that her son's coach, in an organised league, remarked on how much the boy improved. All in all, the sessions seemed like a great success, not just for Brian but also for a large group of children. Eventually, however, the penny dropped.

It started with a casual conversation between Nigel and another parent who happened to be a barrister. Nigel was asked whether he was part of some organisation and his response was same as he gave to other parents. He explained how it all came about and that he was just making it easier for the children to have a bit of fun.

"You realise, of course," the barrister said stroking his chin, "that if any child gets hurt, you are likely to be liable at law unless, of course, all the parents of these children sign some legally binding waiver."

Nigel looked on in amazement. "To be honest," he replied, "I never thought about that but I suppose I should have known. I guess I figured that children play all the time and occasionally someone gets hurt, but that is all part of growing up."

The Barrister replied, "Yes, that was how it was when we were growing up. But now you see people are looking to blame someone for everything that happens. I must say my own profession has a lot to answer for as well. So even though these children are only having a bit of fun you become a target if anything happens, no matter how innocent it may be."

Nigel thought about that, balancing the risks to himself against the benefit to Brian and, indeed, all of the children. In the end he took a good look at his blanket liability insurance policy and decided to get clarification from his broker. Unfortunately, just after Nigel arranged a meeting to discuss the matter a solicitor acting on behalf of the school system contacted him.

The message from the school was clear. While they had no difficulty with local people using their pitches and fields, they could not permit regular organized activities. If someone were to be injured the school would become a defendant in a lawsuit because, with knowledge of the activity, they allowed it to continue. If, however, Brian were to arrange for proper indemnification and insurance cover, and apply for permission from the

Department of Education, the school might consider allowing the activity to continue.

In the end, Nigel had little choice but to end the sessions. Explaining the situation to Brian and the other children was another matter entirely. There were many sad faces the next Saturday when he sat everyone down and explained that the training sessions would have to stop because there were rules, which would not allow the group to continue to play on the school grounds. After the cries of protest, Nigel explained that he didn't like it any more than anyone else but everyone had to obey the rules, just as they needed to obey their parents.

Brian seemed to understand, particularly when Nigel explained that the two would continue to work together as they always had, just not on the school pitch. Brian was disappointed however because he loved playing with a large group of children for the first time in his life.

As they walked home after the disappointment that Saturday, passing the ball back and forth as they always did, Nigel said, "You know I just had a great idea. If it is all right with your parents, we will go into the city for the Germany friendly at Lansdowne Road next week and, while we are at it, we can find you a proper pair of football boots. How does that sound?"

Predictably, Brian was thrilled and the disappointment of the day was forgotten.

The trip to Lansdowne Road was the first of several trips that soon replaced many of the training sessions. Mr. Blessington and Brian would frequently attended matches played by the various Irish professional teams, particularly Drogheda United, and once they even flew to Liverpool to see their favourite team in action. Nigel always smiled at the memory of that trip.

Although it had been many years since his career prematurely ended, Nigel remained in contact with the club and had been involved in the business end of the operation when he worked for a bank in England. As a result he was well connected with the management and had no difficulty obtaining premium seating in Anfield just behind the team. He also arranged for his for his prize pupil to meet the players in the locker room after the match. Thankfully, Liverpool won easily and the players were in high spirits.

Like any little boy meeting his heroes, Brian could not have been more excited but when he entered the locker room awe took the place of excitement and he stood still with a big smile on his face, smiling and saying nothing. The players, however, soon sorted him out and the captain himself took Brian around introducing him to everyone and showing him all the nooks and crannies of the dressing room. Brian left with an armful of souvenirs, an even bigger smile and memories that would last a lifetime.

Nigel stood aside as Brian enjoyed his experience. It occurred to him at the time that the Liverpool players had no way of realising that this child could quite possibly attain a skill level that would dwarf their professional talents. In fact, he was already well on his way.

Chapter Twenty-one

MARGARET O'NEILL had just finished her tea when the telephone rang. She had an immediate premonition that something terrible had happened and what was worse, a vision of young Brian, who only left her house a couple of hours earlier, flashed through her mind. Years ago, Margaret might have accused herself of being silly, but in the past few years, particularly since the remarkable events that surrounded the arrival of Brian O'Suileabháin in her life, she stopped dismissing these visions.

Margaret was now acutely aware of her unconscious thoughts because they always seemed to be an accurate depiction of what was to come. Perhaps it was her introduction to Brian but Margaret now accepted the she was "fey" as the old ones used to say when she was a young girl, and as such occasionally able to know and understand things before they were actually explained to her. In the past it was a curiosity that often made her smile but on this occasion she was truly terrified to answer the telephone.

Realising she had no choice, Margaret picked up the phone as said softly, "Hello."

The woman's voice on the other end replied, "Margaret, this is Eibhlín, are you alright?"

Margaret took a deep breath and said in a more normal voice, "Of course Eibhlín,"

For a moment Margaret thought that perhaps, for once, her premonition was wrong when the voice in the phone said, "That's better, you didn't sound like yourself when you answered the phone."

But then Eibhlín continued, "I'm afraid we have some bad news here, Margaret. Molly has died."

The old woman put her hand to her mouth thinking how distraught Brian must be. "What happened Eibhlín? She seemed fine when she left here just a short time ago."

"I'm sure she was," her friend replied, "but Molly was over eleven years old which is very old for an Irish wolfhound. When she came back to the house she curled up on her rug in the sun porch and fell asleep. Perhaps she had a heart attack but by the time Brian changed clothes and filled me in on the news, she had passed away. The poor little fellow brought her a bowl of water and then he realised that something was wrong. Oh, Margaret, it was heartbreaking."

"I am so sorry Eibhlín," Margaret said, "How is he taking it?"

"Not well, I'm afraid," was the response. "He is lying over there with his arms around her crying his little eyes out. You know, now that I think about it, this is the first time he has ever cried. But of course it is also his first experience with the death of someone he is very close to. Margaret, I just don't know what to do."

Margaret responded, "Eibhlín, let me think for a moment." She closed her eyes and concentrated. Her friend was counting on her, as was the little boy who had become closer to her than any of her own grandchildren. The solution, when it came, was as much a surprise to her as it was to Eibhlín but she had nothing else to offer.

"This is what I think you should do," she said with a conviction she really didn't feel. "You tell Brian that you called me to tell me about Molly, and I am feeling very sad. After all, I knew Molly since she was a puppy, even before Brian was born. You tell Brian that I was hoping he would come over and we could feel sad together, and maybe that way we would both feel better. I think he will come, I really do. If he does you will have to get Cathal and maybe Paddy if he is around, to find a big box for Molly, wrap her in her old blanket and dig a proper grave in the back garden. Put the box next to the grave and when that is ready, Brian and I will come back and we can have a proper burial ceremony."

"Thank you Margaret," Eibhlín said quietly, "I will give it a try."

Eibhlín walked over and knelt down next to her son. She put her arm around the boy and gently rubbed his back. Feeling his mother so close, Brian shifted his attention to her and she put her arms around him rocking her son back and forth.

"It's all right love, it's all right," she whispered. "You know Molly was very old and tired but now she has gone where all good dogs go. And now she is running and playing with her own mother and father just like she is a puppy again. I know you miss her already but her time came to leave this life and she left with happy memories of all the time she spent with you. Molly had a very happy life and you must always remember that."

Brian cried, "But I don't want her to die."

"Of course not, love," Eibhlín said softly, "Molly was a wonderful and very smart dog but we all must die sometimes and dogs don't live as long as people so her time had come. I know you feel terrible but we all feel the same way. You know I just rang Mrs. O'Neill to tell her about Molly and I think she might be crying as well. Why don't we walk over to her house and maybe you can help her to feel better."

Wiping his eyes with the back of his hands, Brian's crying turned to sobs between which he managed to answer, "Do you really think I can make Mrs. O'Neill feel better?"

"Yes," Eibhlín answered solemnly, "after all the two of you were Molly's best friends. Remember Mrs. O'Neill used to give Molly treats even when she was a little puppy and that was even before you were born. I think you are the only one who can make her feel better."

"Alright" the boy said, scratching Molly's ear one more time before he got to his feet. "What are we going to do about Molly?"

"I'll tell you what," Eibhlín replied as cheerfully as she could manage. "I will walk you over to Mrs. O'Neill's house and leave the two of you together. Then I will come back here and by that time Daddy will be here and I will call Uncle Paddy and the two of them will find a nice box and when you come back, we will have a proper ceremony and bury her in the back garden."

Eibhlín took her son's hand and the two left the house and headed up the roadway to Mrs. O'Neill's house. The mother and son did not speak during the short walk. Occasionally Brian, perhaps remembering some moment with his dog, sobbed and Eibhlín walked along feeling helpless because she could think of nothing she could do or say that would further comfort him.

Margaret met Brian and Eibhlín at the gate and leaning down she hugged the young boy as he began to sob once again. Taking Brian by the hand she led him into the house. On entering the kitchen, Margaret took out some milk and the cookies she knew Brian liked. Looking around, the room looked empty without the big dog under the kitchen table and she appreciated, once again, the enormity of the young boy's loss.

"I glad you came over," Margaret said sitting down next to her young friend. "You know that I feel terrible about poor Molly because just like she was your best friend, she always made me feel special when she sat there under the table. I think she liked me as much as I liked her."

Brian looked perfectly miserable, "What am I going to do without her Mrs. O'Neill?"

She replied, "I know it will be hard for a long, long time because Molly meant so much to you. I remember when my husband Brendan died, years and years ago even before you were born. I remember how much I missed him and I certainly didn't know what I was going to do without him. When I really thought about it I decided that even though he was no longer alive on this earth, his spirit was still alive and that someday, I would see him again. And that is what kept me going when I was so very sad. I think that is what you should think about. Molly is no longer on this earth, but her spirit will always be with you."

"And how is that?" Brian asked quietly.

Margaret smiled putting her arm around Brian's slumping shoulders, "As long as you remember Molly, her spirit will be alive. Think about all those times you ran through the fields, or played hurling together, or explored the woods, or when she met you at school and came here for her treat. All those wonderful times that you shared, those things in your mind mean that her spirit is still alive."

Brian eyes brightened a bit, "I remember the shock that Mrs. McNellis got my first day at school when Molly jumped up and ran to me as I left school. She said she thought she would have a heart attack and everyone laughed."

"You see," Margaret said, "that is what I mean. Molly does not want you to be sad so her spirit is reminding you of all the happy things that the two of you did together. And you know, as long as you think about those times, she will be with you."

"She was a great dog, wasn't she?" Brian said with the beginnings of a smile.

"The best dog ever," Margaret replied hugging the young boy. "You know what I think. I think that we should have a party celebrating what a great dog she was. You invite Katie and Libby and some of the other children who knew Molly from school and we will have a party right here with balloons and cake and Molly will be here in spirit because we will all tell our favourite Molly stories. How does that sound?"

Brian smiled, wiping the remaining tears from his eyes, "I think Molly would like that."

Margaret and Brian spent a long time talking about all the things that Molly meant to them until Margaret looking at her watch and announced, "Where has the time gone. We must get over to the ceremony."

With that she pulled on her knitted cardigan and the two, hand in hand, headed off to the O'Suileabháins' house. When they arrived Brian opened the door for Margaret and they walked through the sitting room into the kitchen. Eibhlín gave her son a big hug, relieved that the tears vanished, at least for the time.

Margaret, Brian and Eibhlín walked out into the garden where Cathal and Inspector Paddy Rice were standing reverently next to a large box that held Molly's body. Her head rested on a small pillow and she was wrapped in her favourite blanket.

A very large hole had been dug in the garden and the box rested at its edge with ropes passed under the box.

On seeing his pet, Brian began to sob, as Eibhlín and Mrs. O'Neill held his hands.

His own eyes tearing over at the sight of his son, Cathal began, "I think it is up to me to say a few words about this wonderful dog since I brought her home to Mother so many years ago. From the days when I was a young boy like Brian, I enjoyed the company of a number of dogs - big dogs, little dogs and all sorts of dogs in between. I can honestly say that I never met a dog that was smarter than Molly. When she came into our house, she made herself right at home. Of course she did eat a couple of chairs while she was teething, but after that she never caused us the slightest bit of trouble. In fact, I am quite sure she knew exactly what we were saying and there was nothing she loved more than taking long walks in the fields, chasing birds and butterflies but always running back the minute we called. And then, when Brian came along, she took over minding him... really mother and I were hardly necessary as long as Molly was around. Molly was a very important member of this family and she will be sadly missed by all of us."

After a few moments to consider what Cathal said, Paddy began directing his comments to Brian, "I couldn't agree more with what your father said about this wonderful dog. You may not know this Brian, but when you were only an infant, Molly helped me solve a very strange case indeed. We all know Molly had a very big nose – the rest of her wasn't so small either – but in this case, I gave her a bit of material and asked her to sniff around and find out where it came from. Molly looked up at me and I think she even nodded her head, but anyway she took a good sniff and went all over checking out the possibilities, like any good garda, and then she went right to the source so I had my answer. I also know that as long as Molly was minding this home, I knew that everyone here, including my favourite sister and, of course, my favourite nephew were safe and sound. I know I will miss Molly because she always welcomed me and I am sure that, right now she is still looking after this house and everyone in it."

Eibhlín then put her arm around her son and said, "You know, Brian that I never thought that your father and I would be lucky enough to have a wonderful boy so we ended up with a wonderful dog instead. But then, a miracle happened and you came along but the amazing thing was that just like we fell in love with you, so did Molly. I know that Molly always had a place in her heart for your father and me, but I have never seen a dog that loved a boy more than Molly loved you. I know that when you were at school, Molly would look at the clock just waiting for the minute she could run off and bring you home. And you know how much she loved to run in the fields with you and chase your sliotar and play all the games the two of you invented. You know, I think the thing Molly wanted most of all was that you would be happy and she would do anything to make you happy."

"I think that even though she is gone, she would still want you to be happy. I know it is hard for you to be happy now that Molly is gone, but you will always have all your memories of this wonderful dog and whenever you feel sad, you should think about all the funny things she did and in that way she will still make you feel happy. I know we will all miss Molly, and no one will miss her more than you, but I think it is wonderful that she lived with us for all these years and made us so happy and that is what I want to remember."

When Eibhlín finished, Margaret put her arm around Brian and said, "Everyone has said such wonderful things about Molly that it is hard for me to know what else to say. You know Brian that Molly used to visit me before you came along and I always knew that she was a kind and gentle dog, full of fun and happiness and very smart. But somehow, when you came along she changed – oh she was still kind and gentle, full of fun and happiness and very smart but now she had a best friend to share her life with. You may not remember, but when you were a tiny infant she used to put her nose next to you and you would reach out and pat her and I could see the way she looked at you, with love and devotion and loyalty. There is nothing more wonderful than the love a boy and a dog share and you were as important to her as she was to you."

"Because of this, it is very sad that dogs live for such a short time compared to people, but that is the way God made things. He sent us Molly for a short time and she brought us great happiness when we really needed happiness. And then he took her back leaving us with so many happy memories that she will live in all of us for as long as we are alive. So I want to remember Molly for being a wonderful and loyal friend to all of us and I want to thank God in a special way for sending her to us."

As each of those present spoke their piece, Brian stood silently sobbing as he stared at his beloved friend hoping that somehow it was all a bad dream and that Molly would open her eyes, jump up and come trotting over to him. Deep down, however, he knew that Molly was gone because he knew that the words spoken by his parents, uncle and oldest friend were true. The group was quiet for a moment and then Margaret gently asked, "Do you want to say something, Brian?"

In response, the young boy broke away from his mother and ran into the house. The four adults looked as each other with very real concern as if to ask, "What do we do now?"

As quickly as he disappeared, however, Brian returned with a sliotar that had not only seen its share of pucks but also had spent a fair amount of time between the big dog's teeth. Approaching the dog's casket, Brian reached in and placed the ball under Molly's chin before he stroked the dog's head and snout for the last time.

Between the sobs, Brian said, "This is for you Molly, so that you will have something to play with and something to remember me by. I know you would want me to be happy and I will try my best but now I am very sad because I miss you so much. You were the best dog in the entire world and you were my best friend. I will never forget you."

Eibhlín and Margaret moved forward together putting their arm over Brian's shoulders as he sobbed his final farewell. Cathal then put a second blanket over the dog and closed the box for the last time. The two men carefully lowered the box into the hole and began to slowly cover it over with dirt. Brian stood silently until the job was finished. Paddy Rice finally broke the silence when he announced, "All right now Brian, you and I have a job to do. We must make a proper marker for Molly's grave then you must plant some flowers on it so it will always be a happy place where you can remember the wonderful times you had. Is that alright?"

As he wiped his eyes in his sleeves, Brian replied in a very quiet voice, "Yes."

Chapter Twenty-two

BRIAN BORU O'SUILEABHÁIN was neatly dressed in his new school uniform, grey pants, light grey jumper, white shirt and forest green tie, as he stood on the front steps of his home while his proud mother snapped away with her camera. Brian tried to be patient, but he had never been one to remain in one place longer than was absolutely necessary. His mother, it seemed to Brian, would not be happy until the photograph she took included just the right light, background and, of course, his perfect expression, whatever that might be. He knew that was her way, very precise in everything she did, which probably explained why so many people valued her intricately crafted silver jewellery. This posing, however, was getting a little old and Brian was relieved when she finally finished...but then she noticed that his shirt tail had made its way out of his trousers so she insisted on just a few more.

"Ma," he moaned, "you don't want me to be late for my first day do you?"

Eibhlín replied, "This will only take another few seconds and the school is only down the road. If you give me a big smile that will be it."

Brian shook his head in frustration but after several more shots, somehow managed a smile that satisfied his mother.

The young man captured on film that day was not particularly tall but he had stretched a few inches during the summer and was probably experiencing a growth spurt. Whatever about his height, Brian was solidly built. His chest was that bit broader and his legs that bit bigger than the other boys his age and all traces of baby fat had long since vanished. Apart from his piercing blue eyes and dimpled cheeks, there was little about the boy that appeared out of the ordinary. He was a typical thirteen year old, seemingly in constant motion, whose shirt tails escaped the minute after he kissed his mother goodbye, and whose red-blonde hair, so neatly groomed for the photograph, reverted to form sticking out every which way when he ran down the road.

Brian decided that he was looking forward to attending this new school because, he concluded, this was a new adventure and novelty appealed to him. At least that was the story he was telling himself to overcome the fear and uncertainty that every young boy encounters on his first day at secondary school.

Brian knew that there would be many other students who were smarter than he was just as there were in the National School where he spent the last six years. His friend Katie O'Donnell with her dark brown hair and greenish-blue eyes who seemed to know everything, not just the things that were in the school books was the first person that came to his mind. Brian knew that he would have to work hard at his studies but then with his mother and father scrutinizing his lessons in gruesome detail every night he wouldn't have much choice. His parents did not always agree on everything, but to his occasional regret, something they did agree upon was their role in educating their son. For some reason, which was lost on Brian, they thought they were just as important as the teachers so school didn't really end until they had their say. As a result, although he might not have been a top student his parents made sure that he would always be above average.

One argument that he was glad his mother won found him attending St. Killians, the County Louth VEC Community College. Brian's parents had plenty of money so they could afford to send him to any of the fee-paying schools where more wealthy people sent their children in the hopes of improving their education. His father attended one of these schools, as well as Trinity College, and was now a professor at University College Dublin so he knew all the right people as far as education was concerned.

What Dr. O'Suileabháin really wanted was for his son to attend the same private boy's school in Dublin that he attended when he was in secondary school. His Da took him to the school one time when they had taken the train into the city to see a hurling match at Croke Park. The school building seemed big and dark and there was hardly a blade of green grass in sight. As if that had not put Brian off, the idea of getting up at the crack of dawn every morning, sitting on a train for probably hours, and then walking miles on city streets to go to a school where he would have nothing in common with most of the other kids did not appeal to him at all. His Da, however, told him all about the interesting people he would meet, people who would be important friends for the rest of his life. He also told Brian about the great sports programmes at the school and that he could be part of a championship tradition in rugby. Now that did appeal to Brian because some of his favourite rugby players on Ireland's side graduated from the school. But then he asked his father about the hurling as well. His father explained that he could always continue to play with the local club but that this school concentrated on rugby.

His mother, on the other hand, liked the idea of Brian attending a local school with local children. The VEC School, she argued, would allow Brian to learn in an environment that included all types of students, including girls, not just well off and well connected young men. His Da had gone like, "But Pet, surely the quality of education at the private school is far superior to that at the VEC. Look at the leaving cert scores and the university placement."

His Ma, however, was not persuaded. "Education," she said, "is more than just what is learned in the books. If Brian works hard he will be successful no matter where he goes to school, and we both know that he will work hard. There are excellent teachers in the VEC as well and if he is not successful, it will be because we did not do our job as parents and not because the school was inferior. Meanwhile he will be educated in an environment that reflects the real world, with children of all skills and abilities, not just wealthy and privileged boys. He will also be able to walk to school and will not have to spend hours of his free time travelling."

Brian suspected that his Da knew that he would not win this argument because once his mother decided on something that was it, as he well knew. Anyway his Da tried one more thing,

"And is that they way you think about my education ... it didn't reflect the real world?"

"Ah Pet," his Ma had gone, "you know that was a different time and different circumstances. What was the right thing for you is not necessarily the right thing for Brian. He will be comfortable among the people he knows and he will not be so exhausted from travel that he won't be able to enjoy his learning experience, not to mention playing hurling for his school as well as his club."

The discussion ended as Brian hoped it would. Whatever about rugby, he loved his hurling, he loved the hills and fields around the Boyne and he loved the fresh air of the Louth countryside. There was a certain security to his life that he had come to appreciate from his earliest memories and although he knew that some day that might change, just like the time when Molly died and his life was totally turned upside down, he wasn't quite ready to move on.

Just as he had done in National School, Brian like the idea of racing through the fields to school with the great Gráinne, who entered his life about six months after Molly died, leading the way, forcing him to run faster and faster just to keep up. At least he would know many of the other students, like Katie and her sister Libby, who came from the towns around Drogheda and did not have grand notions about themselves being from posh places near Dublin. Of course the hours at school would drag on, as they always did, but at least when the day was over he could run over to visit Mrs. O'Neill and tell her about all the interesting things that happened. Mrs. O'Neill would have some sweet like apple tart or chocolate chip cookies and a big glass of cold milk, which would keep him going until teatime. So although he was a bit anxious about his first day in secondary school, Brian was glad that he was attending St. Killians on the banks of the Boyne.

A jumble of thoughts ran through Brian's head as he raced down the road to the school. He certainly need not have worried about arriving on time because running fast and long was one thing that he could do well - that and hurling and most every sport for that matter. Funny that, neither of his parents was even the slightest bit athletic and yet here he was, according to some of his coaches, "a natural" whatever that meant. He did know that he loved nothing better than taking his camán out into the fields and pucking the sliotar against trees, fence poles, utility poles or anything he could pick out, the smaller the target the better. And then Gráinne, or a few years back Molly, would be jumping around retrieving the ball and returning it to him for the next puck... a bit wet and sloppy of course, but that would be great training for a rainy match. He also loved the soccer and working out with Mr. Blessington and he knew that St. Killians had a team so maybe he would get to play that as well.

The great thing about sport, he decided, was that since he was as good as nearly everyone he played with, even those several years older than he was, the big kids didn't torture him even though he wasn't very big himself. On the other hand, the problem was that he didn't like to see other little fellows his age get tortured, just because they weren't so good at sport. It wasn't so bad in the National School but at the college there would be really big kids, six years older than he was and he hoped there wouldn't be too many bullies. Sorting out bullies was the only honourable thing to do but not something he enjoyed doing because it always seemed that he was the one that got in trouble... although big kids didn't like to admit that a fellow his size had sorted them out. "A little less honour and a little more common sense," his father advised on the last occasion. Not that he got into lots of fights or anything; it just annoyed him when stronger kids picked on weaker kids. Well maybe in the community school he would see where his father's advice got him.

Brian slowed down as he approached the school gate. A number of students already arrived but since others were strung out well down the road he knew he had loads of time. Just ahead he saw Katie and Libby walking arm and arm into the schoolyard. Brian knew they were sisters but they didn't look very much alike. Katie was Brian's age, very pretty with long dark hair and big eyes while Libby was a year older but had always been in the same class as Katie. Libby had a round face, short blondish hair and smaller eyes. Libby didn't speak very well, which suited Brian because he hardly spoke at all, but she always had a big smile on her face, which in Brian's opinion, made her very pretty as well.

Brian stopped just behind the two girls, pushed his shirt tail into his trousers and made an attempt to push his hair back into place. He then quickened his pace so that he was walking next to Katie. Brian didn't say anything because he knew his voice would come out squeaky if he tried and he thought that Katie was pretending she hadn't seen him for at least a few steps. Eventually she quickly glanced over at him and after again looking straight ahead she said in a very serious and proper voice, "Good Morning Brian."

Brian mumbled, "Morning Katie," and continued to walk with the girls.

"By the way, Brian," his friend said pleasantly, "I would appreciate it if you would call me Kate from now on."

Brian was a bit puzzled by the request but muttered, "Fine, Kate it is."

Libby looked around her sister and said in a loud voice, "Hi Bri..Bri. School today."

Libby always made Brian smile and this morning was no different. He found his voice and said, "Hello to you Libby. Yes, off to school."

"Do you like my uniform?" Libby asked. "It is brand new and my mommy bought it for me."

"I think it suits you well," Brian replied.

As the trio approached the entrance, the school principal, Mr. Brian Freeman stood, hands behind his back, watching through his office window as students arrived for the new school term. He recognised most of the returning pupils, who were involved in the first year orientation, but paid particular attention to the first year students. They would be adjusting to a new and different educational system and it was his job, together with his staff, to make that adjustment as easy as possible. When the new class arrived each year, fresh and eager, he thought of them almost like a freshly wrapped Christmas package. One never knew what treasures or disasters lay inside.

The three approaching the door were certainly first years. He had met the parents of the two girls, one of whom would probably be a high achiever while the other one should be in the special needs class. The parents explained that although their levels of comprehension were significantly different, the younger daughter, obviously the pretty brunette, was extraordinarily protective of her elder sister and hopefully the girls would be kept together as much as possible.

Freeman had explained that while mainstreaming special needs students was intended to better prepare them for the future, it was important that their education not disrupt that of students who were not in the special needs category. The girls' parents assured Mr. Freeman that Libby would not be a disruption and, perhaps, her sister's presence would provide her a much better learning environment then would be found in a typical special needs class. Although he had his doubts, Freeman agreed to allow the two to stay together, at least during the initial assessment period, and to see how it worked out.

As for the little fellow with the mop of strawberry-blonde hair, Mr. Freeman wondered if that was Dr. O'Suileabháin's son, a Brian like himself. Apparently the boy was the talk of the entire community because even as a young child he had displayed incredible athletic abilities. Possibly not - as the child didn't appear to be very tall - but on the other hand, he carried himself like an athlete. His shoulders had a distinctive roll and he walked with his back ramrod straight and not slumped over like most of the other young men his age. The school had never experienced much athletic success but maybe young master O'Suileabháin, whether or not he was the young man with the O'Donnell girls, would change all of that. Funny thing, Freeman was a classmate of Cathal O'Suileabháin at Trinity and as far as he could remember, the boy's father would have difficulty walking and chewing gum at the same time so he concluded that any athletic talent didn't come from the father …must be something about a skipped generation.

Katie, Libby and Brian walked through the main entrance and into a foyer full of students waiting for the assembly hall to open. It appeared that most of those present were first years, easily identified by their small size, new uniforms and the wide-eyed looks at the unfamiliar surroundings. There were a few older students standing to one side who were chatting away with old friends, perfectly comfortable in the environment. The room was remarkably quiet, considering the number of young people, probably because, like Brian, they all felt a certain discomfort at this new experience.

Several people stared at Libby because she was unique and certainly didn't look like any of the other students. Brian noticed their stares and so did Libby but in her typical fashion, she assumed that their attention was meant to be a friendly gesture so she waved and said hello to everyone she saw. Katie tightened her grip on Libby's linked elbow and stared silently at anyone who might even think about mocking her sister.

A couple of the girls were not intimidated by Katie's stares and walked over to the group. The two girls returned Libby's greeting, introduced themselves as Siobhán Tierney and Maeve O'Brien and asked Libby her name. Libby responded brightly explaining the she was Libby and Kate was her sister. Kate, feeling a bit more relaxed smiled a quick greeting while Libby pointed to Brian and after giving his name, explained that he was their friend. After Siobhán and Maeve greeted Brian they were soon engaged in a pleasant chat with the two O'Donnells and soon all four girls were laughing at one thing or another. This rare sound caused others to look over at the group and soon other conversations started, more laughter was heard and in a short time, everyone seemed much more relaxed.

Throughout it all, Brian remained at Katie's side saying nothing but pleased that he appeared to be part of a group. Although he attempted to convince himself that he was looking after the two girls, in truth Katie – mentally he corrected himself, Kate - was a quite confident even among all these strangers and, as such, she provided him with security and not the other way around.

Eventually, the doors to the assembly hall opened and everyone began to file into the room. Just as Brian was about to enter, two older boys, apparently fifth or six years, approached Brian and lightly pushed his shoulder. "You Brian O'Suileabháin?" he was asked.

Brian said nothing but nodded his head.

The taller of the boys again pushed his shoulder this time a bit harder and turning to his mate said laughing, "He doesn't look all that tough to me."

A puzzled expression crossed Brian's face as he wondered what that was all about. First, he didn't think that he had met either boy so how would they know who he was. Then, he never remembered thinking that he was tough so why would they say that. Seeing the girls enter the hall ahead of him, he promptly forgot about the encounter and rushed forward so that he could keep close to them.

Chapter Twenty-three

THE NEW DARK BLUE FIVE SERIES BMW drove slowly to the gates of St. Killians VEC School. Unlike other mothers who undertook a similar chore dressed in tracksuits and runners the elegantly dressed and carefully coiffed Beatrice Pembroke would not consider venturing into the public domain without looking her best. After all, one never knew who one might encounter, although the chance of meeting anyone of consequence was certainly remote in the wilds of County Louth.

Beatrice looked with dismay through the gates of the utilitarian structure in which her children would be educated for the next five or six years. How far, she wondered, was it possible to fall in the course of six months? It seemed only yesterday that Patrick and she were attending a formal dinner party at the residence of the English Governor of Hong Kong rubbing shoulders, as it were, with all the right people in the colony's high society. Patrick was a senior vice president at the Anglo-Chinese Bank and she was actively involved in the Royal Eastern Golf and Tennis Club. Their son Chadwick was in his first year at the local public school attended by all the better ex-pats. The young man was reportedly well adjusted and, by all accounts, an excellent soccer player.

Their daughter Charlotte, called Charlie much to Beatrice's distaste, was a popular and very pretty young lady who was just finishing her last year of primary school. It had become clear that Charlotte was far more interested in tennis, soccer, field hockey and who knows what all else than she was in fashion and etiquette, proper interests for a well-reared young woman. Beatrice reluctantly tolerated her daughter's peculiar interests because she believed that Charlotte would come around when she was more physically mature.

Such a short time ago, Beatrice and her family were well-connected members of Hong Kong's ex-pat high society. And yet, six months later, Beatrice found herself delivering her children to a common secondary school surrounded by farmers' fields. It was abundantly clear that County Louth, and Ireland for that matter, was a long, long way from Hong Kong or London. As hard as it might be to believe, her sophisticated and successful Patrick was reared in those remote hills and still had sisters living here.

Those few short months ago Beatrice thought of County Louth as a pleasant place to visit for a month or so during the summer months when the heat and humidity made Hong Kong totally unbearable. Her children did seem to enjoy the company of their Irish cousins and other assorted urchins that seemed to roam wild in the fields around Drogheda, but she had never been sure that associating with that type of child was in the best interest of her babies, no disrespect to the Irish of course. Summer associations were one thing, but permanent friendships required further scrutiny.

Patrick, it now appeared, had entertained other ideas entirely. The political situation in Hong Kong, specifically the expiration of the English lease of Hong Kong and its reversion to China, was a constant topic of conversation at the club. Although everyone agreed that it would have little effect on business, as least in the near term, Patrick began to look back to Ireland.

It seemed his native country was in the throes of some type of economic boom and Patrick decided that, if the right opportunity presented, that is where he would rather be. Beatrice was annoyed that he had not chosen to share this opinion a bit before he made his decision but once he had decided there was little she could do. When he finally got around to telling her, he also maintained that the children were now getting older and they would be far better off being educated in Ireland rather than in the totally artificial ex-pat school system in Hong Kong.

Beatrice never expected that Hong Kong would be a permanent home so she had no real difficulty with the concept of a move back home. She also accepted that the children would probably be better off attending secondary school, and indeed university, among their own people. However, in Beatrice's opinion moving back home meant England not Ireland and specifically London, or at least the greater London area. Certainly, she argued, a proper English Public School education would best prepare Chadwick for the future as well as providing a network of friends that he could not possibly duplicate in Ireland.

Patrick countered, as he usually did, by saying that the Irish education he received had apparently done him no harm and what was good enough for him was good enough for his children. He also added that the whole conversation was very theoretical because he had no idea what opportunities, if any, were available in Ireland or England for that matter so the entire discussion was dropped.

Thinking back, Beatrice should have known that change was in the air. After all, she had been married to Patrick for twenty years and she knew full well that when he got an idea in his head, it did not remain theoretical for long. That was one of the things that first attracted her to Patrick. He was decisive and knew what he wanted and then he did what was necessary to achieve his goals. Patrick's courtship of her was an obvious example. She was pleased to recall that she had many other prospects but Patrick was decisive and before she knew what hit her, she was walking up the aisle. The other thing was that he was very good looking, tall and slender with black hair and blue eyes, a perfect compliment, she had decided, to her willowy figure and long ash-blonde hair.

It should have come as no surprise to her that Patrick was offered an excellent position at the Irish-Anglo Bank in Dublin, which in his own words he would be crazy not to accept. Before she could even catch her breath, they were headed to Ireland. Really, it had been much too much, much to fast and she did not even have an opportunity to become properly acquainted with her new home. Although she visited Ireland several times, most of her holidays were spent in rural County Louth where Patrick insisted he could relax and recharge his batteries. Trips to Dublin were few and far between so she hadn't had an opportunity to appreciate what the capital offered. A couple of girls at the club insisted that she would love Dublin because it was in many respects a mini-London with proper clubs, shops, theatre and restaurants. This came as some consolation to Beatrice because her perception of Dublin was more like a provincial British City, a mini-Manchester for example, which held no appeal for her at all. The girls also insisted that she should live on the south side of the city near the coast. They suggested places like Blackrock, Monkstown or Foxrock and so she had attempted to relay this information to Patrick.

Patrick has listened patiently to her suggestions but once again she suspected that he had his own plans. "Remember," he said, "I grew up over there so I would know all about the city. The thing is that we could get two or three times the house for the same money on the north side and the commute would not be half as bad. After all, I am the one who will have to sit in traffic or on a train for who knows how long every morning and evening."

In the end, the agreement, if Beatrice could call it that, was that since his new employment would take him to Dublin immediately, Patrick would arrange things over there while she arranged for the move from Hong Kong. Patrick explained that it was in the best interests of the children to complete the school term in Hong Kong and then they would have the entire summer to settle in before they began again in Ireland in the autumn.

By the time Beatrice and the children finally finished organising, packing and shipping it was early July and virtually all the decisions concerning her new life in Ireland had already been made. In fairness, Patrick purchased a magnificent late Georgian Manor House that had been completely remodelled and updated by the prior owner. The property sat on several acres of land and included a number of smaller buildings with stables and a large courtyard. Beatrice fell in love with the property the minute he showed her pictures so she was delighted when Patrick's offer was accepted.

Unfortunately her new home was far from the south suburban Dublin lifestyle that her Irish friends insisted was the only way to live in Ireland. While the idyllic country scenery near in the Boyne Valley was lovely the social aspects of her new neighbourhood was not quite what she had in mind. In fairness perhaps the house was perfect for Chadwick and Charlotte. The children, after spending the last six years in a cramped urban apartment, were thrilled to be living in what amounted to a castle. Without the dangers of life in a crowded foreign city they were free to enjoy their own spacious property as well as roaming the nearby countryside. In addition they knew other children in the area from their summer holidays so they would quickly became part of the younger community. It was, after all, about the children, wasn't it?

Schooling, however, was another thing entirely and Beatrice was furious with Patrick for making such an important decision without properly considering what she had to say. To Beatrice, nothing could be as important as the children's education and she decided that her son would enrol at one of those private rugby schools that had such an excellent reputation for preparing students for university. She had been told that these schools were the closest things to English Public Schools and she knew without question that Chadwick should attend one of these exclusive, private schools. As for Charlotte's education, Beatrice had been told that the private girls' schools, often run by religious, were where the better class sent their girls.

Rather than recognising the obvious merits of educating their children at private schools, Patrick had taken it upon himself to enrol her precious children at this local community college with its "inclusive programmes," which as far a she could tell meant that everyone regardless of academic ability or social status was accepted. Predictably Patrick pointed out that he attended St. Killians and it had prepared him well so he had little doubt but that the school would serve his children well.

Beatrice attempted to explain that the world was a different place than it had been when Patrick was younger. But then Patrick interrupted insisting that the changing world was all the more reason the children should be not be sheltered in some exclusive private school. In the end, the decision had already been made by the time she and the children actually moved to Ireland so there was little she could do except express her disappointment.

As if to prove that she did have some role in educating their children, Patrick agreed with her suggestion that Chadwick begin secondary school with his sister in first year even though, technically, he had already completed his first year of secondary school in Hong Kong. Beatrice wasn't quite sure why Patrick was not only surprised at her suggestion but accepted it enthusiastically. Usually her ideas were met with a tolerant ear but also a level of scepticism but this time it was different. Secretly she was pleased with his reaction but to her, it only made sense.

After all the children were what Patrick always referred to as "Irish Twins," born within ten months of each other. Somewhere along the line Beatrice heard that you wouldn't become pregnant as long as you were nursing but that turned out to be an old wives' tale, much to her embarrassment. Chadwick started school a year earlier than his sister, as would have been expected, and the pattern continued throughout their primary school years. Chadwick was among the youngest children in his school year and not only was he that bit smaller but at times he struggled to keep up with the other children. The result was that, although he was now taller than most of his contemporaries, Chadwick did not seem as confident or as well adjusted as his younger sister.

Beatrice reasoned that since they were starting in a new school, and a new country for that matter, there would be no stigma attached to repeating first year because he would not have to see his former classmates moving forward without him. As an older student he would be more mature than his classmates, which would ease his transition to a new school increasing the likelihood that he would excel.

Remarkably, Chadwick accepted the decision when it was explained to him. He had always gotten on well with his sister and the idea of joining her in the same class, did not cause him any problems. Besides, he liked the idea of being an older student after years of being on the other end. Or was it, as Charlotte suggested, that he would prefer being in the same class as some of her girlfriends from summer holidays in Louth? Whatever the reason, both Beatrice and her husband were relieved when Chadwick was actually happy with the decision.

And so it was with mixed emotions that Beatrice pulled to a stop as her precious children climbed out of the BMW to begin their first year at St. Killians. Charlotte looked so much like her father, with her slim, athletic build, pale skin, dark hair cut fashionably short and bright blue eyes. Chadwick took after her side of the family with her father's height and her own blonde hair and sun kissed complexion. Despite the good-natured ribbing he took from his father, Chadwick insisted that he be allowed to let his hair grow and his long wavy locks, parted in the middle and pushed back behind his ears, would be the envy of any woman. Actually, she thought attempting to be detached about the whole thing, he was quite a good-looking boy and would probably break a few hearts before he was finished.

The two children said their hurried goodbyes and ran through the gates to the school. Beatrice sighed, checked her rear-view mirror and pulled away from the school. She checked the clock on the car dashboard and realised that they were not exactly early but definitely not as late as the children suggested while they waited impatiently for her to finish her make-up and drive them to the school. Hopefully, she thought, Patrick would see the wisdom of hiring someone to help her around the house and chauffer the children around at least until they had their own cars. The last thing Beatrice would want was to repeat this morning's routine on a regular basis.

Chapter Twenty-four

WHEN EVERYONE HAD SEATED HIMSELF OR HERSELF in the auditorium, the Principal, Mr. Freeman, introduced himself and welcomed everyone to the new school year. "It is always a pleasure to welcome a new class of bright young students to St. Killians... almost as big a pleasure at it will be to see you leave in five or six years time."

The students responded with an uneasy laugh, not quite sure whether the comment was meant to be humorous. Mr. Freeman paused for a moment appreciating that at least his comment wasn't lost on everyone and then he continued. "This is an important day for each of you because you are beginning your secondary school education. It wasn't that long ago, that many children in Ireland never got the opportunity you have and national school was the end of their education. Things have changed now and I am sure you are all excited about the new things you will learn at St. Killians. You are all ready to learn aren't you?"

Not knowing exactly what to say a few mumbled something that sounded like yes. Mr. Freeman was hardly satisfied with the response so he said, "Did you say, Yes Mr. Freeman?"

A few more students actually responded by saying "Yes Mr. Freeman," but obviously not with enough volume or enthusiasm. "A bit louder if you will," the principal ordered.

This time the response was quite loud and apparently acceptable so Mr. Freeman flashed his kindly-grandfather smile and the students seem much more at ease. After a slight pause he continued, "Now even though today is your first day of school there will be no classes and as you probably know formal classes won't start until next Monday. We asked you to come in today because we wanted to introduce you to St. Killians so that when you do come for classes you will know how things work. There are a couple of ways that we do this. First, we have divided your class into several groups of fifteen students and we have assigned each group a teacher who is called the group's tutor. In a few minutes we will assign each of you to your group and you will meet your tutor who will be responsible for you for during your years at St. Killians. If you have any problems, questions or difficulties of any kind, your tutor is there to help you. If your parents have any questions, they will also work through your tutor so you see, your tutor is a very important person in making sure that you get the most out of your years here. Does everyone understand?"

This time the students recognised their cue and said, "Yes Mr. Freeman," in clear voices.

"Very good," Mr. Freeman responded with a smile, "I can see you are very quick learners. Now apart from your tutors we have a programme where an older student will be responsible for making sure that each of you gets to the proper classroom at the proper time. Mr. JP Ready is responsible for this programme so when an older student comes up to you next week, you will know they are there to help. We wouldn't want any of you to become lost because we don't like to call in the sniffer dogs on the first day unless it is an emergency."

Several students laughed at the thought of a sniffer dog hunting down a lost student so Mr. Freeman decided that either his humour was improving or the children were becoming more comfortable, either of which was a step in the right direction.

"Finally," he concluded, "While you are meeting with your tutors, I have asked several older students to set up tables in this room with information on all the extra activities that we have. For example some of you might enjoy singing or playing an instrument and so the school band or choir might be something you would be interested in checking out. Anyway, after you have finished with your tutor, you might want to come back here before you go home and talk to older students or faculty moderators about these programmes. There is no need for you to sign up today or make any decisions because schoolwork comes first and it is important that you speak with your parents before joining anything. These presentations are just our way of introducing you to what the school has to offer and letting you know about these programmes. Does everyone understand?"

Again the response was, "Yes, Mr. Freeman," but this time it was that bit louder and more in unison.

Mr Freeman nodded his approval and after repeating his welcome and extending his best wishes for their success at St. Killians he turned the meeting over to the Vice-Principal, Miss Pauline Dwyer. Brian thought that, unlike the vice principal at the national school, Miss Dwyer was very young and pretty for a Vice-Principal, especially compared to Mr. Freeman and she certainly had a friendly smile. Like Mr. Freeman, Miss Dwyer also welcomed the students.

Miss Dwyer's job was to further explain the whole business about class tutors and class heads. Apparently a teacher called Mr. Sean Flynn was in charge of the entire class of first years and the tutors worked with him as well. Anyway, Miss Dwyer told everyone what they should do if they had any problems with their teachers, classmates or studies in general. She talked about students bullying other students and told everyone how important it was to respect each other. She also talked about fighting and taking drugs and all sorts of other bad behaviour and what would happen if you got caught misbehaving. Brian listened carefully, confident that he would stay on the good side of Miss Dwyer.

Finally, she took out a list of tutor classes and explained that as each name was read out, that person should gather with their tutor near the door of the assembly hall and when the group was complete, the tutor would lead them into a classroom so that they could become acquainted.

Brian listened as names were read out and as each group of students followed their tutor out of the auditorium. His name was read out for the third group and much to his relief it also included Katie and Libby. The group also included Maeve, the girl Libby had introduced, but not Siobhán. The tutor was a very pretty blonde woman called Miss Pamela Byrne and when everyone gathered at the door to the auditorium, she led them into a nearby classroom.

After the students had seated themselves, Miss Byrne asked each person to stand and introduce him or herself. Most of the students, like Kate and Maeve, seemed very confident and when they stood up they told everyone their name in a clear voice. When Brian's turn came, he knew he was blushing bright red. In an attempt to get the ordeal over with quickly, he stood, mumbled Brian O'Suileabháin and sat down. Miss Byrne, however, had other ideas and she asked him to stand again because she didn't quite catch what he said. Having no choice in the matter, Brian stood again and this time spoke a bit more clearly but somehow, his voiced cracked a bit on his last name, which caused some of the other boys to snicker. Brian quickly sat down, glad that the ordeal was over. Libby got up and happily announced that she was Libby O'Donnell, without the slightest bit of embarrassment. The same boys snickered at her as well but were rewarded with a stern look from Miss Byrne.

After everyone was introduced, Miss Byrne started, "I noticed that a few of you snickered when some of your classmates introduced themselves. I want you to know that this sort of thing annoys me a great deal and I can assure you that you do not want to annoy me. This group, my tutor class, is a team and each of you is an important member of that team. I don't care whether you are big or small, smart or not so smart, quiet or loud you are all equal in my eyes and you had better be equal in each other's eyes. That means you do not make fun of each other, you are not rude to each other and you help each other in every way you can. Do I make myself clear?"

A few of the students muttered, "Yes, Miss."

"I don't think I heard everyone," Miss Byrne responded.

"Yes Miss," everyone said loudly.

"That's better," she replied. "Now that we have that straightened out, let me explain how things work around here." With that Miss Byrne explained all about the rules and regulations of the school and handed out papers that everyone was supposed to take home to their parents. She also told them all about the school journal which was a notebook each student was to keep because it was a record of everything they learned.

After that Miss Byrne added, "Now there is one rule that I am a bit of a stickler about and that is the rule against chewing gum in the school. The reason we have this rule is because not only is gum chewing a distraction but it seems that used gum ends up in the strangest places, like under desks or worse yet, on my shoes. And what happens when I get gum on my shoes? I get...."

"Annoyed," the class said in unison in response to her prompt.

"So no gum," she concluded.

One of the boys who snickered during the introductions had obviously been chewing gum but the minute Miss Byrne mentioned it, he stopped chewing hoping that she had not noticed. Unfortunately, he was not so lucky and even though she was looking away from him she spun suddenly and said, "Mr. Kinsella!" Turning she slowly pointed her index finger at him and then directed it to the litterbin. The boy got up and sheepishly deposited his gum in the bin while several other students smiled at his getting caught out.

Just as he had in National School, Brian was determined to pay close attention to whatever the teachers said so he listened carefully to Miss Byrne. When she asked whether anyone had any questions, he thought about it and might have raised his hand but he was too embarrassed to do so because maybe everyone else would know the answer and think he was thick or something. Fortunately some of the other students, like Kate O'Donnell, did ask pretty much the same questions as he was going to ask which made him think that maybe he wasn't so stupid after all.

After spending about forty minutes with Miss Byrne, she told them that they would now be returning to the assembly hall where they could talk to teachers and other students about activities that they might be interested in. Miss Byrne repeated what Mr. Freeman told them explaining more about the school's extra programmes, adding things like the drama society and the various sports clubs. She also repeated that the tables were there so that the students could gather information and then they could think about what programme they might be interested in and speak with their parents before they made any decisions. After they were finished in the assembly hall, they were free to go home and the next time she would see them would be the following Monday morning in the same classroom they were in.

With that, Miss Byrne led them all back into the auditorium where the students joined with the first years from other tutor classes and mingled around a bit, looking around at all the tables. Eventually most of them headed off in one direction or the other as they saw something that interested them. Brian followed Kate and Libby until he noticed that the girls were headed for the Drama Society, which wasn't something that interested him in the slightest. He stood for a moment, looking around pretending that he was thinking about where he might go, when what he was really thinking was, "I hope this bit ends quickly so I can get out of here."

He was just about to wander over to any old table, just to pretend he was interested, when one of the teachers approached him and said, "Brian is it?"

Brian looked up in surprise, "Yes, sir," he answered respectfully.

"I am Mr. Harry McElhatton," he said extending his hand, "a pleasure to meet you."

Brian looked curiously at the man, extending his own hand. His father had explained the importance of a firm handshake so, as he had been instructed, Brian looked the teacher in the eye and firmly shook his hand. "Thank you," he said.

"That's quite a grip you have young man," Mr. McElhatton said with a pleasant smile.

"Yes, sir," Brian mumbled.

Mr. McElhatton said "I noticed you looking around at the various activities here and I thought I might be able to help you. I am the manager of the school soccer team and I have it on good authority that you have played a bit of soccer."

Brian responded with a look of surprise, "Actually, sir, I have never played a match," he replied honestly.

"I see," Mr. McElhatton said with a smile. "You know your friend Nigel Blessington is a friend of mine and he told me that you are quite a good soccer player."

"Well, sir," Brian responded, "Mr. Blessington has taught me a lot about the game but I have never actually played. I know a lot about hurling as well, but I have never actually played that either. So, I don't know whether I am any good or not, although I do enjoy both sports and it was nice of Mr. Blessington to say that I play well."

"Would you like to find out then? ...I mean whether you are good or not?" Mr. McElhatton asked. "We have two teams, an under 16 and an under 18 but to start with, we all work out together. I would really like you to come and work out with the team."

Brian looked at Mr. McElhatton suspiciously before answering with his own question, "And if I am good enough, will I be allowed to play?"

Mr. McElhatton seemed surprised at Brian's response. "But of course," the teacher replied, "Sure why wouldn't you?"

Brian said nothing but shrugged his shoulders looking down at the floor.

"I'll tell you what," Mr. McElhatton, concluded. "You take this paper home with you tonight. If you decide you would like to have a go, you have your mother or father sign the paper and tomorrow, you bring some togs and boots and come out to the school fields at 4:00 in the afternoon. I promise that if you are good enough you will play. Is that fair enough?"

Brian reluctantly took the paper and glanced at it before replying, "Yes sir."

Brian watched as Mr. McElhatton returned to the table that was set up so that anyone who was interested in soccer could find out about the programme. He saw the two older students who bumped into him before the assembly standing behind the table and figured that they were soccer players who came in early to help out and answer questions from new players. If he did decide to play soccer, those boys would undoubtedly be on the team as well, but giving him a push was not exactly the best way to encourage him to sign up.

"Don't be such a baby," he admonished himself. "Big kids always push little ones around and since I am the little kid in this school, I might as well get used to it. Besides, things might level themselves out on the soccer pitch if I am really as good as Mr. Blessington seems to think."

There were three or four other boys standing in front of the table, apparently having a great chat with the two older boys. Brian thought about walking over to join them but he would probably just stand there like some kind of loser and make a fool of himself. He couldn't think of anything he might say even if he did go over. Anyway, the coach told him everything he needed to know so there really wasn't much point.

One of the new students was a tallish fellow with long blonde hair. Brian knew that he had seen the boy around because his hair was hard to miss but it took him a moment to remember where. Brian finally remembered that he saw the boy running around with Katie's gang the last few summers. Libby had explained that the boy was a friend of Katie or maybe his sister was a friend of Katie, he wasn't sure which, partly because sometimes Libby's explanations were a little confusing.

Libby also explained that the blonde boy and his sister lived in China and only came over to visit family in the summer, so if that was true him going to St. Killians didn't make any sense. Then Brian remembered that he heard his mother talking about a family from Hong Kong moving into the old Mansfield Manor House and at the time he half expected to see Chinese people. Brian decided that the boy must be part of that family, moving home to Ireland. He thought about going over and saying something to the blonde haired boy but then he was still talking and laughing with the older boys so Brian decided to wait. Maybe when the boy was alone Brian would introduce himself.

It suddenly occurred to Brian that he had been standing there alone, lost in his own thoughts for a considerable period of time and if anyone noticed they would really think he was strange. Quickly glancing around it appeared that no one was paying him any attention because the few that remained in the auditorium were intent on discussions with the older students and teachers at the various activity tables. When he saw that Katie and Libby were no longer at the drama club table Brian decided to leave and hopefully catch up with them on the way home. After taking one last look around the assembly hall, Brian headed for the door.

Chapter Twenty-five

OUTSIDE THE FRONT ENTRANCE TO ST. KILLIANS a number of first years gathered in small groups laughing and chatting. When Libby saw Brian emerge she immediately waved him over to a group where Libby, Katie, Maeve, Siobhán and a few other girls were gathered. Brian, attempting to appear nonchalant, wandered over as if he had nothing else to do.

As he approached, Brian overheard a pretty girl with black hair say, "Can you believe it? Miss Byrne taught my father history when he was in sixth year here. She looks like she is about twenty-five."

Siobhán replied, "But your father is really old isn't he? Everyone's father is really old."

"Well, pretty old," the girl answered

"She was probably just out of school, her first job or something," Katie remarked.

"Or maybe she is just … very well preserved," Maeve said with a suspicious wink.

Even though the girls were talking about something else, Libby reached out and grabbed Brian's arm and excitedly reported, "Kate and I are going to be in the drama society. Kate is going to be an actress and I am going to be a stage-hand."

Brian thought that he should say hello to the rest of the group first, but he didn't want to be rude to Libby so he said, "That's great Libby. What does a stage hand do?"

Libby replied, "I'm not exactly sure but Miss Murphy said there were all kinds of important jobs that a stage hand does to make sure that the play is successful. What did you join Bri.. Bri Brian?"

Brian felt a bit awkward but smiled at the remainder of the group whose discussion was obviously interrupted by his arrival and Libby's questions. "Nothing really, Libby," he mumbled. "The coach asked me about playing soccer so I might do that."

"Are you a soccer player?" the pretty girl with short dark hair and blue eyes asked politely.

Brian, who was painfully shy at the best of times and had hoped to merely join the group of girls, found himself the centre of attention. His response was to blush and say nothing looking down at the ground.

Fortunately Katie came to his rescue. "This girls, is Brian O'Suileabháin." Gesturing to the girl who asked the question she continued, "Brian, this is Charlie Pembroke who just moved here from Hong Kong. You know Siobhán and Maeve." Katie then introduced the other two girls whose names were totally lost on Brian because he was still thinking about how pretty Charlie was.

Realising that he might be staring, Brian immediately looked to the other girls and smiled a shy greeting.

"Brian, you see," continued Katie with a smile, "according to the newspapers, is already the finest hurler the county has ever produced not to mention being very fast and very strong. Isn't that right?"

"Ah Katie... I mean Kate," he replied blushing bright red. "You shouldn't be saying things like that." Although secretly he was thrilled that Charlie was now looking at him with a bit more interest.

"Not only that," Libby added, "but Bri Bri is related to Cúchulainn and he was the greatest hurler in the history of the world."

Kate looked at her sister in surprise, "Now Libby, where did you ever get that idea?"

"In the newspaper of course," Libby replied defiantly.

"That's not exactly what the newspaper said," her sister replied gently.

"Well it's true." Libby asserted a little less emphatically.

"You may well be right," Katie said ending the discussion to Libby's satisfaction.

"Well since hurling's not until the springtime," Charlie asked, "are you going to play soccer this autumn?"

Brian was just about to answer that he thought he might give it a try when the boy with the long blonde hair joined the group. Placing his hand on Brian's shoulder, he interjected, "So mate are you going to play soccer? Everyone saw the gaffer chatting with you."

This time it was Charlie who saved Brian from his discomfort, "Brian, this very rude boy is my brother Chad, Chad... Brian."

Brian turned to face the young man and shook his hand firmly. He was surprised that the boy's handshake was weak and limp. "Easy mate," Chad said, "no need to break my hand."

"Sorry," Brian replied quickly releasing his grip as he returned his attention to the remainder of the group.

"Quite all right matey," Chad, who was several inches taller than Brian, replied again draping his hand over Brian's shoulder. "So have you actually played soccer or do you pretty much stick to hurling?"

Brian replied, now genuinely embarrassed, "the truth is I have never played a soccer match, or a hurling match for that matter. I have done a lot of training but no actual playing."

"Wow," Chad responded with surprise, "never played huh. So why would the gaffer be begging you to join the club?"

"Don't know," Brian mumbled.

Chad smiled, flashing his perfectly even white teeth for the benefit of girls present. "Stick with me then matey and I will show you how the game is played. Back in Hong Kong I played a good bit and was a starter on the school team. Bagged a few goals along the way as well. St Killians may not play to quite the standard that I am used to but I'm sure there will be a few useful players to support my efforts. Maybe you will even get to play once in a while if we are comfortably ahead."

"Maybe," Brian replied grimly.

Charlie, meanwhile, stood with one hand on her waist while she rolled her eyes to the heavens. "Will you ever get off the stage Chadwick Pembroke; you are embarrassing Brian and me as well. I can't believe you are so conceited. There are probably lots of players as good as you are so why don't you be nice for a change before everyone in the school hates us."

"Sorry mate," Chad replied without the slightest bit of sincerity while he roughly pulled the smaller boy to his side. "You girls don't hate me now do you?"

"Of course not," was the reply from Siobhán and two of the girls whose names escaped Brian.

Chad turned to Kate waiting expectantly, but the response from her was not quite what he expected, "You know you can be a royal pain Chad. Maybe a few lessons from Brian on being nice wouldn't go amiss."

"I see," Chad replied narrowing his eyes. "So you and young Brian here have something going on."

Kate, who always seemed to be in control of any situation, blushed slightly but recovered quickly enough to say in a measured tone, "I didn't say that. What I am telling you is that whether or not Brian is a great athlete, and I suspect that he is, Brian is also nice and if a few more people around here were also nice, we would all be better off. Just so there is no mistake, it is you I am referring to."

Chad narrowed his eyes in what he thought was a particularly attractive pose and replied, "So what you are really saying is that there is still a chance for us, right Kate darling."

"That's it," she replied gathering the girls around her like a mother hen with her chicks. "Let's get out of here before I get sick."

The girls laughed and headed toward the school gate. Libby stopped short and turned to Brian to say goodbye. She then hurried on to join the others leaving Chad standing next to Brian, leaning down on the smaller boy's shoulder. Brian watched them leave and just before they reached the gate he was happy to see Charlie take a peak back at him and smile.

The glance was not lost on Chad who slapped Brian on the back and said, "Now aren't they the hottest flock of birds you ever came across. Did you see the body on that blondie one? And you my small friend aren't you the cock of the roost? First Kate and then Charlie and of course we can't forget Libby. So which one is it going to be matey...don't be greedy. Let me tell you now, you could do worse than my sister, a little skinny for my taste but everyone says she is quite the looker."

Although Brian had always been shy and reserved he was not totally naive. He read enough books and seen enough movies to understand the attraction between boys and girls, but until recently he hadn't given it much thought. The week before school started, his father gave him a book about the physical differences between men and women, sexual relations, the creation of babies and all that sort of stuff. He read the book and discussed it with his mother, who appeared a little annoyed that his father had just given him a book rather than explaining things personally. In the end, his ma sorted out any matters that required further clarification. Brian supposed he should be thankful for the information, which would probably save him from saying anything too stupid if it came up in conversation – although he had a little difficulty figuring out how that might happen.

As he watched the girls receding in the distance he had to agree that they were all attractive. However the whole idea of applying that attraction to what he read about in the book was so far removed from his present life that it did not bear serious consideration. On the other hand, he figured that he knew what Chad was getting at, but then after hearing his soccer discussion, Brian also suspected that what Chad said and what he did might be two different things.

Chad thumped him again on the shoulder and said with what Brian hoped was mock seriousness, "So who is it going to be? Take your pick, although not Kate or Siobhán because I may fancy one of them."

"I like them all," Brian said honestly, "but they are my friends, nothing more. I hope that Charlie will be my friend just like Kate, Libby and the others... so you can pick who ever you like, as long as they can all still be my friends."

"Fair enough," Chad said with a smirk. "You can be their friend and I will take it from there. Meanwhile, I've got to fly."

Brian watched as Chad trotted off in the direction the girls had taken and followed slowly after them. The first day of school was only meant to introduce the first years to the school, its rules and activities and as a result it only took a couple of hours. Brian decided that he would run home, change clothes, collect Gráinne and he would still have plenty of time to visit Mrs. O'Neill.

He looked forward to telling her about his first day because he was fairly pleased with the way it had gone. His first year tutor was very nice, although probably a bit strict; Katie...Kate and Libby were in his tutor class; he met a few new people who seemed to like him especially Charlie; and he may actually get a chance to play organised soccer. He wasn't so sure about Chad but Brian figured he would give him the benefit of the doubt. After all, he was new to the area and probably didn't know too many people. Maybe his peculiar way of talking to people was his way of making friends.

Chapter Twenty-six

CLASSES WOULD NOT OFFICIALLY START UNTIL MONDAY of the following week so Brian looked forward to enjoying the last few days of his summer holidays. He spent the morning playing with Gráinne who loved chasing the sliotar nearly as much as Molly had. Although he had only been a little boy when Molly was alive, he still remembered the way she competed for the ball when he hit it high in the air. He remembered with a smile thumping against her as he stretched to catch the sliotar and he also remembered her thumping that bit harder and knocking him aside when she won the ball. It was just like Mrs. O'Neill said, whenever he remembered those great times, Molly again came alive.

Gráinne was a different dog altogether although he knew that he loved her nearly as much as he loved Molly. Thinking back Brian decided that his parents were very wise in not looking for another dog right after Molly died because he might not have been able to take good care of her while he was still thinking about Molly. As it was, some months later, Brian had been the one to suggest another wolfhound and Gráinne came into his life.

As he ran down the road, Brian compared the two dogs. For one thing Molly had been light grey while Gráinne was light tan, nearly white. Brian guessed that the two dogs were about the same size but maybe because he was smaller when Molly was alive, he always thought of his first dog as being much bigger. Apart from size and colour, Gráinne didn't walk him to school and wait at the gates when the day was over. Brian had no doubt that she could be trained to meet him but his mother said that with more and more cars on the road it might be dangerous for his new dog. Besides, when he started secondary school Gráinne might be confused about going to a whole new school and Brian might have activities that kept him late. In the end, they agreed that Gráinne would keep his mother company during the school day, but the dog was always excited to greet Brian when he came home.

Although Gráinne loved to chase the sliotar, she didn't quite figure out how to catch it in the air so she was happy enough to chase it along the ground and then bring it back to Brian. As a result she didn't compete for the high balls the way Molly had but the Brian figured he was now too big for Gráinne to win many balls even if she could jump and catch. One thing was for sure, however. Nearly anywhere he went, Gráinne trotted along after him. Brian spent many hours training Gráinne and he was particularly proud when people commented on her good behaviour. Like Molly, she was very obedient and if Brian told her to stay, Gráinne would find a comfortable spot and sit or lay down until Brian called for her.

The morning's session with his mighty dog, as always, was great fun. Brian and Gráinne ran nearly a mile to the field near Mr. Blessington's house with him bouncing the sliotar on his camán the whole way. He then spent nearly an hour perfecting his strikes until he was satisfied that could hit an old fence pole he had named "the Hill 16 pole,"- after the stands in Croke Park - from thirty yards nearly every time. Gráinne was quick to retrieve the sliotar so she got plenty of exercise as well. After running home and grabbing a quick bite to eat he was looking forward to the soccer training session.

Even though he knew she would behave and sit quietly watching the session, Brian decided not to bring Gráinne to his first practice with the St. Killians Soccer Team. Brian figured that he would have enough to think about without getting a slagging over his dog. When the time came for him to head off, he put on an old pair of shorts and a shirt under his track suit, packed his soccer boots shin guards and a decent enough soccer ball into a small carryall and went into the sun porch to say goodbye to his mother.

Gráinne whined a bit when she realised that although he was dressed as he always did when he went to train with Mr. Blessington, she was not coming along. Brian gave her a good scratch behind the ears and told her what a great dog she was explaining that just this time he needed to train without her. Gráinne looked up at him and seemed to understand. She settled back onto her blanket and concentrated on the treat that Brian's mother gave the dog to keep her occupied. While Gráinne chewed on her biscuit, Brian slipped out the front door and headed for the school.

Brian reported to the soccer pitch behind St. Killians well before the practice scheduled for 4:00 p.m. and found that no one else had arrived. Sitting on the warm grass, he pulled on his shin guards and soccer boots, closed his eyes and enjoyed the moment. Brian knew he was a talented player but the chance to not only compete but to be part of a team was something that he had looked forward to for nearly as many years as he could remember. The thought that his big day finally arrived gave him a special feeling and he couldn't help but smile. Although he enjoyed the feeling, Brian decided the smile had to go. He certainly did not want anyone to see him with his eyes closed displaying what he knew must appear to be very silly grin so he opened his eyes and began a series of stretching exercises Mr. Blessington had showed him.

As he pushed himself out over his right leg that was extended in front while his left was bent to his side, he remembered Mr. Blessington's advice that the biggest mistake a lot of younger athletes make is to assume that because their muscles are young and supple, there is no need to warm up. Mr. Blessington told Brian that he thought his own knee injury was in part because he had not warmed up properly so Brian decided that he would always stretch. As he was diligently going through the series of warm-ups that Mr. Blessington prescribed Mr. McElhatton, the manager, arrived on the pitch attempting to balance a large canvass bag of balls, several small plastic cones and a clipboard.

On seeing the coach, Brian abandoned his exercises and trotted over to help carry the load. "Ah Brian, thank you," Mr. McElhatton said as he handed over the canvass bag. "I see you have decided to join us."

"Yes sir," Brian replied. "My consent form is in my kit bag."

"Very good," the coach responded. "You may not have played any matches but at least you know about stretching. And Brian, it is all right for you to call me Coach or Coach Mac. That is what all the other lads call me."

"Yes sir ... I mean Coach Mac," Brian replied.

A few minutes later the other players started to arrive, shouting greetings to one another and generally slagging each other. Several players grabbed a ball that Coach Mac had emptied from the canvass bag, joined with two or three other players and began juggling or kicking the ball within the group. Brian watched for a short time, trying to decide whether he should join a group or take a ball by himself. The decision was made for him when Chad Pembroke arrived and confident as you please pulled a ball with his studs and signalled Brian to join him.

"Come on, my small friend," he said with a smile, "and let's see what you have."

Brian was a little annoyed at the reference to his size, particularly because this was now the second time the blonde haired boy mentioned it, but rather than make a point about it, he walked over to where Chad was juggling the ball with moderate success. Brian was a little surprised because after hearing Chad talk, he expected that the taller boy would be able to keep the ball in the air indefinitely, something he had been able to do for ages.

The two were joined by another boy who, like Brian, looked a little unsure of the proper thing to do. Brian seemed to recall having seen him at the first year initiation so the boy probably recognised Chad and himself as fellow first years. After moving apart so the three boys were in an evenly spaced triangle, Brian surprised himself by saying that he was Brian and the third lad was Chad. "Peter," the boy replied with a crooked smile.

Meanwhile Chad was on his third, or maybe fourth attempt at keeping the ball in the air and when it fell once again, he pushed it over toward Brian exaggerating his attempt to make the ball move very slowly as if he were kicking it to a little child. Brian moved up on the ball and crisply passed it with the inside of his right foot toward Peter. The new boy stopped the ball and sent it back to Chad.

"Well that's a bit better than I thought," Chad said with a smile as he again attempted to juggle the ball. Brian set his jaw and said nothing although he had to admit to himself that his newfound acquaintance was beginning to annoy him. Chad noticed that his condescending comment did not bring a grateful smile to Brian's face so assuming that Brian was right-footed he kicked to ball to Brian left with a great deal more pace than was necessary for the short distance that separated the three boys.

The pass did not trouble Brian in the slightest, rather in a move that happened so quickly that Chad barely noticed, Brian's left foot flicked and the ball rolled off the outside of his boot arriving at Peter with perfect passing pace. Again, Peter stopped the ball before kicking it back to Chad, using the toe of his right foot. Brian could tell that Peter was not very experienced but at least he was trying without making a lot of noise.

Chad, however, was another matter. He obviously assumed that Brian's pass to Peter was the result of a lucky bounce so he gave it no credence. When the ball arrived, he flipped it up and headed it in Brian's direction. Calmly following suit, Brian easily nodded the ball to Peter's feet and, once again, after stopping the ball, Peter sent it back to Chad. Chad stood on the ball for a moment looking over at Brian. "You surprise me my small friend," he said with what he thought was a charming smile. "At least you have some basic skills."

Once again, the comment about his size annoyed Brian and he wondered whether the taller boy knew this and was just trying to get under his skin or, perhaps he was just trying to be clever. Brian, however, was not one to make a scene but he did decide to put an end to the whole charade and he knew exactly how he would accomplish that.

Chad rifled the next shot at Brian's chest, expecting perhaps that his "small friend" would dodge away or mishandle the ball. He was however, badly mistaken. Brian took the shot against his chest pulling back at just the right moment so the ball dropped perfectly on his feet. From there Brian expertly juggled the ball several times using both the inside and the outside of both feet, at one point stopping the ball on his foot and rolling it around his ankle to the other side. Brian then popped the ball onto his head where he balanced it for several seconds before allowing it to roll down his back and onto his left heel. The left heel flicked the ball back over his head and it landed on his right foot as if Velcro stuck it there. After another long moment he flipped the ball onto his left shoulder and allowed it to roll over his back to the right shoulder and then leaning back, he stopped the ball in the middle of his chest for another brief moment. After returning the ball to his feet and juggling it several more times circling the ball with his foot between each juggle, he finally stopped the ball on his foot once again and rolled a pass over to Peter who missed stopping the ball completely because he was staring at Brian.

Chad also stood staring, speechless for undoubtedly one of the few times in his life. Brian looked over at Chad without a trace of a smile, and announced in a quiet voice, "My name is Brian, not your small friend."

Although he did not realise it, the remainder of the team witnessed most of the performance and as a result, not only the impromptu passing but also the pre-practice banter came to an abrupt halt. Nearly two dozen students stood frozen in place gaping at Brian.

Coach McElhatton also stood to one side attempting to mask his smile behind the right hand covering his mouth. After letting the whole scene sink in, he stepped forward and said, "All right lads. This young fellow is Brian O'Suileabháin and he knows a bit about playing football. We have a great deal of work to do so let's circle up and start our stretching."

As the team moved into position, most of the players seemed to be keeping an eye on Brian. None of them had ever seen that level of ball control, even those who had been present at clinics given by members of the national team. Although such skills did not necessarily translate into ability on the pitch, they all suspected that, just like Coach Mac said, the boy knew a bit about playing football.

No one was more gob smacked than Chad Pembroke and after recovering from his initial shock, he ran over to Brian and said, "Sorry about the small fellow bit matey. I thought you said you hadn't played soccer."

Brian allowed himself to smile a bit. After all he wanted to be a member of a team, and there was no use staying angry at Chad who had obviously apologised. "What I said was that I had never played in a soccer match, not that I had never played soccer."

"Well why not," Chad asked having regained a great deal of his confidence. "You're great, maybe even better than me."

This time Brian knew Chad was making a joke at his own expense, so Brian just smiled and said softly, "Circumstances, matey, circumstances."

Chapter Twenty-seven

HARRY MCELHATTON shook his head in amazement as he reached for the telephone preparing to ring his old friend Nigel Blessington. Harry had been involved in soccer since he was a small boy. He had never been a great player or anything like that but he loved the game, played at several levels and over the years listened carefully to his own coaches. When he was old enough he qualified for his coaching licence, and over the years took the courses necessary to keep it current and attended more than his share of clinics. The net result was that Harry believed he had a sound understanding of the game and was well equipped to coach at the secondary school level.

After taking the position of maths teacher at St. Killians VEC School, Harry had also taken on responsibility for the school soccer programme and he had now managed the boy's teams for nearly twenty years. The school didn't win very often because it was a smaller school and the better soccer players were more involved with their own clubs. It was a bit of the chicken and the egg. The school didn't win so better players didn't bother coming out and since the better players didn't bother coming out, the school team didn't win.

Then too, good athletes might also be involved in other sports like Gaelic, again at a club level. In addition, County Louth had never been a great hotbed of soccer although one of its native sons was a stalwart defender on the Irish National side and the sport was becoming more popular. The net result was that it was not considered particularly cool to be part of St. Killians Football Club so many students with the time and skills couldn't be bothered to play. Having said that, the team did have a few strong players but success would usually be dependent on depth and not enough good players participated to make the programme a success.

Technically the school, like most of its kind, had four teams: under thirteen, under fourteen, under sixteen and under eighteen. In practice, however, the school only fielded two teams, under sixteen and under eighteen and even that did not necessarily guarantee that the two teams were fully rostered. There were often not enough older students to field a senior team so younger students ended up playing on the senior team with predictable results.

Conversely, in some years there were not enough junior players who expressed an interest so the school did not field a junior team at all and the only opportunity the younger lads had was with the senior team. If there was a full squad of senior players, the younger boys didn't get to play at all. As for the inter-school competitions, it was fruitless to even consider the All-Ireland Cup competition because the single elimination format would mean the season was over before it began. At least the provincial league competition guaranteed three matches but it had been many years since a St. Killians team, at any level, emerged from the group stages.

As he paged through the meagre stack of parental consents that he accumulated before the afternoon's practice, he realised that this year would be one of those years with very few senior players. Remarkably, the girl's soccer team didn't seem to have a similar problem and he half considered poaching one or two of the girls who showed particular talent. Unfortunately, Rob Gunne, the girl's coach was not amused. In short, before the first whistle blew Harry resigned himself to another year in which St. Killians would be lucky to scratch out a draw or two.

All that changed approximately thirty seconds before the first practice began. The boys were messing about as they usually did before the formal practice started. Ordinarily Harry paid little attention to these antics but his friend Nigel mentioned that he was familiar with a first year student named Brian O'Suileabháin and, in his opinion, the boy had exceptional skills. Harry knew that Nigel played professionally in England and undoubtedly knew what he was talking about, so he made a special effort to encourage the young man to participate.

When he met Brian at the first year orientation, Harry's first impression was not overwhelming. The boy was quiet and shy and although he was solidly built young Brian was of average height. Interestingly enough when Harry asked him if he would like to play the boy's only concern was whether or not he would be allowed to compete if he was good enough. What kind of a question was that? He would definitely have to ask if Nigel could explain why a child would require an answer to something so obvious. Harry must have struck a responsive chord because Brian was the first one to show up at the practice and he was diligently stretching when Harry arrived – no doubt a credit to Nigel.

The boy was also courteous and respectful, immediately offering to assist him with the bulky equipment. Now that was something Harry didn't always get from other players. When the other boys arrived, teamed up and began to pass the balls between themselves, he saw that young Brian stood quietly to one side waiting to be invited into a group. Not exactly aggressive, Harry thought at the time.

Ultimately another first year student, a taller boy who also spoke to Harry at the first year orientation, joined Brian. Now this boy appeared to have few doubts about his own ability but from experience, Harry knew that could go either way. The newcomer seemed to have become acquainted with young Brian earlier but about the only thing that could be said about their association was that the taller boy was quite condescending toward Brian. Another first year student ultimately joined the pair and it was quickly apparent that the third boy needed work, a lot of work.

After his initial observations, Harry was paying very little attention to the three newcomers and looked around to see whether there were any surprises among the remainder of the squad. Like the three first year students, players in the other groups made short passes to each other and practiced juggling the ball with their feet, a skill which few had mastered. He recognised most of the boys and was pleased to see that his two strong defenders, John Thornton and Jimmie Rice, and his best striker, Bill Hagerty, all sixth years, had returned to the squad. What brought his attention back to the three youngsters was that suddenly all the remaining groups fell silent, stopped their drills and stood staring at the three first year players, or more precisely, at young Brian.

For some reason that was not immediately apparent, Brian was juggling the soccer ball with incredible skill using his feet, head, neck, shoulders, chest and even heels. In all his years of studying soccer, Harry had never seen a display of control to rival Brian's performance, and that would include seasoned professionals and trick artists. After about thirty seconds, or perhaps it was much longer, young Brian stopped the show, announced to the taller boy that his name was "Brian" and not "my small friend" and prepared to carry on like nothing unusual had happened. It was quickly clear that the purpose of the exercise was to end the condescension and in that Brian was most assuredly successful. In addition he attracted the attention of several other players. Obviously impressed, some of them came over to have a word.

"Hey kid," big John Thornton asked, "where did you learn to do that?"

The young fellow replied quietly, almost in embarrassment, "Just messing around. It really isn't anything special because I don't have much use for it on the pitch."

"Still, pretty impressive for a first year," the older student conceded.

Whatever about the practical usefulness of these tricks, Harry concluded that anyone who possessed such remarkable ball skills could probably play the game and hopefully lead St. Killians to glory, or at least a couple of wins. Blowing his whistle Coach Mac announced the beginning of the training session.

Harry's suspicions about the boy's ability were ultimately born out as the practice progressed. Throughout the stretching exercises, general warm up and drills, Brian listened carefully to Harry's instructions and executed to perfection. In the past Harry occasionally had difficulty with some players who messed during what they decided were the boring parts of the session. He had no such problems with his young superstar even though the drills were probably boring for a player of his skill. What was even more surprising to Harry was that the other players, even those who had played for several years, were watching Brian, concentrating on the drills, and attempting to duplicate his skills. The result was a coach's dream; a training session that was crisp, orderly and effective, just as the coaches' clinics insisted they should be.

As was his practice, each training session ended with a full-field scrimmage and for the first time, Harry got some indication of what the presence of Brian O'Suileabháin might mean to the team.

Most of the older players had established themselves at various positions so Harry simple instructed them to take red vests and then he assigned them to their accustomed spots. The red vests were what he would have expected to be his starting eleven, based on prior years' experience, while those that remained were either newcomers or the prior years' substitutes. When the red team gathered around their keeper Harry assessed the remaining fifteen players and starting with Brian, asked whether each player had a position he preferred. Brian responded without hesitation, "mid-field." The response surprised Harry because most skilled young players fancied themselves strikers since there was more glory in scoring goals. The taller first year student with the long blonde hair quickly stepped forward and volunteered for that position.

When everyone was assigned a position and the second team donned their yellow vests, Harry gathered everyone in the middle of the pitch. He announced that since this was the first scrimmage he was interested in seeing players moving to open positions and making short, crisp passes, not dribbling, shooting or even scoring. When he blew the whistle signalling the beginning of the scrimmage, most of the players promptly forgot his instructions. The older players tried to establish their superiority by dribbling around the less experienced yellow team. Most of the yellow team seemed more interested in kicking the ball down the field as quickly as possible regardless of the presence of an intended target.

Although he was tempted to blow the whistle and start over, Harry decided to allow the scrimmage to continue so the players would realise how futile their efforts were. Here we go again, he mumbled to himself and then, remembering his potential saviour, he looked to the middle of the pitch locating Brian. To his amazement, the young man was standing at midfield looking around as if he was trying to figure out what the game was all about. Oh, great, Harry thought, he is even more lost that the rest.

"That's enough," he decided putting the whistle to his lips, but then the ball made its way to Brian's feet. Instead of kicking it away, the young man controlled the ball deftly stepping around any attempt by the red team to dispossess him. He didn't attempt to progress the ball, but his control was such that he might as well have been holding the ball under his arm.

Brian's head, however, was up looking at his teammates. He pointed his finger at an open spot to his right instructing one youngster to move while he told another to find an opening on the other side. The youngster on the right did exactly what he was told and Brian rolled him a pass while Brian moved into the spot vacated by the red player who had run back to challenge the ball. The recipient of the pass prepared to give the ball its customary kick down field when Brian yelled "Back." The boy dutifully froze in his tracks and rolled the ball back where Brian again took possession. Once again Brian effortlessly controlled the ball until he was able to instruct another player to move into an open spot.

Harry watched in amazement as the yellow team put together six or eight passes in a row. They didn't progress very far but the players quickly got the idea that they should move into an open spot and once they received the ball they should look to pass it back to Brian who would inevitably have moved to open area. Brian would shout "back," "left," or "right" to identify his position so that the receiving player could concentrate on the pass.

Frequently the player making the pass would not even look to see if Brian was where he asked for the pass but trusting the confident instruction, delivered the ball back Brian. On occasion, a yellow-vested player made an errant pass and possession was turned over to the red team. Since the reds were still more interested in demonstrating their moves, Brian simply darted in and took the ball back. In time other yellow players began to move into open positions copying Brian's moves and soon passes were being made without Brian's intervention.

The play got ragged at times, especially when the red team members, frustrated with their lack of possession, began to aggressively tackle yellow ball handlers. But, eventually the red team recognized the effectiveness of the yellow team's tactics and began employing them as well. As a result, it was not always so easy for Brian to retrieve possession after it was lost. Remarkably, even though little effort was made to progress the ball toward the goal, both teams were working hard and players appeared to take great satisfaction from moving to an open position or making a good pass.

Harry stood back, arms folded, his whistle hanging unused from his neck. This young man Brian, in a few short minutes, accomplished what he had tried to teach for twenty years. Although their ball control skills frequently let them down, both red and yellow sides actually resembled a team.

While Brian was no longer involved in every pass, he was unquestionably in charge, controlling play on the yellow side and merely by his presence in the vicinity, intimidating players on the red side. At one point, he took possession and indicated that the boy with the long hair, Chad, should make a run up the right touch line. The boy followed the instruction without hesitation and Brian sent a perfect pass between two defenders. Chad caught up with the ball and sent a wild shot in the general direction of the goal, but that lesson was not lost on either team.

As the practice moved toward its conclusion, the ball was smoothly moving up and down the field and a few reasonable shots were actually taken. With a general lack of ball control and a number of longer passes that were a bit optimistic, much of the play was still ragged but when he finally blew the whistle to end the scrimmage, Harry was more encouraged than he ever thought possible.

Harry gathered the players on the middle of the pitch and congratulated them on an excellent practice. "Well done lads," he concluded. "For a first practice the movement and passing were excellent. If we can improve on our ball control and shooting, we could have a great deal of fun this year."

The players hooted in triumph and headed for the touchline. As Harry watched, attempting to restrain the broad smile that threatened to break out on his face, lads from both sides were introducing themselves and patting each other on the backs. Particular deference was reserved for young Brian and everyone seemed to have a word for a person who apparently had become their young leader. John Thornton, who was not only tall but strongly built seemed to take a particular interest in young Brian and chatted amiably as they left the pitch.

Harry was still shaking his head in amazement as he dialled Nigel's number. "Nige, Harry here. Where in God's green earth did you find that boy?"

On the other end of the line Nigel laughed, "So you have seen young Brian in action."

"Yes," Harry replied. "Incredible, absolutely incredible. His skills, his control, his passing, his leadership on the pitch...my wildest dreams come true."

Nigel replied, "Yes, I thought you might like him. Years ago, when he was very young, I saw him messing around with a hurley and sliotar and it was clear to me that he was an incredibly gifted athlete. I wasn't sure whether he knew anything about soccer so I invited him to kick the ball around. After that we worked out together for a time but his skills were so natural that all he really needed was to understand the nature of the game. As you can see, that also came rather easily."

Harry agreed, "But he also listens carefully and follows instructions. Why he probably knows more about actually playing the game than I do and it is apparent that there is not much I can teach him. My guess is that he could probably take over any game and score at will."

"But he won't," Nigel said quickly. "Don't sell yourself short Har. This boy is special and he is talented but he is far more interested in being a part of a team than seeking personal glory. If he was interested in personal glory he could probably run track because he is faster than any kid I ever saw, but that is not our Brian. Being part of a team is something you can help him with. Sure he could score at will, and your school would win the cup, but if you tell him to do that, you will lose him. My advice is to work with him but let him lead from the middle. You know Roy Keane is his favourite player, so let him be a Roy Keane."

"Thanks Nige," Harry replied. "I appreciate your advice almost as much as I appreciate your sending me the young man. Roy Keane, huh. You know that boy can be far better than Roy Keane ever dreamed of being... in fact he might be already."

Excerpt from the Local Newspaper

> *Drogheda News*: In a shock start to the schools soccer season perennial group bottom dwellers St. Killians Community College began the season with a convincing 5-2 victory over last year's beaten finalists St. Josephs College of Dunleer. St. Killians' goals came from five different players, Bill Hagerty, Jim Rice, Tom Mulvey, Paul White and Mike Fitzgerald but the man of the match had to be first year student, midfielder Brian O'Suileabháin. Young O'Suileabháin played with the poise of a seasoned professional controlling the play and distributing pinpoint passes to his teammates.
>
> When interviewed after the game, Coach Harry McElhatton complimented his young star,

"Unquestionably Brian is an important part of our team, a piece of the puzzle that we have been missing for the past several years. He also brings a certain level of confidence to our more experienced players who realise that with Brian, ball service will be there. I think that confidence is reflected in some good finishes by five different players. I know I am certainly looking forward to seeing how far this team can progress."

Tom Crotty and Terry Finnegan were on target for the Dunleer School.

Chapter Twenty-eight

PAMELA BYRNE had been teaching history and geography at St. Killians Community College for nearly twenty-five years. She had entertained opportunities to move to other schools, both private and VEC, but the rural environment of County Louth suited her. Unlike her counterparts in the big city schools, traffic was seldom a problem and it never took more than thirty minutes to drive from her home on Dublin's north side. In addition, Miss Byrne was now teaching the second generation in many families so there was also a familiarity with the parents, which also made life easier.

Finally, teaching on the banks of the Boyne, in what was effectively the cradle of Irish Civilization, was a history teacher's dream. Teaching history in an urban environment seemed somehow very theoretical but when you could look out the window and see where the ancient Celts lived, or where King Billy fought King James, history came alive. She hoped that her enthusiasm and passion for her chosen discipline made it easier for her students to learn.

The students were, of course, her priority. Although Miss Byrne always wished that the summer holidays extended a few more weeks, she did look forward to the opening of the new school year. She particularly looked forward to the arrival of the new first year class because for the most part they were an unknown entity. As she looked into their anxious faces Miss Byrne wondered what surprises lay in store for her. Would these children be bright and receptive or dull and disruptive? Which students would be the leaders and which would be the followers? A disruptive leader might mean a long six years but a class led by industrious students was a pleasure to teach.

It never took long to make an initial assessment and Miss Byrne quickly decided that the new class had definite possibilities. Maybe it wouldn't be as good as her "babies" of a few years before, but the class had some strong personalities, all of whom seemed to be interested in applying themselves to their studies.

The history class she was about to teach was a good example of the entire first year class. It included a particularly bright young woman named Kate O'Donnell who was already establishing herself as a leader. Kate was undoubtedly attractive but she was not the slighted bit affected and she seemed to get on well with everyone in the class. Perhaps one reason was her close association with her sister Libby, a child with Down syndrome. Libby's happy disposition seemed to attract a wide range of children and once Kate established that these children were not a threat to her sister, they all got on famously. As a result, wherever Kate and Libby went, a half a dozen others were sure to follow. And because Kate was always well prepared and was responsive in class, that behaviour became "cool" so the others tried to copy her.

The class also included a couple of boys who probably watched too many movies about California high schools. They decided that they would be the stereotypical athletic heartthrobs and hoped that their behaviour, occasionally disruptive, would impress the girls. The leader of this group was a boy called Chad Pembroke who was slightly older than the other children, but undoubtedly good looking with long blonde hair, nearly to his shoulders.

Miss Byrne quickly decided that she might have to "put the schmock on him" but for the most part her efforts were unnecessary. The reason was that, unfortunately for Chad, his sister Charlotte was also in the class. "Charlie" was a good friend of Kate and Libby and she brokered no nonsense from her brother. If Chad's behaviour became a little too outrageous, Charlie was quick to straighten him out. In addition, it seemed to Pamela that despite his attempts at being cool, Chad was attracted to Kate, as were most of the fellows. Chad quickly realised that disruptive behaviour would not impress Kate in the slightest, so after a couple of failed attempts, for the most part he fell into line.

And then there was Brian Boru O'Suileabháin. Now this young man was a bit of an enigma. Miss Byrne knew from the faculty lunchroom that he was quite possibly the greatest athletic talent that had ever graced the halls of St. Killians. This level of athletic talent often translated into popularity and a leadership role, but Brian was very quiet and reserved and seemed happy enough to silently follow Kate, Libby and their gang like a well-trained dog.

Even though he was not particularly tall – although Miss Byrne noticed that he was experiencing a growth spurt typical for boys that age – the other boys treated him with a great deal of respect. Normally smaller boys were the targets of physical horseplay, generally harmless enough, but even boys in the upper classes gave Brian a wide berth. It was as if they saw something in his eyes, perhaps silent and deadly, or perhaps it was his athletic skills. In any case they apparently decided not to subject him to the tests that most of the others endured. Miss Byrne, however, could not see anything threatening about the boy. Like many boys his age Brian was cute with bright blue eyes, red-blonde hair with an unrepentant cowlick, and dimples that were present even when he wasn't smiling.

Brian was also a model student at least with respect to his work and classroom behaviour. Miss Byrne suspected that his performance was a credit to his parents, Cathal and Eibhlín O'Suileabháin. Within the first week of classes they arranged to meet with her to discuss what was expected of not only Brian but also themselves.

Miss Byrne had actually been a student of Dr. O'Suileabháin at UCD and she was both impressed and flattered that he would take the time to seek her advice on educating their son. The results spoke for themselves. Brian never missed a class, was always completely attentive and never caused the slightest disruption. His school journal was a model of precision and it reflected a serious effort to neatly and carefully display what he learned. Miss Byrne could find no fault with his performance as a student...with one notable exception. In the weeks of teaching Brian history and geography, he had never once opened his mouth in class.

Miss Byrne believed in a form of the Socratic Method rather than just lecturing the students. History, she explained to all her classes, was more than just a time-line of people, places and events. She attempted to get the students involved in lively discussions eliciting their opinions on the reasons for historic events and encouraging them to use their imagination in reliving history.

In most cases, there was an initial reluctance to become involved in these discussions but after a few weeks, inhibitions disappeared and nearly everyone had something to offer. Even reluctant students usually joined in with a small bit of encouragement. Miss Byrne attempted to draw Brian into these discussions but his furious blushing and obvious discomfort made it clear to her that his time had not yet come. In time she began to wonder if he would ever have enough confidence to speak out.

Miss Byrne's thoughts were interrupted by the bell marking the beginning of the class so she collected her thoughts and entered the classroom, closing the door behind her. The class rose to greet her and on her direction, sat down as the lesson began.

"Today we will be discussing life in Celtic Ireland," she began focussing the student's attention on a large poster of a crannog that she had hung at the front of the classroom. "Who can tell me about this picture?"

Several hands went into the air and Miss Byrne asked Charlie Pembroke to respond. "That is a crannog, Miss, where the Celts lived. It was like an island surrounded by a wooden fence with houses in the middle. The houses were made of wooden poles with sticks and mud walls and ceilings."

"Very good," Miss Byrne replied writing and underlining crannog on the blackboard. "Now, you are a Celt living in a crannog, three thousand years ago. Tell me what it was like."

For a moment there were no hands so Miss Byrne moved over to the poster and pointed to a cross-section of a house. She then prompted her class, "Well now, where was the light switch for electricity?"

The suggestion caused a number of twitters among the students and Libby said, "Sure they didn't have 'lectric lights back then."

"You are absolutely right, Libby," the teacher replied to her beaming student. "No electric lights, she wrote under the word crannog, much to the amusement of the class. "What else can you tell the class about living in a crannog...Anyone?"

Again she looked around for a raised hand but when none appeared she began to think about offering some more hints or approaching the discussion from another angle. Just as she was about to turn around she thought she saw Brian O'Suileabháin's hand, barely visible over the shoulder of the boy in front of him. Looking again she clearly saw the hand and wondered for a moment if she was hallucinating. ... No definitely not.

"Yes, Brian," she said trying to contain her curiosity.

"Well Miss," Brian began staring intently at the poster, "the round houses inside the crannogs were very smoky because they had a fire in the middle to keep people warm and the smoke went everywhere. There was a hole in the top so some smoke went out there but it was still smoky. The ceiling was not brown like in that picture but it was black from all the smoke. Lots of people had red eyes like you get when smoke gets into your eyes and a lot of the older people couldn't see very well because of all the years in smoky houses. They also seemed to cough a lot, probably from all the smoke."

Miss Byrne listened in amazement. Suddenly aware of the fact that her expression might be reflecting her surprise, she turned quickly and wrote 'smoky' under crannog. "Excellent Brian," she said, "anything else."

"Yes" the boy replied solemnly, "the houses had the most peculiar smell. People didn't take that many baths back then especially when it was cold, and sometimes they used animal skins to keep them warm, which you couldn't really clean. And then the smell of smoke got into everything especially the animal skins and peoples hair, so when you put everything together, there was a very strong smell."

Miss Byrne wrote 'strong smell', underlying strong on the blackboard.

Turning to Brian she again attempted to mask her amazement, "Very good, Brian. Have you been to Ferrycarrig or one of the Celtic interpretive centres?"

"No, Miss," he replied seriously leaving no doubt that he was telling the truth.

Miss Byrne has assumed that his knowledge must have come from such a source, although she could not recall any interpretive centre that provided so visual an explanation, and his response took her by surprise. She certainly did not want to do anything that would discourage Brian's continued participation, especially since the other students were obviously infatuated by his insights. As much to buy time as anything else she said, "Tell us more about the smell."

Brian's forehead was knotted in concentration as if he were trying to remember something but after a moment he replied, "I think that the first time someone smelled a Celtic house they might think it was a terrible smell, but people lived with it their whole life and they got used to it so after a while no one seemed to notice. I don't think it was a nice smell for us but for the Celts it was the smell of home so for them it was nice."

Miss Byrne leaned forward with her elbows locked and both hands on her desk as she listened closely to what the boy had to say. In all her years of teaching, this was definitely a first... a student whose creative imagination was so advanced that one would swear he was speaking from his own experience. Not wanting to let the experience pass she continued, "And the people, Brian, what were they like?"

"Well," he said, searching his memory for the right description, "most of them were short, at least not as tall as we are. They didn't cut their hair so it was a bit wild. The people mostly had light brown or reddish coloured hair but sometimes you couldn't really tell because it was dirty. Some of the younger men also bleached their hair white but I'm not sure why they did that. I don't think their teeth were that good, especially the older people because they didn't have dentists or toothbrushes. Most of the older ones only had a couple of teeth in their heads. It didn't really matter because they didn't eat that much meat, except for special occasions and the porridge and bread didn't need that much chewing. They were very nice, especially to their children and babies and gave them lots of hugs and kisses. And then I think they sang a lot when they were happy or when they were sad."

Brian paused for a moment and then he concluded, "I think that is all I can think of at the moment."

"Thank you very much Brian," Miss Byrne responded. "If you don't mind me asking, have you read about these things you told us in a book?"

"No miss," he replied looking directly at her with his big blue eyes.

Suddenly realising the source of his knowledge she said, "Of course. Your father must have told you about life in early Ireland. He is a Celtic scholar isn't he?"

Brian blushed, "Yes, Miss, he teaches about the Celts, but he didn't tell me about what the people were like or what it was like to live in ancient Ireland. We don't talk about things like that at home."

"But, how is it that you know all these things?" she asked.

"I don't know, Miss," he answered obviously perplexed. "I suppose I just thought about what it must have been like."

Miss Byrne smiled, "Well thank you for telling us about the Celts, Brian. Your answer was the best I have ever heard."

Brian blushed even more at the compliment as Miss Byrne composed herself to continue her lesson on the Celts. She noticed that several of the students were as surprised and impressed as she was by the exchange and it took them a moment to redirect their attention from the back of the room where he sat, head down. She particularly noticed that both Kate O'Donnell and Charlie Pembroke, both very bright students, were among the last to return their attention to the front of the class and they smiled slyly as they did so.

The meaning for the smiles was not lost on Miss Byrne who decided that there must be far more to young Brian than meets the eye. Perhaps she was doing him a great disservice in thinking that he merely followed the girls around.

The remainder of the lesson was a bit of an anti-climax as Miss Byrne found it difficult to concentrate on her lesson plan. She just couldn't shake her surprise at what just occurred. It wasn't only the descriptions, which were historically accurate, perceptive, and imaginative but the manner in which they were presented. And then, as if to top it all off, it was Brian Boru O'Suileabháin, quiet, shy and invariably mute Brian O'Suileabháin who painted so brilliant a picture. Well, just about when she thought she had seen it all....

The class ended and Miss Byrne exchanged greetings with several of the students as they departed for their lunch period. Among the last to leave was her newest prize pupil who scurried past with a shy smile, hoping it seemed that he would avoid further conversation. The last thing she wanted was to discourage him from further participation so she said softly, "Well done, Brian."

The young student turned back and smiled.

When the last student left, Miss Byrne locked the classroom and walked in the direction of the staff room. Although she greeted a couple of students and fellow teachers along the way, she was having a great deal of difficulty getting the classroom exchange out of her mind. There were without doubt things that Brian said that would be found in any number of books, but then he had mentioned things like the specific nature of the smells and the affection that the Celts had for their children. Where had those things come from?

Miss Byrne took her books into the teacher's common area and placed them in the pigeonhole that was designated for her use. She then sat down at the table in front of the boxes collecting her thoughts. Finally her curiosity got the better of her and she rang Mrs. O'Suileabháin.

The telephone was answered on the third ring and after the greeting Miss Byrne said, "Hello Eibhlín, this is Pamela Byrne from St. Killians."

"No, no nothing is wrong. Quite the opposite in fact."

"Of course I understand. After all this is the first time I have rung you."

"Well this might sound a bit strange but Brian said the most extraordinary things today in history class. The fact that he said anything at all would in and of itself have been big news but we were speaking about the life of the ancient Celts and I asked the students to imagine they lived in those times. I then asked them to describe life in a crannog. There weren't any volunteers until he spoke, for the first time since he walked into my class."

"Yes, I know he is very self-conscious but hopefully the experience today will give him the confidence to participate a bit more."

"No, no. You see his descriptions of life in ancient Ireland were not only historically accurate... at least to the extent that we can surmise... but were so perceptive and, frankly, so personal that you would have thought he had lived in those times."

"Yes, I certainly agree that idea is a bit around the bend. I was just curious whether you had any idea where he might have come up with these ideas. Perhaps a book or from speaking with your husband."

"I see. Your husband keeps his professional life completely separate from his home life. Brian did mention that Celtic Studies is not something that is ever discussed in the house. Might Brian have wandered into his office?"

"Off limits... Yes. I'm a bit the same way. Not particularly neat but I am organised in my own fashion and I don't want anyone touching anything because I know where everything is."

"Sports books... I see. Yes, I suppose that the reading habits of most young fellows would not be particularly academic."

"So I have heard. It sounds like he is very active and gets plenty of exercise. But I must say you must be doing an excellent job, "pinning him down" as you say for those couple hours every evening, because his homework is exemplary."

"No, that's it. His participation today was not only unexpected but so outstanding that my curiosity got the better of me and I thought that you wouldn't mind me ringing you."

"No, not at all. Thank you. I wish all the parents were more like Dr. O'Suileabháin and yourself."

"Bye...Bye... Bye."

Chapter Twenty-nine

MARGARET WAS SWEEPING THE AUTUMN LEAVES from her porch when she caught sight of a familiar strawberry blond head running up the laneway. Because of his soccer and other school activities, she didn't see Brian as often as she had when he was in national school, but he was still a frequent visitor. When he did appear, he brought a special joy to her day and she sometimes longed for the days when he was just a little fellow and a day seldom passed when she was not blessed with his company. But her Brian was now growing up and she was delighted that he was becoming a wonderful young man.

Soon after he began secondary school, Margaret considered that perhaps Brian had outgrown her usefulness to him. Rather than inflicting what she thought might become an unwanted obligation, she told Brian that she knew he was very busy with school, new friends and his sport so he shouldn't feel obligated to visit her if it was not convenient.

The look of horror that crossed his face at the time still brought a smile to her ancient face. "Obligation" he said in sincere shock, "Mrs. O'Neill, you are part of my family... like... like my granny. Since I don't have any grannies that are still alive, you are the only one I have. And I love visiting you and talking about all sorts of things. Sometimes, when my mind is confused you always seem to have the right thing to say. Plus... where would Molly and now Gráinne be without you. Mrs. O'Neill, I love you."

The response brought tears to her eyes and after thanking him for saying such kind things Margaret explained that she loved him too but she knew he would be very busy now that he was in secondary school and she just wanted him to know that she understood perfectly if he couldn't make it over as often as he used to. Brian replied that he also knew he would be busy but he loved visiting her and he hoped she didn't mind if he popped in whenever he could. That seemed to resolve the matter and, true to his word, Brian did call in frequently and when he did, the visit made the old woman's day.

It occurred to Margaret that the boy that arrived at her gate that day, followed closely by his beloved wolfhound was more a young man than a boy. He was apparently in the midst of a growth spurt and he was now taller than she. On the other hand, Brian's blue eyes still sparkled, his hair was still unruly and the dimples on his cheeks were as prominent as ever. Unlike many teenagers, the boy's growth did not seem to give him a long and gangly appearance rather; his proportions did not seem to change at all. As he grew taller, his neck and shoulders also broadened and his arms and legs appeared to be more muscular and well defined.

When she mentioned her observations to Eibhlín, the boy's mother agreed completely reporting that she put it down to his suspected genetic background. She guessed that in Celtic Ireland survival required that a boy develop into a man very quickly and Brian's growth reflected his heritage. Although Eibhlín also suggested that it might have something to do with the fact that not only did Brian eat like a horse but his enthusiasm for nearly non-stop exercise and training had not waned in the slightest. Margaret laughed as her friend pondered when it would be that her son became one of those teenagers who lie around and do nothing.

Despite his current growth Margaret decided that it was improbable that Brian would grow taller than six feet but she suspected that his final height would be within an inch or two of that mark. Whatever about his height or physical structure, Margaret had no doubt that he would be a fine looking man, nor did she doubt that his kindness and good nature were a permanent part of his character.

As usual, Brian greeted Margaret with a big kiss on the cheek while Gráinne furiously wagged her tail. Since he had grown taller and stronger, Brian developed the habit of picking the old woman up as he hugged her tightly...but not too tightly. As Margaret gloried in the greeting she could not help to marvel at the combination of factors, parents perhaps three thousand years old and intelligent and loving foster parents in a modern rural environment, which produced this wonderful young man.

Since the day was fine, Margaret directed Brian to her garden table and hurried inside to produce the milk and sweet that had become a tradition. Gráinne too, anticipating her treat, sat patiently next to Brian facing the door from which Margaret would soon emerge.

After they settled in their chairs, Margaret commented on how well Brian looked and asked him how school was going.

"Couldn't be better," Brian replied, the remnants of his first drink of milk clinging to the sides of his mouth. "Actually I enjoy my classes more than national school because the teachers treat us more like grownups. Of course the work is harder but I guess all those study hours my ma and da make me put up with are paying off in the long run. I guess it is easier to concentrate when you know what the teachers are talking about."

"And what is your favourite subject?" Margaret asked.

It certainly didn't take Brian long to answer that question, "History, definitely."

"That was my favourite subject as well," Margaret said. "Although back when I studying years and years ago, there was a lot less history to learn about."

"Ah Mrs. O'Neill," Brian replied with a smile, "you aren't that old, and besides I'm sure you had to study about the ancient Celts and that is my favourite bit so far."

"Yes," she said in mock seriousness, "I think I did come after the ancient Celts. And what is your teacher like?"

Brian replied, "I have a really neat teacher called Miss Byrne and when she tells us things, it is really like listening to a story. Plus we all talk about why things happened so it is more than just memorising dates and events like in national school. That makes it much more interesting."

"And do you talk about things as well?" Margaret asked trying to hide her surprise.

Brian, thinking about his class participation, blushed slightly. "Yes, as a matter of fact I do," he said definitely. "Not all the time, but once in a while anyway."

Margaret smiled placing her hand across her young friend's arm, "Of course. You must also give the other students a chance to speak."

"Exactly," Brian replied with a broad smile. He knew that Mrs. O'Neill would know exactly how shy he was and that speaking up in class was something he was reluctant to do. A bit more seriously he continued, "But I do add the odd comment here and there."

Margaret responded, "That is very good to hear because participating in class is an important part of the learning process and it sounds like your Miss Byrne knows all about that. What type of things do you talk about?"

Brian thought about that for a moment before answering, "Oh you know all kinds of things. The first time I said anything a few weeks back I was really scared that I might say something wrong or that the other kids would laugh at me but after a while I realised that everyone says things that are wrong and everyone laughs when that happens so it is nothing to worry about. That first time, though, I think I was right and so no one laughed."

"And what did you talk about?" Margaret asked.

"You know," Brian replied scratching his head, "that is a funny one. Miss Byrne was talking about the ancient Celts, you know three thousand years ago and she asked if anyone could tell what life was like for those people. Well, no one seemed to have any ideas and I don't know what came over me but the next thing I knew my hand was up in the air. I thought Miss Byrne was going to die of the shock of it because I hadn't said anything before that."

"So what made you put your hand up," Margaret prompted.

Brian answered, "Now that's the funny bit. For some reason I actually knew the answer. I don't know how, but it seemed that I knew what life was like for the ancient Celts... at least some of it. I know that Miss Byrne wanted us to use our imagination in trying to figure out what life was like and I guess she thought that was what I was doing. But the thing is, I never gave it much thought and I would never have said a word if imagination was all there was to it. It was like I opened my mouth and out it came, without me hardly thinking about it."

Margaret suddenly remembered her visions those many years ago before Brian came into her life. She could see herself holding the tiny baby with the extraordinarily perceptive eyes. If the boy's background was what she and Eibhlín suspected, however improbable, Margaret wondered exactly how many of those perceptions were indelibly etched in his subconscious. While those thoughts were still being teased out in her mind, Margaret realised that the conversation stopped and Brian was looking at her with some concern.

Quickly recovering, she said, "I was just thinking about what you said and life among the ancient Celts. What kind of things did you tell the class about?"

Brian thought back to his classroom experience, "Now that I think about it, what I told the class about was what someone might see or smell or hear if they ended up in a crannog three thousand years ago. Even though we read about other things later, I didn't say anything about how they grew crops or made bread or made jewellery out of gold or fought battles because those things didn't occur to me. All I could think about was seeing, hearing and especially smelling. I think the other students enjoyed that bit because can you imagine the smell of a place that was always full of smoke and where no one took a bath, at least in the winter. Some of the others were still talking about the smell for days after and we all got a great laugh out of it."

"Well, whatever you might think of it," Margaret responded, "it seems to me that you must have a very good imagination."

"Maybe so," Brian said thoughtfully, "but the thing is it didn't seem like I was talking from what I imagined. It seemed like I was talking from what I remembered and that is what made it seem so real. Don't you think that is strange Mrs. O'Neill?"

"Indeed I do, Brian. Indeed I do," Margaret answered. "But the important thing is that you participated and shared what you thought with the class and, in that way, everyone learned something. I think that is what Miss Byrne wanted to happen."

"I think you are right, Mrs. O'Neill," Brian said with some conviction.

"So have you had anything else to say in the class?" Margaret asked.

"Well," he replied slowly, "I am still a little shy about saying anything but it isn't as bad as it was before the first time. I do say something now and again but I have never been so positive about what I was saying as I was that first time. It's ok though because I am not as afraid to say something that is wrong, now that I have said something that was right."

"Now that's a very good attitude," Margaret replied rubbing the boy's forearm. "Now tell me, how are your friends the O'Donnells."

"Kate and Libby? Sure they are in fine form. When I am not playing sports or working out, I sometimes hang out with their gang and they don't seem to mind. Kate is very popular at school. Of course she is very pretty and with Libby around there is always lots of fun and stuff. There are a few other regulars like Charlie Pembroke who I guess is Kate's best friend."

"Oh, yes, Charlie the soccer player is that right?" Margaret asked.

Brian's tell tale blush needed little interpretation. "Yes, she is probably the best player on the girls' team, both under sixteen and under eighteen. She is mostly left-footed, which other girls aren't used to and she is also very fast so she is fun to watch. I think she is probably better than her brother Chad, although you wouldn't want to mention that to him."

Margaret smiled at her young friend's attempt at nonchalance. "Tell me this. How is your friend Chad?"

This time Brian smiled and shook his head. "Well you know, Chad is Chad. At least he doesn't call me "my small friend" any more. But he still thinks he is a much better soccer player than he really is. In fairness he has scored a few goals in practice matches and when that happens, there is no living with him because he relives every detail with anyone who will listen. Fortunately Kate and Charlie are pretty good at sorting him out."

"Well maybe that is just his way of trying to be popular and make friends," Margaret offered.

Brian thought about that for a moment before replying, "Maybe so. Chad is not that easy to figure out. I think he kinda likes Kate because he talks about her often enough. But then sometimes he pretends like she isn't there and spends loads of time talking to another girl called Siobhán. Now that doesn't bother Kate in the slightest but I know her well enough to know that trying to make her jealous isn't going to make Kate like him any better. Who knows, maybe it is Siobhán he is interested in after all. You never know with Chad."

"So do you... ah... hang out with Chad?" Margaret asked.

"Not really," Brian replied, "except when I am with the gang and he happens to be along. The thing is he is into all sorts of things like television, video games and music and I couldn't be bothered with all that. I would rather be working on my soccer or hurling or running with Gráinne or even just working out with the weights my da gave me last Christmas. We are just interested in different things."

"I can understand that," Margaret replied. "But you know he is also new to the area and he didn't go to National School here so he could be a bit lonely even though he might not show it. I think you should be especially nice to him, just in case, after all, you are teammates."

"You know me," Brian said with a smile. "I try to be nice to everyone. Even though it can be a little tough with Chad, I will do my best."

"I'm sure you will," Margaret said, again marvelling at the wonderful young man who had actually said he loved her and called Margaret his granny.

Chapter Thirty

THE SUCCESS OF ST. KILLIANS' SOCCER TEAM, led by their young superstar, created a predictable interest in the programme. In prior years the team would consider itself lucky if more than a dozen supporters stood near the touch lines watching the matches and most of them would have been related to the players. As the word of the team's success spread that number grew so significantly that spectators were now three and four deep along the lines and, in their efforts to see the action, were making it difficult for the linesmen.

Although unexpected expenditures were the last thing that the principal needed, Brian Freeman ordered the erection of temporary stands at the school's field to keep supporters and curious on-lookers from spilling out onto the pitch. In truth, he had little choice and now Mr. Freeman's difficulty was replacing the expenditure in his already tight budget. He even seriously considered passing a basket like they do in the church. On a positive note, as his vice-principal Pauline Dwyer pointed out, the publicity would certainly do the school no harm. He did, however, draw the line at a request by the media that they should be provided with an elevated platform at the top of the bleachers, equipped with tables and chairs, from which they could report on the action.

While most of the supporters were attracted by the team's recent results there were a few who backed the team from the first match. Charlie Pembroke, an excellent soccer player in her own right, had always attended her brother's matches. Because her loyalty was not usually reciprocated by Chad supporting her efforts, and because she had better things to do with her time, Charlie decided that she might attend, if it was convenient. But then Brian O'Suileabháin appeared on the scene and her curiosity overcame her annoyance with Chad.

Since she didn't want to appear to be too interested, she talked Kate and Libby O'Donnell, Siobhán Tierney, Maeve O'Brien and a couple of other girls into joining her. Charlie knew Siobhán had a thing for her brother, so that was no problem, but Kate and Libby and never seen a soccer match and hadn't the slightest interest in the sport so that was a bit more difficult. Ultimately, she convinced Libby that Brian would really love it if she supported the team, knowing full well that where Libby went, Kate was sure to follow. After that first match, however, Kate was a willing participant. And as for Libby, she was always the first supporter at the field and when the stands were erected, she claimed the best seats, the top two rows in the centre of the pitch, for the girls.

As a result, the other girls could make their way at their own pace assured that the seats would be waiting for them. Of course it didn't take long for the other students to recognise that those particular seats were reserved, even if Libby was not there to make the point. As for Libby, she was not the slightest bit bothered by the fact that she had to sit alone for at least a half-hour before the match, because Brian always came over and spoke to her and just before the kick-off he waved up to her in the stands.

One crisp cold autumn afternoon the girls sat huddled together in their accustomed seats. Although there was still a bit of warmth in bright sunshine, the chill in the air reminded everyone that winter was not far off. On the pitch, the referee blew his whistle and the match began

Charlie watched the match intently, a true student of the game, while the other girls chatted about any number of things. When they first started attending, Charlie was annoyed with her friends because she couldn't understand how anyone would make the effort to brave the elements and then not watch the match. After a few matches, however, she didn't mind because she was perfectly willing to trade the girls' company for their total lack of appreciation for soccer. Occasionally, however, she was surprised.

"It's hard to believe, Charlie" Kate said quietly on one such occasion, "that the fellow in the middle of the pitch, is our Brian. It's like, like he's totally in charge, not a bother to him."

Charlie smiled without taking her eyes off the match, "For a boy who wouldn't say boo off the pitch something must happen to him when he crosses the line. Look at him directing traffic, even telling the sixth years where they should go."

Hearing the last remark, Maeve leaned over and said, "I'd like to tell a few sixth years where they should go as well." Both Kate and Charlie shook their heads in unison.

Just then Brian anticipated a lane opening up and his pass was perfectly timed to meet the onrushing striker who found himself with a clear path to the goal. As the crowd roared, he took two touches but just as he was ready to shoot, he lifted his head at the last moment and his strong shot passed well over the bar. The crowd groaned while the striker banged himself on the forehead, fully aware of his mistake. When he looked up to Brian to apologise for blowing a perfect opportunity, he was greeted with an encouraging smile and handclap as the young midfielder back peddled into position for the goal kick.

"See that," Charlie said encouraged by Kate's interest in what was occurring on the pitch. "Brian saw that passing lane open even before it was there and the pass could not have been more perfect. But then that shot... terrible... you just can't lift your head or the ball will go high every time."

The technical comment was a bit beyond Kate's comprehension, but she had her own observation, "Did you see how that sixth year, Stephen, looked at our Brian like he was begging forgiveness for messing up the shot and then there is Brian telling him it was alright. Who would have thought it?"

Not to be left out, Libby added, "You know what I heard. I heard some of the older boys saying the Bri.. Bri.. is a legend. What do you think that means? I thought legends were old or dead."

Kate turned to her sister and replied, "It's like slang Libby. It means he is a better player than everyone else, not that he is old or dead."

"He is good, isn't he?" Libby said happily.

"Oh he's good all right. And will you look at his body," Maeve said. "Look at the definition in his legs and then there is his arse. Did you ever see anything so beautiful?"

All the girls smiled at the remark, even Kate, but she quickly replied, "What are you like Maeve? Will you ever get off the stage? People will hear you."

"Just what I would expect out of you," Maeve replied with mischievous grin not the slightest bit concerned that she might be overheard, "but I dare you to say it isn't true."

Kate said nothing but rolled her eyes, which sent everyone into a fit of giggles.

Charlie looked over at her friends and said, "You know girls, there is a fairly good match going on out there, if you would care to look."

Just then Brian launched a perfect pass from nearly the centre circle toward the right flag. Chad Pembroke was playing the wing and he gathered the ball in stride and headed toward the corner. Chad lost his opportunity for a quick cross as the defender scurried back into position. Still in possession, Chad faced the defender faked to the left and attempted to dribble around his opponent. Unfortunately, he was quickly dispossessed and his plea to the referee for a foul was totally ignored. He stood for a moment with a shocked look on his face but when he realised that no one was paying any attention he hustled back to defence. In the stands, Charlie shook her head and covered her eyes.

Siobhán, however, was quick to come to Chad's defence. "Did you see that Charlie? Chad was hacked. Why didn't the ref blow the whistle?"

If she expected sympathy from the player's sister, Siobhán was mistaken. "Actually," Charlie replied, "Chad should have crossed the ball immediately because he had two teammates in the box but either he wasn't good enough to do that or he decided to put on a show and he definitely wasn't good enough to do that. In the end, he ran into the defender not the other way around. That would never be called a foul and I am a little embarrassed for his whinging about it."

"Oh... never mind," Siobhán said, apparently missing the point. "Well he certainly is the best looking boy on the pitch." The remark brought more giggles from the girls. Libby added, "Well he does have very nice hair."

"Thank you Libby," Siobhán said.

"His legs are a bit skinny for my taste," Maeve added with a smirk.

"They are not skinny," Siobhán responded indignantly. "He is just tall. Kate, what do you think?"

"I think he is a fine looking boy," Kate replied without elaboration.

"And not a short little fellow like Brian," Siobhán added defiantly.

Even Charlie was distracted from the match by that comment. "Now Siobhán," she said. "There is no reason to get on Brian. Besides he isn't short at all, not anymore. He has to have grown three or four inches in the last month and I doubt he is finished."

"And he's very nice," Libby added.

"And he shows up at all my matches," Charlie said emphatically.

Just then, Brian ran an overlap into the left corner. He juked the defender beating him to the end line and headed along the line toward the goal. Just before he was closed down by the centre back and keeper, he expertly flicked the ball over their heads and Billy Hagerty, who found himself all alone in front of the open goal, made no mistake heading the ball into the back of the net. The supporters stood and cheered as Brian and the rest of the team congratulated Billy as they ran back for the restart.

When the match restarted, Siobhán turned to her friends. "Why is it always about Brian?" she asked. "Did you see that goal? Wasn't that a brilliant header?"

Even Kate with her limited knowledge of the game stared at Siobhán, her mouth open in mute surprise.

"Because," Libby said triumphantly, "Brian is a legend!"

All the girls laughed at Libby prompt proclamation except Siobhán who rolled her eyes and shook her head.

Maeve, who was a great one for stirring the pot, poked Siobhán in the ribs winking at her when her friend reacted and said, "So Charlie... Brian attends all your matches does he? You wouldn't be a bit sweet on him would you? Would you like to share some news with us...perhaps you two are an item."

Although she recognised the question for what it was, Kate looked over at Charlie curious to hear the response.

Charlie's pale white skin took on a reddish hue as she attempted to ignore the remark. "If you don't mind, I am trying to enjoy this match. And if you really want to know, Brian is a friend, nothing more. He attends my matches because he likes to watch soccer, and we are also pretty good, in case you didn't notice. He also watches me play because I watch him play, unlike certain unnamed relatives of mine, so there."

"All right, all right," Maeve replied pleased that her remark had its intended effect, "no need to get your knickers in a twist."

Charlie shook her head in disgust and returned her total concentration to the action on the pitch.

Just then, Brian intercepted an errant pass from one of the central defenders, cleanly beat the other defender and sailed in on the unprotected keeper. Realising that a score was inevitable, the keeper was undecided whether he should come out to cut the angle or remain back. A bit late he moved toward the onrushing player keeping his body square to the goal as he had been trained. Brian moved toward the left bringing the keeper with him and faked a shot to the near post. The keeper dived in that direction and Brian rolled the ball to the right, directly into the path of Chad Pembroke who had no choice but to kick it into the net.

Chad, having seen entirely too many premiership celebrations, ran toward the stands, emulating an airplane, until he slid to a stop in front of the supporters. The other players, including Brian, gathered around him patting him on the back and messing his hair. The referee blew his whistle threatening a card for excessive celebration, and that, along with Coach Mac's admonition brought the celebration to a close.

In the stands, Siobhán was jumping up and down as if Chad just scored the cup winner. She stumbled a bit against her friends who could only smile at her enthusiasm. Eventually they were able to pull her down into her seat before Siobhán fell into someone, but she continued to clap and shout.

"So now Charlie," she said after catching her breath. "What do you think about that?"

Charlie looked at her friend seriously wondering whether she had seen anything at all, bar the actual delivery of the ball into the net. Deciding probably not, she answered, "Actually Siobhán, the goal was well taken. Even more important, Chad seems to know where his meals are coming from so he was in the right place at the right time."

Siobhán was satisfied, although confused by the answer, but rather than seeking clarification, she turned to Libby, and asked, "Tell me now Libby. Who is the legend now?"

Libby smiled pleasantly and replied without hesitating, "Brian is the legend!"

Of course the comment set all the girls laughing happily and even Siobhán had to join in. Kate looked over at her sister with genuine love and affection. For all Libby's difficulties she could not have been blessed with a more perfect sister and, it occurred to Kate, that Libby was a lot more perceptive than any number of people seemed to think.

The match ended with St. Killians winning four goals to one. As they walked down from the stands, Charlie recognised that despite the score, the match was entirely one sided. St. Killians would undoubtedly have scored several more times if Brian's teammates had converted half the chances he presented to them on a golden platter. It would have been an absolute massacre if Brian decided to put the ball in the net himself instead of relying on the boots of his teammates but in the end the scoreline would reflect once again, that the best player on the team had not scored a goal.

It frustrated Charlie to see that despite his incredible talent and the success of the team, her friend Brian had never scored. She knew, however, as did anyone else who understood the game that his lack of goals was entirely his own choice because, at the schoolboy level of competition, Brian could literally score at will.

As she watched Brian trot over to join the coach and his teammates at the centre of the pitch, Charlie thought about this strange boy. Strange in a good way, she quickly corrected herself. He was undoubtedly the finest soccer player she had ever seen and yet, he had no ego when it came to personal accomplishment. Meanwhile several of the other players, particularly her brother Chad, basked in the glory of their meagre efforts.

In fairness several of the older boys understood exactly what was going on. It didn't seem to bother them at all that this first year student was the heart and soul of the senior team. In fact the central defender, John Thornton who was about the biggest and strongest sixth year boy in the school seemed to have adopted Brian and wouldn't allow anyone to take the mick out of him. But then after the past few years, the older boys, more than anyone else, were probably enjoying the first success the school had ever experienced. In any case, there was no doubt that Brian was in total command on the pitch directing the play of his teammates, including boys five years older than he. And yet when he joined the gang he was totally shy and reserved, perfectly content to let the others lead while he seemed to enjoy just being in their company.

As Charlie headed in the direction of the school she glanced back and noticed that Kate was looking at her. Charlie's first reaction was to blush as she thought that Kate probably saw her staring at Brian. Trying to hide her discomfort, she smiled pleasantly and linked arms with her friend. Kate smiled back and said, "He really is quite magical isn't he?"

Somehow the comment seemed perfect so Charlie hugged Kate's arm tighter and replied, "Yes, magical."

Chapter Thirty-one

BRIAN HAD SPENT THE LAST HOUR running with Gráinne and he felt particularly good. As much as he enjoyed practicing and playing soccer, as a member of a team St. Killians, he still loved being on his own with his dog, the perfect feel of a camán in his hands running through the fields overlooking the Boyne without a care in the world. The problem with soccer training sessions and matches nearly every evening was that he felt that he was ignoring his great friend Gráinne and he missed his solo sessions with his dog, his hurley and a wet, sloppy sliotar.

Early in the school year it had been less of a problem because it was still light when he finished practice, although his mother never could quite understand how he would have enough energy to run with Gráinne after soccer practice. But as the days shortened, the early darkness meant that there was little time for such sessions except on weekends. Today was different because Coach McElhatton gave the squad a day off since the girls were playing a group match in their own league competition.

Brian had structured his outing so that it worked its way back to the school where he knew the girl's match, although it might not draw the crowds that attended the boy's matches, would be fun to watch. He tried not to miss any of the girl's matches because they supported the boy's side and besides, he knew that most of his gang would be out cheering for their friend Charlie Pembroke.

As the pair approached the pitch, Brian and particularly Gráinne always attracted attention. By now the students and staff at St. Killians had become accustomed to seeing Brian in the company of his famous hound but the dog's size still caused a stir. In addition to being very large, she was also so docile that no one hesitated to greet her and Gráinne gloried in the attention. The students, particularly the first years, had adopted Gráinne as sort of a mascot and she seldom missed a soccer match.

Remarkably, Gráinne seemed to know when St. Killians scored as she barked happily while everyone else cheered. One of his friends from the first year class designated himself as the official Gráinne minder when Brian was playing actual matches. After the first few practices, Brian even felt comfortable enough to bring his dog to training sessions because he knew that she needed no minding. On his command Gráinne would sit by his kit bag and watch the action until the session was over.

"As if the boy isn't famous enough," Mr. Freeman the school's principal remarked, "he has that massive hound to attract attention."

Pauline Dwyer, the assistant principal replied, "I sincerely doubt that is intentional. The last thing Brian would do is to try to attract attention. Just not in his nature."

"I suppose you are right," Mr. Freeman conceded. "Still and all, if you gave him a sword instead of the hurley, and maybe young Pembroke's long blond hair and a headband, he would look just like that sculpture of Cúchulainn and his dog."

"I see what you mean," Miss Dwyer agreed.

Oblivious to either the comments or attention his arrival with Gráinne might bring, Brian arrived at the pitch, hurley in hand, and wandered over to the stands several minutes after the match began. As soon as he approached the pitch he stopped and watched a bit of the play. Matching the success of the boy's team, the under eighteen girl's team was within a drawn match of advancing into the knock-out stages of the provincial competition and it was quickly clear that they would have little difficulty with the afternoon's opponent.

Unlike the boy's team, the girls under eighteens were mostly fifth and sixth year players and there were plenty of girls competing at all levels. There was, however, one first year student playing on the under eighteens and that was Charlie Pembroke. Her selection to the senior team reflected her obvious skill on the pitch and not some need to fill a roster spot. Although she may not have had all of the ball control skills of the older players she was extremely quick and fast and speed was one thing that no amount of experience could bring or coaching could teach.

Charlie played on the left wing and when she made a move to the outside, everyone rose to their feet because they knew she would be running free in a flash. If she was closed off, her cross would undoubtedly be perfect for the onrushing strikers. If the central defenders did not move over she would be quickly in on the keeper and her strong left boot directed the ball to the back of the net on a number of occasions.

Brian knew that Coach Mac tried to convince Coach Rob Gunne, a former professional footballer who was in charge of the girl's teams, that they should rock the boat a bit and see what would happen if Charlie played lift wing for the senior boy's teams. Coach Mac insisted that she would be in no danger of injury on the wing and since she was quicker than anyone on his team except Brian, she would be a valuable addition. Coach Gunne was having none of it because Charlie was his leading scorer and the girl's programme, he insisted, was just as important as the boys; perhaps even more important because there were far more girls participating in the sport.

Brian watched as Charlie made one of her signature runs down the wing, crossing the ball at just the right moment but, unfortunately, Maria Mendoza missed judged her header and the ball passed harmlessly over the bar. While the ball was being retrieved and placed for the goal kick, Brian and Gráinne walked over to the stands where Kate, Libby, Siobhán, Maeve and Chad were sitting were sitting in their accustomed seats at the top, middle of the bleachers. The girls greeted Brian pleasantly and he smiled, returning their greetings.

Chad, apparently delighted to be the only boy among the group of girls looked over at him with a reluctant hello suggesting that he join them. Brian thought it bit funny that Chad should be the one to invite him to join his friends when he knew he needed no invitation but that was Chad. Besides, his classmate had been a little cold to him since Coach Mac decided that Chad would be better off actually playing with the under sixteens rather than sitting on the bench with the under eighteens.

Nevertheless, Brian thanked him for the invitation but explained that Gráinne was not too good on aluminium bleachers. He did climb onto the seat at the end of the third row while his wolfhound made herself comfortable in the grass below. Seeing him sitting alone, Libby came over and sat next to him, so closely in fact, that she nearly pushed him off the seat.

"How are we doing?" he asked.

Libby smiled happily, "Great Bri. Bri. Couldn't be better."

Brian looked at her and slowly replied, "Ah yes. That's good. And how is the team doing."

"We have two goals and the other team have none. Charlie made the first goal and Sheila Connolly made the second." Libby replied.

"Already," Brian said. "I thought I only missed a few minutes."

Libby replied, "You did, but the girls are really good, aren't they?"

Brian agreed and sat quietly concentrating on the match. A few moments later he became aware of the fact that Libby was staring at him curiously. He returned her look wondering what that was all about. It didn't take long to find out.

"You like Charlie, don't you Bri. Bri."

"Of course I do," Brian replied. "And I like Kate and you and Siobhán and Maeve and Chad as well. Why do you ask?"

"No reason at all," Libby replied mysteriously. "When they said you liked Charlie, I told them the same thing you said so I was right, wasn't I?"

Brian had become accustomed to conversations with Libby and he knew that she would occasionally say things that didn't make a lot of sense to him. He suspected, however, that he knew what the girls meant by "like" but he didn't want to upset Libby by explaining the matter to her so he agreed that she was correct.

As they sat in companionably silence watching the match, Brian though about what Libby said. If the truth were known, he was probably as confused as Libby. He really did like Charlie in a special way because like him, she loved soccer, and she was so much fun to be around. But he also liked Kate in a special way because she was so smart and seemed to look after everyone in the gang, especially Libby. For that matter he liked Maeve because she was always trying to stir up trouble, Siobhán because she was very pretty and Libby because she was always happy and had a lovely smile.

He enjoyed the company of all of his friends even though when he was with them he still mostly stood around listening and laughing at their carryon. In the end he saw no reason to pick one over the others, if that is what the girls thought "liking" required, because they were all his friends and the last thing he wanted was to lose any of them. Some of his other classmates had boyfriends or girlfriends and were seen as a couple but he couldn't see any reason for that when, for the first time in his life, he had lots of friends and could not have been happier.

A few minutes later, Charlie scored again. Well really she was crossing the ball and everyone went after it but for some reason nobody touched it and the ball hit the ground and the back post after which it bounced into the goal. Charlie looked over at the bench and the stands with a big smile on her face and raised her two hands in the air as if she was saying that she didn't have a clue how that happened. Everyone on the sidelines laughed and clapped but no one louder than Libby.

When the restart got the game going again, Libby asked, "Brian, when I start playing soccer will you come out and cheer for me?"

Brian looked at his friend with a puzzled expression and said, "Of course, Libby. Are you going to play soccer?"

"Yes," she replied, "and I'm going to be in the Olympics."

"That's great," Brian said with a smile. "And when did you decide all this."

"Well," Libby began dramatically. "Last night my daddy and I were watching the television and there was a show about Special Olympics and you'll never guess, they were playing soccer. So I said I would love to play soccer like you and Charlie and Daddy went, 'so why don't you give it a go.' I thought that was the silliest thing Daddy ever said because I am a bit fat and I can hardly run never mind kicking the ball around so, of course, I laughed. But .... Daddy wasn't laughing; he was serious so after a while I stopped laughing too."

Libby paused and watched the match for a while but by now, Brian was curious so he prompted, "And, Libby, and.... What did he say?"

"Well," she began again launching back into her story. "He asked me if I really wanted to play soccer and I said I would love to play more than anything in the world and so he asked if I was willing to work really, really hard to get a chance to play and I told him I thought so, so he said then if that is what I wanted there is no reason why I shouldn't play. Well..." she continued dramatically, "that sounded all well and good but I said how? And he said that first I would have to go into training like all good athletes so now, every evening after tea, he and I go for a long walk and sometimes we even jog as well. He said when I am in shape he will sign me up for soccer and if I work really hard, I will be in the Special Olympics. Can you believe it, me in the Olympics?"

"Of course I can believe it," Brian replied. "Especially if you set your mind to it. And when you start playing I will help you and I'm sure Charlie will as well."

"Oh Bri...Bri..." she said happily squeezing his arm. "That would be great."

On the pitch the whistle blew for half time and Brian's friends in the bleachers came down to stretch their legs. After giving Charlie a congratulatory salute they wandered over to where Brian and Libby were sitting.

"So what are the two of you plotting?" Chad asked.

"Nothing," Libby replied simply.

"Libby?" Maeve asked making a funny face as if she were accusing her friend of telling a fib, which found Libby giggling in spite of herself.

"I am going to play soccer too," she announced proudly. "And I was just telling Brian all about it."

"She's in training," Brian stated. "And when she is ready to start playing we are all going to help her."

Chad looked dubiously at Libby and Brian but then Kate stepped in as she usually did and explained, "Actually Libby is training with Daddy five evening a week with a long session on Sundays, and since he used to play with Bohs, he knows what he is doing."

"Hey that's great," Siobhán said, "pretty soon you could be playing with Charlie."

"Right," Chad said sarcastically.

"Or even with Chad," Maeve said even more sarcastically obviously striking a nerve with Chad whose lips tightened into an angry glare.

"Enough" Kate said quietly. "I think it is great that Libby wants to play and we should support her rather than starting a row."

Chad was not quite through, however, and he snarled at Maeve, "The only reason, Miss Know-it-all that I am playing with the juniors is that there are too many strikers on the senior team. If I had told the gaffer I was a midfielder, like Brian here did, I would be playing on the senior team. Isn't that right Brian?"

Chad stared at Brian daring him to contradict what he had said.

Brian knew that Chad's statement was a bit of a stretch but the last thing he wanted to do was make a scene by telling the total truth so he tried to think of another way. The pause had become a bit uncomfortable when Brian finally answered, "Well Coach Mac did say you had some excellent skills and I'm sure if any of the strikers were not able to play, you would be the first one called up."

"There you have it," Chad said triumphantly, obviously deciding that in some way Brian supported his own justification for the demotion. "Anyway, since the juniors aren't going to make it out of the group stages, I will probably be brought into the squad regardless."

In truth, Brian thought that life would be a lot easier if that actually happened. If Chad was actually as good as he thought he was maybe the juniors would have won more often, but Brian had learned to accept Chad as he was. Having him on the bench for the senior side was undoubtedly better than listening to him moan and groan about how he was being mistreated.

Meanwhile the second half was just about ready to start but rather than going back up into the bleachers the whole group decided to stay with Brian, Libby and Gráinne. Predictably the second half was like the first and the score would have been much worse if Coach Gunne had allowed the starters to play for more than fifteen minutes of the second half. Brian could not help but be impressed by the play of the senior girl's front line because once a chance presented itself, Maria Mendoza, Sheila Connolly and Charlie of course, seldom missed. If a few of his own teammates could concentrate on finishing the way the girls did, his team would be even better.

After the match ended and Coach Gunne finished meeting with his team for some final words, Charlie ran over to where her friends were standing near the corner of the pitch.

"So lads," she said flushed with the excitement of the match. "What do you think?"

"Were you playing out there?" Maeve asked with a shocked look on her face.

Libby quickly replied, "Of course she was, silly, and she was brill, wasn't she Brian?"

Charlie looked at Brian eagerly anticipating his approval and he did not disappoint, although he self-consciously directed his response to Libby, "Yes, absolutely brill. The boys should have a winger as good as Charlie."

Excerpt from the local Newspaper

> ***Drogheda News:*** The surprise soccer success of the year, the St. Killians Reds cruised into the semi-finals of the provincial U-18, League

Championship with a convincing 3-1 victory over Tallaght Community College. Once again, the man of the match was Brian O'Suileabháin who effortlessly controlled the middle of the pitch and directed the offence with precision passing seldom seen at secondary school level. In truth, the result flatters the Tallaght School because St. Killians were unable to finish several clear chances.

This caused Coach Harry McElhatton a great deal of concern as he told this reporter, "We were lucky today because Tallaght did not generate a great deal of offence. At this level of the competition you have to take your chances. As I told the boys, after the match in the final rounds of the league the defences become tougher and every half-chance is important. We cannot afford to waste them like we did today. I can assure you we will be working on finishing."

Billy Hagerty, Kevin Buckley and John Thornton scored for St. Killians; the later on a thundering header from O'Suileabháin's corner kick. Sean Carroll scored for Tallaght.

In the girl's U-18 quarter finals, St. Killians drew two all but dropped a heartbreaking penalty shoot-out to Marian College of Bray. Charlotte Pembroke and Sheila Connolly scored for St. Killians while Maggie Ryan and Maria Totti scored for Marian.

Chapter Thirty-two

PAMELA BYRNE joined her colleagues Ailish Callaghan and John McVee in the staff room at St. Killians Community College for lunch. As usual several other regulars would undoubtedly join the three, as the group of long time teachers were, without question, creatures of habit.

"Rough day?" Ailish asked as Pamela collapsed into the seat.

Pamela replied, "Not so bad but long. I have parent-teacher conferences this evening and you know how they tend to drag on."

"One of the great joys of being a class tutor," John remarked, "meeting with less than enthusiastic parents many of whom would rather not be there. I remember one mother saying that she didn't know why she was even there at all because once her darling son set foot in the school, he was our responsibility, not hers."

Ailish responded, "Now John, you know that is definitely the exception. Most parents want the best for their children and are seriously interested in their children's education."

"Fortunately," John agreed. "Anyway, it usually comes down to the children. You can tell by the way they respond whether their parents are likely to be interested and involved. So what are your urchins like this year?" he asked Pamela.

"Well this year isn't so bad at all," Pamela said. "My first year tutor class is really quite good and if they continue to develop they could be among the best classes I ever had."

"They'd never replace your babies!" John answered in feigned shock.

"Well they do have a way to go but you never know," Pamela replied. "Anyway, I am kind of looking forward to meeting Brian O'Suileabháin's parents. I had a nice chat with his mother Eibhlín some time back and I have little doubt that she is not only interested but also very involved in Brian's education. And his father taught me Irish history at UCD, although I doubt that he remembers."

"Oh yes, Brian O'Suileabháin," Ailish said, "that would be our aspiring young soccer superstar. I must say he is certainly putting St. Killians on the sporting map. We have been in the newspapers more in the past three months than we have been in the past three years."

"And my husband says that he is an even better hurler. You know my Paddy, those Cork fellows and their GAA." Allison Baker said announcing her arrival. "So we'll probably have the newspapers camped out here all year."

"I hope that doesn't annoy our esteemed leader, Brian Freeman. You know how he likes the spotlight." John said with a smile.

The group was joined by Kathleen Cameron who caught the last few remarks and asked, "So how is young Mr. O'Suileabháin performing as a student?"

"Well, I have no complaints," Pamela replied. "He is always very attentive in class and his homework is always letter perfect. When I asked him about that he said that his parents make him study for two hours every school night. If he has finished his work or doesn't have any work, they dream up things for him to do or find him books to read. Can you imagine that...two hours...a night? I'm not sure young Brian is thrilled with that but there is no doubt he is prepared for class. The only thing is that he is very quiet. But then every once and a while he comes out with amazing insights. John, you have him for religion, don't you?"

"I do," John replied, "Same thing, very attentive, very well prepared but getting him to participate is like pulling hen's teeth. I think he is still a bit self-conscious but he will probably grow out of that. You know the type, not a peep when they are in first year but you can't shut them up five years later."

"According to Harry McElhatton," Kathleen added, "he is not shy on the soccer pitch. A natural leader was the expression used."

"I suppose he is comfortable on the soccer pitch, but not quite so comfortable in the classroom," Pamela suggested.

"Speaking of young Mr. O'Suileabháin and soccer, I was looking out the window during lunch break the other day and I saw him out on the fields," Ailish remarked. "And you know what he was doing?"

"Training no doubt, or running with that massive beast of his," John quipped.

"You mean Gráinne," Pamela stated. "She is wonderful. An absolute dote. One of these days I'm going to get a wolfhound of my own."

"As I was saying before I was so rudely interrupted," Ailish said with mock severity staring at John McVee...

"Well you did ask," he interjected meekly.

"As I was saying, I saw Brian out on the field kicking a soccer ball with Libby O'Donnell. I stood there for five minutes with my mouth wide open. She isn't exactly an athlete as you well know, but he was so patient it was unbelievable. No matter how bad her aim he chased the ball down and kicked it back to her. They were laughing and having great fun the whole time."

"Libby O'Donnell," Pamela said. "Another of my lassies although I think Brian knew her from national school. Whatever else about Brian; everyone seems to think he is nice. You know how the girls are about fellows and I'm sure we all hear descriptions from time to time, but the universal description for Brian is: 'he is so nice.'"

"You know," Kathleen added, "a few of the girls seem to think he is cute as well. Something about those big blue eyes and his dimples."

"Cute and nice," Ailish summarised, "a deadly combination and long may it continue."

"Don't forget, no trouble in the classroom," Pamela added.

John McVee interjected, "Speaking of Libby O'Donnell, she isn't sick or anything is she. She seems to be losing weight."

"Typical John McVee," Ailish replied shaking her head. "Here the poor girl loses some weight, which is undoubtedly a good idea for her, and you think she is sick. Although it might not occur to someone of your build, some people actually want to lose weight."

"Actually, I know a bit about that," Allison Baker's sister Ciara Baker stated as she sat down. "According to her sister Kate, Libby is in training with her father and they are walking or running every evening with a long walk on Sunday afternoons."

"Training for what?" John asked.

"Playing soccer of course," Ciara replied. "Sure isn't the whole place going soccer mad?"

As Pamela left the staff room heading for her first afternoon class she couldn't help but smile thinking about the lunchtime conversation. She had been teaching at St. Killians for nearly twenty-five years, literally since it opened, but she had no doubt that in the years to come the current school year would be among the most memorable and the current first year students would be equally distinctive. For a school that was vaguely aware that some male students played soccer, it had indeed become soccer mad, and that was unquestionably down to the arrival of Brian O'Suileabháin. Even Libby O'Donnell, God love her, had caught the bug. But the girl's team was also flying high, thanks to another first year, Charlotte Pembroke.

Charlotte was among Pamela's history students and it was easy to see why she was so popular among her classmates. Charlotte had a slender athletic build but was quite attractive with stylishly cut short black hair, pale skin with just a smattering of freckles across her nose and cheekbones and dark blue eyes that always seemed to twinkle. Despite this, and perhaps because she was a bit of a tomboy, Pamela doubted that Charlotte realised how attractive she really was. The young woman also displayed a great sense of humour, much of which was directed at herself and she seemed to get on with everyone. She did have a cross to bear and that was her brother Chad, also in first year, and he was another kettle of fish altogether.

Chad was a remarkably good-looking boy, and unlike his sister, he obviously knew it. He was tall and thin with grey eyes and long blonde hair that he tended as carefully as any girl. Because of his good looks, a number of the other first years, and a few older students as well, seemed to swoon in his presence, which did nothing to undermine his ego. As a result rather than being himself, he seemed to be putting on a show when he interacted with his fellow students.

Chad established himself as the leader of several lads who appreciated that he attracted the girl's attention, but Pamela doubted that he had any real friends. That was unfortunate because on the few occasions she had spoken with the boy, when he was not among his mates, she found him pleasant and respectful. Although he feigned superiority and indifference she could almost see that Chad longed for the type of friendships his sister enjoyed; he just didn't understand how to go about it. Pamela would often see Chad hanging around a group of very popular students that included Charlotte, Kate and Libby O'Donnell, and a couple of others - remarkably including Brian O'Suileabháin. The group seemed to tolerate his presence, but only just. Still, it would have been easy for Chad to ignore the group and if he didn't see something he liked.... then again a couple of the girls were very attractive.

The class leader was undoubtedly Kate O'Donnell and because she was in Pamela's Tutor Class, Miss Byrne could appreciate her talents. Not only was Kate very attractive with straight, long dark hair, blue-green eyes and a face and features that wouldn't look out of place on a model, but she was very bright, certainly among the best students Pamela had ever encountered. In a few years Pamela could easily see Kate doing very well on her honours leaving certificate and taking her pick among the disciplines she could study at university. Kate's sister Libby informed Pamela that her sister was going to be a doctor and Pamela did not doubt that for a moment.

In addition to being very bright, Kate seemed to be someone who looked after her friends, helping them whenever that was required. It was clear that Kate had been looking after Libby, who had a mild form of Down Syndrome, since Kate was old enough to understand her older sister's condition, and it seemed only natural that she would assume the role among her friends. Whether it was Brian O'Suileabháin's shyness, or

Maeve O'Brien's troublemaking, Kate was always ready to assist, or perhaps, protect was the more appropriate term. Kate's leadership was quiet and understated which undoubtedly made it even more effective.

Actually, the fact that Kate O'Donnell had been established as a class leader was the primary reason Pamela had such high hopes for the first year students. She recalled a few years earlier when a young man who was a total messer, and that was being charitable, established himself as the class leader. The boy never really matured and as a result did not approach his potential; yet a number of his classmates continued to follow him. As a result, the cool thing to do was to be disruptive, take the odd drink or two and generally appear disinterested in either school or schoolwork. When the class finally graduated, Pamela was delighted to see the back of them. Few had been serious about learning and attempting to teach over the disruptions made that one year Pamela would prefer to forget.

On the other hand, her "babies," as Pamela's colleagues would remind her, were a class whose leaders were popular, involved in extracurricular activities, and good students and the entire class seemed to look out for each other. As a result they were a pleasure to teach. Pamela hoped that the current class could be like her "babies."

When classes ended Pamela Byrne stopped in the staff room, checked her messages and collected materials that would be required during the parent-teacher conferences. She would be meeting with the parents of her tutor class and had accumulated notes from other teachers so that she discuss the student's performance in every subject. There was a great deal of preparation involved but Pamela didn't mind, particularly if the parents were truly involved in their children's education.

The first people she would meet were Brian O'Suileabháin's parents Cathal and Eibhlín. Even though she met his parents early in the school term, before she had really become acquainted with Brian, Pamela was a bit nervous about the meeting. Dr. Cathal O'Suileabháin was a lecturer at University College Dublin when she was studying history and there was always something intimidating about meeting with one's past professors. It seemed like, no matter how long she had been teaching, when confronted with one of her professors she suddenly reverted to her prior experience as shy student, terrified that her performance would not be good enough to satisfy her teacher. Fortunately she had done well in Dr. O'Suileabháin's class.

Brian's parents arrived early for their appointment, which was always an encouraging sign. Rather than make them wait, Pamela was happy to invite them into her tutor classes' room.

"Welcome," she said shaking each of their hands. As was often the case, Pamela looked at the parents trying to see if she could spot physical characteristics that were inherited by her student. Apart from the strawberry-blonde hair, which Brian probably inherited from his mother, she could see few similarities. Dr. O'Suileabháin was tall and gangly with a long thin face, greying hair that had once been dark and brown eyes. Eibhlín was short and round with a rosy complexion, curly red-blonde hair and green eyes. Although they may not have looked like their son, it quickly became clear that they were most interested in his welfare.

"Thank you for seeing us," Eibhlín said with a smile that was probably a permanent fixture on her face.

"Yes," Cathal added, "we appreciate the opportunity to discuss our Brian's progress since our last meeting... hopefully it is progress."

Pamela directed the couple to chairs that were set in a small circle, "Of course Dr. O'Suileabháin, Brian is a pleasure to teach."

Cathal looked more closely at Pamela and recognition finally registered. "Ah yes, Miss Byrne," he said with a smile. "I do seem to remember a student of mine who bore a remarkable resemblance to you what, four or five years ago."

Pamela smiled, "Well, try twenty four or twenty five years ago."

Dr. O'Suileabháin shook his head in what appeared to Pamela to be genuine amazement, "Not possible. You are entirely too young to be that Miss Byrne."

"I'm afraid I am," she replied basking in the compliment.

"Well, at least we know our Brian is in good hands," Cathal said seriously. "I recall you being quite a diligent student."

Pamela, blushing slightly and realising she was regressing into 'shy student mode,' responded, "Well the subject matter and the presentation interested me a great deal so that made it a bit easier."

"Thank you." Cathal replied graciously. "And by the way, please accept my apologies for not recognising you when we met some weeks ago. It must have been your youthful appearance."

"Will you go on out of that?" Pamela replied happily.

"But enough about the old days," he continued. "What about our Brian? What can we do, or should we be doing to make sure he makes the most of his education? I must admit I am a bit at a loss when it comes to secondary education."

"I would have to say, that isn't reflected in your son's performance," Pamela said. "Very few of my students are as well prepared for class. The reports from the other teachers are virtually identical to my observations and I can only assume that is because you work with him at home."

Eibhlín responded, "We do check his homework every evening and long ago we established a routine that includes a quiet period of study after tea. When school is in session we actually sit down with him and we read or work as well so it has become a natural part of our lives – something we do as a family. You see, Brian is a very active child and the study period is the only way we can slow him down long enough to help him concentrate on his studies."

Pamela smiled, "Is there any chance you could convince a few other parents that an evening study time is a good idea? Brian has obviously benefited."

"Thank you," Dr. O'Suileabháin said, "but what else can we do?"

Pamela consulted her notes, "I spoke with most of Brian's teachers and they all agree that he is always prepared and attentive in class. The only complaint anyone seems to have is that he is very quiet and seldom participates in class discussions when the teachers engage with the class. Now I know that this is simply a matter of self-confidence because many first year students are also very quiet. No one knows your son better than you do so perhaps you may have some ideas, or perhaps it is just a matter of time and development."

Dr. O'Suileabháin stroked his chin and considered what Miss Byrne said. "I wouldn't say he is quiet around the house so perhaps it is just a matter of comfort and confidence."

"Maybe if talked more about the class discussions that would help," Eibhlín suggested.

Pamela nodded her head appreciating these parents' interest and concern. "I know I spoke to Eibhlín about this some weeks back, when Brian not only participated but made some remarkable observations about life in early Celtic Ireland. That seemed to be a subject that he was completely comfortable with so maybe with comfort will come confidence. But he did say something interesting when I spoke with him about it. Brian told me that you don't discuss Celtic studies at home even though you would undoubtedly be an incredible resource on the subject."

"Yes," Dr. O'Suileabháin replied. "My difficulty, not my son's, is that my life has been dedicated to the study of Celtic Ireland and while I greatly enjoy my work, I consider myself one dimensional in some regards and I wouldn't want to foist that on my son. While I am gratified at his interest, although I'm not sure where it comes from, I want him to be well rounded, unlike his father, and to that end, I keep my professional life as an educator in Celtic Studies separate from my role in educating my son."

"But perhaps he has inherited the bug from you?" Miss Byrnes inquired.

"Perhaps," Cathal replied with a smile. "At any rate, it would do no harm discussing the matter with him… along with our more general talks about classroom participation. If I made a concerted effort to avoid Celtic overload, perhaps we could have the best of both worlds."

Eibhlín added, "You see, Miss Byrne, Cathal and I came upon this parenting business comparatively late in life. In fact the arrival of our Brian could not have been more of a surprise. We have our theories about good parenting, and of course we have read everything we could get our hands on, but theory and practicality can be two different things. As a result, we are always interested in hearing what people who deal with children all the time, teachers or other parents, for example, have to say."

"Quite right," Cathal added. "Brian is our most important priority at this time. Anything that we can learn to help in his education and development is most valuable information. For that reason we really appreciate meeting with you and we are most encouraged by your interest in our Brian."

Pamela smile warmly thinking that if all parents were like this couple, her life would be a doddle. "You can certainly be assured of my interest," she said. "Brian is a delight to teach and a wonderful boy. As for your own role, you know your son far better than I do, but I can't imagine anything you could or should be doing that you are not already doing. I honestly wish that all the parents were as concerned and active as you are."

"Thank you for that," Eibhlín said with a smile.

"Is there anything else we need to know about?" Cathal asked.

"No, not at all," Pamela said rising from her chair. "Well, perhaps one more thing... more curiosity than anything else... Do you have any theories on how Brian became such an incredible athlete? His skills and abilities have obviously turned this school upside down."

Cathal laughed, "Your guess is as good as mine. I could say he works out and trains during all of his spare waking hours, because that is the truth, but he has had these incredible abilities from, literally, infancy. So, I would have to say it is hereditary. Having said that, neither Eibhlín nor I have an athletic bone in our bodies and we are not aware of any distinguished athlete in the past few generations of our families. So it must be a rather recessive gene or something like that."

"You see," Eibhlín added, "the very existence of Brian in our lives is so remarkable that we accept everything about him as a wonderful surprise... of course some things are more surprising than others. The thing is, Brian is Brian and we love him unconditionally so athleticism is just something that happens to be part of the package. We have talked to Brian about this and, hopefully, he understands that his skills are only a part of him and that he shouldn't let them define him, if you know what I mean. I would hope that he will always be very level-headed about his abilities and not allow them to overshadow his wonderfully good nature."

Pamela nodded her head in agreement. "Well, I must say that so far, it would appear that there is very little chance of that. Although he is well respected by all the students for his athletics, he is also well liked by his classmates. "Nice" seems to be the applicable term which does mean a great deal to children in their early teens, so it seems to me you have done an excellent job as parents. The young man is a pleasure."

"Thank you," Eibhlín replied, shaking her hand. Dr. O'Suileabháin added his thanks and handshake as Pamela opened the door to the classroom.

"Thank you both for coming in and if you ever have any questions or if I can be of any assistance, please don't hesitate to contact me," she concluded. "Here is a card and I have included my mobile phone number on the back."

When the door closed behind them Pamela Byrne walked over to her desk to prepare for the next meeting. There were times when she wondered whether she made the right decision in entering and remaining in the teaching profession. This was not one of them.

Chapter Thirty-three

BRIAN FREEMAN had been the principal of St. Killians Community College since its inception twenty-five years earlier but in all those years he had never seen such excitement, and indeed spirit, among both students and staff. The school's senior boy's soccer team reached the finals of the Leinster Championship, rarefied air for a team that had never previously made it out of the group stages. The match would be played that evening at soccer grounds in Dublin and nearly the entire school was planning to support the team.

As he walked through the hallway, students were actually offering friendly greetings instead of looking away as if they feared that catching his eye might result in some admonishment. The hallways were festooned with banners and posters wishing the team the best of good fortune in the up-coming battle against the goliaths of boy's soccer, St. Finbars College of Delgany. He recalled that once he had been interviewed for the position of head master at that prestigious, male only, institution.

He had been impressed with their campus and facilities and the success of the soccer and rugby programmes, perennial contenders for provincial and national honours, ensured a strong school spirit. The alumni included many well-known figures from the world of politics and business that were committed, financially and otherwise, to the schools continuing success. As a result, the pay was significantly better than what he could expect to earn with the VEC and he was sorely tempted to make the move. It had been a tough decision but Wicklow was a long way from his home in Louth and ultimately he decided there was something a bit pretentious about being a head master; he would rather be a principal.

As he walked the halls of St. Killians he thought it ironic that these years later the dominance of Finbars was being challenged by this total dark horse from Louth. He could nearly imagine the head master of Finbars making the same walk. Mr. Freeman did not believe that the students of that school experienced the excitement of the Killians students; after all he had attended a school similar to Finbars. He sincerely doubted that the hallways were so elaborately decorated. The presence of girls with their enthusiasm and artistic talent were a bonus not enjoyed by all-boys schools. At Finbars, victory was not a hope, but an expectation. While the players would be particularly greeted that day, their supporters would say, "Do the business!" rather than "Good luck!"

All things considered, he far preferred the electric atmosphere of St. Killians, although in the unlikely event that they were successful, he would probably have to have his vice-principal, Pauline Dwyer, reshuffle the entire schedule so they could have some type of celebration... speaking of putting the cart before the horse.

Just ahead, Mr. Freeman saw the boy of the moment, Brian O'Suileabháin walking with Libby O'Donnell. He thought that the two, who were obviously good friends, made for a strange pair. Everyone they encountered wished young Brian good luck, patting him on the back or, in the case of several boys, thumping him on the arm. A few girls even gave him a good-luck kiss on the cheek. Brian went from one furious blush to the next mumbling his thanks under his breath, obviously embarrassed by the whole thing. Libby, on the other hand, seemed to accept the good wishes on his behalf, loudly thanking everyone and flashing her permanent smile. The two students, Mr. Freeman decided, were the most exciting additions to the student body that he could ever recall.

With young Mr. O'Sullivan the reasons were more obvious. He was an incredible athletic talent but he was so shy and reserved that he displayed none of the ego and confidence that most anyone in similar circumstances might demonstrate. As a result, he was well like and well respected by nearly all the students. A few might be a bit jealous of his talents, but even the senior students accepted and protected him. Libby was also well liked and well protected but for an entirely different reason.

When Mr. and Mrs. O'Donnell approached Mr. Freeman and suggested that although their elder daughter experienced Down syndrome, they wanted her to remain in the same classes as their younger daughter Kate, even though Kate was obviously a top student. Mr. Freeman had been reluctant at the time but allowed the arrangement more as an experiment than anything else. When the assessments were made several weeks after classes commenced, he expected to require a change.

He recalled with amazement the uprising within his staff ranks, led by Pamela Byrne, her history teacher, and Nicola McElroy who taught religion, when he suggested that she be moved. He assumed that, at best, the young woman would sit quietly at her sister's side and not disrupt the class, just as her parents promised. Mr. Freeman was surprised to learn that, according to these well-regarded teachers, Libby had become a valuable member of the class.

It seemed that she certainly was not a disruption but frequently participated in class discussions. As Nicola put it, "Libby is not afraid to state the obvious which occasionally eludes more gifted students." Pamela also explained that Libby brought a different perspective to class discussion and the result was a better learning experience for everyone. Both teachers agreed that other students would frequently tutor Libby, which helped them to better understand their own studies. The child would never be an honours leaving certificate candidate but she was learning and, amazingly enough, helping others to learn as well, so she had been allowed to stay in the higher class.

Mr. Freeman knew that Libby and Brian had been friends since their early days in national school but he was still amazed to see them two together. Libby was vivacious, friendly, talkative, outgoing and totally lacking in any athletic ability while Brian was the exact opposite in every way. And yet, the two of them were not only friends but among the most popular students in the school. As Mr. Freeman continued down the hallway, he slowed his pace so that he could enjoy following their progress and their interaction with the other students.

Eventually, he turned into the corridor leading to the staff room feeling as good as he had in some time. Seeing Rob Gunne who coached the girls' teams and knew a thing or two about football, he asked, "So what is your honest opinion about our chances?"

Rob turned from checking his pigeonhole and replied, "Honest huh. Well Harry has some pretty solid sixth years but unfortunately none of them have much experience at this level. Of course, he has Brian O'Suileabháin who has no experience at any level but is undoubtedly the best player any of us have ever seen. If Finbars can shut Brian down, we are in for a long evening."

Mr. Freeman nodded, appreciating the validity of the coach's perspective. "On the other hand, no one seems to have been able to shut the young man down, even though he has been closely marked by two and three players."

"True enough," Gunne agreed. "But then we haven't played a team of Finbars quality. Several of their players have a chance to play professionally possibly even in the UK. And then there is the experience factor. Most of those boys are sixth years and have been playing together, and winning competitions, for years. I would think that they could make it difficult on our young Brian."

"I see," Freeman replied, his good feeling of the past several minutes gradually fading.

Gunne continued, "And then there is our inexperience. Even if Brian opens them up, our strikers will still have to finish and we have missed our share of open nets."

Freeman sighed, "Well, Rob, thank you for your optimism. You have certainly given me a good feeling about our chances."

Gunne laughed, "Well you did say honestly. On the other hand, you never know and that is why these seemingly one-sided games are actually played. Maybe our boys will take it to a new level and with a bit of luck, you never know what might happen."

As Mr. Freeman headed for the couch where he hoped to enjoy his lunch, it was obvious that the majority of the staff did not share Gunne's lack of optimism. The match was the sole topic of conversation and all the teachers were looking forward to attending and, hopefully, celebrating a victory afterwards.

Brian Freeman smiled at their enthusiasm. He didn't even want to think about what the same staff room might be like on Monday if the team was beaten, or even worse, drubbed. As he looked around basking in their high spirits he concluded that although ignorance might be bliss there had to be some benefit to their positive thinking. At least he fervently hoped that was the case.

Chapter Thirty-four

MARGARET O'NEILL carefully tuned her kitchen radio to the Louth Community Radio Network before sitting down to enjoy her evening tea. The programme playing included her favourite traditional Irish Music but that was not the reason for her listening. A special programme would be starting soon and she didn't want to miss a second.

Her adopted grandson Brian stopped in to visit her earlier on the crisp November afternoon accompanied, as always, by the his great hound Gráinne. As usual, the two enjoyed pleasant chat with Brian filling Margaret in on everything that was occurring in his life, particularly at school. Although she knew that Brian was not a brilliant student, with dedicated parents like Cathal and Eibhlín, Margaret also knew he would be successful. And with his hard work, it seemed that Brian was enjoying his first year in secondary school. Of course she knew that he was still painfully shy but he had friends to "hang around" with as he so aptly put it. Despite the friends he still spent a great deal of time on his own enjoying the open spaces, running and training with Gráinne. Margaret had long since concluded that those sessions would always be part of his life.

Brian's big news was that the school soccer team made it to the provincial finals and that Brian was an important member of the team. Because Margaret followed the progress of St. Killians in the Drogheda Paper, this "news" came as no surprise to her, but she listened carefully enjoying Brian's enthusiasm. Margaret smiled when she recalled the understated way in which he described his role. "Well, Mrs. O'Neill," he told her, "I don't score any goals but I do help the other players score and the team is winning so that is what really matters."

You would have had to spend the last three months on another planet not to know that her Brian established himself as the most talked about athlete ever to play in the county. Even Ray the postman, knowing her close friendship with Brian, sang his praises in terms she could not even imagine. "He dominates," Ray said. "I don't miss a match because he is so fun to watch. Why he is in complete control from the first whistle and now the team has become so accustomed to his game they know they will get the right pass at the right moment. That is the reason the team wins and young Brian doesn't even take a shot. Magic, Mrs. O'Neill, pure magic... and even more amazing is that here he is the leader of the pack and only in his first year."

Margaret never thought that she would hear it said her shy, reserved Brian was a leader but Eibhlín explained that once he stepped out onto the pitch, he was a different boy all together. He became confident, assertive and most definitely the leader of the other boys. It seemed that no one, even students five years older than Brian, objected to his role because although they all knew that although her son could probably score at will he always put the team first, making sure that everyone was involved. In fact, Margaret knew that he had never even scored a goal because he was too busy passing the ball to his teammates.

Margaret would have loved to see Brian play but she had long since decided that she would rather remain at home and enjoy the young man's first hand reports of everything that transpired in his life. Besides, as she entered her ninetieth year she thought she was a little old to be standing or sitting out in the cold autumn air for hours at a time. Brian seemed to understand this just as he seemed to enjoy telling her about everything that happened. If she were actually present, that would hardly be necessary and they both would be deprived of those wonderful moments.

Earlier in the day, Brian did explain that the provincial final would be broadcast on the community radio station so "if she had nothing better to do" she could always listen. She assured her young friend that nothing short of her house burning to the ground would stop her from tuning in, and now she eagerly awaited the start of the coverage.

At precisely 6:25 the distinctive voice of legendary sports commentator Jimmy McGrain welcomed listeners to live coverage of the final.

"We are here live under the lights at Dalymount Park to bring you the Leinster provincial final of the Under 18 schoolboy's league between St. Finbars College from Delgany, in Wicklow and St. Killians Community College from Drogheda in Louth. The sky above is black and moonless but the weather forecast is for a dry evening during which the champion of Leinster school soccer will be crowned. While both teams must have visions of lifting the cup, one might be tempted to believe that this match will be as one-side a final as could possibly be imagined. After all St. Finbars are the two-time defending cup holders and are seeking an unprecedented third title in a row. The St. Finbars squad is easily two deep with experienced fifth and six year students at every position. Three of their starters, including keeper Brian Moore have been called to play internationally for Ireland's under-age teams. Coach Michael O'Leary told me earlier today that this is the most talented group of players he has ever been around. As a group the St. Finbars Bulldogs have never lost a match because according to Coach O'Leary, they will do whatever it takes to win. Certainly St. Finbars must be considered the prohibitive favourites but, of course, the winner will be determined on the pitch and not on the form."

"Oh my," Margaret O'Neill said out loud, moving her serviette to her lips. The announcer certainly wasn't giving St. Killians much of a chance. She could just imagine a group of big strong men lined up against her little fellow and his mates. "Well," she announced to the radio, "it could be David and Goliath."

"On the other side of the ball we have St. Killians Community College whose victories in the past four years can be counted on one hand. That was, however, as they say in the town lands around Drogheda, "BB" which means Before Brian. Killians

has been the shock of schoolboy soccer in the county, or perhaps even in the country because they have gone from being an undisputed doormat to an undefeated finalist, all in the space of one season. Unlike Finbars, Killians is short on both depth and experience as thirteen of its twenty players are under sixteen and two of those are under fourteen. Only six of the starting eleven are fifth or sixth year students. Undoubtedly those six include two exceptionally strong defenders, big John Thornton, called Thunder by his teammates and Jimmie Rice who is as smooth as Thornton is strong. The front line is anchored by sixth year, Bill Hagerty who seems to have an instinct for the net when the opportunity presents itself and led St. Killians in scoring during the present campaign. The success that the Killians Reds have enjoyed this season must be attributed to the emergence of Brian O'Suileabháin at midfield. He is only a first year student and would normally play under fourteen, but it quickly became clear that his level of play was far superior to that of youngsters his age. Coach Harry McElhatton immediately promoted young Brian to his senior squad and the young man has dominated every match since. Throughout the group stages and the knockout rounds of this competition, despite double and indeed triple teaming, no team has been able to stop young O'Suileabháin who has controlled the middle of the field linking the strong defence with Killians strikers. It will be interesting to see how the vastly more experienced St. Finbars Bulldogs compete with this young phenomenon. The question will undoubtedly be answered tonight as the teams are receiving their final instructions and kick-off is only minutes away."

While the radio station made its commercial announcements, Margaret turned the volume up, just that bit more. She couldn't believe that she was so nervous because, after all, she knew very little about sport in general and nothing at all about soccer. Her Brendan, God rest his soul, was a GAA man in the days when GAA and the English sports did not see eye-to-eye. As a result, Margaret had never seen a soccer match and the only things she knew about the game were Brian's excited reports. It did seem to her that St. Killians would have their hands full with an opponent so much older, stronger and more experienced. She knew that Brian was also bigger and stronger than he was six months ago, but some of those St. Finbars boys would be four or five years older than he was.

Margaret's thoughts were interrupted as the voice of Jimmie McGrain returned to the air.

"St. Finbars has taken the initial kick-off moving from my left to right and has quickly advanced the ball up the right wing. O'Brien is cut off in the corner by White and he passes the ball back to Ntumba at midfield. The Nigerian born midfielder dribbles the ball toward the centre circle, where he is dispossessed by Brian O'Suileabháin. O'Suileabháin controls the ball while his teammates move forward and then passes to Donovan, his partner in mid-field. The ball is returned to O'Suileabháin, oh my, he is clattered by Jason Smith. The referee gives Smith a few strong words but I would have thought that tackle merited an immediate yellow-card. Smith did not come remotely close to getting the ball but seemed satisfied in taking young O'Suileabháin's feet out from under him. In my experience, a good referee should announce his control over a match at the beginning and allowing that type of play can only create difficulties as the match progresses. O'Suileabháin seems no worse for wear and takes the free kick, a perfect strike to Mulvey on the wing. Mulvey takes the ball into the corner and his attempted cross is blocked over the end line by Murphy. Mulvey lines up to take the corner kick and Thornton moves from his centre back position to the top of the penalty box. Mulvey sends his cross in but it is too close to the keeper Moore who fists the ball out, directly into the path of Brian O'Suileabháin. O'Suileabháin sends the ball in toward the post, where Hagerty just mistimed his jump and the ball skimmed off his head and out for a goal kick. Oh my, O'Suileabháin is down again as he was hit very late by Stephen Murphy but it appears that the referee has missed that one altogether and O'Suileabháin jumps up and returns to his position. Well early on, it seems that

a pattern is developing. Finbars has apparently decided that the best way to cope with Brian O'Suileabháin is to mark him closely and to tackle him at every opportunity. The difficulty they seem to be having is that because of the youngster's skill, the tackles are either late or illegal."

Margaret listened as Jimmie McGrain described what appeared to be an even match with neither side asserting any great advantage. She cringed every time Brian touched the ball because it seemed inevitable that the announcer would follow the report of his possession by announcing that some St. Finbars player came in with a strong tackle. Even McGrain seemed surprised at the referee's reluctance to issue warnings about these tackles. Margaret wasn't quite sure what a tackle was because she thought soccer did not entail tackles, at least not like Rugby or GAA. She began to be concerned at the number of tackles that Brian was taking and could only envision her young friend stretched out on the ground after each attempt. For her, half time and even full time could not come too quickly, regardless of the outcome.

"Well the whistle has blown signalling half-time at Daly-mount Park in what, it must be said, has been a brutal first half. Although both sides had chances the story of the first half has been the punishment meted out to young Brian O'Suileabháin by the St. Finbars team. It seems that their tactic has been to take him out of his game by tackling him from every imaginable angle whenever he touches the ball, in many cases illegally or well after the ball has been passed on. The result has been innumerable free kicks which have completely upset any flow to the match. If this is what the Finbars coach means by doing whatever it takes to win, this reporter is not impressed. In fairness, Killians have not exactly been choirboys themselves and a couple of their players have not been reluctant to clatter Finbars players in retribution for the assaults on their young leader. The referee has issued two yellow cards against the Finbars Bulldogs but that total could, and perhaps should have

been eight or ten cards. It would seem that he has lost complete control over this match. Both yellow card recipients have been replaced so Finbars has no player on the pitch playing on a yellow. John Thornton is carrying a yellow card for Killians but he is obviously too valuable to be replaced. To be honest I don't know how many more brutal tackles young O'Suileabháin can take and it seems only a matter of time before Killians will be worn down by Finbars' relentless attacks."

As the radio station broke for commercial breaks, Margaret stood and stretched her legs. She was now seriously worried about what was happening in the soccer match. She knew that her Brian was very fit and could probably run all day without tiring but the idea of boys much older and much stronger running into him every time he touched the ball filled her with fear for his safety. Brian so wanted to compete and be part of a team that he was thrilled to be playing at St. Killians. However, Brian was still a young boy, naïve in so many ways. He seriously thought that all athletes subscribed to a code of honour and fair play and she wondered how he would react when faced with what seemed to be a win at any price attitude. Margaret could only hope that the match would end quickly and her young friend's enthusiasm would not be totally destroyed.

"Well, it's another free kick for St. Killians. The first twenty minutes of the second half have not changed St. Finbars' approach to the match as they have continued to disrupt the flow of the game by tackling young Brian O'Suileabháin with increasing ferocity. By the time the free kick is delivered, usually with amazing accuracy, St. Finbars has reset its defence, which has so far been able to deal with the threats. It seems that Finbars has decided to play nearly its entire team behind the ball, defend vigorously and count on its experience and strong goalkeeper to defend what may well be a match decided on penalty kicks. In fairness to the referee, three yellow cards have been shown to Finbars players, which are an improvement on the first half, but not, in my opinion, a completely appropri-

*ate response. The supporters from both sides, it seems, have
expressed their disgust at the Finbars tactics and every time
O'Suileabháin is tackled s chorus of boos rain down on the St.
Finbars team. Unfortunately, this seems to have had no effect
on Finbars' approach to the match."*

*"Play has resumed with a St. Finbars goal kick and Moore
sends the ball well past the centre circle. The ball is headed
strongly by Thornton to O'Suileabháin who turns against
Bradley, steps over the ball and easily leaves the defender behind kicking out at a ball that isn't there. O'Suileabháin takes
two steps up the field and, oh no, he is brutally taken out at the
back of his knees by Tony Bradley. There was absolutely no attempt to win the ball. That tackle was quite simply an assault.
Whether out of malice or pure frustration, Bradley kicked out
at the back of O'Suileabháin's right knee and the young man
is hurt. Certainly that must merit a straight red card from the
referee who is running over to confront young Bradley. Unlike
all the other occasions, when he jumped up without complaint,
O'Suileabháin is still down on the ground clutching his right
knee. Oh, no, here comes Thunder Thornton going after Tony
Bradley and the fists are flying. Both teams have joined the
melee, as the referee and both linesman have waded into the
middle of the pack, blowing their whistles and trying to restore
order. I would be remiss if I did not say that this altercation
is the predictable result of the referee's failure to take control
of the game in the first ten minutes. I am also surprised that
Thornton or one of the St. Killians players did not more seriously retaliate before this, in response to the manner in which
their young star has been tackled but, perhaps, that can be attributed to disciplined coaching. It had to boil over, however,
and now the referee, linesmen and coaches are trying to restore
order."*

Margaret sat tensely, her handkerchief over her mouth,
shocked at what was being described. Her Brian was lying on
the ground, injured and the young men who were supposed to
be involved in a sporting competition were fighting like young

hooligans. It was the last thing she expected and she felt almost as badly for young Brian as she had when his beloved Molly died. "Please, God" she whispered, "let him be all right."

"Well order has finally been restored at Dalymount Park and the referee is consulting with the linesmen. The referee is calling John Thornton and Tony Bradley over and is marking in his book. Both have been given straight red cards and are finished for the match. Jimmie Rice, St. Killians captain is now having a word with the referee, well perhaps more than a word. The referee is going to his pocket, oh dear; Rice has also been show a red card, undoubtedly for dissent. That will leave Killians defence in tatters. The medical staff is still tending to Brian O'Suileabháin and a stretcher is being called. He is certainly also finished for the night. I'm not sure who is available to replace the young superstar but with the loss of their strongest defenders the remainder of the match will be played ten against nine and one would have to assume that St. Killians hope for an upset is over."

"O'Suileabháin is being stretchered off to the sideline in the company of Coach Harry McElhatton. Clearly the young man is in some discomfort but he appears to be trying to explain something to his coach. The stretcher is deposited near the St. Killians bench while the physio continues to attend to Brian O'Suileabháin. The referee is consulting the Killians manager obviously asking if a substitute will be sent on. It appears that McElhatton is not prepared to make a substitution although I can't see how his young star can return to the action. At any rate, the match will restart with only eight players competing for St. Killians".

Margaret listened, almost relieved that her Brian would no longer be subjected to continuing abuse. She could only pray that his injury was not too serious. She also hoped that the experience would not change his love of the game.

"Well, folks, there are only fifteen minutes left in the match and it is clear that St. Finbars has abandoned its strategy of playing for a tie and winning on penalty shots as they are pressing forward against what would appear to be a defenceless opposition. It is really a shame that this match should be reduced to this sham but Finbars can take no glory from their certain victory. Their tactic of conceding free kicks at every opportunity rather than allowing for a free flowing match may be strictly within the rules but it has made a mockery of the game and serious questions must be raised about the referee's refusal to show far more yellow cards."

"There is the first goal of the match. Jack Murphy sent a long cross from the left corner, which was headed home by Stephen Long. Clearly St. Killians no longer have any answers for the Finbars attack. Killians takes the restart, Donovan passes the ball back to White who sends the ball down the right wing toward Mulvey but he overshoots the target and the ball goes over the touchline. Throw in to Finbars. Doherty takes the throw, in to Long who makes an unencumbered run up the middle of the field. He passes over to Ntumba who jukes past his defender and slides the ball across to Murphy who is unmarked on the back post. Murphy passes the ball into the back of the net. St. Finbars two, St. Killians nil."

"It looks like St. Finbars is going to send on its final substitutions now that the game is effectively over. I'm not sure why Coach Harry McElhatton has not replaced young O'Suileabháin except, perhaps to prove a point because even if he were replaced the match has effectively been over since the young man was injured and Killians two senior defenders were sent off. At any rate John Dunphy and Sean Walton come on for St. Finbars. And... wait a second... Brian O'Suileabháin has apparently recovered enough to re-enter the contest. He is stretching his right knee and the referee has signalled him back onto the pitch. Unfortunately there are only five minutes left in the match, plus at least a couple of minutes on injury time and I can't imagine the difference that the young man might make, particularly with a clearly damaged knee."

Margaret stared at the radio with a look of horror. No sooner was she able to relax as whatever damage had been done, when her Brian was being sent back out. Whatever was the coach thinking? Clearly it would make no difference to the outcome and the boy had already been injured badly enough to require a stretcher to remove him from the pitch. Now he was being sent back out for the final few minutes.

"Well this is certainly a shock. Brian O'Suileabháin has returned after sustaining what appeared to be a very serious knee injury. The referee has signalled a restart and Jim Donovan touches to ball to Hagerty who immediately sends it back to Brian O'Suileabháin. O'Suileabháin moves forward deftly stepping over an attempted slide tackle. He dribbles past the centre circle and into Finbars territory. Dunphy attempts a slide tackle but O'Suileabháin holding the ball between both feet jumps high in the air and over the top of the sliding Dunphy. If that young man is still injured, you couldn't see it in that move. O'Suileabháin is fronted by Nolan but the Killians midfielder spins past and Nolan reaches out and grabs the young man's shirt. O'Suileabháin pulls away, oh my goodness. The referee has blown his whistle. It's a free kick to Killians but the referee certainly should have played the advantage. I would have thought it is a little late to be initiating a quick whistle. Killians is lining up quickly, while Finbars are taking their time setting up a wall. It is O'Suileabháin who will take the kick as he stands along behind the ball. The referee blows the whistle and O'Suileabháin steps forward and launches a left-footed rocket that... yes... it bends over the wall and into the top left corner of the net. The keeper had no chance to stop that shot and suddenly it is two to one. Surprisingly enough that, my friends, is the first goal Brian O'Suileabháin has scored for his school. Finbars is in no hurry to restart the match with only three minutes remaining but the referee is warning them to move forward. Long takes the restart, sends it forward to Walton who kicks the ball all the way back to the keeper. Moore holds the ball but he is pressed by Hagerty and he finally sends it way up

*the field into the Killians' half. Brian O'Suileabháin rises above
everyone and heads the ball into an open area to his right. My
goodness, I don't know much about vertical leaps but his boots
must have been at least three feet off the turf. O'Suileabháin
wins the chase to the ball tipping it just out of reach of the
sliding Walton. O'Suileabháin has some room to run down
the right touchline and he spins away from the sliding Long
and then counter-spins against Nolan who was clearly trying
to take him down like a rugby player. I have seen Pele, George
Best and Diego Maradona at their best but I have never seen
anything like this. Young Brian O'Suileabháin appears to be
in some sort of trance, anticipating every attempt to take the
ball and countering it with a combination of remarkable ball
control, perfectly time touches and a series of spins that have
left the St. Finbars defenders clutching at air. You can't tackle
what you can't touch. Shane Barry is the last defender and he
squares up against O'Suileabháin. Oh my.... What a move.
O'Suileabháin stepped over the ball and back-heeled it over
Barry's head and now he is one-on-one against the top schoolboy goalkeeper in the country. Moore comes out to cut down
the angle... it's no contest. O'Suileabháin has chipped the ball
over Moore's head and the ball is in the back of the net. The
score is tied, two all. Remarkable, absolutely remarkable. I
don't know how else I can put this but I have never seen anything like this in my entire life and as the listeners will well
know, I have been covering soccer for forty years."*

*"I'm sure you can hear the roar from the stands as those
who remain, apparently even St. Finbars supporters, are on
their feet roaring their approval. Hagerty has run into the net
and retrieved the ball running it out to the centre of the pitch.
There is no doubt that St. Killian, or should we say Brian
O'Suileabháin wants one more shot in the waning seconds of
the match."*

Margaret sat in her chair not knowing whether to laugh or
cry. Her Brian was apparently not hurt as badly as the announcer first suggested and for that she was relieved. On the

other hand, she could only wonder what was transpiring on the field. The announcer said that Brian seemed to be in a trance and all Margaret could think about was Cúchulainn and his "red mist." The legends reported that Cúchulainn could summon a type of trance, which, once entered, left him invincible. Had Brian summoned the same legacy inherited from his father three thousand years earlier? Was he really performing impossible feats? If so, what would people think about her young friend who was hardly more than a boy? "Too early", she thought, "much too early."

"We are into injury time and St. Finbars restarts the match. Coach McElhatton is shouting at his players to attack the ball while Coach O'Leary wants his players to play keep away. Walton kicks the ball over to Dunphy then to Nolan and here comes a wave of Killians players Dunphy kicks the ball back toward Long who has lost the ball over the touchline. Throw in to Killians. Mulvey takes the ball obviously looking for O'Suileabháin. He takes the steps and heaves the ball a long way toward the middle of the field. O'Suileabháin again rises high in the air and this time takes the ball on his chest coming down in full control. With due respect to the St. Finbars players I think they know they are in trouble. The young man's jaw is set and he appears to be staring straight ahead looking neither left nor right although clearly he sees everything and knows exactly where everyone is positioned. O'Suileabháin begins his run chipping over an on-rushing Nolan, catching the ball on the top of his right foot and spinning to the left avoiding the challenge of Stephen Long. Three St. Finbars players are moving forward in tandem, but O'Suileabháin rolls the ball between Dunphy's legs, into an open area to the left. He sprints through the defenders and chases the ball down as it nears the left touchline, where he again squares up to the defenders. Coach O'Leary is screaming for his players to get back and it looks like there are now nine Finbars and a half dozen Killians boys in the box with Ntumba challenging the ball. Certainly not much room for O'Suileabháin to operate. Ó

Suileabháin's head is up as he moves toward the end line, check that, he stepped over the ball with his right foot and heeled the ball with his left leaving young Ntumba lunging toward the end line. O'Suileabháin takes two steps toward the box and shoots with his right.... What a shot...oh my... unbelievable... it's in the back of the net...it's in the back of the net... now I have seen everything... The shot took off like a bullet toward the right post and at the last possible moment seemed to bend high into the right corner. The keeper was planted in the middle of the goal but the ball arrived so quickly there was nothing he could do. Sean Walton, guarding the back post, jumped but the shot was well over his head. Brian O'Suileabháin picked the only possible spot through the Finbars defence and executed the bending shot, on the run, with a precision that would leave David Beckham standing in awe. The crowd is on its feet roaring, clapping and stamping their feet in approval. St. Killians have taken the lead three to two and this time it is St. Finbars rushing for the restart. Unfortunately for them, the referee is looking at his watch and there can't be much injury time left. He may allow the restart but not much more. Dunphy kicks the ball forward to Nolan who sends it long up the touchline toward Ntumba who is immediately confronted by O'Suileabháin. Ntumba looks for an outlet and pushes the ball to his left, right onto the right foot of O'Suileabháin who anticipated the move and, once again, takes control of the ball. O'Suileabháin moves to an open spot and stops. He is standing still, his right foot on the ball, making no attempt to advance. O'Suileabháin is staring straight ahead and seems to be daring the St. Finbars players to have a go at taking the ball. Somehow, I don't think there will be many takers. The referee has put the whistle in his mouth as he checks his watch one last time...and there's the final whistle and St. Killians are the Leinster under-eighteen league champions by a score of three goals to two."

Margaret put her hands over her mouth in excitement. She was so completely exhausted that she felt like she played the entire match. Her mind was a jumble of emotions from excitement, to relief, to concern so she tried to concentrate on the important thing. Her wonderful Brian apparently came through his ordeal intact and she could only imagine the excitement he must be experiencing.

Chapter Thirty-five

BRIAN O'SUILEABHÁIN found himself standing in the middle of the pitch, surrounded by his teammates while supporters streamed down from the stands. From the shouts of celebration, it was clear that St. Killians won the match and they were now the newly crowned Munster provincial champions but he was a little vague on exactly how that happened. He did remember lying on a stretcher on the sidelines as a doctor examined his right knee. He also remembered looking up at the scoreboard and seeing that his team was behind by two goals with just over five minutes to play.

Remembering his injury, Brian reached down placing a hand on each side of his right knee. No question about it, the knee definitely hurt, an experience that was entirely new to Brain who never experienced even so much as a sore muscle. Looking up at the scoreboard, he saw the final posted, St. Killians 3 - St. Finbars 2. So by what miracle, had his team overcome a two goal deficit in the final minutes? Perhaps, just as Mr. Blessington had suggested, the team had enough confidence to mount an improbable comeback even while he was injured and unable to play.

Brian's teammates where climbing all over him mussing his hair and slapping him on the back so obviously they thought he had something to do with the result. In all honesty, however he couldn't remember anything since he was stretchered off the pitch and Finbars scored their two quick goals. How could he possibly not remember those last five minutes? Rather than appear to be a complete idiot by asking someone, Brian decided to accept the score for what it was and he smiled happily, joining in the celebration.

Billy Hagerty jumped on his back in celebration, reminding Brian of his sore knee, and he winced with pain. "The knee lads, the knee," he groaned.

"Sorry mate," Hagerty replied puzzled at Brian's reaction. There certainly didn't seem to be anything wrong with the knee when his teammate single-handedly took over the match not ten minutes earlier.

Big John Thornton ran over when he saw his young friend's pain. "Still hurts, huh?" he asked. "

"Brutal," Brian replied with a crooked smile.

"Must be a delayed reaction." Thornton concluded as he took his position at Brian's side, intent on protecting him from any unnecessary jostling.

Brian looked over at the big sixth year and said, "By the way, thanks for defending me out there. A little over the top, but much appreciated anyway."

Thornton smiled mussing Brian's hair, "No worries mate," he said with a smile.

Brian looked around the pitch to see that most of the supporters had left the stands and were dancing and shouting among the players. A few Finbars players also joined in and were shaking hands with their adversaries. None of them seemed particularly interested in actually approaching Brian and his big bodyguard but they congratulated him from a distance by giving him the thumbs up.

He looked over at Coach McElhatton who was being interview by someone with a microphone. Brian tried to move a bit closer to hear what was being said, hoping that he would discover how the game was won, but between the crowd and the noise he could not make out the conversation. This was undoubtedly the most peculiar thing that ever happened to him.

Brian realised he was standing with a goofy smile on his face watching everyone celebrate and despite applying every effort at his disposal he still had no idea what had occurred. Finally, his gang, Kate, Libby, Siobhán, Maeve and Charlie arrived and immediately took turns hugging and kissing him on the cheeks.

Brian turned a bright shade of crimson and half-heartedly objected, "Ah lads, you'll get all sweaty and smelly."

"We don't care, Bri.Bri..." Libby said saving her biggest and best hug for last. "You were great...just great."

Looking around at his friends who hemmed him in on all sides he quietly said to Charlie and Kate, "I know this sounds very strange, but I honestly can't remember what happened in the last five minutes of the match. Please tell me before I lose it completely."

Kate and Charlie looked at each other in amazement and then back at Brian. Quite apart from the fact that Brian was not the type who would joke about such things, it was clear from his expression that he was quite serious; he really didn't remember.

Trying to explain further, Brian whispered, "I... I just don't know... I remember sitting on the stretcher with my knee killing me and seeing the scoreboard when Finbars were up by two and the next thing I knew, everyone was on the pitch celebrating."

Kate linked her arm on his right side and replied, "You won the game, Brian – all by yourself. You scored three goals and you won the game."

On his left side, Charlie copied her friend in linking his arm and elaborated. "You jumped up when St. Finbars were making their final substitutions and told the coach that you were ready to play. Then this look came over you like you were in a trance or something and after the restart you took on the entire Finbars team by yourself, dribbling over and around them like they weren't there. You scored the first goal on a free kick over the wall into the top left corner, you chipped the keeper on the second and you bent the third into the right corner from play. It was absolutely amazing. And you really don't remember anything."

Brian looked blankly at his friend, "I promise Charlie, I don't remember anything. Maybe I was in a trance or something."

Kate pulled Brian tightly toward her and said, "I don't think anyone minds that Brian. Everyone is saying that it was the finest display of soccer they have ever seen."

"But my knee," Brian protested. "It was killing me when I was on the stretcher and it is still killing me."

"Maybe it is like mind over matter," Maeve suggested. "Maybe when you went into the trance you forgot all about the knee."

"Who cares," Siobhán offered. "Brian, you were brilliant, the team won the championship and we should celebrate."

That seemed like a good idea to Brian but as the group walked toward the exit he stopped, "One more thing lads... please don't say anything to anyone about my not remembering. I feel like a right eejit as it is without everyone else knowing about it."

The girls promised that it would be their little secret and again began the trek across the pitch. This time their progress was interrupted by the arrival of an official and very harried looking man wearing some sort of earphones and a carrying a clipboard. "Sorry young man," he said, "but we need you to give a radio interview."

Brian looked up in surprise and then at his friends before responding, "Me, radio, you must be joking. I'd be so nervous, I'd probably... well I'd be too nervous. Tell them to talk to Jimmie Rice, he's the captain, or Billy Hagerty, he's a great talker."

"I'm sorry young man," the man replied officiously, "but you will have to do the interview so if you don't mind following me."

Brian looked to his friends obviously terrified about giving the interview, particularly as he didn't even remember the game's conclusion. In response, Kate stepped between Brian and the man and said, "No, I'm sorry... but perhaps you did not hear or understand Brian. He does not want to give an interview and there is no reason why he should be required to go on the radio. As you can see, Brian's knee was badly injured and the most important thing is for us to get him home so he can pack the knee in ice. Please tell your supervisors that Mr. O'Suileabháin has declined the interview because he prefers to let his play on the pitch speak for him. That is all."

Retaking Brian's arm, Kate turned her back on the man who stood in shock, his mouth hanging open. The remainder of the group followed Kate's lead and reconvened their march toward the exit. Maeve, Siobhán and Charlie were doing their best to squelch the howls of laughter, which they knew would come as soon as the radioman headed back to the presenter. Brian and Libby were looking at Kate in amazement while Kate tossed her head as if what she had said and done was the only possible response and nothing could have been more natural.

Eventually Maeve announced that the radioman was trotting back with the bad news and all the girls began to giggle. "That was great," Libby said patting her sister on the back. The rest of the girls also marvelled at the way she so coolly disposed of the nuisance and Brian expressed his thanks as well.

"Right, I could just see it," Maeve said with a mischievous grin. "The radio guy goes, so how did you do it, Brian... and Brian goes... do what? And the radio guy goes score those final three goals... and Brian goes what three goals? And the radio guy goes the three goals that won the match... and Brian goes... What match... and the radio guys goes..."

"Enough" Charlie said as the whole group, Brian included, were laughing at not only what Maeve said but her exaggerated portrayal of Brian as sort of a punch-drunk fighter.

Brian looked around at his friends and decided that about the luckiest thing that had ever happened to him was taking Mrs. O'Neil's advice and making friends with Libby. Now he had five close friends and any number of others who were friends as well.

Just as the group reached the exit, they were joined by Chad who ran up from behind jumping up on Brian's back. "The knee," several of the girls shouted in chorus.

"Sorry mate," Chad replied, "I thought you had shaken off that tackle. Well done, by the way."

"Thank you, Chad" Brian replied. "The knee is still a bit sore."

"Well it won't stop you from celebrating now, will it?" Chad asked. "My folks have invited everyone over, win or lose, and my recruiting efforts have been fairly successful. Nearly everyone is coming."

Brian replied, "Well I don't think a shower first would go amiss. I wouldn't want to put everyone off their food."

Chad laughed, "No problem old man, it will take everyone a while to get there anyway."

Outside the stadium, Brian and his entourage encountered Brian's parents, Cathal and Eibhlín chatting pleasantly with Chad and Charlie's parents, Patrick and Beatrice Pembroke. The couples met at earlier matches and although they weren't exactly social friends, they had their children's schooling in common – and of course soccer. Mr. Pembroke, smiled broadly when he saw the group of students and announced, "Now there's the man of the hour." He extended his hand, which Brian shook firmly after he disengaged from Kate freeing his right arm.

"Well done young man," Mrs. Pembroke added, her arms crossed against the chill in the November air.

Brian's mother, Eibhlín rushed forward to embrace her son, while his father stood next to Mr. Pembroke, smiling broadly. Brian returned his mother's embrace but winced when she shifted from side to side. Stepping back quickly she exclaimed, "Brian, pet, you're hurt. Is it the knee?"

"Still a bit sore from that knock," he replied.

"Sore," Cathal said, obviously concerned. "You are having trouble standing up. We must get you to the hospital immediately."

Brian, seeing the party he was so looking forward to fading away, immediately protested, "Ah no, Da. It's just a little stiff. Kate figures it needs to be iced down and if it is still sore in the morning, then we can talk about the hospital."

"So Dr. O'Donnell," Cathal said addressing Kate with a smile, "is that your professional opinion?"

Kate blushed slightly but immediately responded, "Yes, Dr. O'Suileabháin, ice for the first twenty-four hours to keep the swelling down and then heat to improved the circulation. Perhaps the hospital will be necessary but with our health system, you know you would only be sitting there for hours on end and it would probably be the morning before they got around to you anyway. It is far better that the patient be comfortable with his knee elevated and iced as soon as possible."

Brian and his friends were staring at the normally serious Kate admiring her cheek and wondering what had gotten into her. The adults were suppressing grins but were also impressed at the manner in which she delivered what sounded like perfectly reasonable medical advice.

Mr. Pembroke replied, "Excellent Dr. O'Donnell. Your diagnosis and treatment wouldn't be in any way compromised by the party that you don't want your friend to miss."

"Absolutely not," Kate replied with a flip of her hair. "The best interests of the patient's health always comes first."

Everyone laughed at that except Kate who was doing her best to keep a straight face.

"I'll tell you what," Eibhlín announced. "We will take our young hero home so that he can clean and we can make up a few ice packs. We will then drop him down to the Pembroke's and pass him into the care of his personal physician and she had better be sure that he sits quietly, as difficult as that might seem, with his leg up and the ice firmly in place."

"Sounds like a plan," Patrick added, "with one modification. Cathal and Eibhlín, you are most welcome as well. There will be a number of other parents in attendance and we have plenty of room so we won't be in the young people's way, or more importantly, they won't be in our way."

With that, the group dispersed and headed for their cars looking forward to meeting up again shortly. As he left the girls Brian turned back to Kate and quietly said, "Thanks again Kate. That's twice you rescued me. I don't know what I would do without you."

Chapter Thirty-six

IT WAS PAST NINE O'CLOCK by the time Brian and his parents arrived at the Mansfield Manor House where Chad and Charlie lived. No one seemed concerned with the time because it was Friday and everyone could have a lie in the next day. Brian struggled to balance on an old pair of crutches that his father dug out of some musty closet. The crutches were wooden and the rubber supports that went under the armpits were cracked and rock hard. The rubber grips were also well past their sell-by date and Brian was disgusted to be seen with such monstrosities. Brian was perfectly willing to limp along but his father informed him in no uncertain terms that taking his weight off the knee and using the crutches had become a non-negotiable condition for their attendance at the Pembroke's party. Although he had been hurting for only a few hours, Brian was already impatient and couldn't bear to think what it might be like if he was forced to hobble along for days, or even weeks. At least his father did promise that he would get proper crutches at the hospital.

Apart from the mouldy old crutches that were neither comfortable nor cool he was also annoyed that Gráinne was to be left at home, despite Brian's insistence that she was practically part of the team. "I know they have a posh house," he complained, "but she is hardly likely to relieve herself on their carpets." Unfortunately that was also a non-runner. And then of course there was the shopping bag filled with smaller plastic bags of ice and wrapped in towels that would be applied as soon as Brian found a seat. All in all Brian was beginning to think that the "conditions" for his attendance at the party were beginning to get a little much.

Patrick and Beatrice Pembroke greeted the O'Suileabháins at the front door and brought them into a large foyer where Cathal presented the bottle of wine he brought for the hosts. The five were joined by Charlie who emerged from a staircase leading to the lower ground floor. The young woman in her stocking feet ran toward her parents and slid across the tile floor to a stop next to the recent arrivals much to the displeasure of Beatrice who rolled her eyes and shook her head.

"Our daughter, Charlotte," she announced with a sigh. "Charlotte, you do remember Mr. and Mrs. O'Suileabháin."

"But of course," Charlie answered. "Hi Mr. and Mrs. O. Come on Brian. The gang's all here."

"Right then," Patrick Pembroke concluded, "Cathal, Eibhlín step this way. We have been formally banned from venturing into the lower floors of the house and apart from the meet and greet, our heirs have been banned from the upper floors."

Cathal followed his host replying, "That sounds like a reasonable arrangement."

Eibhlín handed her shopping bag with ice to Charlie and told the girl that she was counting on her to be sure Brian's leg was elevated and packed with ice at all times.

"No worries, Mrs. O," Charlie replied with a smile. "I'm sure Kate and I will take good care of our injured warrior."

With that they headed for the stairs, Charlie leading the way. Just as they reached the stairs Charlie looked back and noticed that Brian was trying to figure out how to descend stairs using the crutches without killing himself. "What are you like," she said in mock exasperation. "You have to carry the crutches in one hand, hold the rail in the other and hop down. Haven't you ever used crutches before?"

"No," he replied with an embarrassed smile. "And I hope I won't ever have to use them again."

At the bottom of the stairs, Charlie and Brian passed through a small corridor with doors on either side and then through a door directly ahead into a massive family room with all the accessories anyone could imagine. One corner held an entertainment centre with a big-screen television and state of the art sound system. The room also included a bar area with a number of comfortable seats and the other end of the room held an American style pool table and very professional looking dart board. Along another wall were an assortment of old fashioned arcade games and even a pac-man and a lady pac-man table, which obviously predated the birth of any of the children. Nevertheless, from the attention they were receiving, pac-man had hardly gone out of style.

There were about thirty or forty young people in attendance, mostly first year classmates from St. Killians. In addition, a few older players and friends also chose this party over any number of others that were undoubtedly taking place throughout the townland around the school. When Charlie and Brian came through the door everyone started clapping, much to Brian's embarrassment. Charlie, however, waved her hand in the distinctive manner of a beauty queen or the queen of England, thanking everyone for so warmly welcoming her arrival. "But I was only gone for a moment," she said in mock astonishment so the cheers for Brian immediately turned to boos for Charlie, which suited Brian just perfectly.

Kate and Libby hurried over to join Charlie in escorting Brian into the party. Nearly all the guests came over to greet Brian and to congratulate him on the match so for the moment, he was the centre of attention. The trio opened a path for Brian and escorted him to a large brown leather recliner near the entertainment centre. "Your throne," Charlie said presenting the chair with a flourish.

"Yes, for a king," Libby added.

Brian handed Libby his crutches and took his seat while Kate relieved Charlie of the shopping bag. In a few moments she elevated Brian's legs and arranged an ice pack for his knee, holding it in place with one of the towels Brian's mother had provided. When she finished her ministrations Kate sat on the arm of the chair and asked Brian if he was comfortable.

Brian replied, "Perfect, thank you Kate. But really, I'm fine so please stop fussing over me. I think there is a party going on."

Someone cranked up the sound system and a number of the guests began dancing, while others returned to the pool table, pinball machines and the dartboard as the party resumed.

Brian was just getting comfortable when Siobhán and Maeve rushed over. "Food and drink," Maeve announced. "His lordship requires food and drink."

"What would you like, Brian?" Siobhán asked. "They have all types of snacks and the pizza will be here in a little while."

"Really, I'm fine," Brian replied embarrassed that his friends needed to look after him.

"Right," Maeve said sternly, "we will decide what you need and if you don't like it, it is your own fault." With that the two went over to the food table and packed a plate with small-spring rolls, sausages, chicken nuggets, chips and carrots and after retrieving a can of 7-Up from the refrigerator they delivered their treasures to Brian.

"So do you want this or not?" Maeve asked waiving the plate under Brian's nose.

Brian smiled happily, realising he was actually famished, and answered meekly, "Yes please.... Miss."

Maeve looked sternly at Brian and replied, "Don't take that tone with me young man or I will dump it in your lap."

"Sorry," Brian replied now smiling broadly while everyone laughed.

"That's better," Maeve replied setting the food down on the flat armrest and handing him his drink.

The party continued and everyone seemed to be having a great fun. Since most of the guests came over to chat with Brian at one point or another, Brian decided that perhaps the knee was definitely a blessing in disguise, at least for the party. Most of the kids were dancing and singing and the entire middle of the room was transformed into a dance floor. Brian knew that he would have been entirely too embarrassed to dance because even though his mother tried to teach him a step or two, he just didn't seem to be able to make his feet follow the beat of the music and. On top of that he didn't know what to do with his arms and hands. Sitting in the lounger with his icepack was a perfect excuse for not dancing. Then again, he didn't have to start any conversations because lots of his classmates came over to where he was sitting and chatted with him. As a result he was getting to know them a little bit better and he figured that it would be easier to go up to them the next time he saw them.

He did notice that Kate, Charlie, Libby, Siobhán and Maeve were keeping an eye on him making sure he had plenty to eat and drink, especially after the pizza arrived. All in all, he did feel like a king on his throne because he was being so well looked after. Brian decided that he had seldom been happier, at least in the presence of so many people.

Siobhán, standing next to Brian, filled his cup for the umpteenth time, when she asked Charlie, "So what's with your brother. He hasn't budged from that pinball machine for about an hour."

"I think he is jealous of Brian," Charlie replied. "He has always fancied himself the big athlete and I think it has finally dawned on him that our Brian is a little out of his league."

"Jealous?" Brian asked genuinely surprised. "Sure I can play soccer but he is tall and handsome and much smarter than I am plus he has no trouble talking to anyone about anything while all I do is stutter and blush. And did you see him dance a while ago. I wish I could do half the things he does."

"It's a guy thing," Charlie answered. "At least a guy thing for my brother who wants to be the best at everything. Don't worry, he'll be fine once he sorts things out in his head."

"You know what I think," Maeve said. "I think Siobhán should go over there and flirt with him. You know Siobhán, he fancies you."

Siobhán replied, "Right, me and anyone else with a pair of boobs. Ooops sorry Brian, girl talk."

Brian blushed slightly and closing his eyes, he shook his head. Although his face used to turn the brightest shade of red and there was nothing he could do to hide the shocked look on his face he had become accustomed to hearing this "girl talk," so the bright red became a moderate shade of pink. In a way he was flattered that the girls didn't seemed to mind his hearing their comments even though they always apologised and made it appear to be a mistake.

"Nevertheless," Maeve responded, "off you go."

Siobhán sigh deeply, tossed back her long blonde hair. "The things I have to do," she moaned. Siobhán then walked over to the pinball machine with an exaggerated sway of her hips.

Maeve, Brian and Charlie watched as Siobhán stood next to Chad, walking her two fingers up and down his sleeve and whispering something in his ear. At first, Chad shook his arm as if he was trying to chase her away but she persisted and Chad, smiling sheepishly allowed himself to be pulled onto the dance floor.

"You see what I mean," Maeve said as the three watched this very attractive couple spinning with clear expertise. "Nothing a little TLC wouldn't cure."

When the dance was over, Siobhán dragged Chad over to where her friends gathered around Brian's chair. "You see," she said, "and we were all worried about him when all he needed was a little push."

Chad quickly regained his confidence and putting his hand out to shake Brian's he said, "Again, great job old man. I was going to stop over earlier but it's tough to fight off the crowds." Brian shook Chad's hand noticing that his grip had improved significantly since the first time they met.

Brian responded, "Thanks Chad. What I would give to be able to dance like you. You look like you should be on television or something."

"Well, you did get injured playing soccer, so you can hardly dance," Chad replied stressing the "playing soccer." To anyone other than Brian the comment might have sounded slightly bitter, but that didn't seem to be what Brian noticed.

"Even if I were fit as a fiddle, I couldn't even begin to dance like that. Where did you learn those moves?" he asked.

Chad hesitated blushing slightly. "Mom and Dad," Charlie interjected. "Especially Mom. She a great one for proper social behaviour and she thinks dancing is a great social skill but Chad took to it better than I."

"It is a great social skill," Siobhán added quickly, "and Chad is excellent."

"My Ma tried to teach me as well," Brian said in sympathy with Chad, "but if I listen to the music, I can't think about what to do with my hands and feet and if I think about my hands and feet, I don't seem to hear the music."

Suddenly appreciating his superiority in a least one discipline, Chad responded magnanimously, "Well, perhaps Siobhán and I could give some lessons, when you recover of course. It might be an interesting way to pass a cold, wet winter's evening."

"I don't think even you could help my dancing," Brian replied, "but if the gang is keen, I will give it a go."

"Sure why not," Maeve added. "Might be a bit of craic."

Siobhán looked over at Kate and Libby who had just rejoined the group and when Kate agreed and Libby clapped her hands in delight. "Right then," Siobhán stated, "in a few weeks when things get back to normal we will open the school."

Chad smiled broadly apparently pleased that the group would be learning from him, or perhaps that at least for the moment he was even a part of the group.

Kate, meanwhile, stood back with her arms folded, studying Brian. What an incredible boy he was. And not just the athletics, which she knew defied explanation. How could anyone be so incredible nice? The only person she knew that was nicer than Brian was Libby, but then sometimes Libby didn't know any better. Maybe Brian, like Libby, was slightly challenged but she hardly thought that possible because, apart from athletics, in every other respect he was perfectly normal. He was just so incredibly nice, or perhaps, she decided, naïve might be the better description. The problem with that, as Kate well knew from her years with Libby, was that people who were too nice, or too naïve could easily be taken advantage of or even hurt without ever realising it was happening.

It was clear to Kate, and she thought anyone else who cared to pay attention, that Chad was very jealous of Brian and had been even before Brian's athletic talent was revealed. Why? Because Chad, despite all his apparent confidence was insecure and unhappy with himself while Brian, shy and quiet Brian, was comfortable with himself. Chad tried too hard to impress his friends and was unsuccessful while Brian didn't try at all but was completely successful. Chad was tolerated while Brian was well liked. As a result she really didn't think Chad liked Brian very much, but that was completely lost on Brian because he was so incredibly nice, or so naïve.

The dance business was a perfect example. Just by being himself, Brian drew Chad back into the group by flattering him about Chad's ability, and his own inability, to dance. He had restored Chad's confidence, and probably bravado, and yet, Kate knew for certain that Brian's reaction was not calculated, he was just being Brian, just being nice. "Brian, Brian Brian," Kate thought to herself, "What are we going to do with you."

Kate was shaken from her reverie by Libby, who suggested that all those fit enough should have a group dance. Brian could watch how it was done.

That sounded like a great idea, especially to Chad who would be surrounded by five beautiful girls. As they headed out onto the dance floor, Chad, fully a head taller than the girls, looked around to be sure that others at the party saw what was happening. Brian sat in his chair, smiling happily and clapping his hands to what he thought was the beat of the music.

Chapter Thirty-seven

THE FOLLOWING DAY BRIAN AWOKE to the not unpleasant feel of Gráinne's long tongue licking his face. He was surprised to see that it was light out because usually this time of year he awoke before sunrise, even on Saturdays. Brian remembered that it was well past midnight before he went to bed and concluded that he had probably just been very tired.

As Brian stretched he recalled the dream he experienced that night. Brian did not consider himself a dreamer, or if he did dream – he learned that everyone dreams – he hardly ever remembered what his dreams were about. Usually he was asleep the minute his head hit the pillow, slept soundly and awoke bright and early in the morning remembering nothing about his sleep. That was the reason his dream the past night was so clearly etched in his memory.

Brian closed his eyes and remembered that his dream found him back in Celtic times just like he studied in Miss Byrne's history class. He remembered all kinds of strange people like a tall man dressed in a long flowing purple robe trimmed in gold with two huge moustaches falling over the edges of his mouth. The tall man was standing next to him with his arms crossed and a stern look on his face as if he were protecting Brian from someone or something. Brian also remembered a number of women, dressed in woollen skirts, whose heads were covered with woollen shawls. They seemed to be mixing something like nuts and herbs in small bowls and they were chanting all kinds of strange things.

Brian seemed to be in the middle of everything sitting in a leather reclining chair, just like at the Pembroke's, with his legs up on the footrest. Now that was really strange because he was quite sure they didn't have leather recliners in Celtic Ireland. In his dream he had no idea where he was, or what was going on because it was so strange, but somehow it wasn't at all scary. As a result he wasn't the slightest bit afraid and it all seemed so comfortable and safe.

Thinking about his dream caused Brian to begin to doze again, but this time Gráinne's licking was a bit more urgent, accompanied by a low whine. Brian reached over and scratched his dog's ear. "All right, girl," he said, "I'll get up now but couldn't you let me get a few more hours of sleep, just this one time."

As he pushed the duvet back, Brian looked over at his alarm clock and was shocked to see that it was already well past noon. At first he thought that perhaps the clock stopped because he never, ever, slept for twelve hours but it was light out and the clock was definitely running so he must have really slept it out. Brian pushed the duvet off and jumped out of bed stretching as he did so. Twelve hours, he kept thinking to himself. I slept for twelve hours.

Brian took a couple of steps toward his bedroom door, intent on visiting the toilet, when he nearly tripped over one of the crutches he used the previous night. Looking down at the crutch reminded him of his injury and he immediately reached down placing a hand on either side of his right knee. Whatever swelling he experienced the previous night was definitely gone. He flexed his leg back and forth, and could not even feel a twinge. Deciding to push a little further he squatted down, easily returning to a standing position without the slightest discomfort. After that he jumped up and down a couple of times but still... no pain and no stiffness. It was as if he had never been injured.

Smiling to himself, Brian thought that was the best possible news. It never occurred to him that his recovery was anything out of the ordinary, rather he just assumed that he was a quick healer and probably hadn't been injured that badly in the first place. Thinking no more about it, he went into the bathroom and took a long hot shower, suddenly looking forward to the visits he planned for the day.

Eibhlín smiled when she heard the shower amazed that Brian had finally arisen. She nearly went in to check on him because she knew her son never slept so late. Eibhlín decided to give it a few more minutes because she figured that between the match and the party he must have been exhausted, although in truth she had never seen that either. In any case, the rest would certainly do his knee no harm. "Breakfast," she said to herself. "A great fry-up is just the ticket."

Several minutes later Brian emerged through the kitchen door, his red-blonde hair still damp from the shower. "Ma," he announced giving her a big hug and twirling her around as he often did, "That smells gerrrrate."

Eibhlín smiled happily but stopped short the minute her feet hit the ground. "Brian, your knee," she exclaimed.

"No worries," he replied, "it feels great, like nothing happened."

"But it was badly swollen last night," she said as she reached down and placed her hands on his knees, first one and then the other. Clearly there was no difference between the two.

"I must be a quick healer," Brian replied as he took a long drink of milk and began to eat the corn flakes that his mother put out to start.

Eibhlín returned her attention to the cooker putting the finishing touches on the breakfast, complete with two eggs cooked just like Brian preferred.

"I still think we should have it looked at," she replied, at the same time realising that, considering her son's ancestry and amazing talents, she should not have been surprised at his remarkable recovery.

"We'd be thrown out of the surgery," Brian replied with a laugh. "There is nothing at all wrong with me. Watch." With that he jumped up from his chair and began a wild dance around the kitchen throwing his legs every which way. He concluded with his interpretation of a Cossack dance doing deep knee bend and throwing his legs out. He wasn't very good at it so eventually he fell on his bottom while Eibhlín could only laugh in amazement.

Cathal, wondering what the commotion was all about, arrived just in time to see the dance and, like Eibhlín his immediate concern was the knee. Rather than saying anything he looked quizzically at his wife. "Cured, it would appear," she said through her laughter. "You know our Brian. Now here's something to keep you going," she concluded handing Brian his fry.

"Remarkable," Cathal muttered as he returned to his study.

When Brian finished breakfast and put his dishes in the dishwasher, he grabbed a sliotar and his camán, whistled for Gráinne and headed for the door. As had been his normal mode of travel since his earliest days, Brian did not merely run from one place to another, rather he ran balancing the sliotar on his hurley or pucking it high into the air and then sprinting forward to catch it before it hit the ground. Gráinne, meanwhile, would run along next to him and part of Brian's challenge was to handle the sliotar despite her bumps along the way.

Brian's first stop, just down the road, was at the Blessington's. It had been some time since his last training session with Mr. Blessington but he frequently called in and talked soccer with his first true coach. As always, Mr. Blessington was delighted to see him and welcomed Brian and Gráinne into his kitchen.

"Well my friend," Nigel began, "I saw the match the other day and I must say I was very impressed with your performance."

Brian looked at Mr. Blessington in surprise, "you were there? Why didn't you come down after the match?"

"Well, I was going to," Nigel replied, "but then you seemed to be surrounded by a bevy of beauties and I certainly didn't want to get in your way."

"Ah no," Brian said blushing slightly, "those are just my mates. They wouldn't have minded at all."

Nigel smiled, "Your mates huh. I don't recall having such good looking mates when I was your age."

"Ah Mr. Blessington," Brian said again blushing.

"Anyway," Nigel said, "the match wasn't that great with the way Finbars played, but what came over you at the end."

After confessing to the girls and getting a general idea as to what had occurred, Brian decided that he would have to come up with some reasonable explanation rather than telling anyone else that he didn't remember. Even Mr. Blessington might think that his spacing out would be very strange. "I don't really know," Brian began honestly. "You know they were hacking at me from the first whistle and I guess eventually I just lost the head. Especially after they speared my knee from behind. You know, I have always made the pass, just like you taught me, but for some reason, I just couldn't let Finbars win because of the way they played."

Mr. Blessington stroked his chin considering what Brian told him. "That is just about what I thought," he replied.

"You know," Brian continued, "I think I wouldn't mind losing if the match was sporting and both teams played honourably, but I guess I sat there on the stretcher and got madder and madder as I saw the clock ticking. Do you think I did the wrong thing Mr. Blessington?"

"No," Nigel replied. "I can completely understand what happened and I suppose if I were in your boots, I would have done the same thing. You should know, however, that you have created a whole new set of problems for yourself."

"And how is that?" Brian asked, genuinely puzzled.

"You see Brian," Nigel explained, "before that match the press was beginning to take notice of you because of your skills and teamwork, which was only to be expected. I even heard about you from people that I know in soccer circles, but the general consensus was that you were a promising talent that everyone should keep an eye on for the future."

"I guess I knew that," Brian said modestly. "I know I was in the paper and some of the kids at school made a big deal out of it. That is one of the reasons I hang around with my gang who I have known for ages. I guess I never thought much about what other people might think."

"The problem now," Nigel continued, "is that news of yesterday's match is spreading like wildfire, even as we are sitting here. I know that the match was videotaped and within a matter of days, every professional club in Europe will have seen it. As a result they will no longer see you as a young player who might develop, but a young player who could already compete at the highest level."

"No," Brian insisted, "I'm just a kid."

"Doesn't matter," Nigel said with a smile. "Professional clubs like Liverpool have development teams, and they sign young fellows who are barely older than you are. That way, they have them tied up when they are young so that other teams can't ask them to play when they get older."

Brian appeared amazed at the news but he stated, "Well, I'm not going to sign up with anyone so that should take care of that. I haven't even had a chance to play hurling."

Nigel laughed, "Of course you're not. That isn't the problem. You see everywhere you go from now on the newspapers and the television stations will be following you around. All kinds of people are going to be offering you and your parents all kinds of things, even a great deal of money, for you or your parents to sign this or that. It is just something that you will have to get used to."

"And all because I scored a few goals in a school match?" Brian asked genuinely surprised.

"Well, in fairness, it wasn't that you scored, but the way you scored that has created the interest," Nigel replied.

"So what should I do? You will help me won't you Mr. Blessington?"

"Of course I will," Nigel replied. "The first thing is that I should speak with your Mother and Father and explain what is going to happen, because I'm quite sure not only the press but also professional scouts will be at your house later today, if they haven't arrived already. Perhaps I can help them understand the process so they will know what to do. But that is the easy part."

"And what is the hard part?" Brian asked.

"You are the hard part," Nigel said with a smile. "I know what you are like Brian. You have been reared properly and you are very courteous particularly to adults. Your friends like you because you are nice and I have never seen you be rude to anyone. Now these are wonderful things and I am quite sure that your parents are very proud of the way you are growing up."

Brian's expression remained one of confusion but he thanked Mr. Blessington for the compliment.

Nigel thought for a moment before continuing, "I hope you will understand what I am saying because this is very difficult. You see many of the people who you will meet as a result of yesterday's match, are not like you at all. They may seem nice, and of course some of them are. Most of them are not really interested in you but are only interested in your skills as a soccer player because they think they can make money because of your skills. All they need is for you to agree and since you are so nice, you might think that going along with them is the right thing to do. Do you understand?"

"Not really," Brian replied. "Do you want me to stop being nice? I'm not sure I would like that."

Nigel shook his head, "No, no, no... never stop being yourself because that is what makes you special. Let me think if I can put it another way. Oh yes. Remember yesterday's match? You played the way you always play, with great sportsmanship and... ah... honour. But what happened was that the other team was playing an entirely different game so in the end you had to change the way you played and that is what you did. You didn't do anything wrong, you played fairly and properly, but you didn't play the way you usually play because that was what was necessary. Isn't that right?"

Brian thought about that for a moment before agreeing, "Yes, something different did come over me," he said with a smile.

"Well now," Mr. Blessington continued, "you must do something different with all the strangers who will come up to you just like you did something different last night."

"And what is that?" Brian asked.

"Right then. Listen carefully," Mr. Blessington said pulling his chair a little closer to the table. "Of course you must always be courteous but you must also be firm. What you must do is walk away. Walk away every time. Even if a television camera or radio microphone is put in front of you, you must simply say, 'I'm sorry, sir or ma'am, I have nothing to say.' If someone from a newspaper wants to ask you questions, you say the same thing, 'I'm sorry, I have nothing to say.' If someone who is not from the press wants to talk to you or give you something you must say, 'I'm sorry but you will have to talk to my parents.' Every single time you must be courteous, but you must walk away. Can you do that?"

Brian nodded his head, "I think I can. But what about the school newspaper? One of the girls who runs the paper said she wanted to do an article about the team and she wanted to talk to me next week."

"Of course that's alright," Nigel replied. "As long as it is only the school newspaper. Everyone else, even people who are introduced to you by your fellow students, you must be courteous but walk away. Can you do that?"

Brian smiled remembering the way Kate handled the radioman after the Finbars match. "I think I can. And I know just the person to help me if I run into any problems."

Brian then explained about Kate and Nigel agreed that she was just the person for the job. Mr. Blessington said that maybe it would be a good idea if Kate rang him on the telephone so he could explain what was going on so he gave Brian a business card to pass on to Kate. Mrs. Blessington arrived with two cups of hot chocolate to fight off the chill of the day and Brian and Mr. Blessington chatted for a while about the state of the premiership.

Just as he was about to leave, the telephone rang and Mrs. Blessington answered, handing it over to her husband.

"Cathal O'Suileabháin, for you," she said simply.

Nigel took the phone and said, "Cathal?"

"Yes, but he is just getting ready to leave."

"I'll check." Placing his hand over the receiver he told Brian his father was on the phone and wanted to know where he was going next. Brian explained that he was going to visit Mrs. O'Neill and Cathal passed that information on.

After a moment, Mr. Blessington said, "I'm not surprised, Cathal. But RTE and BBC, wow... Brian and I were just talking about that."

"I know, I know. It must be a bit intimidating and I wouldn't want Brian to walk into that either. I'll tell you what. Why don't I tell Brian to stay at Mrs. O'Neill's until you ring and give him the all clear? Meanwhile, I will drop over and help you handle the press. I know a bit about that from my football days."

"Ah no. It's no problem at all."

"No, No... No problem. Anyway, I am partly to blame with all those training sessions.... Not that it wouldn't have happened eventually."

"Right then, I'm on my way and Brian is off to Mrs. O'Neill."

As they left the house together Nigel said, "The press... right on time." Brian thanked Mr. Blessington for all his help and headed up the road while Nigel trotted toward the O'Suileabháin's house.

Chapter Thirty-eight

Margaret O'Neill, put her brush in the corner, quickly removed her apron hanging it on the peg near the door, and opened the back porch door to welcome her Brian. She hoped he would call and knowing the young man as she did, was not surprised when she heard a happy bark as Gráinne entered the garden.

As always, Margaret was greeted with a big hug, although she did notice the Brian was that bit gentler than he had been when she was a young one in her eighties. Gráinne too, greeted her excitedly, accepting the soup bone that she knew would be her treat.

"You'll never guess," Brian began, "but the televisions stations from both Dublin and England are camped out in front of our house. Mr. Blessington has gone over to sort them out."

Margaret hurried around putting together her customary snack for her adopted grandchild and replied, "I'm not surprised. It seems that after last night you are becoming quite famous."

"I am not," Brian said laughing.

"Well," Margaret said, "according to the radio station that I have been listening to all morning, some people might not agree with you."

"Really," Brian said in amazement. "Well, I suppose Mr. Blessington was right after all."

"And what did he say?" she asked.

Brian answered, "He said the press and everyone else would be after me so I'd better be ready."

"And how are you to be ready?" Margaret inquired curiously.

Brian answered quickly, "I'm to be very polite and courteous but say, 'I'm sorry but I have nothing to say.'"

"That sounds like good advice," Margaret replied.

"It suits me to a tee," Brian said. "I would probably get all embarrassed and say something stupid if I had to answer any questions. Hopefully Kate will help me because she is very smart. She rescued me from the radio station last night so I know she is good at that. Mr. Blessington thought it was a good idea and he will probably talk to her as well."

"And the knee," Mrs. O'Neill asked. "How is the knee?"

"Never better," Brian said smiling as he flexed his right leg. "You know it was all puffy and really hurt last night but when I woke up this morning, it was fine. I think I must be a quick healer."

"That is surprising," Margaret replied. "Usually knees can take quite a long time to get better and sometimes it is even necessary that the doctors operate. Did you take anything for the knee or did anyone treat it?"

Brian answered, "No, not really. We put some ice on it after the match and the plan was to go to the hospital this morning but when I woke up it felt perfectly normal so that was the end of that. Funny thing though, last night I dreamed that I was in ancient Celtic Ireland sitting on a leather recliner, of all things, and there were all sorts of women looking me over. Maybe they cured me."

"Maybe they did," Margaret replied with a smile that covered her true thoughts... 'maybe they really did.'

"So if your knee was swollen and hurt last night, how did you manage to play after the boy from St. Finbars ran into the back of your leg?"

Although Brian decided not to tell anyone else about his inability to remember the last five minutes of the match, Mrs. O'Neill was not just anyone else and anyway, he usually told her everything. "To be honest Mrs. O'Neill," he said. "I don't know. In fact I don't remember anything that happened in those last few minutes. One minute we were losing two to nil I was lying on a stretcher looking up at the scoreboard clock which said there were five minutes left. The next minute everyone was pounding me on the back because we won."

"And you don't remember anything?" Margaret asked.

"Nothing," he answered. "In fact I had to ask Kate and Charlie and they were the ones who told me about the goals that I guess I scored. Maeve said I was probably in a trance or something. Isn't that the strangest thing you have ever heard?"

Mrs. O'Neill said nothing for a moment but she was thinking that no, that wasn't the strangest thing she had ever heard, not even close considering how her young friend arrived in the first place. In fact, she had long since stopped being surprised at anything that happened to her precious friend. "I must admit, it is very strange," she finally agreed. "Since you were injured before the goals you must have been in terribly pain but the announcer said that you were playing as if you had no pain at all. Especially for the last goal which would have been kicked with your bad leg."

"I don't know," Brian said shaking his head. "As hard as I have tried, I just can't remember anything at all. Maybe I was in a trance. Do things like that happen?"

Mrs. O'Neill replied, "I suppose they do, Brian. I remember reading a story a few years back about a man who was working under his car when the jack slipped and the car fell on him. Anyway his wife heard him screaming in pain and she ran out and saw what happened. She didn't even think, she just ran over and grabbed the side of the car and picked it up like it weighed nothing at all and that was how she saved her husband's life. Later she couldn't remember a thing and could hardly even rock the car, never mind pick it up so maybe she was in a trance just like you."

Brian thought about what Mrs. O'Neill said and finally replied, "Maybe so, but mine was a little different because I know I could probably score the goals like everyone said I did. I just wouldn't ordinarily do that because soccer is a team sport and the proper way to play the sport it to pass the ball and work together."

"Yes, of course," Margaret replied. "But maybe when you were injured by that unfair tackle, it made you change the way you play. Since it was not the way you usually play, you didn't remember it happening."

Brain agreed, "I suppose that could happen. Maybe it was like Cúchulainn and his red mist. When he was in danger or got very angry because his opponents weren't fighting with honour, he changed the way he fought and he went into a trance and then no one could stop him. Maybe it's a bit like that."

Mrs. O'Neill looked down at her hands folded on the table for a long time and then she looked up into Brian's bright blue happy eyes and she said, "Yes Brian. It could very well be a bit like that."

FINIS